D0414828

The author is a retired university professor who worked most of his life abroad. He has published four scientific books, forty scientific articles and six novels. All of his books are based on places he has lived so the background is accurate as are the historical details. During this time he witnessed the corruption among both leaders and diplomats while seeing the horrors of violence and war. He observed people's ability to find kindness and courage even in the face of death.

This book is dedicated to the people of Burma especially to Daw Lynette A Tun Tin and friends who showed me the real country, her love and friendship which I have never forgotten.

Robin H Meakins

# BURMA AND THE JADE TREE

AUSTIN MACAULEY
PUBLISHERS LTD.

A CIP catalogue record for this title is available from the British Library.

ISBN 978 184963 612 4

www.austinmacauley.com

First Published (2014)
Austin Macauley Publishers Ltd.
25 Canada Square
Canary Wharf
London
E14 5LB

Printed and bound in Great Britain

# Acknowledgments

The author wishes to thank his son Tim Meakins for the excellent maps and Vicky for commenting on the typescript. The photographs are from the author's own collection. I hope that I have done justice to the people of Burma and all those who fought for Britain during her longest war. Most of the post war part is based on my experiences as a teenager living in Rangoon and many of the people I knew who I have never forgotten.

# Contents

A Map of Burma and East India, 1940 to 1946

# Part One

# 1
# 1781. The Imperial City of Peking

*On the road to Mandalay,*
*Where the flying fishes play,*
*An' the dawn comes up like thunder*
*outer China 'crost the Bay!*

Rudyard Kipling (1890) '*Mandalay*'

Whoosh. Crack. Bang. Flash. The sky was suddenly filled with cascades of many coloured lights as exploding rockets sprayed the darkness with star-like patterns telling Peking, the greatest city on earth, of the approach of an Imperial caravan. This signal made people tumble out of bed, while others, already awake, started to do their allocated tasks. Everything in the Emperor's domain worked in the most efficient way. There was no fuss, no shouting, just everyone working together so that everything was ready to receive the caravan.

The Burmese jade merchant Maung Win Tun Tin rode in the caravan dressed in a thick woollen coat as protection against the cold night air. He was amazed at the massive firework display lighting the dark morning sky that only the Chinese could have invented, and whose magic illustrated their power. They were a very modern society that prided itself in having medicines to treat all ills, produced great art and literature, and a mighty military that roamed the Orient. Their large, ocean-going junks sailed everywhere, even to places where the people had brown skin, or were white, looking like ghosts. It was all recorded for those with the right connections and training to read in thousands of scrolls kept in well-maintained libraries.

The caravan accompanied the fireworks with the music from small gongs, followed by the haunting sound of the long temple horns whose noise reverberated in the early-morning mist. The standard- bearers rode ahead holding high the flags of the Emperor Qianlong and General Lin Po identifying the jade caravan as the one that was three moons overdue. The news of the pending arrival of the caravan spread throughout the city. This was a time of great commercial opportunity, as there were hungry travellers to feed, goods to buy and sell, and perhaps people to rob. The caravan came from Burma, transporting one large and two smaller jade boulders. After a journey of over thirty moons, the last few miles seemed to take hours for the thousand men, two hundred horses, a hundred oxen, and ten wagons to arrive inside the city walls. Then the workers were paid off, and the soldiers sent to their barracks.

Maung Win travelled with the laden wagons as they wended their way over the narrow, cobbled streets of Peking before entering the gates of the Imperial jade warehouse. Once inside the compound, the experts examined the boulders to value and weigh them prior to payment. Then, they argued about who would be allowed to cut the boulders. After this, the carvers examined the rock structure to determine the best way of cutting it to yield the finest stones. Each carver hoped to obtain the most precious of all jade, owned only by the Emperor and the highest mandarins they called fei cui. With the right help, they vied for pieces of such jade of the deepest colour, without flaws, and translucent as such stones were rare. They would prove pleasing to the Emperor and rewarding for his artists. As Maung Win left the warehouse, he smiled at the mandarins trying to move and weigh the jade boulders. He knew that they would find a way to value the boulders, though it may take days. Still, that was their problem not his.

It was the end of a long journey that Maung Win did not wish to repeat. He was only thirty but felt much older as the journey had aged him. Now his back ached, and his hands had deep calluses from holding the ropes to keep their precious cargo safe. His hair was dirty and unacceptably long, nearly touching his neck. The grime from the journey embedded into his hair, his clothes, and his skin itched, caused by the lice and fleas infesting his clothes. Therefore, he had to find good lodgings where he could soak his body in warm water, remove all pests and be massaged by a nubile woman. It was not a sexual thought but a wish for comfort and companionship. Drinking tea and talking with an intelligent would be most acceptable and help him relax before he slept.

Luckily, an Emperor's guide took him to a large house inside a walled courtyard which was the hotel for honoured guests. Once inside, he was taken to a reception area where he was undressed and bathed. His old clothes were removed and burnt while he lay in a metal bath filled with warm water. Two women washed his body and combed his hair with soap and the oil of the chrysanthemum removing all fleas, lice and nits before cutting it and massaging oil into each strand. Once clean, he was given a new Chinese silk gown and slippers before being shown to his room and taken to the dining room. Then he was served a huge choice of the best freshly cooked Manchu foods and the finest rice wine. Afterwards, he was led to his room where a young woman comforted him before sleeping by his side. Next morning she massaged his body before giving him acupuncture to alleviate the pains from the journey. This luxurious attention made him feel like nobility and delighted to be the Emperor's guest in Peking.

Now relaxed, Maung Win remembered how the adventure had started when he was visited in Burma by envoys of the Emperor of China wishing to purchase the largest jade rocks he had for sale. After many cups of tea, they decided to buy two huge boulders for four hundred pieces of gold. They paid half on collection and promised the balance would be paid when they arrived in Peking. Within two months, a large caravan arrived from China to transport the boulders to Peking. Then Maung Win rode with the caravan on the long journey to Peking to collect his money after the boulders were valued by the Emperor's mandarins. The journey started on the east bank of the Uru River near Maung Win's secret jade mines at Mogok that he worked with the consent of the local hill people. This was a wild area where the hill people were headhunters. The tribes tolerated Maung Win as he traded fairly with them and gave them goods as payment for their accepting him. Thus, no one else could enter the lands around his mines without fear of either being driven away or killed. No Burman

(Bamar) or Chinese had succeeded in working the mines and so the secret of their location remained his alone. The hill people escorted him on his travels inside Burma in return for gold and other luxuries. They only left him when they reached the mountains leading to China.

At times, the journey appeared to be impossible as they slowly moved the gigantic rocks – the largest the weight of fifty men – on huge wagons through forests, down mountain slopes, and across wide rivers. It was complicated by the need to travel as secretly as possible to avoid unwelcome attention from the many bandits who roamed the area.

The Chinese used relays of horses to pull the priceless cargoes that were assisted by hundreds of labourers. This was just one of many caravans that the Emperor of China sent to collect precious items. The distance they must travel was less than that covered for centuries by the silk caravans to the north, but the terrain was different. Never before had anyone moved such a mighty load over the high mountains linking Burma to China. Indeed, nobody but an Emperor would have ordered such a dangerous and expensive venture.

The human cost was enormous. The ropes cut into the flesh of the men lowering the cargo down the slopes making them turn red with blood, and many fell to their deaths. Often they overcame landslides blocking their way, and avoided boulders suddenly released by the rains to shoot across their path that destroyed everything in their way. The rocks panicked the horses so that some fell down the ravines to die on the rocks below.

Maung Win marvelled at the skills shown by the Chinese. To cross running mountain rivers, they first sent men upstream to check the weather and warn of flash floods approaching the caravan. In places where the river was very wide or the ravines too deep, they built bridges. Teak trees were cut down to make beams that were assembled in sections, lifted into place by ropes and levers before being secured to each other to form a bridge. Then each horizontal part was supported from below by wooden struts or stone pillars.

Each bridge took weeks to build, as it had to be strong enough to support the weight of the cargo. They were built so well that today some still exist and are used by drug smugglers and renegades.

Everyone, including Maung Win, toiled from dawn to dusk until night fell, and then they ate and rested. Every night they posted guards to defend their cargo from bandits wanting part of the treasure. All such attacks were repulsed, but weakened the caravan from loss of people and supplies. During one attack, fifty bandits stole ten horses and killed thirty men. The cost was small but it was an affront to the Emperor, and promptly punished. General Lim Po dispatched his cavalry to track down and kill their attackers, and returned with the horses. It was his duty to punish all who attacked the Emperor's column. However, of the fifty soldiers who left on the sortie, only thirty returned. It was a disaster but saved face – what we call honour. If he failed to punish their attackers, the Emperor would banish or execute him because he never forgave any affront, as the God King must always to be seen to be omnipotent.

The Emperor Qianlong of the Qing Dynasty loved objects carved from Imperial jade also known as fei cui. Jade was part of the Chinese culture though it was mined in the foothills of the mountains north and west of Mogaung in the realm of King Hsinbyushin of the Third Burmese Empire. Both men were powerful with empires that bordered upon each other. There existed an uneasy peace after the Chinese army was defeated by the Burmese to last even after the Burmese King Hsinbyushin attacked the Siamese lands around Ayutthia. When the Burmese King captured the Siamese artists and skilled carvers and took them to his capital to start a new phase of Burmese art and culture, the Chinese said nothing. Therefore, the Burmese King Hsinbyushin allowed the Emperor to convey the jade boulders to Peking. Both men liked jade, but by letting the Emperor have the huge jade boulders, Hsinbyushin hoped to keep the Chinese away from his lands.

The Chinese called ordinary jade chen yu, and used it for jewellery, marks of rank, and sacred carvings, with the finest pieces valued above gold. They named the objects necessary for life after jade, so the penis was known as the 'jade stalk' and the vagina the 'jade gate'. For did not the jade stalk place the seeds of men into that perfect jade garden (the womb) of women to produce life born through her jade gate? Indeed, it was and so it would be until the end of time.

The colour of jade varies from black to nearly white, but the most precious is imperial jade or fei cui that is a deep green. The best fei cui has the colour seen in the brilliant emerald green of the kingfisher's neck plumage and it was that jade the Emperor Qianlong desired above all else. He obtained old pieces and new pieces, carved as well as plain. All were for his pleasure, to be fashioned as he wished. They were carved into objects of outstanding beauty and delicacy to last forever. Some were inscribed with poems or carved into jade stalks or smooth egg shapes to give sexual pleasure. The Chinese crushed the smallest chippings into a powder to use as an elixir to promote health and longevity.

After a week, Maung Win was rewarded for his efforts when a mandarin arrived with the final payment for the jade boulders. It was more than he expected. There were a dozen horses and a wagon loaded with five hundred pieces of gold, the finest silk cloth, and thirteen pieces of normal jade. In addition, there was the unusual gift of twenty pieces of fei cui and items normally reserved for the nobility. There was an imperial silk coat with embroidered golden dragons as worn by mandarins and the burial jade that signified eternal life, consisting of small jade plugs, which upon death were put into his body apertures. For instance, a jade cicada was placed under his tongue to preserve his Chi or bodily vital spirit, and a round jade piglet would be laced to his right hand. The cicada signified rebirth from the soil, and the pig an increase in the family size and wealth. They were gifts that the Emperor usually only gave to a great man.

The final gift was a girl Mai Li, dressed in a red silk cheongsam with a long slit down the side to reveal her slim legs. The colour red was associated with happiness and pleasure. As was the tradition, she carried her dowry of ten carved jade horses, a set of the finest porcelain, fine silks, and medicines. Nothing was said, as she bowed deeply to her new master, trembling at the thought that he might reject her. She was Chinese, but not from the ruling class, so rejection could result in her becoming the plaything of a soldier or merchant.

She waited with bowed head, praying to her ancestors that he accepted her so that she could reward him with love and care. He did not have to feed her a lot as she ate no more than a sparrow and was very quiet and well behaved. She silently vowed that even if he whipped and beat her, she would not cry out or cause any problems. Please, please dear beloved ancestors, make him desire me – if only for the moment! In that sincere plea, the spirits gathered around her and granted her wish.

Maung Win accepted her as a wife, for to refuse could be fatal, and anyway, she was young and very pretty. She was so small and doll-like that she could not eat much and would help him pass the time while the carvers transformed his jade into objects of pleasure and great value. Therefore, as was the custom, he accepted her with a deep bow and placed his stone marker, or chop, around her neck. It was not like a brand but more like a small necklace that bound her to him and him to her. It was their ritual, their way, just as in other places and at different times, people exchange rings. The chop allowed Mai to buy things without money, and provided her some protection from thieves and other unpleasant characters.

For the next three months, Maung Win and Mai lived by the city's Jade Gate near the workshops of the carvers of jade and ivory, and the markets where the merchants sold silks and incenses. It amused Maung Win that Mai's jade gate gave him such joy while they lived so near the Emperor's Jade Gate. He loved her small perfect frame and little bud-like pointed breasts that responded eagerly to his caresses. They would make the beast with two backs well into the early hours. Sometimes she let her long black hair cover her firm breasts to excite him. At other times, her laughter radiated joy around the room, making him content. When Mai was asleep, or pretending to be as is the way with women, his eyes feasted upon her creamy body, so silky to the touch, and hoped that she would give him a child. He loved his other wives, but simply adored Mai. He knew that he was ten years older than her, and yet she made him feel young again. When, at last, Maung Win was asleep Mai would thank her ancestors for giving her so much pleasure and a good man. She asked for his seeds to grow inside her jade garden to become their child who they would cherish. When all was quiet, she lit a scented joss stick and placed it in the sand before a statuette of Lord Buddha. Then she meditated upon the goodness found by all who followed the true path.

Maung Win commissioned the jade carvers to produce twelve jade trees of life with many branches to denote his family. They carved each piece of fei cui into a tree topped with an orb mounted on a central trunk to denote the man as head of the family. Under these were four branches, one each for his two wives, one for Mai, and another, in case he should need another woman. For a man in his position must always be aware that women were attracted to him, or his wealth, and that he may still succumb to her charms. Under the top branches, there were two more rows of branches before the tree's roots descended into the large base mounted in a container to store the spare leaves. Each twelve came with forty small jade leaves each with a thin gold band to hang them from the branches, two leaves for each member of his family. When completed, they wrapped each jade tree in silk, then in rolls of paper, before placing them in a wooden box. In Burma, he would get the trees blessed to become the medium to communicate with his ancestors and descendants. One tree would be put in a place of honour, with a leaf for each wife and on the branch below a leaf for his three sons and four daughters. Then each of his family would wear the second leaf around their necks as a talisman for protection. When his children married, he would give each of them, a tree with the understanding that it was passed to their children. For when one died, the leaf must be removed and given to the next born.

Maung Win left nothing to chance, so he took Mai to an old Chinese soothsayer to have their fortune read. The soothsayer touched his long grey beard as he looked into the couple's eyes and examined the palms of their hands. Then he tapped a cage to inform his trained bird to select a tiny scroll from a pack of them in a container, the obedient bird picked at different scrolls before lifting one up in his beak for the old man to take, unroll, and read his prediction. It read: You will be happy in a distant land where you will raise two children. Your dynasty will flourish until the sun dies and the earth returns to God.

Maung Win had the smaller jade stones engraved with his stamp of authority or chop. It stated his name in both Burmese and Mandarin, followed by this inscription: Jade is a blessing when given, a curse when stolen or demanded. Remember this well for it is like me a good friend but terrible enemy. It comes only from the blessed mountains of Burma and we, the Burmese, let no man take it from us.

The remaining jade pieces were carved into horses, images of Buddha, and a mongoose killing a large cobra. The last image was very precious in his eyes as it signified the success of the smaller good mongoose over the bigger evil snake. The carved statues of Buddha could be sold in Burma, though he would give the biggest to the King and another to the nearest shrine. They crushed the pieces of jade left over from the carving into a fine powder that Mai used to produce an elixir to make Win's jade stalk strong and pleasing to her. Some say that helped make a child; it must have worked for after ten moons Mai gave birth to a daughter and a year later a son.

The Chinese believed that the great philosopher K'ung Fu-Tse, often called Confucius, who lived from 551- 479 BC likened jade to virtue. After his death, his students compiled his sayings into the Confucius Analects. Of jade, he said: When polished and brilliant the whole is pure, its compactness and hardness are a sign of intelligence, its edges do not cut but are strong like justice. Its colour represents loyalty. Its interior shows its many flaws clearly for all to see while its transparency signifies sincerity. It is an iridescent brightness born of mountain and of water that shows both its goodness and is a sign of chastity.

In time, the jade trees passed down the family from father to son or daughter. In 1922, Maung Win Lynette, a descendent of Maung Win and Mai married Paul Anderson and received from her father Maung Tun Tin one of Maung Win's jade trees to keep the tradition alive. Therefore, when her children were born, a jade leaf was added to the tree on branches under those for Paul and herself. When her children left home, they wore a jade leaf around their neck as a talisman to protect them from evil. While in the Anderson's sitting room was a teak corner cabinet with glass windows that contained several pieces of old cream coloured ivory that included a large ivory tusk, twenty carved into a bridge and a statuette of the goddess of love and happiness. Alone on the top shelf was Maung Win's jade tree with four leaves – one each for Lynette, Paul, their daughter Mai, and son Peter. The jade tree was never just an ornament, but the protector of their spirits. Lynette had three fei cui horses, that she knew could only be sold when the family was in need, but not just for financial gain because to do so was 'bad joss' (bad luck). She never told even her husband their worth except to say that they were of sentimental value. She knew that one of the Ching horses could fetch a thousand pounds or enough to buy a large house. It was her insurance policy for the future prosperity of her family, in the same manner that the leaves of the tree protected her loved ones from evil. Their value was impossible to tell, as none of the London museums had any fei cui jade.

When in need of guidance, Lynette would light a joss stick and pray before the jade tree to evoke the spirits of the ancestors to help her through difficulties. To do this, she needed perfect silence to enter a spiritual trance-like state. Therefore, she meditated when everyone was out or at night when all were asleep. Occasionally, while meditating, she would fall into a trance to see images of her family back in Burma, her children at school, or signs of danger. At such times, her spirit travelled through the ether to commune with her loved ones. She did not, as you might think, take narcotics, nor drink more than the occasional glass of wine. Lynette was clairvoyant with that ancient gift of communication through the mind and spirit that most of us have lost or never had. In truth, the jade tree gave its protection and advice, even an insight into events happening miles away. It is hard for those without a deep belief in the divine to understand that such things exist, but they do. For it is written that there are only three great virtues: faith, hope, and charity and the greatest of all is charity. Charity is kindness, giving to the needy, and the gift of love that transcends all others – that of understanding.

# Part Two

# 2
# Boxing Day 1941: Rangoon, Burma

While in Britain, people sat around the fireplace recovering from the little Christmas feasting that rationing allowed, others were in far-off places trying to save the Empire. Peter Anderson flew for weeks with the other aircraft from his wing to his mother's homeland, Burma. He was tired of scanning his mirror and looking into the sun for a foe, as yet unknown. All was quiet, as few pilots would attack a wing consisting of thirty dirty, but fully operational, RAF Hawker Hurricanes. Soon the odds would change, as like a Roman gladiator, each pilot would fight his opponent to the death when only God knew who would die or live. Peter had so much to do but could not control his destiny. If he was to die, it should be up in the air… free like a bird and not in a muddy trench or in the cold, cruel sea. It was better to die quickly like a grouse shot from the sky during the glorious twelfth of August.

Peter's love affair with planes started when he met the gorgeous Gertrude while visiting Uncle Jeremy in Shorcham-on-sea on the Sussex coast. It was love at first sight as she waited in all her splendour on that green field. She was Jeremy's only true love, his companion, and plaything, indeed everything he adored, responsive to his wishes, reliable, and very exciting. What more could anyone want?

A DH Tiger Moth similar to *Gertrude* at Shoreham Airfield.

Gertrude was a silver painted aircraft – or more correctly, a de Havilland Tiger Moth biplane with two open cockpits. She introduced Peter to that most exotic mixture of pleasure and science found only in the world of flying. Then he experienced that sensual feeling of looking down upon the world beneath from the purity of the sky. Here, there was nothing to disturb his thoughts, just the humming of the engine and the whistling of the wind.

Jeremy took Peter over the sea before teaching his nephew how to fly. Peter was such an enthusiastic pupil that Jeremy enjoyed teaching him, and they spent most of their spare time with Jeremy and Gertrude. Weeks turned into months as Peter learnt to take off, land, stall the engine, and cleverly recover the aircraft from a spin. They would loop the loop or fly upside down, held in only by their seat belts. They flew in the sunshine, in rain, over sea and land. To Peter this was heaven, and Uncle Jeremy knew it.

Uncle Jeremy was a solicitor whose life revolved around work, his lady friends, and flying. He had a rugged appearance enhanced by facial scars from some injury obtained while flying in the Royal Flying Corps during the Great War. He never talked about it, and no one dared to ask. It was enough that he had the DFC and bar with the retired rank of Wing Commander.

Jeremy disliked the idea that pilots were a special class. In fact, he hated anything that separated him from his fellow pilots, who were his only true friends. Many were mechanics, farm labourers or landed gentry. Whenever asked to help, each of them would roll up his or her sleeves to fix another's machine. They were a strange group of kindred spirits who, when it was too dark to fly or work on their aircraft, would sit around the bar and talk about flying. Few planes were new, as most were rebuilt ex-warplanes kept airworthy by skilled hands. If you could afford a motorbike, then an old plane was cheaper. The biggest expense was fuel; therefore, many pilots shared an aircraft.

At school, Peter wondered why some students proudly showed pictures of themselves at pro-Hitler rallies in the black uniforms of their fascist tribe. Why was Sir Oswald Mosley and his Blackshirts of the British Union of Fascists allowed to roam the land? Their code of 'Might is Right' attracted bullies as well as those of the upper class who feared communism and their own workers. They terrorised foreigners by breaking their shop windows and beating up everyone they did not like, often paid by the rich and famous. Many celebrities such as the society sweethearts, the Mitford sisters thought Hitler was the solution to all of their problems. The night war was declared with Germany many people burned their black uniforms and fascist photographs, as few dared to support Moseley for fear of ending up in prison. Indeed, many fascists ended up in prison, while others fled on ships and aircraft to America, taking suitcases swollen with the family silver. A dockworker commented that the ships were full of rats abandoning Britain, but no one would miss them. Many wondered what new problems the war would bring and how they would cope. Mothers worried, as all men of fighting age were required to register for military service or were sent to the nearest training camp.

Everybody was on the move, or knew someone who was. People dug bomb shelters in their gardens or converted the wine cellar to protect their families. Windows were fitted with blinds so no speck of light could help enemy bombers. Woe betides anyone who let light seep through the blinds as the wardens enforced the blackout with vigour. Many people dug up their flower gardens to plant fruit trees and vegetables in the hope of avoiding starvation.

As an officer cadet in the Auxiliary Air Force, Peter flew or enjoyed a great social life. His unit had their own pack of hounds and hunted on horseback any unlucky fox that came their way. Peter avoided the hunts as he found them barbaric by saying he could not ride. While at hunt balls, he enjoyed dancing closely with a young lady, inhaling her perfume, and stealing a kiss between dances. Wine flowed, and the music played on as they had fun, ignorant of the terror ahead. It was surreal; nothing seemed to matter during the Phoney War. Few cared that the poorly equipped allied armies in Europe were due for a thrashing from the modernised German army.

Then Peter was posted to RAF Shoreham to train to fly Hawker Hurricanes. It was like old times, as Wing Commander Jeremy Anderson ran the base and had Peter, together with another trainee, James (Jim) Ashton billeted with him. Jim and Peter became good friends to drink in the Officers' Mess or go to a seashore pub to play darts. All too soon their training was over, and they went first to a squadron in Kent and then on to Burma. Peter's greatest advantage over his fellow pilots was his fluency in Japanese and Burmese. His Burmese mother, Lynette, taught him all the languages she knew and liked to practice her Burmese on her children while promising that one day they would visit her family in Burma, but they never did. It was just too far away and there was not enough time, or money, for the journey.

Now, flying over Burma, he wondered if he would fit in. He did not like school, especially the arrogant selfish students. Whenever his mother thought, he was getting too big for his boots, she would smile and say, 'Even the smallest ant has value in the sight of God, and one must not forget that. The good you did yesterday is gone and now only what you do today matters.' His mother was raised a sincere Catholic, though she kept many of the Buddhist ways. She would never kill a fly and on her own was a true vegetarian, but with the family, she cooked a great Sunday roast dinner and a goose for Christmas. The goose was purchased already prepared for the oven.

At the outbreak of war, Peter's sister, Mai, married Lieutenant Charles Brighton of the Gurkha Rifles. The wedding was magnificent with his sister looking beautiful in her white lace dress. Only their father, Paul, worried that the war would make his daughter a widow. Everyone present could see that both Charles and Mai adored each other. Later, Mai told her mother that she had no regrets, as it was better to have one day of blessed happiness than a hundred years of regret. She knew that soon Charles would leave her behind as he joined his regiment to India. Likewise, Paul was certain that Mai intended to get pregnant to have part of Charles with her throughout those lonely dark days, and longer nights, to come.

Suddenly, the sound of the wing commander's voice reminded Peter he was at war and ordered to descend to one thousand feet over the sea, turn due north over the city and land at Mingaladon airport. Below was the wide Irrawaddy delta with its lush green vegetation. Occasionally, a village or road became visible, or a flash of gold reflected from the bell-shaped pagodas. Soon they flew low over the harbour and Rangoon with its wide streets overlooked by the golden Shwe Dagon pagoda, and the Prome Road lined with flowering trees that flashed their red and blue colours in greeting. On the ground, people looked up and waved at the RAF planes while spies noted the aircraft type and their numbers to send to the Japanese.

'Blue squadron, lower your undercarriage, and land in pairs.'

Peter replied, 'Blue Two. Roger, over and out.'

Peter lowered the undercarriage until the wheels clicked into position, reduced airspeed, adjusted the flaps, and let his Hurricane descend in line with the rapidly approaching runway. The hardest thing about flying was making a correct landing at an unknown airfield. His approach was good as his aircraft touched down with only a minor bounce. As he got out the ground engineers checked and refuelled the plane while the armourers cleaned and loaded each gun with new ammunition belts.

'The speed the ground crews are preparing our planes probably means there's a flap on,' Jim stated.

'Let's hope that we get forty winks before then!' Peter replied.

'I must stretch my legs after sitting for so long. Do you want to come with me?'

'Yes let's take the long way to the arrival's hut.'

Therefore, they walked with the warm, soft afternoon breeze running through their hair on an airstrip set for war. There were anti-aircraft guns guarding the sky and machine gun posts in concrete bunkers defending all the approaches from the ground.

'It is a strange way to visit my mum's country!'

I bet you never expected it to be like this.'

'That is true. I just hope that I see more before it's all over.'

'You will see more of the land. It'll take a golden bullet to get us.'

'Peter be careful. It is never wise to tempt fate.'

They were silent as neither knew what to say.

'I wonder what Christmas is like at home.'

'It is bloody cold and raining, with everyone sitting around a meagre fire pretending to be warm, with their teeth chattering! Here we have it all with no rationing or working in an office filing endless pieces of useless paper. It is warm with free food, uniform, and accommodation for us to enjoy. All we have to do is fly their aircraft, so what more could any man desire?'

'Family, friends, Christmas carols; mistletoe, and chestnuts roasted on a roaring fire with a glass of fine wine, a beautiful woman and song!'

'You're just bloody greedy. Be thankful for what you've got.'

They laughed at life and continued to walk as they passed the aircraft that included old RAF American F2A-2 Brewster Buffalos parked alongside two newer RAF American Consolidated-Vultee A31 Vengeance dive-bombers. Nearby were three P40 Curtis Tomahawks of the American Mercenary Air Force or Flying Tigers. The arrival of thirty Hawker Hurricanes mark II was a much needed and welcome addition to the defence of Burma. The Englishmen had not seen a Brewster or a Tomahawk before, but they knew that the old Brewster was a poor combat aircraft. They hoped the strangely painted P40

Tomahawks were as fast as they appeared while painted like a shark with white teeth and red mouth. It was an unusual sort of camouflage in a very strange war!

On reporting to their commanding officer, they were given quarters, ate a meal of bangers and mash, and retired for the night. They washed, cleaned their teeth, and went to sleep. Jim dreamt of being with Jane walking through the long grass by the river. Would he see and kiss her again and would she still love him? It was times like these when the loving attentions of a soft woman were all any man needed before facing the reality of his own death.

Peter dreamt of sitting in the garden chatting to his parents as the birds sang and the blue sky gave a sense of peaceful bliss. Somehow in his heart he knew that they would all meet again, in this world or the next. For around his neck Maung Win's ancient jade leaf spun its magic, giving him peace of mind, and protecting him from the forces of evil gathering around.

Before daybreak, their dreams were interrupted.

'Wakey! Wakey! Rise and shine! Let's be having you. The food is served in ten minutes. Morning briefing at seven sharp – and gentlemen don't be late!'

They were up and in the mess in minutes. It was a rush, but they were used to running from place to place. Everything was hurried whether eating food, going into combat, or trying to catch a few, most blessed, minutes' sleep. To survive, one overcame the lack of sleep and ate whenever possible. In the Officers' mess men of various nationalities ate their bacon, sausages and eggs with brown sauce, washed down with sweet cups of tea.

In the briefing room, the CO entered; pipe in hand, with a well-cultivated smile that calmed all around him. He said, 'Good morning gentlemen! Welcome to the turkey shoot, as our American friends call it.'

Everyone politely laughed and began to feel more confident as the CO updated them on the situation. 'The Japanese Imperial Army has entered southern Burma from Siam through the Three Pagodas Pass. The Siamese military dictator Phibun Songkhram surrendered, giving the Japanese all the assistance that they could possibly need. So you will be pleased to know as of now Burma is the front line, and we are on our own.'

The CO noted the latest arrivals, youthful and neat in their new uniforms, a contrast to the old hands with their worn flying jackets and prematurely aged faces. Within days, these newcomers would look like the others, or be dead. Lost youth is the price of war. He knew that he would never meet some of them as the fighting was so intense that many would not survive the week. The survivors had to fly by the seat of their trousers to bring back crippled machines and catch some sleep before returning to the fray. Hair would grow long, with faces taut and pale from lack of sleep and cordite. While their new leather flying jackets would become worn and patched as day in and day out they lived and slept in them. It was the awful truth, made worse by being outnumbered fifty-to-one. The enemy knew that they outnumbered the British in the air and on the land, so they would continue their relentless attacks until they had conquered all of Burma. He slowly lit his pipe, took a puff, and continued the briefing. 'The Japanese Army's tanks, artillery and bombers must be destroyed. At this moment, their air force is not well organized, and if you are careful you can shoot them down just like at the funfair. The Buffalos and Tomahawks will defend Rangoon while the new Hawker Hurricanes will attack the Japanese bases in Siam. Remember, no heroics. Blow the buggers up and get your aircraft back even if you have to carry it. Sadly, we have more pilots than aircraft so beware of enemy fighters that are fast and hunt in groups. Gentlemen, I wish you all good-luck.'

Then the Squadron Leaders issued their individual orders. 'Gentlemen the tactics are simple. Fly high before bombing your target and then regain altitude. The secret is speed, so like a cat burglar, strike before they know what has hit them. Obey strict radio silence as the Japanese listen. Do not yell out as you go in, and no victory rolls until the bloody war is over. Each Hurricane is supplied with a pair of 250-pound bombs, one under each wing making her heavier and slower to respond. So take off carefully. Whatever you do, drop the bombs before you return, preferably on the enemy.'

They smiled, while inside feeling uncomfortable knowing the warning was real. It would be a disaster if they bombed their own people and in the chaos that surrounded them, anything was possible. They heard that the enemy bombing of Rangoon on 23rd and 25th December killed over seven thousand people. The Allies lost ten planes but destroyed fifty enemy aircraft. This kill rate was excellent in most theatres of war, but not good enough in this situation.

Maps in hand, they walked to their planes looking like schoolboys, out for a stroll in the sun. Peter was five feet ten inches tall, slim, with black hair, dark skin, and large brown eyes. James was two inches shorter with long fair hair, and unusually green eyes.

'It is funny that I am not afraid. However, I feel so damn thirsty that I could drink a pub dry, and my hands are very clammy. It must be this damned heat.'

'I feel like that. I hope that I can remember the way back.'

Alongside their aircraft, they turned to grin at each other, feeling safer knowing the other was by his side. A friend in need is a friend indeed, especially when death lurked nearby. The squadron leader led his squadron down the runway followed by the others. Adrenalin flowed through Peter's body making him feel awake and exhilarated. The sensations of movement took over as his plane rolled down the runway, gained speed and lifted off into the air. The squadron leader's aircraft led the squadron down the runway followed by the others. The Hurricane mark IIA fighter-bomber was equipped with twelve wing-mounted .303 (7.7mm) calibre Browning machine guns and two 250 lb bombs. The Rolls Royce Merlin engine purred as it powered the aircraft upwards to 34 000 feet at 328 mph. It is said that pilots who flew Spitfires claimed it was a better fighter than the Hurricane. It was probably true, but the Hurricane was the workhorse, the plane for all weathers and for most jobs. She had an operational range of 500 miles compared with 400 for the Spitfire. The Hurricane had a fuselage consisting of a metal frame covered with wood and fabric so that most enemy bullets went straight through without causing major damage.

The squadron flew eastwards towards the airfields marked roughly on their maps. All too soon they were ordered to follow their leader in pairs. So Peter flew alongside Jim in the third pair. He fused his bombs and set the two switches on the selector panel to the 'On' position. They descended rapidly over an airfield full of burning planes, while rocked by the anti-aircraft fire exploding around them. Peter dropped his two 250 lb bombs onto the enemy before climbing away. Seconds later came the explosions followed by a shock wave that threw the aircraft all over the place. Then it was all over, and everything was quiet.

'Nice work chaps – now home. Watch the sun for bandits.'

On the flight back to Mingaladon no one spoke. The pilots scanned the sky for enemy fighters that did not materialise. So this time they all arrived back unharmed.

Peter Instinctively touched the jade leaf around his neck and felt its power. It was as though his ancestors supported and guided him throughout the day and night. Maybe they were here as birds, as spirits, or just in his mind. It did not matter as it made him feel good to know that he fought for the British and the Burmese, as both were part of him, as he was of them. Back at Mingaladon, the ground crew inspected each aircraft before refuelling and rearming them ready for the next sortie.

That night in the Officers' mess, they sang around the piano and drank whatever was available. The alcohol and the singing seemed to take them home and make them forget. Both Peter and Jim fell to sleep, slightly drunk, and grateful to have survived their first raid.

# 3
# The Shwe Dagon and a Moment of Peace

*Then, a golden mystery upheaved itself on the horizon – a
beautiful winking wonder that blazed in the sun, of a shape
that was neither Muslim dome nor Hindu spire… 'There's
the old Shway Dagon', said my companion… The golden
dome said: 'This is Burma, and it will be quite unlike any
land you know about.'*

Rudyard Kipling (1889) *From Sea to Sea.*

A week later, everything changed as the previous night's raid was hell, with
most of the surviving aircraft returning with no ammunition. On the way back
from bombing a Japanese Army Division they were attacked by enemy aircraft
diving from the sun so that many Hurricanes were lost or damaged. Now every
mission was dangerous as they flew against the more numerous enemy.

On returning to base Peter noted that most planes were damaged, two pilots
wounded and two others missing, never to return. One plane landed on the
runway like a drunken duck on a frozen lake ending up intact but with her pilot
dead in the cockpit. The fatally injured pilot had obeyed orders to bring his
aircraft home and died doing so. The aircraft was repaired to take another
gladiator into the hell of combat.

Only one of the squadron's aircraft was operational after the worst day so
far but there were more to come. Next morning Peter and Jim were given the
day off while the engineers struggled to repair their aircraft. It was a bit like
putting Humpty Dumpty back together again. However, they would work flat
out until they succeeded.

Peter and Jim were tired of the Officers' mess and wanted to do something
unusual. Then they met Daniel Combs and his Karen wife, Anna, who offered to
show them around the city. Daniel made everyone feel good; nothing was too
much trouble, and anyway; he loved Burma as much as he adored Anna. The
young pilots accepted the offer and were soon in Daniel's Chevrolet driving the
fifteen miles down the Prome Road to Rangoon. They drove along roads lined
with flowering trees such as red flowers of the flame of the forest, the blue of
the bougainvillea and the sweet-scented frangipani. Peter noticed the brightly
painted trucks and buses, and large-wheeled wooden carts pulled by water
buffalo and cattle. That morning everybody was on the move at a gentle, but
respectable pace. Women carried their children on their backs protected from the
sun and rain by brightly painted umbrellas as men on bicycles pulled passengers
in rickshaw-type taxis. Everywhere they looked there were Buddhist priests, or

pongyis, with shaven heads in saffron robes walking around with bowls asking for alms. The city was vibrant and full of colour as the brightly-coloured flowers mingled with the dress of the people.

Daniel Coombs parked his car at the foot of the Shwe Dagon pagoda where the golden stupa rose like a giant finger from its hill top platform pointing up to the sky. After passing through an arch guarded by a pair of huge chinthes, the mythical lion dog of Buddhism, they climbed the hundreds of steps to reach the temple. The golden bell-shaped stupa enticed them upwards like a light to their moth-like curiosity. Its gold sides reflected the sun's rays, giving an aura of beauty and mystery. It is one of the great wonders of the world, like Venice from the sea, or the pyramids of Egypt.

Burmese women in traditional dress at the Shwe Dagon Pagoda.

On the stairs, Anna stopped to buy joss sticks and a bunch of fresh flowers. It was hot and humid, making them feel tired even though there was a cooling soft breeze. So Peter and Jim stopped half-way up to let Anna and Daniel catch their breath.

'Wait and let us older folk catch up.'

'Sorry Daniel! I've never seen anything so beautiful.'

'I have and she's by my side,' Daniel added putting his arm around Anna's waist.

Anna looked embarrassed as Daniel did not normally say such things in public. So, like most women, she changed the subject. She said, 'the temple, or pagodas, of Shwe Dagon is built on a hill 180 feet above Rangoon. It has a central stupa or spire that is 785 feet in circumference and 300 feet tall.'

'That's enormous. It must be the biggest ever made,' Jim said.

'It is the biggest functioning pagoda complex in the world, though I am told the ruins of Angkor Watt in French Indochina, and the ruins at Pagan cover a greater area.'

'I am glad that Anna knows about the temples as it makes it ten times more interesting.'

'She is an expert who visits here once a week,' replied Daniel.

Smiling and full of hope, they climbed onwards and upwards towards the clear blue sky. All around them the birds sang in the trees, and monkeys ran around up and down the stairway. At the top, they reached a large courtyard on which stood many smaller shrines that encircled the main stupa. The courtyard gave people access to every shrine where they freely intermingled with the *pongyis* (monks) with their shaven heads, and saffron coloured robes.

Peter and Jim were totally enchanted by the beauty of the temple complex and the colours of everything. It was very bright, so alive, and above all a timeless place of peace. Here they were in a dream world while all around them war raged as men killed each other with a violence that was alien to this Shangri-la. Women, some with children, knelt in front of the small temples in their best clothes to pray and give an offering. Girls with cheeks smeared with white cream laid flowers or lit scented joss sticks. A few men came with offerings and prayers before going off to work. Peter admired the small, slim shape of the young Burmese (Bamar) women with their rounded faces and glorious long black hair rolling down their backs. Peter felt that they were like his mother. On the other hand, Jim saw them as small, fragile dolls, full of beauty and grace that were well worth fighting for. Indeed, they were doing just that.

Meanwhile, Anna went across to a white-painted shrine containing a small Buddha to kneel and place four joss sticks in the sand jar in front of it that she lit while chanting quietly. As she rose she placed one bunch of flowers by the statuette of Buddha and bowed her head.

'Lord Buddha who has always guided my people I beg you to listen to my prayers. I ask you to bring peace to this land. If it is your will stop the killing and let us return to your grace. The path we must live is full of suffering but with good deeds and thoughts, I will walk it for the betterment of all people. I ask you to look down on us and protect these two boys who fly to save us from the invaders. Protect Daniel and give us a child for me to bring up in our images. Allow me to follow the path to righteousness and know the true joy of being a woman with the man I love.'

Anna joined the others inside the largest temple room that was dominated by two large gold images of Buddha and many smaller ones, some made of gold, and two of white porcelain. Lord Buddha looked like as a young man with a serene smile on an oval face, in a cross-legged sitting in the lotus position, usually with a jewel on his forehead between the eyebrows. The right arm folded as if his hand was holding his leg. The whole body was slim and full of grace. The face added both mystic and serenity to his image. Buddha always looks slightly downwards with clear brown eyes either side of a majestic nose with a small mouth and chin and long earlobes.

'Your Lord Buddha is very beautiful unlike the fat grinning, images of the Lord Buddha from China,' Jim remarked.

'To us Theravada Buddhists this is how Buddha should be. We cannot understand the Chinese fat, rich old man with a cynical smile. Lord Buddha gave up his princely riches and all earthly pleasures to spend his life in contemplation and helping all to follow the true way to salvation. His image looks down upon us with love and kindness to enter our very being and to guide us through the trials and tribulations of life,' said Anna.

She lit a joss stick in front of the large Buddha and then continued. 'Lord Buddha is our guide to perfect happiness through the four noble truths. Namely: Life is suffering. The origin of suffering is desire and only be ended by its control. And there is a path that leads to the suppression of suffering.'

'Well that's enough preaching for today,' Daniel butted in.

'Anna what do you mean by the true way,' Peter asked in a desperate attempt to understand this ritual – that was part of his own heritage.

Anna looked for Daniel's approval to continue, which he happily gave with a silent nod and a smile. Rarely did a young man sincerely want to know such things, and yet Daniel sensed Peter's need, but did not know why.

'The path of deliverance in Theravada Buddhism is known as the Noble Eightfold Path. It consists of eight principles. You should try to have: the right views, the right intensions, the right speech, do the right actions, have the right livelihood, put in the right degree of effort, be of right-mindedness, and carry out the right contemplation. Most important of all one must respect the life of all creatures, you must meditate on your life and improve yourself, and lastly: you must give alms to the poor and care to those in need,' continued Anna.

'If you do all of these things, then you reach nirvana, a Buddhist heaven,' said Daniel. 'If not, you will be reincarnated. If you are good, like Anna, you return as a rich and honourable person. If you are a sinner, like me, then you will be a slimy slug, an ant, or even a slithering snake.'

Anna was not amused, so she gently but firmly slapped his wrist. For no one, not even her beloved, must tell God what to do or cast themselves down into the depths of hell. It was asking for something bad to happen, and soon it would. At times like these, she had great difficulty in coming to terms with being a Christian while following the true path of Buddha. Indeed, she took the best from both to have a fulfilled life, full of kindness and understanding, generous and yet not condescending.

On leaving, Anna said 'On top of the stupa is a green light formed by the sunlight passing through one of the biggest emerald's ever found. It is said this pagoda contains five thousand diamonds, two thousand rubies, sapphires, and topazes. The Shwe Dagon has more gold than does the Bank of England.'

'Burma must be Britain's richest colony,' said a surprised Peter.

'It probably is, as Burma produces most of the world's supply of jade and rubies and is the fourth biggest oil producer. All Burmese can read and write, and many train in our colleges and universities for higher office. We also produce the finest teak, rubber, and fine works of silver and jade.'

'We grow two crops of rice a year. Whatever you plant in the ground will grow, because it is hot and rains one hundred inches a year!' Anna added with a disarming smile.'

'Leave a spade in the garden for a week, and it will grow back into a tree,' added Daniel.

'What Daniel says is true. This is a land of miracles; whose magnificence is sometimes overshadowed by greed of people and corruption.'

'It is fantastic to be here. So peaceful and yet somehow I feel that I have been here many times before,' Peter commented.

'I often feel like that. Maybe it is what the French call déjà vu.'

'You're all silly,' Jim joked. 'He's seen the Shwe Dagon and the Sule Pagoda from the air probably fifty times.'

After leaving the Shwe Dagon, they drove off to explore the city. They lunched at the Strand Hotel before visiting Scott's market where they walked between stalls displaying colourful silk and cotton wraps called *longyis*. On some stalls were beautiful teak carvings of elephants, chinthes, and strange mythological creatures next to boxes of scented joss sticks. Nearby were the silver and gold sellers with gracefully fashioned objects. Some made rings from gold melted down from bits of old Queen Victoria gold rupees. In more secure shops, merchants sold sparking cut emeralds, rubies, and star sapphires along with objects of many shades of jade. Peter had never seen so many shades of jade that varied from near white to jet black and of course; the best is the green variety.

Afterwards, they went to the Rangoon Sailing Club on the shores of the Royal Victoria Lakes where Peter and Jim went sailing while the others rested in the shade. Around them, people relaxed in deck chairs sipping fresh lime juice and iced tea, playing mah-jong, or quietly reading a book. As the little boats caught the wind to skip across the still waters of the lakes, they felt only the sun on their backs and a slight breeze on their faces. It was a little paradise in the middle of a terrible storm. Then they were taken back to the Strand Hotel for a drink and to talk about their experiences among well dressed with men in waistcoats and the women with flowers in their hair.'

'We try to look clean and tidy. What we wear are *longyis,* and not sarongs, and made of cotton, satin, or silk and worn around the waist like a skirt. Above the *longyi* a woman wears a muslin or cotton blouse with a high neck known as the *aingyi*, fastened across the front and to one side, usually the left. Over this may be worn a little white coat known as a tamain. The men may wear a waistcoat with a wrap turban according to their tradition. Burman (Bamars) and Karen wear the wrap-around hats while others use leather hats.'

Under a rotating ceiling fan blowing down cool air, they sat drinking refreshing cool, lime juice. Daniel said that one never drank alcohol during the heat of the day as it leads to dehydration and premature death. Indeed, all *pukka sahibs* and their *burra memsahibs* would sit on the veranda of the Rangoon Club watching the sun go down over the yardarm to drink their gin and tonics. Lesser mortals came to the Strand Hotel or other bars to have their regular tipple. The sunset drink was, like the Spanish afternoon siesta, a traditional thing that the Right Sort of Chaps did. Many a wild native pye-dog, some riddled with fleas and rabies, had been known to scuttle to the side of the road as another drunken pukka sahib raced his car carelessly by after having the infamous 'one more for the road'.

Daniel thought many of the *pukka sahibs*, and their *burra memsahibs* were a disgrace to Britain, as many despised the Burmese, especially women like Anna married to a white man. Having sex with a native was politely ignored but totally accepted as what happens to men or women in those hot, lusty climates. Often visitors to the government houses, during both day and night, came to service the carnal desires of the administrators. This caused no real problem because, even if a baby was born, the Burmese would adopt the child, for were they not a blessing from God to be loved and cherished? Children of mixed marriages in England, or among society in Burma, were called half-castes, or the French word chichi, and shunned.

The Thankin nationalist, established in Rangoon College as an independence movement, disturbed Daniel because he did not know what they wanted. Burma already had self-government while remaining a colony. However, to the Thankins this was not enough, so some enlisted in the Japanese puppet Burma Independence Army.

The activities of the British Colonial Administration did little to make the Burmans (Bamars) like them. Instead, the Burmese despised the pukka sahibs in their white shorts and helmet-like topis. They did not understand why the Scots, the Irish, and the Welsh never called themselves British and blamed all failures on the bloody English. A Burman (Bamar) would dislike, or look down on, a tribesman from the Shan, Karen or other states. However, he would never let any foreigners hear him say so. It was, according to Oriental custom, just a matter of face.

The trouble with the British Raj was the lack of loyalty to anyone or anything. If the enemy wanted to know anything, all they had to do was ask their waiter friends. The club bar boys made a good income from reporting what the drunken men, or their gossiping women, discussed. They knew how many ships, tanks, and aircraft the Raj had in Burma.

Sly Boy was a spy who used his youthful looks, soft seductive voice, and sexual skills to infiltrate the establishment. He was on intimate terms with various ladies, but especially a colonel's wife. When her husband was away, Sly Boy would meet her insatiable sexual appetites and in return, she told him everything she knew. When she was satisfied and asleep, a state marked by a series of bull-like grunting snores, Sly Boy would photograph all documents and maps in her husband's study. If she had caught Sly Boy, he would simply kill her. So, the Japanese had all the information they needed and planned the invasion of Burma down to the smallest detail, working on a timetable where failure was unacceptable and defeat unthinkable.

That night Peter and James felt content for in one day, they knew more about Burma and the Burmese than many ever learnt. They fell in love with Burma and to some extent with Anna. If you had been there you would have done the same.

Before going to sleep, they prayed for protection during the stormy days ahead, for Burma to stay free from the Japanese and for angels to guard their new-found friends, Daniel and Anna. Alas, for all their prayers life was about to take a terrible turn for the worse. Even the jade leaf around Peter's neck would need all of its magic to keep him safe. For now, the devil and his terrible dogs of war in the form of the Japanese army raced towards them, devouring all in their path. No man or beast was safe. Even the hermits living in the hillside caves meditating for the good of the world would suffer in the coming barbarity. Death was all around, but few saw the signs.

# 4

# The RAF's Last Stand in Rangoon

*For it's Tommy this, an' Tommy that, an' "Tommy 'ows yer soul?"*
*But its' thin red line of 'eroes' when the drums begin to roll.*

Rudyard Kipling (1890). '*Tommy*'.

Everything was rapidly changing as Peter and Jim waited anxiously for the generals to act, unfortunately when they did it proved ill-advised. Now the evil god chaos raised his ugly head, causing confusion. Peter was shocked on hearing that the Japanese annihilated the 17th Indian Brigade on the east bank of the Sittang River after the bridge was prematurely blown up. Most of the six spans of the 1, 650 foot long bridge survived; one fell into the river; two were damaged, but not destroyed. With no bridge to cross the river, the 17th Brigade could not retreat, though some troops were evacuated on boats, while others drowned trying to swim the fierce waters of the Sittang River. Therefore, the abandoned soldiers together with the British 7th Armoured Brigade had to fight five Japanese divisions without support, as if someone had wiped their existence off the slate of life. Many died or were captured, while a few escaped northwards. Most of those captured would die or become crippled from hunger and torture when forced to work on the Death Railway from Siam to Burma.

The Japanese engineers repaired the Sittang bridge in two days to allow their army to advance the 120 miles to Rangoon. Nothing could stop them as they swarmed over the land like a mass of South American army ants devouring all in their path. As if in a Greek tragedy, the British generals failed to establish defensive positions and gave the enemy all the time they needed to advance. For reasons that no one has ever explained, General Alexander ordered his armies and air force to abandon Rangoon and retreat to newer positions. It was as if he lost hope. The British Empire was collapsing like a house of cards while people died, and others drowned their sorrows in another gin and tonic.

Peter's squadron was ordered to abandon Mingaladon and go north to Magwe. The pilots flew there along with some of the ground crew and essential supplies in the few transport aircraft. However, the others escaped using every form of transport available to arrive at Magwe in small isolated groups; the less fortunate were captured or died. In the new base, the engineers with their screwdrivers, spanners, and hammers kept the RAF flying against all odds and in all weathers. The armourers maintained and rearmed the machine-guns at every opportunity, for their lives relied on speed and a few aircraft to defend them.

Now the RAF attacked the advancing Japanese army, Mingaladon airport, and Rangoon docks, while giving cover to General Alexander's army as it continued the long retreat out of Burma. The soldiers hoped to reach a place where they would be allowed to fight. While marching, a few waved at the RAF planes to make Peter think that the British Tommy was beaten, but not destroyed.

In stages, some of the army retired to protect the oil fields around Yenangyaung on the eastern banks of the Irrawaddy. The rest crossed the Irrawaddy and Chindwin rivers to reach the Chin Hills and Assam. The organisation was so poor that many wondered if the generals had sold them to the enemy. Maybe they were cowards, or Churchill had decided that after the capture of General Percival at Singapore, he would not risk losing anymore. Now the morale of the British troops, including the air force was at an all-time low where the only one you trusted was the man standing or flying by your side.

Before the war, the Burmah Shell Oil Company's oilfields at Yenangyaung made Burma a major oil exporter. Now the retreating British could not allow the oil wells, and storage tanks to fall into the hands of the enemy. If captured, the oil would supply all of Japan's fuel requirements for their advance into India. Therefore, the British filled up every fuel tank and empty container with fuel before carrying on their exodus. At least now, they had enough petrol in their vehicles to reach India.

Everyone waited for the order to counter-attack, but it did not happen as the Japanese raced towards their objective – the oil fields. On 14th April, at Myingun, the King's Own Yorkshire Light Infantry (KOYLI) fought a defensive action that kept the enemy away from the oilfields. Then on 15th April, the order was issued for a civil engineer and a Royal Engineer to demolish the oil fields. They reacted immediately by placing explosives around the hundreds of well shafts to destroy most of them. In some cases, they dropped explosives down the shafts to seal them off and placed others on the storage tanks and refineries. After withdrawing to a safe distance, the explosives were detonated to turn the oilfields into a towering inferno that burned for weeks, fed by tons of crude oil. Yellow and red flames from the fires rose high in the sky while plumes of black smoke cut out the rays of the sun, with fumes that burned one's lungs, skin, and eyes. This meant that when the Japanese reached the oilfields, all they found were burning wells and twisted buildings, but no oil. This was a major setback, as now they had to wait for fuel to reach them by road from Rangoon. One reason for capturing Burma was that the Burmese oil would fuel the Japanese war machine.

The RAF at Magwe was overstretched with most of their aircraft covered with patches over the bullet holes, and fitted with old parts made serviceable by good engineering. They were operational, but would not be acceptable to any aircraft inspector. Where spare parts did not exist, they were made, or taken from another wreck. Now each aircraft was held together by what was known as string and sealing wax; looking mottled and dirty, but they worked.

Peter's luck ran out when attacked by a pair of Nakajima Ki 43 Oscar aircraft diving from the sun. There was no excuse for him not seeing them; except he was very tired and not watching for anything above him while flying by instinct, low on ammunition, and watching the fuel gauge. Suddenly, he was aware of an Oscar chasing Jim's aircraft and fired on it hoping to give Jim a chance to escape. Then the second Oscar sent a stream of lead into Peter's aircraft that tore into the engine and the wing. Luckily, no bullets hit the cockpit, though in seconds, black oil covered the windscreen, making it difficult to see. Peter glanced at the altimeter that showed five hundred feet – too low to parachute out. Now all he could do was to try to coax his broken plane to land on any flat piece of land – that is, if he could find some. Instinctively, he touched the old jade leaf around his neck for his ancestors to guide him to safety. It gave him hope that he would survive.

Matters became worse when the engine oil hit the hot exhaust cowlings and turned into flames. The engine struggled, making a series of splutters as the pistons ceased before the plane started its final spiral descent into the ground. Just in time, Peter saw a flooded paddy field to land his aircraft. The aircraft bounced off the irrigated rice field to send a cascade of water into the air and make a sleepy water buffalo race out of the field in sheer panic. Then she bumped and scraped her undercarriage on the mud before ending up nose down in the earth.

Uninjured but miles from home, Peter climbed out of the cockpit and over the burning wing to escape. He reached a wooded area when the plane exploded as the flames reached the aircraft's fuel tanks. Peter looked back at the burning remains of his trusted aircraft with tears in his eyes. He had lost a friend, and now he was alone for the first time since arriving in Burma.

Peter knew that he must move fast before the black smoke attracted the enemy like wasps to a jam pot. He had sent no May Day signal, as who could save him? During the last days of the Raj in Burma, he was just another person lost in action, presence unknown. Head down and arms pumping, he ran as fast as he could until exhausted, then he rested briefly under some trees where the ground was drier.

After ten minutes, he started walking only to stop to check his compass and move in a north-westerly direction. He was scared and prepared for the worst. As they say, his number was up as death was probably inevitable. On day two, he stayed away from the roads and paddy fields, preferring the seclusion of the shrub land. He thought he could reach the Chindwin River and even the hills of Assam. He ate a dry biscuit or some chocolate from his emergency pack while still walking. All this activity soaked his body in sweat and made his parched throat feel like leather, while his feet started to swell. Foolishly, he consumed all his water during the first day, and now had none.

By the fourth day, his senses played tricks with his brain as simple noises such as the chattering of a nearby monkey, and the wind in the trees made him jump out of his skin. Everything was new and unfamiliar making him aware of the danger lurking around. He kept a look out for snakes, or insects that bit and irritated his body, or an enemy behind each tree. The whole world was against him and only his own actions guided by the spirits of the jade leaf could save him.

Slowly, he was going mad in this maze of warm, damp greenery... Then as if in a dream, he heard a distant murmuring of British voices. His heart raced at the thought that he had found a column of retreating soldiers to hold his breath and listen, not daring to believe what he heard. There was nothing – just the loud sound of his heart beating within his terrified body and tears formed in his eyes, as he knew he was going insane. For didn't the Greeks say. 'Those the Gods love they first make mad?'

Then he heard a baby cry, and a woman said, 'Hush little darling, mummy's here.' It was real, and he was not dreaming. But what did it mean?

He wondered if they were soldiers, or more likely POW's being marched to some unknown fate. So he carefully crawled forward on his stomach to part the long grass to see what was making the noise. He could just make out a scruffy-looking white woman carrying a child whose existence warmed his soul. To think that in this hell, she gave such love to one so small and helpless! Maybe even the dogs of war would allow them to find peace and perhaps the chance to start a new life and forget their predicament. He said a short prayer, just as he felt the cold steel of a sharp knife touch his throat.

It was over.

'Please be quick for my God will understand and accept me in the next life,' he muttered. 'Dear Mary Mother of God, pray for the forgiveness of my sins, as I forgive those who sinned against me.'

As quickly as it came, the knife moved away. Terrified, Peter turned to see a small native with a short, muscular white man grinning down at him.

'Calm yourself, lad. Your prayers are answered. We all are sinners and for the moment; all prayers are gratefully received.'

'I hope so, sir,' Peter replied. He was stunned by this chance meeting, when so easily the blade could have killed him.

'Sorry about the knife, but you could have been the enemy.'

No problem,' Peter managed to say, though he was not sure that he meant it.

'Glad we found you before the enemy did. Well, I'm Pip, Pip Palmarino. I was a Sergeant Major in 'the Royal 'Ampshire Regiment during the Great War, and now the self-appointed leader of our little group of refugees. There is me, Pip's Man and my friend Margot Blanch, who are trying to take these people to safety in India. We started the journey in two trucks that ran out of fuel, so we took to Shank's pony and, like our ancestors, marched off into the unknown.'

'It's good to meet you sir.'

There was no question about Pip being genuine, as like so many Hampshire people, he dropped his 'h's at regular intervals.

'You can't call me sir. From your flying jacket, I can see you're an officer. Are you going to join us – unless you 'ave a better idea?

'Yes please. Joining you is the best thing to happen to me for days.'

Let me introduce my friend and guide, he is a Naga with an unpronounceable name and likes to be called Pip's Man. He is no one's servant and is the best next thing to 'aving an escort of Nepalese Gurkhas. He is a loyal friend, and I am told makes a very bad enemy.'

'I'm Peter Anderson and delighted to meet you. You have saved my bacon.'

'Well let's 'ope so, but there's a long way to go just on a song and a prayer. We don't 'ave much, but we share what we've got. I hope that's all right?'

'Very much so, it sounds totally smashing.'

'If you still 'ave any medicine please give it to us, for we suffer from everything you can imagine from Delhi tummy, fevers, jungle sores, cuts, and despair.'

'I have some quinine, bandages, and morphine in my survival kit.'

'Good man! Give it to our Karen nurse, Anna.'

To Peter's surprise, the nurse was Anna Coombs, and both were pleased to know that the other was alive. It is strange how friends meet at times of danger. It is not accidental but an act of God. Anna greeted him with tears in her eyes and a hug. She was like his sister, who when grieving would sob and shake but say nothing. Where was Daniel?

'Thank God, Peter, you're alive. So many have died and alas more will follow. The devil stalks this land, destroying hope and people who once tainted can rarely be healed. Even the tears of Lord Buddha will take many rivers to wash us clean of the blood and treachery that set brother against brother.'

'You are a sight for sore eyes Anna. It seems ages since Rangoon, and yet it is only such a short time since the world went crazy.'

'God always sends a friend to one in need, so he has sent you to me and me to you. It will help us like wounded birds fly away from the fires of hell. No one should have to exist without hope of a life everlasting and peace of mind.'

Anna shook and held Peter tight as tears of grief washed down her cheeks onto his face and they both shared a deep unspoken sorrow.

Peter noticed Anna had cut off her lovely long black hair to look more like a man. He did not like her short hair, but she was still beautiful. She looked older as if she had lost part of her life as the vibrant, happy young wife he once knew. Now she spent all her energy helping others while ignoring her own needs. Her eyes were sunken into her skull, and her soft face wore a mask of sadness. He realised Daniel must be dead or a prisoner, and knew it was wise not to ask. He felt that if she wanted to tell him about Daniel, it would be fine. Likewise, if she did not, he would never ask.

# 5

# A Stroll in the Jungle among Friends

*Tous pour un, un pour tous.*
(All for one, one for all.)

Alexander Dumas (1844) '*The Three Musketeers*'.

The refugees moved north-west, spurred on by the fear of capture. The nearness of the enemy was a constant worry, especially when they saw the sky lit at night by the fires from burning villages, heard the sounds of gunfire, or an enemy aircraft roaring across the sky in search of a target. It was sticky, hot, and miserable. Perspiration moistened everyone's body, draining valuable salts and water and weakening them. Cuts festered to form jungle sores, and when they waded through streams, many large, black leeches attached to their legs to suck their blood.

Peter felt the grass cut his legs and the weight of the child on his back bore down like the sins on the back of a pilgrim. He grinned and carried his burden with fortitude knowing it was the same for the others. To stop was fatal, so no one spent long when answering the call of nature. Where Pip went, they followed in search of a safe haven like ships in a storm on an uncharted coast looking for any port, not caring where.

'Come on, you lot, and keep moving! We must go further before we can safely rest.'

No one replied but smiled at the ex-soldier and well-known elephant hunter. They knew that Pip Palmarino did not wish to become a guest of the Japanese Imperial, and so felt that, like Moses leading his people across the Red Sea; he would get them to safety. They were right to trust him, as he was the only one who knew the jungle well enough to survive. Two years previously, Pip was charged by a man-killer elephant, aimed his gun and fired. He killed the bull, but the dead beast pinned Pip to the ground. Pip took two hours to pull his body free of the elephant and two weeks to drag his injured body to the nearest village.

The refugees were a mixed bunch of civilians who were abandoned by the British during their chaotic retreat. A few died on the way, and others joined them in their exodus to find safety. They carried the little they owned after abandoning the trucks and discarding most personal effects. Many kept a crumpled photograph in a pocket, a charm around their neck, or their favourite walking stick. Most of them had only the clothes they wore. One middle-aged English schoolteacher made a yoke, from which she carried her bundle of spare clothing and extra things for the women with children. At a distance, she looked like a local labourer carrying goods except for her thick red hair, pale skin, and deep-set green-blue eyes. They were innocent lambs waiting for the slaughter with only their feet to save them. It was an unusual type of war that required a very different type of hero.

Four hours later Anna Coombs checked out a village. No one asked her to do the negotiations, but she did, as being a Karen, she spoke most Burmese languages. She discovered that, for the moment, they were safe with no signs of the enemy. The friendly villagers brought food and water while two men led them to a clearing away from the village where they could lie down, stretch their tired legs and wash their hands and faces.

It was all civilized, very British, though many were of the refugees were from different nationalities and cultures. They fed the children first before taking a small portion for themselves. They were so well-disciplined and shared everything, so Peter failed to realise that they were in a state of shock. None had ever gone for a walk into the jungle, except for their leader, and most had lived comfortably attended by servants, and enjoying the best food and drink that money could buy. They quietly suffered from the effects of prolonged fear and tired muscles that were slowly becoming strong again.

'Will we go back to get my Teddy?' little Timmy said to Peter.

'Of course we will return. It is just a matter of time; you wait and see. Now don't worry your head about such things and get some sleep, for soon we will be on the move again. I bet your Teddy's safe and well.'

'Will the Japanese eat us when they catch us?'

'Don't be so silly. Who would want to eat a skinny little thing like you?'

'Peter. Will they cut off your head when they catch us?'

'I hope not. I quite like my head where it is, thank you.'

'Will you stay and help us?'

'You know I will if you stop talking.'

There was silence as the little orphan Tim fell asleep, leaving Peter to wonder how sad it was that this six-year-old feared the advancing Japanese. Later, Peter learnt that Tim had seen his father beheaded and his mother raped and killed, so now he rarely spoke to anyone. Peter could not imagine what such horrors had done to such a little boy. Perhaps Tim thought Peter was his new father. That suited both of them.

Fear and the taste of defeat had become as infectious like a plague that entered the soul leaving nothing untainted. Peter had hoped the British Army would counter-attack, but realised just how unprepared they all were and how easy it had been for the invaders to occupy southern Burma.

He was awakened only minutes after getting to sleep by Pip holding his elephant gun.

'Sorry to wake you, but we must go. It is important that we leave no trace of our visit as I don't want the villagers punished for 'elping us. It would be wrong, and I won't let them suffer for our stupidity.'

Peter rubbed his eyes and jumped up.

'Yes, of course! I will stay and make certain nothing of ours remains behind. Then I will easily catch up with you slow coaches.'

'You'll do fine. You must keep the rest together and stop them getting depressed. While they all believe we will get to India, we have a good chance. When they stop believing, we will all die – or worse still be captured.'

'Will we make it?'

'Did 'annibal cross the Alps?'

'Of course he did.'

Then, if we reach the safety of the jungle by dark, we will survive. People say the jungle is our enemy, but it isn't, for the jungle is neutral. While we're in the jungle, shadows conceal us from most eyes. One good thing about the jungle is that it will supply all our needs for food and water.'

After they left Peter picked up a cigarette butt, a handkerchief, and a top off a can of corned beef. Then he moved quickly, hoping to find Pip's people, as on his own, he would get lost. He felt vulnerable when he entered the edges of the jungle with their tall trees and sparse undergrowth.

'Come Peter sahib, must walk faster or we both miss Sir Pip.'

It was Pip's Man who was quiet, well behaved, with a grin that lit his whole face and exposed a few missing teeth. He had no shirt, exposing the tattoos that covered his body from his neck to his waist. In his belt was a small knife, and over his shoulder was slung a crossbow with a quiver full of bamboo arrows.

'Thanks for waiting.'

'No talk but come quickly so we catch up to Pip.'

'OK, I'm coming,'

Twenty minutes later they re-joined the party. All were pleased to see them, especially young Timmy, who ran up to Peter and held his hand while Pip's Man just walked on, nodded at Pip, and disappeared ahead into the gloom. Tim had adopted Peter, whether he liked it or not, and so Peter had to take care of him.

A further ten miles into the jungle they came upon Pip's Man cooking the carcass of a barking deer. Around the fire was a feast consisting of fruits, water, and a place to sit. The smell was fantastic.

'Is anyone hungry?' Pip asked.

So they sat down to rest or play with the children. The venison was magnificent and the fruits delightful. The only thing that was missing was an ice cool gin and tonic, though one suspected that Pip could have found one if he wanted to. By tradition, they never drank until the job was done and the sun well below the yardarm. Even before the food was eaten the fire was extinguished, the ashes hidden, and again, all signs removed.

Then Pip addressed them. 'We are safe in the jungle as we can't be seen from the air but must avoid main tracks and villages. 'Owever we must learn the ways of the jungle. Make no noise when you can hear no jungle sound. Stay silent for a moment and listen to the normal noises of the jungle.'

Everyone did as they were asked and heard the noises of the insects, the wind in the leaves of the trees high above, the monkeys chatting away, and the tapping noise of the water dripping through the canopy down to the ground.

'When noisy soldiers are near the animals will stop talking, and it is quiet. Then stay still and as quiet as a mouse.'

'So the animals will warn us,' chipped in young Timmy.

'Just so Tim, they'll warn us if we let them. While Pip's Man will guide us across this featureless jungle to where we'll find safety.'

'Sir Pip, we now go, chop chop! Our cooking fire will attract the yellow devils.'

Pip said nothing, just nodded as both men went to scout a safe way ahead, closely followed by the group.

One night Margot took Peter into the jungle away from prying eyes and told him about Anna. She had noticed, as indeed, they all had, that Anna and Peter knew each other.

According to Margot this is what happened.

Anna's life with Daniel Coombs, a young British engineer, was as happy as this world allows. They were deeply in love and radiated a happiness that affected all around them. It should have never ended since it was paradise. They lived eight miles north of Rangoon on the Prome Road in a lovely bungalow. Anna and her sister ran a health clinic next door, while Daniel worked in the dockyard. One fateful morning Anna woke up feeling full of love, goodwill and joy in her newly found knowledge that she was carrying Daniel's child. After working in the clinic she sat on the veranda with her sister under the frangipani blossom and waited for Daniel's return. She wanted to surprise him with her good news.

She had heard that the Japanese army was advancing but was sure that the British would hold them back long enough for everyone to leave. It was unthinkable that the British Empire could be defeated by the Japanese.

The women greeted the British Army lorry that stopped at their bungalow but were horrified when from it appeared ten Japanese soldiers pulling Daniel with them. He was tied up and covered with blood from many beatings. Anna tried to help him but was held back by the soldiers. The Japanese officer placed Anna and her sister near her kneeling husband to watch him cut off her beloved's head. Daniel looked into her eyes until the moment he died. Anna felt Daniel's soul entered her so that together they would travel until time stood still to meet again in the next life. Daniel's blood covered the two women, so they sank into a form of despair so deep that few survive.

Now oblivious to everything, the two sisters were beaten and repeatedly raped then left for dead. Two bundles of joy that had never hurt a fly were left broken on the ground in pools of blood while ants crawled around them. Even the vultures stayed away, as if forbidden by God to touch the flesh of the innocent. Only that strange cry of the male crested tuk-tu lizard broke the silence, as if telling the world of the horror that was all around.

An hour later and purely by chance, Pip came along to check that Daniel and Anna had left, as he heard the Japanese were in Rangoon, or if they needed help. He could not believe the carnage that lay before him. In the clinic were the bodies of two nurses and an orderly, left where they had been butchered. Then he found the remains of his friend Daniel, and Anna's sister and just wanted to vomit. Still in shock he saw Anna's body move and picked her up in his arms to wash away the blood. Her chest moved slightly as she struggled to breathe. Thank God she was alive!

Slowly, Anna became conscious, saw Pip's face and smiled.

'Pip, don't leave me -- I am so cold and very afraid.'

'I wouldn't leave you, lass not in a month of Sundays.'

Sadly, Anna remembered her loss and yet too weak to cry could only reply. 'It would be good leave, for the light has gone out of my life.'

Pip swallowed back his tears, for indeed the days of sunshine were over to be replaced by the clouds of war, and the despair of the dispossessed. It was all happening too quickly and so violent. Still, there would be time to consider what had happened; and it was not now. They must leave, but first he must bury his dead friends.

Pip carried Anna to a safer place away from the horror that had filled her eyes and half-blinded her with pain. Somehow Pip stole four trucks and set about collecting those wanting to escape.

Anna did not say that she had lost Daniel's baby as it was too personal to tell anyone, even dear Pip. Much, much later Anna told Margot.

Anna became a tower of strength, helping the women with the children and scouting nearby villages for assistance. She said that God spared her so that she could help the sick to reach safety. In her behaviour, there was not a single trace of self-pity, just plain common sense. Her smile and her fortitude proved magnetic winning everyone's love and trust. If you were ill, you asked Anna. If you were full of despair or afraid, she would cheer you up.

Few knew her story, for if they did, they would know that they were in the presence of one of God's beloved. She was an angel with torn wings and soiled body, but was a light to all who met her. Years later when she was old and lame people were amazed at her kindness and smile even when obviously in pain. Her goodness and belief in God inspired everyone.

She kept the scant medical supplies for the seriously ill while treating each symptom as they developed with sound reasoning, disinfectant, and traditional remedies. Her knowledge of herbal plants helped when the Western medicine had long been used up.

Later, Margot asked how Peter knew Anna, so he told her about the day in Rangoon and the Shwe Dagon pagoda.

'Now, be strong,' Margot said. 'Do not think that it is by chance that fate has sent you here. You have to help us get everyone to safety.'

So Peter helped Anna with the children and helped her to collect herbs for medicine and the fruits, nuts, and fungi for food. They learnt to laugh together and support each other as dear friends should. In some way, both regarded the other as a sibling to whom they could tell anything. And so this pure love grew between two people thrown together by the horrors of war. Inevitably, a time came when Anna took Peter into the forest where they could be alone to hold and kiss each other in the way that shy teenagers do. Timidity gave way to desire as clothes were gently eased away, and eager hands explored each other's body. Peter was aroused by her soft silky skin, and marvelled at her generous pointed breasts. After a while, she guided his manhood into her and felt a woman again as both moved together in that ancient ritual called love. Now he knew how special it was to make love to a woman. It was indescribably beautiful, so natural and yet so very personal. Only God could have made such a perfect act, such a loving feeling, and such a glorious expression of endearment, which left him exhausted but deeply calm.

Like all good things, it was over too soon, though he could not let her go. He had never felt so complete, part of another or strangely content. They felt at peace, yet strong enough to face the ordeals that lay ahead. Afterwards, Peter felt a bit guilty that he had sinned and hurt her. Anna felt his youthful sense of wrong and set his mind at ease.

'You and I must take what little joy we can and savour it like a good wine or a great vision. Tomorrow we may die, and until then others rely on our strength. Life is to be enjoyed – let's be glad that we have made each other happy.'

'Oh yes you have. I will always love you, Anna, until the day I die.'

'Silly man – you do not love me but only think you do. You will remember me, as I will you for in a time of danger, you were my friend. When I needed loving, you gave me your body so that we will always be a part of each other.'

With that they returned to the group to sleep, content with being alive even though they were in the middle of nowhere. In the following weeks, they slept next to each other like all the other couples; No one commented as they were happy to see the two find some consolation in each other's arms. For it is written in the sands of time that life is just a short journey that starts with the pain of birth and ends in the agony of death.

To the end of their long lives, they remained in contact as friends, apart but linked together, forever by a thin silk web of love and shared experiences. They were the lost children who war made prematurely old and yet not mature enough to know their own minds. They were adrift in uncharted waters trying to save others and give them hope.

Pip taught everyone the ways of the jungle, the names of the trees, what fruits could be picked and what animals could be eaten. Once a king cobra came near the group while they slept so that Pip killed it with his curved jungle knife, in fact, it was a Gurkha Kukri. Quickly, the twelve foot long snake was skinned, cut into pieces and placed in the cooking pot. This they enjoyed believing it was a 'wild chicken' stew, and afterwards most slept. Others sat to listen to Pip talk about the snakes of Burma. There was the deadly Russell's viper, the small poisonous kraits, the cobras, but above all the magnificent king cobra. Pip said that most deaths from snakebite in Burma were caused by the five-foot long Vipera russelli or Russell's viper, that was distinguished by three rows of reddish-brown spots outlined in black and again in white. However, many snakes like the common krait rarely bit anyone.

Cobras fascinated Peter from the time his mother told him stories of snake charmers. Later, his father gave him a signed copy of Rudyard Kipling's Jungle Book, written in 1894, which told of snakes. Now he heard that the king cobra, or hamadryad, (Ophiophagus hannah) was the world's largest poisonous snake, which guarded her eggs until they hatched. They feed on small rodents and other snakes, but rarely attacking humans. The Hindus respect the Hamadryad because legend says the adult will suck the milk from a cow without harming her. The jungle was a good provider, but according to Pip's Man, it must be honoured and respected. As you go by a banyan tree, you should say a prayer to the jungle gods, known as nats, because they live there. Indeed, the many-branched, one hundred foot tall and ten feet wide banyans, whose aerial roots hung down towards the soil beneath, were the ideal homes for anything. The banyan tree is a mulberry called *Ficus bonghalensis*, or sometimes *Ficus indica*. It is important to the traditional peoples of the Burma-Siam region for its unusual shape and for its ability to survive nearly anything. Many tribes put small parcels of food and other gifts in the trees to please the gods and to ask for their help.

Peter learnt to recognise the wild rubber plants, the *Cinchona* plants whose bark gave quinine, even how to cut open and eat the stinky durian fruits. There were plantations of the quinine-producing *Cinchona* trees established around 1890 in parts of Burma, India and Java in order to treat malaria.

Most trees found in the jungle were the Burmese teak *Tectona grandis* and the ironwoods with their huge buttress–like roots. The leaves, fruits and all other edibles kept the group healthy, their diet occasionally being supplemented by meat when hunting proved successful. The jungle floor was soft under their feet and usually dry. Once they rushed to higher ground as waters from a nearby stream broke their banks and rushed over the jungle floor like an incoming tide. From the top of the hill, they looked down as the raging waters swept away many small animals and snakes.

Soon they felt safe when waking up to the distinctive calls of Hoolock Gibbons in the trees high above them as they played their daily duet at the break of dawn. Now and then they saw the images of small animals gliding from tree to tree, a hundred feet above them, or came across a tapir or a deer. Often the ground birds such as the peafowl and wild pheasant were added to the cooking pot. Strange many coloured fungi grew out of the moist earth. Some were deadly poisonous while others highly edible, even delicious.

Sometimes they found a clearing where dead trees had fallen so making a hole in the canopy that let in the sun light. On the tops of the fallen trees, there were orchids and strange hairlike, parasitic plants known as epiphytes that normally lived a hundred feet above the ground in the canopy. There were so many beautiful orchids that for days the ladies and the children wore them in their hair. It was a simple, gesture, but it made everyone happy.

One night a large Bengal tiger wandered towards them while stalking a barking deer. The magnificent yellow-striped beast must have picked up their trail and was preparing to have them for dinner – or was it for breakfast? Slowly, the hundreds of pounds of muscle sniffed the air and bounded towards the refugees. Pip levelled his elephant gun as Pip's Man aimed his crossbow at the carnivorous feline. Then a pair of barking deer broke cover and distracted the tiger, who gave chase with leaps and bounds before jumping on the back of the largest deer dragging it to the ground before killing it. It was over in seconds as the deer was picked up by the neck and carried away into the distance.

'The tiger probably 'as young nearby and is taking 'er prey to 'er lair. See what a little deer can do by giving up his life so that we may survive?'

'I doubt that,' Margot added with a grin. 'More likely the deer saved the tiger's cubs from starvation.'

On another occasion, the jungle noises suddenly stopped to be replaced by the sounds of something large moving through the undergrowth. There was a crashing of trees, and a trampling of the ground that Peter had never heard before. Pip's Man seemed totally disinterested in the noise, but Pip was worried. Maybe it was a Japanese tank or a tractor. It certainly wasn't Burmese for only a few local people could afford such a machine or the petrol to run it.

'Stop and be still,' Pip whispered.

They obediently stopped and sat down quietly. Even the babies seemed to know when to be silent as none cried. Pip moved slowly forward, not standing nor crawling, but crouched down with his rifle ready. Pip's Man followed, arrow strung in crossbow, while Peter held his revolver. They found a hastily abandoned Japanese campsite and saw why. It was because a herd of wild elephants had passed through the camp on their way to bathe in a nearby stream. The elephant spoor was everywhere, as were their footprints on the trampled ground with broken trees. The elephants had routed the Japanese but who would return to collect their belongings once the beasts had gone.

Pip laughed. 'See, Peter, even God's animals are on our side.'

'No, Sir Pip, the jungle is neutral. Though maybe our nats have been watching over us,' Pip's Man said. Then he walked further down the beaten track to see if there were any Japanese nearby.

'Shouldn't we go back as the others must be worrying?'

'Yes, we should. I did not realize that the Emperor's thugs we're so near. However, you must not tell the others it could make them give up just when I am beginning to feel that we can make it. Fear fogs the brain leading to self-destruction, so we must control it fear, or be ignorant, to survive. It takes a very brave person to be afraid and still remain courageous.'

They rapidly collected the cans of food, blankets, and a pair of boots that could fit someone, leaving no trace behind them. It was essential that their presence remained a secret as the Japanese soldiers were all around them.

Most days went by peacefully so that at night, they slept while taking turns being on guard. Pip's Man made the smokers local cheroots. After the war, some of them bought their Burma cheroots from a tobacconist in London's Burlington Arcade. It was a little vice that reminded them of a time in a distant land where they defied all odds and lived to help others. No one could tell who smoked a cheroot, so they would ignore any butts left behind.

Days turned into weeks as they crossed Burma. Every day, Pip, Margot, or Pip's Man went out hunting for food, leaving Peter in command. The one thing that marked the passage of time was that the children grew bigger. Babes became toddlers; toddlers grew strong from walking, and teenagers became adults. Even here the clock of life still carried on its inevitable progress towards the end. It was not easy, and often they went hungry when fruits and nuts were difficult to find or the hunting party did not return for days.

Once Pip returned with cans of food and metal drinking bottles full of water, together with a bottle of quinine to cure malaria. Anna gave it to the sick and the children as a bitter tasting drink consisting of a few drops of quinine in water. It was a lifesaver.

'How did you get it? I bet the Japanese did not give them to you.'

'Well. Pip's Man is damn good with that crossbow, so the enemy saw nothing before they died.'

'But why take risks? When they are missed, we'll be hunted down.'

'I'm not stupid. We walked south and across the river to where they are camped and caught them resting. We 'ad no choice, as without quinine or finding some *Cinchona* bark, malaria will kill us. I knew that the Japanese carried medical supplies with them, so it was our only 'ope.'

As the journey continued they became part of the jungle. The women wore their skirts loosely around their waists like the traditional Burmese *longyi*. Everyone wore headgear such as a cap, a scarf, or a self-made turban. At every stop, shoes were repaired. Clothes quickly washed and dried to become faded, taking on a sandy shade that blended with their surroundings. Pale skins became tanned making them look healthier and a bit like Anna. Muscles replaced flab. Beards grew on previously clean-shaven faces. So that their rate of walking increased to that of an infantryman. Former bank managers collected fruits and wood along with a riverboat sailor, a cook and a nanny. The Burmese, British, French, a couple of Dutchmen and a talkative Italian chef were just Pip's family, and would remain so for as long as they lived. They swore like troopers, looked like pirates, and worked like bees.

# 6

# At Last they reach Nagaland and Safety

*A good man and woman are worth a thousand unwilling conscripts.*

Like the gradual progression of light during a winter's dawn, the dark forest gave way to the half-light of the woodland and then into long, forgotten sunshine. Now the undergrowth was so thick it had to be cut away to let the refugees pass. Then the vegetation became sparser as they started the slow climb up the foothills covered with grass and small trees. Everyone was happy to see the sun that it helped them forget there were fifty miles more to go. They climbed the slopes as thick mud grabbed at their feet or sometimes a person would slip to slide on their backsides down a few feet before starting to climb up again.

Now there were many insects, especially mosquitoes that bit their bodies while their legs were covered with black blood-filled leeches. The sun drained the moisture from them to leave cracked lips and dry skin. At each stop, they lit cheroots to burn the leeches, so they dropped off leaving behind a bleeding hole as cuts were bound and feet rested. Thorns and other objects were picked from the skin and forgotten before grabbing a few minutes sleep.

Three days after leaving the jungle, they met a patrol of Naga warriors armed with old-fashioned rifles and crossbows. Pip's Man smiled with joy, exposing not for the first time, the many gaps in his teeth. There was a great deal of slapping of backs, grinning, and laughter as he sat down with the newcomers and chatted away for what seemed to be hours while the group rested.

Each Naga tribe had different traditions and leaders. Some Naga chiefs had approached Ursula to lead them after the British left, so they could fight the Japanese and their Burman (Bamar) allies. The Naga, Karen, Shan, Kachin and Chin did not like the Japanese or the southern Burmese they called Burmans (Bamars). They considered the Burman (Bamar) lazy and arrogant, while the latter thought of the others as primitive and uneducated.

So Miss Ursula Bower established a Naga force to carry out work for the British. The Naga warriors loved the challenge and the thought of combat as it was part of their ancient tradition of headhunting before being converted to Christianity. However, they still respected their nat gods as well as the new religion. The Naga group was incorporated into V Force commanded by the popular former Deputy Commissioner for Nagaland, Charles Pawsley and run by Ursula Bowers. They collected information on the enemy positions, their numbers, and could identify each Japanese division. Slowly, the British started to trust the local people and obtain accurate information where before unfounded rumours of Japanese superiority destroyed the morale of the retreating army.

The Naga warriors could travel silently like shadows in the night to work behind the Japanese lines and accurately record the enemy's movements. They showed Pip the way to safety before going as suddenly as they had come. A day later they found the village of twenty thatched basha huts at the top of a hill consisting of a hundred people. The compound was full of animals and children playing as if nothing had changed in a thousand years, maybe it hadn't. A village banyan tree was decorated with food offering to the nat gods, for the Naga lived as one with nature. They kill only for food or to protect themselves. Snakes, however poisonous, are shooed away so that they may keep the balance of nature by killing off the rats. The gentle breeze through the trees played a sweet serenade on the little metal objects hung from the trees.

It was heavenly and the first time they felt safe since leaving Rangoon. Only a few died; however, many would suffer for decades from prolonged attacks of malaria, but all bore the scars of the time before they joined Pip. They would never forget the sound of bombs, the shrieks of 'Banzai!' and the murder of their friends. Many had lost loved ones and everything they owned, but were glad to be alive.

Pip's Man left the refugees with some Naga men and women as others helped the refugees find shelter in the huts and brought water for drinking and washing. The Naga women giggled at the unusual sight of well suntanned, muscular memsahibs in their ragged dresses. Happily, the group sat down en masse and rested. While the refugees slept, the Naga removed their shoes, which were later returned, crudely but effectively repaired. Though the European women spoke no Naga and the Naga women no English, somehow they communicated by gestures, so that eventually all of their needs were met. Everyone enjoyed their first real wash since the journey began. Then the children slept while the adults rested and talked about everything and yet nothing. Hope seemed to shine all around as if they had found the Holy Grail.

Painting of Naga Headman.

Peter noticed these Naga people were different to Pip's Man. The headman wore his robe over one shoulder, unlike any Burmese dress, and on his head wore an ornate leather hat adorned with bird feathers. His ears were pierced with long bush pig horns in each lobe. The chief's wife was naked above the waist only wearing a *longyi* and some large silver bands on her forearms. Around her neck were necklaces of coloured cords and beads. She wore her long black hair uncut and tied back to reveal a series of silver earrings that reached down to her shoulders.

The villagers feasted the refugees on roasted wild pig, rice, fruits, and freshly made bread to treat them like heroes. By the time the feast was over, the tribal chief sent a messenger over the hills to the British garrison to come and collect the refugees. While they waited to be collected, the women tried to make themselves as respectable before giving up and resting. They sat down on the woven reed mats under the shade of the village huts and enjoyed that deep sleep only known to the weary. The children and their elders slept watched over by Pip, Margot, Peter and Anna like the guardian angels that indeed they were. All four were totally burnt out but were not going to sleep until their flock was transported to safety.

Just as the sun rose over the hills four Bedford three-ton army trucks arrived at the village to collect the refugees. So they said their farewells to the Naga villagers with hugs and waves before being helped into the trucks. For the first time for months, the group was separated when divided to go into the trucks, they started to feel the loss of the others with whom they had shared so much. They knew that too soon they would be on their own and with mixed feelings, they fell silent, pondering their future and remembering the bitter past. As they left the village, Peter noticed that Pip's Man remained with his people, keeping a couple of Japanese rifles. Pip and Margot said nothing, so Peter decided that silence was the best policy.

In the garrison, Peter was whisked away to Calcutta with only time to give Anna, a big hug and his address, asking her to write. Anna did until eventually death parted these two dear friends and jungle lovers. Leaving Anna created a hole in Peter's life that he vowed not to fill, but like so many people, he was soon to break his vow.

Peter hoped that Pip, Margot and the others, especially young Timmy and Anna, would be safe. He would always remember carrying Timmy, through a jungle with leeches stuck to his legs and his belly rumbling with hunger. Well, it was something to tell his grandchildren, if he lived long enough to have any.

After the war, a young man (the author) asked Pip Palmerino and Margot Blanche why few knew their story. They just smiled and poured him another large glass of cool lime juice slightly laced with gin. Then Margot changed the subject by showing him her latest oil painting of a beautiful Burmese woman in traditional dress. If you see her paintings, you will notice that she has captured for time immemorial the beauty of the Burmese people, and the land that she loved right until death took her on that last journey. For after the war, she and Pip lived together in a beautiful bungalow on the old Prome Road eight and a half miles north of Rangoon.

During the chaos of the British Army retreat out of Burma, half a million civilians made the journey to India. Some travelled by road and train, arriving at Akyab and taken by boat to Calcutta. Others walked the journey in groups varying from ten to two hundred. People talked of Captain 'Elephant' Bill Williams, who transported a hundred people and over a hundred working elephants out of Burma. This made Peter wondered why no one referred to the elephant hunter who led a hundred people out of Burma over six hundred miles on foot. However, Williams and Palmerino were as different as chalk is to cheese. Both were the great men who do famous deeds when the world is thrown into a state of insanity, and all systems descend into mindless chaos.

The British Army failed to hold the important river towns of Shwegyin and Kaing. If they had crossed the Chindwin at this point they could have held the town of Kalewa for weeks. Why did not the generals, or the tank commanders supply or steal river craft to carry the tanks and other vital equipment over to the west bank of the Chindwin River? Likewise, there are no reports of scouts being sent forward to capture, organize transport or even build rafts that with line and tackle would have saved more equipment. The Japanese light tank, the Ke-Go, had a similar performance to the British Stuart tank with a crew of four with one 37mm gun and two 7.7 mm machine guns. The US built M3 Stuart had thicker armour and could travel at 40 mph while the Ke-Go had a speed of 35 mph. By not allowing the British tanks to fight the weaker enemy ones, General Alexander again lost an opportunity to show that the Japanese army was not invincible.

On 12th May, the Japanese captured Kaing to find two thousand vehicles, a hundred and ten tanks, and forty artillery pieces abandoned. Most were destroyed, but not all. General Sukurai's forces were tired but triumphant having marched for one hundred and twenty-seven days, fought thirty-four battles and covered fifteen hundred miles at the rate of thirty miles a day.

The Japanese never expected to capture Burma but only to occupy the southern part to obtain the oil. However, when the British garrison surrendered at Singapore, and they captured Rangoon, the Japanese decided to annihilate the British to rule the whole Orient. So the Emperor ordered the advance into India, and his field commanders to stop the British from retreating to India. Now the arrogant white men with their cartoons of Japanese soldiers as bespectacled monkeys hanging from trees would pay for their racism and stupidity. The Japanese had both the experience in warfare, and the best equipment that was often assisted by a few eminent British business men.

# 7
# And the Rain Keeps Falling

*Still falls the rain -*
*Dark as the world of men, black as our loss -*
*Blind as the nine hundred and forty nails*
*Upon the cross.*

Dame Edith Sitwell (1940) from *Night and Dawn.*

Peter was sent to a new squadron based in north-east India and equipped with brand new aircraft. Now every flight was different, as either the weather or the duties changed. The climate of northern Burma and eastern Assam made flying hazardous. The rising hot air formed thermal currents that lifted the aircraft up, only to drop without warning a few hundred feet after the plane passed them. Pilots had to contend with strong winds, violent electrical storms and torrential rains. Peter learnt to navigate by compass bearing and dead reckoning as ground signs were few and far between.

The only thing stopping the Japanese advance into India was a series of positions running from Kohima in the north, down to the Arakan coast in the south. The positions known as 'boxes' held small groups of troops tired of retreating and prepared to stand up against the undefeated Japanese Army.

Then the first monsoon of the year arrived to change everything; streams became rivers, and roads churned into mud. This deluge of water affected everyone by hindering the defences while slowing down the Japanese advance, giving both sides a needed lull in the fighting.

Peter told nobody except his CO and Jim, of his time with Pip Palmerino. He heard people talk about the group of refugees who walked out of Burma while collecting clothing, cigarettes, and food or even making toys for the new arrivals. The fact that they could survive being chased by the Japanese Army lifted everyone's spirits. Their story started to make the disillusioned soldiers believe they could fight and defeat the Japanese.

While talking to a sergeant, Peter was surprised to hear the strength of his sergeant's feelings. The sergeant said, 'I thank God for old Palmerino because he proved that we can win this war by bringing all those people to safety. If an elephant hunter can keep the Japanese at bay, then we can give them something to worry about. He deserves a bloody great medal from His Majesty at Buck House, but I am sure the generals are never going to acknowledge his heroics.'

Peter just smiled. He secretly agreed that, if the Army had more people like Pip Palmarino and fewer old school tie types with yellow streaks running down their backs, the Japanese would not have taken Rangoon in the first place.

Peter and Jim now patrolled the sky fifty miles into Burma looking for enemy aircraft and protecting the Bristol Beaufighters as they attacked the

Japanese supply routes. As the enemy advanced they brought in newer fighters to protect their slower Sally and Betty bombers. The latter made easy targets if one avoided the gunfire from the turrets mounted on top, on both sides, and in the tail. The normal sortie involved strafing and bombing river barges carrying the Japanese across the Chindwin. At other times, they destroyed trains and railway bridges, or vehicles carrying supplies to the advancing army. The longest flight was when they escorted the C-47 Dakota transport aircraft airlifting supplies from Northern India across the mountains of "the hump" into China. This supplied the Chinese Army of Generalissimo Chiang Kai-Shek's Koumintang (KMT) under the US General "Vinegar Joe" Stillwell. It was a milk run, as they were only needed near the Chinese bases where the enemy fighter aircraft waited for them. On arrival in Chinal, the planes were re-armed and refuelled while the cargo was removed before they flew in a group back to India.

For Peter and Jim, it was a time of waiting, for reflection, and to meditate in preparation to fight for King and Country. When it was too difficult to fly they read, swam, or had a sing song in the mess. It was a hard time as the older pilots were reminded of their dead or missing friends.

Peter tried to improve his Burmese and Japanese and often sat with the Intelligence officers as they interrogated a Burmese informer to make certain that the translator was accurate. Everyone feared being sabotaged by nationalists making many suspicious of the Indian Army, the Gurkhas, and especially the Burmese. It was all ill-founded because the Karen, Naga and Chin were vehemently pro-British, as they feared the Burman (Bamar) from the South and the opium growing Shan to the east. The Christian and Animist Naga did not like the Buddhist Burman (Bamar).

Jim and the CO played golf around the edges of the airfield, while the ground crew played cards or again rebuilt an engine, machine gun, or whatever took their fancy. The engineers were brilliant repairing and maintaining the aircraft in spite of the dust, temperatures and humidity.

Peter liked talking to the cockney Alfie Stokes, he was the mechanic that kept Peter's aircraft flying. After one sortie, Stokes remarked to Peter, 'Sir, I hoped you would stop collecting 'em moth 'oles. It's a bloody job getting enough fabric to fill the gaps. It's not Whitechapel! I'm more of a tailor than an engineer.'

Peter replied, 'Well let's change places; you fly the aircraft, and I become the tailor. Then you will get the thrill of the kill, and I will get some sleep.'

'Thanks for the offer, but not bloody likely sir! Fighting is for young heroes like you and repairing for us old codgers.'

'Well if you insist, I suppose I must keep on flying and wait to learn the art of being a tailor.'

'That's right sir. Don't worry about me as I replace more 'oles in your plane that in any other.'

'Well I do my best, but the moths keep eating away at the old fabric.'

'These holes in your aircraft are big enough for squirrels or mice to get through. Just come back safely with your plane in one piece.'

'I know you will do your best Stokes; then I promise I will try to avoid damaging my plane.'

Then Alfie Stokes chuckled as he set about fixing Peter's plane for the umpteenth time.

Often Peter touched the jade leaf around his neck to feel good and try to communicate with his ancestors and through them with his mother. He never knew it, but she saw him and was glad.

He regularly wrote home and sometimes received letters from his mother and sister, but father never wrote unless something was wrong. He kept in regular correspondence with Anna, who had joined the nursing corps in India. Peter loved hearing from her and knew that he would always remember her. When he closed his eyes, she filled his senses with joy to give him hope that the human race was worth dying for.

At last the British restocked their arsenals and assembled food supplies to allow each position to withstand a long battle. Trenches were dug deep into the hard stony ground on mountain sides, and artillery positions established to fire down on the valleys below. Everyone knew the Japanese must cross the Chindwin River and go through the disease-ridden Kalewa valley to attack the British defences. So they established fields of fire to give the Allied defenders the advantage in the inevitable round of battles to come.

This was a different army from the one that retreated across Burma. They had lost over thirteen thousand men as either dead or missing, while only inflicting five thousand Japanese casualties. Now they were harder, more experienced, and fitter with access to shelter; supplies, medicine and armour when previously they had none. The morale among the British increased knowing they had the advantage, because the enemy had to climb up to Allied positions. No one dared mention that the Japanese still had more soldiers than they did.

Everyone benefited from taking the daily dose of mepacrine to prevent malaria, and the improved sanitation that reduced cholera and typhoid cases, though tick typhus was still common. Then more aircraft arrived to operate from the large bases deeper inside India and from smaller ones in the Assam hills. This made Peter think that maybe they were no longer the Forgotten Army.

Supplies were taken up the muddy steep, and narrow roads to the defence zones termed administration boxes. The materials came on trucks, on the backs of mules and carried by men. This operation did not stop when the monsoon rains turned the tracks into mud and dangerous, skating rinks. Whatever the weather, the ordinance had to get through, and it did. When the monsoons came, over thirty-five inches of rain fell soaking everyone and everything.

The Chindits under Orde Wingate caused havoc behind enemy lines. Their first raid around Indaw disrupted the supply route to the Japanese forces attacking Stilwell in the north. It was a major success, though the Chindits suffered severe losses due to disease, lack of supplies, and inadequate equipment. The Chindit raids shocked the Japanese making General Mutaguchi change his plans. He turned his main attack away from Stilwell and his Chinese army in the north to the west towards the British. He decided to try Wingate's methods by sending his divisions into the jungle with only light provisions and expecting them to live off the land. The lack of accurate information and supplies was to cost the Japanese dearly in the months that followed.

# 8
# All Power Corrupts, but Some Faster than Others

The Flag of the Japanese puppet State of Burma.

The leaders of the Burma Independence Army (BIA) met as students at Rangoon College where they established the Thankin movement which trusted the Japanese to liberate Burma and give them independence. They were Aung San, Ne Win (Maung Shu Maung) and U Nu who later helped the Japanese invade Burma through the Three Pagoda Pass.

Colonel Suzuki Keiji visited Rangoon in 1940 as a representative of the Japanese newspaper *Yomiuri Shimbun* under the alias of Minami Masuyo and recruited many Thankins as Burmese allies. In Siam, Colonel Suzuki Keiji commissioned the Thankin Thirty Comrades as officers in the Japanese Army then adopted the Burmese name of Bo Mogyo (Officer Thunderbolt). The Thankins were known as Bo (Officer) and carried out the ceremony known as *thwe U Thauk* (the drinking of the blood). During this ceremony, the Thirty Comrades cut a finger and collected their blood into a bowl, added alcohol and drank the mixture. It was an unusual ceremony for Buddhists but then war is a strange and foreign land. When Japan declared war on the Allies, Colonel Suzuki formed the Burma Independence Army (BIA) with himself as commander and Captain Kawashima (Bo Aye) as his deputy. Aung San (Bo Te Za) was a Major General, who with Suzuki led the Japanese invasion force through the Siamese towns of Raheng and Mae Sot into Burma. Bo Ne Win with a Japanese lieutenant arranged the sabotage of communications around Moulmein to keep the British unaware of the invasion.

The Japanese 55th Division, led by General Takeuchi attacked the city of Moulmein on 18th January meeting light resistance from the 3rd and 7th Burma Rifles. Bo Ne Win's sabotage caused panic throughout Moulmein City making defence nearly impossible.

Afterwards, the invaders travelled north, only meeting heavy resistance at the Sittang Bridge before moving on to capture Rangoon. Here the Japanese disbanded the Burmese Independence Army to form a smaller Burma Defence Army (BDA) under Bo Te Za (Aung San). If that was not demeaning enough, the BDA was ordered to destroy all pro-British forces. Now even the most junior Japanese soldier was treated with more respect than the BDA. Rape and robbery became common, and the sanctity of the monasteries no longer respected.

The Japanese became concerned on hearing that many Burmese doubted their good intentions. So they appointed, the former premier of British Burma, Ba Maw, as the new *Adipati* (Head of State) of an Independent Burma. They chose the ideal man because when he was defeated in Parliament in 1939, he joined the Freedom Bloc that opposed any Burmese involvement with the Allies in World War II. During 1940, he was imprisoned for sedition by the British in Rangoon Gaol where he was liberated by the Japanese.

The *Adipati* studied at Rangoon Collegeas well as at the universities of Calcutta, Cambridge, and Bordeaux. With all his education, he never believed in anything and changed sides when profitable. He opposed the British move to make Burma a separate nation, and realising his actions were unpopular, changed his mind to join the pro-separatists in a coalition government as Minister of Education. In 1937, he became Burma's first Prime Minister until defeated in 1939. Now Ba Maw assembled a government of nationalists and appointed Aung San as Minister of Defence and head of the Burma Defence Army (BDA) and Thankin U Nu as Foreign Minister. He made them all instruments of Japanese colonialism.

The arrival of the Japanese secret police the Kempei-Tei left an indelible mark on a nation of mostly pacifist Buddhists. To the Burmese, the idea of killing people by torture or cutting off their heads was unheard of. To make things worse, many sadistic and less educated of their people joined the Kempei-Tei as interrogators, informers and torturers. Anyone who showed strong Anti-British feelings, and could speak some English and Japanese, was recruited as a local member attached to either the Army or the Kempei-Tei. They were issued with uniforms and taught how to extract information using every means possible. The Japanese managed to find the usual vermin that all society has hidden away; the bullies, the sadists, the cheats, and the over-ambitious. Ba Tin was an unimpressive student who seduced women, preferably married ones, and gambled. When he had run out of money, he obtained it from his parents, friends; alternatively, he stole it. At fifteen, he sold his mother's ruby necklace for a few hundred rupees, telling her that her maid, Daw Kyi, had stolen it. So Daw Kyi was sacked. Her only crime, if crime it be, was that she refused to sleep with the young master. Unlike his cousin Peter Anderson, Ba Tin from an early age was a seducer of women, especially if it provided money or power. He loved both, but preferred power.

He stole from everyone, even taking the money and jewellery offerings from the temples. Once he was nearly caught by a *pongyi* (monk) while trying to steal from the Shwe Dagon Pagoda, so he never went there again. He felt no guilt at stealing from the *pongyi kyaung* (monastery) for, if reincarnation was true, he was already going to come back as something awful. He read Burmese poetry about corruption among the *pongyi* and how they stole, had women and lived well from the donations of the poor. His favourite writer was the brilliant Thankin Thein Pe Myint whose book Tet Pongyi, which ridiculed the corruption in the monastic orders. He did not like the British or that aunt had trained as a nurse before marrying an Englishman. When he heard that his younger cousin, Peter was a pilot, he hoped they would meet so that he could kill him. He really disliked mixed-race people as he thought they diluted his family ancestral stock.

One morning, Ba Tin was caught robbing an old Burmese man by a Japanese policeman. When the victim told the Japanese that he was a thief, he replied that the man was a British spy. Ba Tin was arrested, pushed into a cell and made to write a statement. When they found that he could write Japanese and English as well as Burmese, they were impressed. But should he be put to work as a labourer like most common criminals or could he prove useful? So they needed to test him and show all that he was a friend of the Japanese people.

Ba Tin was interrogated by Major Hitaki wearing the black uniform of the Kempei-Tei, an open-collared white shirt and peaked cap.

'Come here,' Hitaki screamed at Ba Tin.

'Coming Major-san,' Ba Tin answered, bowing deeply.

'Why did you steal from the old man?'

'He lied to you, mighty Major-san I am no thief.'

'No! You lie.'

'Please, Honourable Major-san, I will do anything. Just let me go.'

'Maybe I will, or I could make you work on the docks as a coolie carrying the boxes from the ships to load on the waiting the trucks.'

The idea of being a coolie made to work faster – speedo – the Japanese called it, horrified him. Ba Tin avoided any form of physical labour.

The Major pondered for a while. Could he use this man or should he be sent to a work gang? If he risked using him, then Ba Tin must prove his worth.

'How can I trust you?' he asked. 'You obviously are educated, and we do not have enough people who speak our language as you do?'

'Oh Major-san, you can trust me. I will do anything for you. I speak Japanese, English, Burmese, Karen, Chin and Hindi. I would be good for you and would work very hard at all times.'

'You will do what I say without question, ah so?'

'Yes, I will do whatever you desire without question, Major-san.'

'If you disobey me, I will simply cut off your head. You agree?'

'Anything you want, I will do without question.'

After the Major left, Ba Tin was fed and given a clean light black uniform to wear together with long boots, a leather belt with holster and a pistol. Then he was taken to Rangoon market where a crowd surrounded the man he had robbed. The old man knelt on the ground with his hands tied behind his back near Major Hitaki.

'Ba Tin of the Kempei-Tei was insulted by this British spy and so I, Major Hitaki, demand he dies by the hand of the one he tried to harm.'

The crowd looked at Ba Tin in his black Japanese uniform with loathing.

The Major walked over to Ba Tin while taking out his long Samurai sword and whispered into his ear. 'Do exactly what I say, or you will take the old man's place and be executed.' On saying this, the major laughed before adding. 'For us there is nothing simpler than cutting off the head of one's enemy. By doing this you will please me and put fear into the hearts of our enemies. For from this day forth all will remember you and tremble.

There was a deadly silence while the crowd wondered if any Burman could ever do such a thing as even the dacoits did not behead people. They decided that it was just another game.

Ba Tin felt the pistol pressed against his back as he took the sword and lifted it. He knew that if he killed the old man, no Burmese would trust him, but he would gain the support of the Kempei-Tei. Without a moment's hesitation, he swung the sword and cut off the old man's head. He felt no remorse for the victim, only pride that it was done with one stroke. The blood on his clothes proved his power of life and death over the people, and he enjoyed the feeling as he started his descent into sadism. He did not notice the look of disgust and horror on the faces of his people, or the pleading look in the eyes of his innocent victim.

On his way home, he noticed that when anyone saw the dried blood on his uniform, they moved out of his way as news of the old man's execution spread through the streets. So when they saw any Burmese in Japanese uniform, they felt a mixture of shame and fear.

Within a week, he was promoted to be Bo Ba Tin and given quarters next to Rangoon Gaol. At first, he would just beat up his subjects and deprive them of sleep. Then he learnt to use his pistol to kill, wound, or scare his victims and reduce even the strongest person to a useless wreck. The more pain he inflicted, the greater was the pleasure that proved much better than having sex.

Too late Major Hitaki realised that he had produced a monster, so he posted Bo Ba Tin to the BDA suppressing pro-British Karen rebels in the hills bordering Siam. He was the ideal person to terrorize people, rape, torture, and burn their houses. Anyway, it would get rid of him as the major was concerned that Ba Tin had not obtained a single piece of valuable information, even though he had carried out over one hundred interrogations and executions. Major had learnt from his time in China that it was better to scare people into submission than to kill them as frightened people cooperate. Dead people cannot be useful and often have relatives who hate you.

As fate would have it, Ba Tin did not join the BDA, but was transferred to the Western Front, where information was needed. Translators into Japanese of English, Burmese and other dialects were few, making Bo Ba Tin a valuable commodity. The High Command decided that Ba Tin was cruel enough to get any Tommy to talk. He was needed, as the Japanese was in unknown territory where information was proving difficult to obtain. Previously, the BDA supplied information but here the tribes were often pro-British. The rumour machine that undermined the British so effectively in Lower Burma did not work in the north and west.

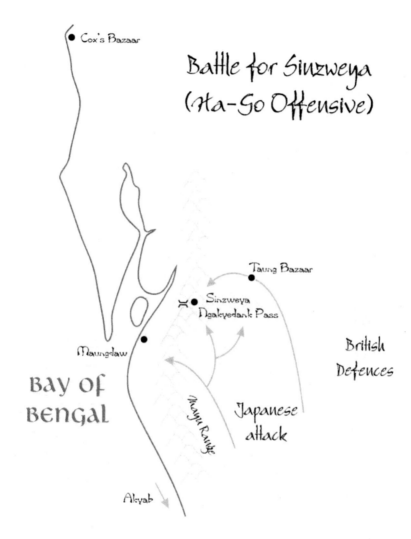

Battle for Sinzweya
(Ha-Go Offensive)

Cox's Bazaar

Taung Bazaar

Sinzweya
Ngakyedank Pass

Maungdaw

British
Defences

BAY OF
BENGAL

Mayu Range

Japanese
attack

Akyab

# 9

# The Arakan Peninsular and the Battle for Sinzweya

*Nobody can run forever.*

After months of frustration, Captain Charles Brighton was ordered to take his Gurkha soldiers south to defend Sinzweya near the Arakan peninsular. He was delighted as it was a change from retreating across rivers and through the jungle when ordered instead of being allowed to fight the enemy. He feared his men, whose motto was 'Better to die than be a coward', were beginning to think all the British were without honour.

Sometimes, like when they crossed the Chindwin, they found themselves without a line of retreat. No one had arranged barges, boats or bridges, so he sent swimmers across the river with ropes to erect a rope bridge so that each man could pull himself with his equipment on the rope across the deadly waters to the other side. It was dangerous and very wet, but luckily, he lost no one. His men grinned when he got his legs wet crossing the river. Once the Gurkhas found and destroyed a Japanese jitter party of six soldiers behind the British lines. Instead of congratulations, GHQ decided the enemy was attempting to cut them off and ordered another withdrawal. Life was controlled by a mixture of bad decisions, panic and an inability to let anyone stand firm and fight.

Charles felt a sense of destiny when General Slim took over command from Alexander. Though General Alexander had the nickname of 'Lucky', he certainly had not passed on any of his luck to his men. Slim was rumoured to be a soldier's soldier, though only time would tell. Maybe they would no longer run like rabbits and attack the enemy before Japan ruled not only Burma but also India.

Once Charles overheard Corporal Joe Brown, a territorial soldier from the Royal West Kents, talking to his mate. He said, 'So they've removed old General Alexander, and not a bloody moment too soon. So maybe now we can have the tools and be allowed to fight.'

'Well, with Slim we might have a chance.'

'I want to fight to make the Japanese pay for making me walk across Burma.'

'Maybe it'll be a bit more positive, so that we see action.'

'My old man fought in the Great War, and survived. So will I, I just want a chance to use my rifle having lugged it across Burma.'

'I would like to get the rabbit Alexander, slimy Mountbatten, and new man General Slim down here to show 'em what war's really like.'

'Make the bloody generals walk up to their waists in mud?'

'I think it would do them a lot of good to walk through the mud, sleep on the ground, and smell the cordite and the rotting bodies of those poor sods who died at their command.'

'Well let's get on with the war before we are charged with treason.'

'It isn't treason; it is the bloody truth!'

Charles smiled as they expressed exactly what he felt.

Days later they reached a valley of dried paddy fields surrounded by heavily wooded hills. This was Sinzweya so the Gurkha soldiers set about assembling supplies, digging trenches and building machine-gun nests to stop any Japanese attack. Each position or box had many trenches reminiscent of WWI that were surrounded by barbed wire. However, unlike Flanders, here there were no continuous defences, but staggered positions with a clear field of fire that would hopefully stop the Japanese. Most of the soldiers were pretty confident that they would stop the Japanese. Most felt that if they attacked, they would be assisted by the other groups. Between the Gurkha and the Japanese were six defensive positions held by seasoned soldiers of 89th and the Indian 7th divisions.

The Gurkha soldiers were eager for battle, sharpening their curved kukris ready for the kill. Charles admired these 5 feet tall soldiers who were so courageous, and yet when not fighting could be so naughty. Maybe they just liked to work and play hard. He felt safer knowing they were on his side. He had fought with them for the last six months and knew that they stood their ground when attacked. Everything was ready with the Vickers heavy machine-gun nests established, and the lighter Bren guns placed around the perimeter.

On 6th February, the Lee tanks of the 25th dragoons arrived, each having a 75 mm hull-mounted gun with another 35mm on the turret and four 7.62 mm machine guns. They were rapidly camouflaged to act as mobile bunkers.

At first, Japanese fighters strafed the positions until the RAF responded. Within days, the RAF shot down sixty-five enemy aircraft and only lost three of their own, so that they dominated the skies.

Peter escorted the Dakotas on their supply runs or flew against the Japanese Air Force, who now had new, faster fighters such as the Tojo. The Spitfire was magnificent in combat, which meant life was simple. However, it is only when you think that everything is easy that things go wrong. By the morning of 6th February, the Japanese passed north through the lines of the Indian 7th division to capture Taung Bazaar before turning south towards the Sinzweya admin box. During the night of 7th, the battle started as, like ghostly images, the Japanese attacked the eastern side of the box.

'For God's sake wake up, there's lots of Japs coming at us from the east,' Private Jed Miller said shaking Corporal Joe Brown awake.

'Easy Jed, I can see them. Just stay calm and wait for orders,' Corporal Brown replied knowing that he had the situation under control. It was totally unexpected, as any attack was supposed to come from the south.

As the enemy came into range of the rifles, the corporal acted.

'Men aim carefully, independent fire at will, one shot per target.'

Then, there was the noise of sporadic rifle fire as each man selected a target, waited and shot him before moving on to the next. Thus, the Royal West Kents (RWK) and the West Yorks (WY) held the line against the advancing enemy.

'What we need is for some bloody officer to order the tanks and artillery to open fire.'

'Jed for Pete's sake shut up! Wait until you see the whites of their eyes and shoot the little buggers before they get you.'

'Sorry, Corporal.'

Someone must have heard, because the 75 mm guns of the Lee tanks suddenly erupted with devastating fire into the enemy, causing them to fall and retreat. It was time for action and someone yelled, 'Kents – it's up and at 'em! Pick your target and take him out.' So that night the RWK and WY soldiers drove the Japanese back.

'Well, we held them! It wasn't so bloody impossible after all.'

'No Corporal! I just hope I get a few more of them before they get me.'

'Don't be silly. Who wants you?'

'So we just sit and wait for 'em, eh, Corporal?'

'Before you can say Bob's your uncle, they'll be back. Just you mark my words.'

Charles and his Gurkha soldiers watched Ammunition Hill and the surrounding area to prevent any enemy getting near the munitions.

The Japanese circled the admin box while a hundred of them captured the hospital. Here they disarmed and tied up the prisoners, collected the medical supplies and set up defences against a counter-attack. When it came it was a solitary Bren gun carrier, which was driven back by grenades.

'They will send the tanks against us next Commander-san.'

'No. The fools will not fire onto their own wounded. They are so stupid. Wars are not won by the faint hearted!'

The Japanese interrogated the captives with such vigour that their screams were heard 300 yards away at HQ. Still the British Commanders did nothing, hoping that by daylight, they could save their men.

Before dawn, the prisoners were lined up in a nearby valley and machine-gunned down. The Japanese were in such a hurry that they failed to notice that three men were still alive. Then they killed the wounded lying helpless in their beds in an orgy of mindless brutality.

After repeated attacks, the RWK and WY recaptured the hospital and pushed the enemy back. To their horror, they found in the hospital the mutilated bodies of thirty-one patients and four doctors. The first man to enter was only sixteen; on seeing the carnage he ran outside and was sick. The next man seeing the horror made the sign of the cross and vowed revenge. When the others heard or saw what had happened, anger rose up inside them like never before. This was no longer any general's war. It was personal as the enemy butchered their mates.'

'They are pagan bastards!' one soldier yelled.

'No one can help any nip when I find him for I'll have his bloody guts for garters,' another replied.

'There is no use in surrendering to the bloody savages! So we had better stand and fight.'

'Yes Sergeant, give us a chance, and we'll settle the score.'

'Now it is, as it should be, Death to the Enemy.'

Behind the hospital, they found the bodies of the others with their hands tied behind their back and cut to pieces by machine-gun fire. To everyone's amazement they found three survivors; they were shot but still alive.

'Sir, there's three living.'

'My God, only three did you say? How many are dead?'

Thirty-five died in the hospital and fifty more outside, sir.'

The dirty little bastards must pay for this. No one, but no one kills medics and our wounded. Tell the men to give no quarter, and make sure they know what has happened. I want everyone to know the Japanese are savages who kill and mutilate the injured, just as we heard they did in China.

The effect of the Japanese brutality on the defenders was to have an important bearing on the course of the engagement. Within hours, everybody knew what had happened at the hospital. They felt sick down to the pit of their stomach before becoming angry and itching for revenge. Even the tired and disillusioned wanted to fight rather than be tortured and shot. There was to be no prisoner of war camp for them. If the Japanese wanted a contest with no quarter given, then the Allied soldiers accepted the challenge while vowing to show the enemy no mercy.

On 9th February low flying Dakotas dropped supplies by parajute. The parajute was made of Bengali jute and cheap to produce. The problem was that the cargo fell more rapidly than those with a silk parachute. In the Dropping Zone (DZ), the wise looked upwards to avoid being crushed into strawberry jam under a falling canister. Only when the last one had landed were the containers collected. Each airdrop increased the men's morale. They felt that at last someone cared and maybe would let them stand and fight. Perhaps they would even defeat the Emperor's men. The troops were impatient to get at the enemy and did not like waiting like live bait for the tiger to come and slay them. The Gurkha soldiers were no exception to the rule. They hated to wait for anything and were always worried that they would be forgotten, or even not trusted enough to fight. However, they had all enlisted under the British flag in the Indian Army to fight as their parents had before them.

'Captain Brighton,' said Havildar Temasen.

'Yes, Havildar Temasen,' Charlie replied to his sergeant.

'When will we get our chance to fight?'

'It will be at any moment.'

'Sir we want to die fighting as men. We do not want to be captured, tied up and shot.'

'I can't see anyone being able to tie you up, Havildar.'

'Nobody is going to tie me up, sir! I would kill the first man who tried with my teeth, if necessary.'

At that point, Charles was ordered to hold the Ngakyedauk Pass at the western entrance to the admin box. Now they were taking the fight to the enemy, as General Slim promised. Someone likened being inside the admin box with very little cover, to a grouse during a grouse shoot, except that the grouse probably has more places to hide. One problem was that the wooded hillsides overlooking the box afforded good cover to both defender and attacker alike. The steep sloping hills were crisscrossed with mule tracks and the trail down to the Ngakyedauk road. The winner would be the side that held the road and occupied the hillsides. It all depended on logistics and timing. The supply route could prove a weakness in the British defences.

'Havildar Temasen,' Charles called out.

'Yes, sir.'

'Assemble the men to leave in ten minutes, we're to hold Ngakyedauk Pass.'

'Yes Sir.'

'We will show them what a Gurkha soldier can do,' Charles added.

Charles looked at his men and saw the impish grins. They liked what he had said. Rapidly, the Gurkha soldiers picked up their rifles, machine guns and one Piat anti-tank gun before moving silently to take up their new positions. Once in their correct position they lay in ambush and instinctively touched their kukri as they waited. It was as though they were praying to some Hindu god. As darkness came, each Gurkha made himself nearly invisible by moulding their bodies to the ground or hiding in the undergrowth while hardly breathing. Nothing stirred as they waited for the expected night visitors.

They did not have long to wait.

The first infiltrators came over the Ngakyedauk Pass to snipe down on the British positions. How ignorant these westerners are thought a sniper, as he took aim at his target. He awaited the signal to start firing. He was tired and hungry but knew that soon they would take the British camp and then there would be rations for all.

When they identified an infiltrator, a Gurkha was sent after him. No order was spoken, just a hand pointed and a nod given.

'Don't fire unless you have to. Use your kukris,' Charles ordered. It was imperative that their positions were kept hidden for as long as possible.

Charles watched through his binoculars as each Gurkha in turn stalked his allotted target. It was like watching the loyal mongoose hunting a snake. The hunter silently and slowly approached his target by sliding on his stomach so low that often he was completely hidden. When ready, he rose and attacked the unsuspecting prey. There was a brief flash of light as the kukri slashed into the enemy and then not a sound. The Gurkha searched the body for documents, water, and medicines, while removing weapons and ammunition. As quietly as he had advanced on his prey, he would return and report back. For the first few hours, the Gurkha soldiers quickly eliminated all the infiltrators. After a few minutes, the Japanese infantry advanced with fixed bayonets slowly down the pass. They were cautious, expecting to find a British position guarding the road. It was so quiet that they decided the position must be further downhill towards the base, and were unprepared for battle when they walked into the waiting Gurkha soldiers.

The first wave of attackers was repelled after being severely mauled. However, now the enemy knew their positions and sent in wave after wave of Japanese infantry. By sheer weight of numbers, the Japanese gained the middle ground to come closer to the camp. It was now down to hand-to-hand combat as the Japanese long bayonets fought against Gurkha kukri and bayonet. For one moment, it looked as if the Gurkha soldiers were being beaten.

Then Havildar Temasen took twenty men to attack the Japanese flank. Charles was too busy fighting to notice the disorder Temasen caused. The Japanese hated the Gurkha soldiers who cut into them with their little swords and destroyed everything in their path. Seeing his men hesitate, the Japanese lieutenant tried to rally them by drawing his Samurai sword to attack the leading Gurkha. It was a futile gesture for as he attacked one Gurkha, he turned his back on another one who killed him, so that his men retreated in disorder.

The third wave of infantry now advanced on the Gurkha positions with cries of *'Banzai, Banzai'*. This and the blowing of bugles, was meant to send fear into the hearts of the enemy. However, the Gurkha soldiers ignored this childishness.

'Keep firing. Don't let them escape,' Charles ordered.

The Gurkha soldiers advanced with sheer determination to bloody their kukris.

'Now draw your kukris.' Then the remaining kukris were taken out and held high for all to see.

'Charge!'

The Gurkha fighters raced onto the enemy with kukris cutting and slashing so that within minutes, the enemy was either dead, wounded, or had run away.

'Gurkhas come to me,' ordered Charles.

They fell back to their position, carrying their wounded with them. The enemy had gone as suddenly as they had come. All that remained were the bodies of the dead and dying.

The wounded were taken to the hospital, while the guns were cleaned, and kukris sharpened before returning them to their scabbards. For the next two weeks, few kukris were replaced unused. The sight of a Gurkha with kukri in hand was terrible to observe, especially if you were their target.

'Havildar Temasen, it is time to set sentries and clear up.'

'Yes sir.'

'It was a bloody good show. You attacked at just the right moment. We were getting a little worried down here.'

'That's me, sir, always on time, never late or early.'

At that moment, Charles felt proud of his men. He watched with wonder at the loving care they gave their weapons, especially their kukris. At times, when they put their kukris back in the scabbards without having drawn blood, they would cut their finger as if it was their sacred duty so to do.

While some of the Royal West Kents were guarding a dried out seasonal riverbed, or chaung, they shot two Japanese infiltrators. The next night they intercepted and killed another group of forty. On searching the bodies of the enemy, they found a map marked with the enemy assembly points prior to attacking the admin box. So using this information, the RWK soldiers ambushed the Japanese before they could join up with their colleagues.

Meanwhile, another Japanese force, the Sugiyama battalion, was routed by the Dragoons' tanks. The outcome of the battle was uncertain as both sides were sustaining heavy casualties with very little ground being taken or held. The Japanese command was angry at being held up by this small position supplied from the air in what they called the *ento jinchi sakusen* (the cylinder position operation). He was surprised his night attacks were repelled with so many of his men dead or wounded. It was not as easy as he had come to expect.

After each skirmish, the British gained confidence as they realised that they could hold their positions and defeat the so-called 'invincible' enemy.

On the nights of 14th and 16th February, Colonel Tanashashi sent three battalions against the admin box in two separate charges. They were ordered to carry out rapid, near-suicide attacks. The stillness of the night was broken by the sounds of bugles and cries of *'Banzai!'* as the Japanese charged the admin box. The British repulsed the attack as star shells from the tanks lit up the night sky and machine-gun fire mowed down the assailants. The three Japanese battalions had nowhere to hide and nothing to do but fall back.

This was not to be any one-sided battle. Japanese Zeke (Zero) aircraft strafed Ammunition Hill, hitting some supplies, while the Japanese captured C Company Hill from the West Yorkshires, coming within 500 yards of the Admin Box HQ and overlooking the new hospital. So the West Yorkshires were ordered to retake C Company Hill. As they advanced, the 75 mm guns of 25th dragoons' Lee tanks shelled the hill killing many of the enemy soldiers and tearing into the woodlands. The tanks stopped firing only as the West Yorkshires reached the foot of the hill. Then their commanders watched them through their binoculars take the hill at the bayonet point. They captured the hill but at a cost, half of them dead or wounded. In reply, the Japanese attack faded away as they withdrew, badly battered. The Japanese had no more ammunition for their howitzers or their mountain guns. So the British set about chasing them out of the battle zone.

The Japanese were beaten because they lacked anti-tank weapons and underestimated the allied forces' ability to fight. Life for the Japanese columns was hard; having run out of munitions and food, but their mistake was the killing of the prisoners in the hospital. This action gave the British soldiers no alternative but to fight to the death. So murdering and mutilating the sick and non-combatant medics melded the allied forces into one body that was not going to surrender, and who were determined to defeat the Japanese. The British soldiers' distrust of the Gurkhas faded away as a new army was born. Charles felt that his fellow officers would stop referring to him as the Johnny in command of a little group of wogs, but he knew the snobs would not change. For them, the Regular British Army was for gentlemen, and the Indian Army was where foundlings and upstarts ended up. Charles felt that they would have to rethink their racism or at least acknowledge that the Indian Army was as equally brave when tested under fire.

The air supply system nearly failed when on 8th February, the leading aircraft turned back without dropping any supplies. The next day a senior American officer, General Old, personally flew the plane that made the first drop. The lesson was learned, so that fighter support was given to the cargo planes, and more ground sorties carried out on enemy positions by the air forces.

Not far from the battlefield, a Japanese officer, Major Suki, arranged for his wounded men to go north. He was pleased that the trucks full of wounded were not attacked from the air. In fact, they were left in peace to save the wounded and repair the damage done to their equipment. He had thought that none of his men would survive the ferocious British onslaught. His fellow officers were too savage. In China, he learnt that it was not a good idea to terrorise one's opponent, as a cornered dog always turns on his attacker. He kept his thoughts to himself because others may consider them to be treason. He did not consider himself to be a butcher but an expert in logistics who tried to maintain a chain of supplies over this extended supply route. As he made his way to the east, he vowed never to allow his men to commit crimes against nature. If they lived and were allowed to escape to safety, he would do his best to fight a proper war.

He would always remember the cry from a British soldier while under attack. 'Don't let the buggers get near. If they catch you, they will butcher you like they did the men in the hospital!'

Another shouted as he charged, 'Give no quarter. Kill them like they did our boys!'

Major Suki remembered his days in England learning the language and attending a short course on logistics. He loved the country with its green fields and friendly people. It was strange that when he was a child Britain was their ally against Russia, and now they were his enemy. There was nothing that he could do about the way things were, so he set about his duties praying silently that soon the killing would end.

# 10

# Every Ace can be Trumped

Over the Arakan, the RAF Spitfires were faster than their opponents' aircraft and their pilots determined to reduce the size of the enemy air force. By anyone's calculations Peter recorded more than the six confirmed kills required to make him an ace and so was awarded his DFC. Sometime he would have to go to India and collect it, but for now there was a lot of flying to do, and so little time.

A flight of Vickers Supermarine Spitfires.

At the beginning of February, Peter was promoted to a Squadron Leader in command of nine Hurricanes. The squadron consisted of three experienced Sergeant Pilots and six new Flying Officers. With his command came that most unwanted responsibility of babysitting the young officers. Peter preferred the company of the more mature Sergeant Pilots to the arrogance of his junior officers. Many of them shot down at least fifty enemy craft but were not honoured. This may have been either because the records were lost during the war, or because they were only Sergeant Pilots.

Peter wanted to treat all of his pilots equally, but the RAF would have none of it. The Flying Officers had one mess tent, the rest another. Too many senior officers considered one Flying Officer worth ten Sergeant Pilots. In fact, the opposite was true. If you said so, you became an outcast for wanting to mix with the ranks. After the war, the official RAF list of aces often omitted the sergeant pilots and especially men like Carey, who single-handedly out fought the Battle of Britain aces.

So between the sorties against the enemy, the Hurricane pilots were put through their paces. The young officers disliked Peter, but soon respected the man they called 'the straight-laced old fart'. They failed to realise that he was only a few years older, but thousands of years older in experience.

The new pilots learnt about their aircraft and its good and bad points. The problems of flying in difficult conditions were taken in one ear and straight out the other. Still, Peter had done his part, and it was up to the new boys to put it into action. If they got it wrong, they would probably be dead or crash. In war situations, their behaviour would determine their survival. They taught the pilots to identify the enemy aircraft, their code names and how to distinguish between friend and foe. By the time you could see the red circles on the wings you were too close, so aircraft recognition was vital.

Luckily, most Japanese planes looked different to the allies' aircraft. Peter showed them the profile of the Dakota and compared it with the Sally enemy bomber. He explained that the Dakota was the main workhorse of the Allied Forces in Burma. It was 64 feet long with a 95 foot wingspan and could carry four tons of cargo such as two light vehicles or 28 combat men at a slow airspeed of 180 mph for up to two thousand miles. The Sally bombers were equipped with nose and tail gun turrets with a 250 mph. Peter explained that the fuel stored in the wings, and the fuselage over the central section of the Sally made good targets.

The newcomers tended to sleep off the effects of the previous night's alcohol during most lectures. However, they always woke to hear the details of their opponents' fighters. They heard of the Zekes, usually known as Zeros, adapted from its Japanese name *Reisen Kanjikisen* (Zero Celebration Carrier-based Fighter Airplane). It was named in 1940, the year that marked the two thousandth anniversary of the legendary Jimmu becoming Japan's first emperor. The Zekes were fast, reaching 340 mph and climbing at an astonishing three thousand feet per minute. Each aircraft had two 7.7mm machine guns synchronised to fire between the propeller blades and two 20 mm Oerlikon cannons mounted on the wings. He pointed out to the rookies that the 7.7 mm machine guns were the same calibre as the British .303.

Then the intelligence officer briefed the newcomers and old hands together, about the newer enemy aircraft, especially the new Nakajima Tojo. 'You can outfly the Zekes, keep up with most Oscars, but beware of the Tojo. They are new, fast, and highly manoeuvrable.' He pointed to a diagram of the Tojo and its silhouette from all angles and said, 'Gentlemen note the all-metal Tojo aircraft has tapered wings and body. The cockpit is high above the large engine cowlings and behind the wings. It looks more stocky compared with the streamlined Hurricanes and Spitfires, but don't let looks deceive you. This bird can really move. The large radial engine in front rules out any frontal attack, especially as their machine guns can fire between the propeller blades.'

Looking around to make certain his audience was awake, the boffin tapped the diagram and continued. 'The Tojo has two 7.7mm machine guns and two 20 mm cannons. However, some of the Tojos have a new 40 mm cannon. It can reach over 380 mph and climb at four thousand feet per minute. Compare this to the Spitfire mark V with a max speed of 365 mph, similar weaponry, and rate of climb. So you're equal, though it would be difficult if you got a Tojo on your tail. The Hurricane and Beaufighter should avoid all Tojos – or if you cannot, then dive down on them from above. Remember it has a 70 mph advantage and is very agile.'

Their orders were to prevent enemy aircraft from attacking the British positions and protect the Dakotas. It proved difficult, as the enemy attacked in waves of seventy aircraft. If the army was to hold their ground, they must be supplied from the air. The odds were not good, but better than in Rangoon. On the morning of 10th February, Peter took off with two other Hurricanes to patrol east of Sinzweya while the rest of the squadron protected the Dakotas. Only when he was airborne did he realise that he left the jade talisman on his bed. It was not a good omen, but it would be there when he returned.

The role of Peter's section was to report, or intercept and break up, any concentration of enemy aircraft approaching the British positions in the Arakan. They climbed to twenty thousand feet and scanned the sky above and below them for the enemy. Twenty miles east of Sinzweya they found a group of Sally bombers with a Zeke fighter escort. They had to be dispersed or destroyed before they could attack the British bases.

'Red Leader to Red Section,' Peter spoke into his intercom. 'Ten bandits at five o'clock.... Go in fast and leave without any heroics. Good luck. Over and out.'

'Roger orders understood, Red One going in.'

'Red Two going after the little ol' foxes. Tally ho.'

The three Hurricanes dived down on to the unguarded backs of the enemy bombers hitting two Sally bombers before doing a loop and attacking the Zeke escort. On the second run, they hit three aircraft and may have downed one of them. Then they fought the Zekes for a few minutes that seemed like eternity. Luckily, all three came out intact with the usual collection of moth holes.

'It was a piece of cake!' Red Two said to Red Three.

'That was fun.'

'Stop chatting, check fuel and ammunition levels,' interrupted Peter.

He was concerned that his two young officers were still thinking that they were after a harmless fox and not an enemy with the ability to kill. They must have used up at least half of their fifteen seconds worth of ammunition.

'Roger, Red Leader, everything OK,' replied Red Two.

A few seconds later Red One confirmed the same. So they continued their mission flying eastwards to intercept a second wave of enemy aircraft flying low beneath them.

'Red Leader to Red Section,' Peter spoke clearly into his intercom. 'Attack the three bandits at three o'clock.'

Peter started his dive, aiming for the side of the first Zeke so that his bullets would hit the engine or the pilot. The latest Japanese aircraft had armour behind the pilot's seat making it difficult to get a good shot from behind. So he flew closer to pour all his fire into the enemy and do the maximum damage. As he closed on the Zeke, Peter could see the face of the enemy pilot. Just as the pilot saw Peter, he felt the bullets rock his Zeke. It was ripped to pieces before it dived away in flames. Peter hoped the pilot bailed out safely but did not see any signs of a parachute opening.

Immediately, he pulled his joystick back to regain height before attacking the next targets. He was distracted by his section shouting at each other over the intercom as they swooped down, firing on the enemy below them. They failed to cause any serious damage as they were overexcited, having thrown caution to the wind. They came in too fast, firing early and then climbed rapidly before and trying a tail shot in. At last, one of them lined up a Zeke and blasted it out of the sky. If he had been any closer he would have been hit by the metal thrown from the dying plane.

Peter noticed that Terry Woods was chasing a retreating Zeke. This was a bad idea when there were more bandits than RAF planes around.

'Woods, do not follow the bandits but join Red One to return to base.'

'Roger, Red Leader, you are a spoilsport!'

'Maybe, but this is an order, Woods, so break off and return to Base.'

'Roger.'

Then Peter saw two Oscars and what was probably a new Tojo coming towards them. He knew that Red Two had no chance against these faster planes.

'Woods, you have a couple of Oscars and a Tojo approaching you.'

Woods climbed and together with Red One flew away towards their base. Unfortunately, neither pilot looked back to see if Peter was behind them. They were too inexperienced to know about looking after each other and working as a team. They never thought they were responsible for anyone, including their Squadron Leader. Maybe if they had thought about it, things would have been different. However, in war, as in life, maybes never change a thing.

Peter looked around and seeing nothing turned westwards towards Cox's Bazaar. The fuel gauge showed a quarter full, and his ammunition enough for the journey.

Stealthily, a Tojo aligned itself behind the Hurricane and fired. Then Peter felt the first salvo of bullets cut into his aircraft as she shuddered under the impact of all that lead but still remained intact, as most went straight through the fabric-covered wings. Rapidly, Peter responded by pulling back the joystick and climbing as fast as he could in the hope of shaking off his attacker. The Tojo pilot was excellent, too bloody good as he climbed to remain behind Peter. Damn, thought Peter, the only thing left to do was shake the Tojo off. So he swerved to the right, and to his horror saw the pursuing Tojo copied him. When he dived to the left, the Tojo followed. It was as if the two planes were connected by a piece of string, for where the Hurricane flew the Tojo followed. Up and down they went, then dived to the left and climbed to the right.

It was a deadly dogfight in which Peter was the hunted, and the hunter had the advantage. He tried to make a dummy roll to the left, quickly straightened up and turned to the right. Unfortunately, the Tojo did not fall for it and remained right on his tail. The chase continued for a few minutes until the inevitable happened. The Tojo's twin cannons destroyed part of the Hurricane's starboard wing. The Hurricane started to pull to the port side. Peter noticed his fuel gauge dropping as the fuel spurted out of his pierced fuel tank. Then the Hurricane started a final dive towards the ground, rotating slowly.

Peter put his arms above his head to open the cockpit canopy that proved difficult to move, but it did. He felt dizzy but climbed out of his seat. Immediately, the air stream pulled him free of the spinning machine as it hurtled downwards. He fell fast as he moved his right hand across his chest to locate the ripcord ring to release his parachute. His fingers found the metal ring and pulled it.

Damn it, open! Now he was gathering speed and dropping fast. Soon he would lose consciousness and die.

'Blessed Mary, full of grace, please hear my prayers.'

He did not finish his childhood prayer as suddenly he felt a jolt under his armpits as the parachute opened and started to break his descent.

'Thank you God.'

For one second, he felt the joy of drifting towards the earth with his parachute and worried the Tojo would shoot him while in the air. However, the Tojo pilot was far away chatting to his fellow pilots about shooting down a Hurricane.

As the ground approached Peter tried to remember what his instructor had told him about bending his legs and rolling once he landed. As he looked at the ground, it seemed to be approaching much too quickly. Then he hit the soft ground with a thump and immediately tore off his parachute before running away as fast as he could. He knew that he could live off the land, but first he had to get as far away as possible from his crashed plane. Soon the area would be swarming with enemy soldiers looking for him. As he ran he realised that he had landed badly, hurting his left ankle and bruising his side. Still, whatever the pain, he must leave the place.

After running for an hour he stopped and took his bearings. He realized that he must be about fifty miles east of the Sinzweya, which meant that the Japanese army was between him and the way home. So he decided to strike north in the hope of meeting up with the Chin resistance fighters or else getting through to Assam.

The ground was hilly and difficult to traverse. For each mile as the crow flies he walked two extra miles through the thick scrub. He was not equipped for this mission only having his service revolver but no jungle knife. When he stopped he checked his .28 Webley revolver, making sure that all the six chambers were loaded. If necessary, he would shoot a few of the enemy before he died. In the cold of that first night, he missed the protection his jade leaf gave him to be afraid of what the future would bring.

On the second day, he ate some jungle fruits and drank water collected from leaves. His legs and hands were badly cut by the sharp leaves of the shrubs and long grass. It would be quicker going through the paddy fields, but then he would be easily seen. His left ankle was so swollen that he cut the shoelaces to loosen his shoes. Then he slept for an hour before the noise of breaking vegetation and people approaching woke him. He lay very still hardly daring to breathe, as twenty Japanese soldiers passed within a hundred yards. They joked and smoked cigarettes as they moved westwards. Peter counted twenty of them as he lay still until they were out of sight. Then he continued travelling north, knowing the nearer he got to Assam the less chance he had of being captured.

On the third night, he saw some Burmese wearing white silk longyis holding little lanterns in their hands calling out to him. He could not say why, but they gave him hope so he followed the distant, inviting lights. As morning came he realised that he had walked all through the night following some apparition. Bloody sleep walking at my age he said to himself. He rested for most of the day before continuing his journey. Again, he saw the lights, which he decided must be the lights from glow-worms flying in the branches of the banyan trees. Still it was a bit magical and made him feel more confident about his future.

One thing started to bother him. It was simply this, when he had passed a banyan tree that held lanterns, they vanished and others appeared ahead. As he walked away from the first banyan tree towards the next lanterns, he had turned around and found all the lights behind him had vanished. Peter reasoned that the noise of him passing by the tree stopped the glow-worms from shining. He saw a trail of twinkling lights leading into the far horizon and wanted to get there, feeling then he would be safe.

He should have remained feeding on the occasional fruits and travelling by night aided by his magic lights. However, for no reason, except that he was hungry and his ankle hurt, he did not. Instead, he started a circular search for a food supply and came to a village in a small clearing. So he decided that this would do as a place to beg for food from the locals. It was risky but maybe someone would help him.

He could not have chosen a more terrible place or time. Before he reached the first hut, he felt the cold steel of a bayonet touch his face and looked around to see three Japanese soldiers. They forced him to put his face down on the ground while they searched him. Nothing was said as a hard boot pinned him to the ground while someone removed his revolver, money, survival rations, and his watch. Only then was he allowed to sit up with his hands on his head.

A Japanese officer appeared, pistol in hand, and his sword dangling from his waist.

'Ah so-ka a pilot. You be good you *okayge*. Be bad *ashita mati mati.*'

Peter did the only thing possible and put his hands by his side and bowed his head.

'Food Captain-san?' Peter asked, making gestures like rubbing his stomach and putting a finger in his mouth.

'No food for you, *okayge*!'

Then they tied his hands behind his back before throwing him into the back of a truck, where he was on the floor with two other prisoners. Sitting either side of them were four soldiers with rifles and a man in a black uniform with a short truncheon. When Peter tried to sit up, a truncheon knocked him down.

'*Yazume. Yazume. Ashita mati mati,*' shouted the man in black.

'For God's sake lie still, or the little shit will beat the hell out of us,' whispered a prisoner.

'No talk! You talk. *Ashita mati mati.*'

They remained silent as they were transported to an unknown destination.

Back at Cox's Bazaar, two young officers were in trouble. When they had landed they were full of what great pilots they were to shoot down a Zeke and a Sally. Then they waited for Peter's aircraft to return. It did not. Peter must have been shot down or run out of fuel.

Soon they stood in front of the CO and Peter's friend Squadron Leader Ashton.

'Flying Officer Simmons! Please explain where and when Squadron Leader Anderson disappeared?'

Simmons was Red One, and the most responsible of the pair.

'Sorry sir! Red Leader told us to return to base as our ammunition and fuel were low. We assumed that he was right behind us.'

'You assumed! You didn't even bother to look in your mirrors to see if he was near you. You thought that the silly old fool could look after himself.'

'It wasn't Simmon's fault, sir,' butted in Red Two, Flying Officer Woods.

'Woods, did I give you permission to speak?'

'No sir!'

'Well shut up both of you. Not only have you lost your Squadron Leader, but you have lost my friend. You two better pull your socks up and wipe your noses before I have you grounded. Then you will receive a rifle and help defend the base.'

'Yes, sir.'

'Now go off to be debriefed and report every detail that you can and do not claim a hit unless it is confirmed. I somehow doubt if anyone wishes to confirm a kill considering you lost your Squadron Leader. We do not need any more arrogant fox-hunting snobs out here with their bloody tally-ho! We are not any old chap; we are all fighters prepared to serve or die. The Japanese has excellent pilots, and unlike your poor little fox, they kill. For God's sake grow up before it is too late.'

The two youngsters left Squadron Leader Ashton with their tails between their legs and hoping that Peter would fly in.

Jim Ashton felt the loss of his friend quite deeply as it was his experience that few downed pilots survived the jungle. Peter had survived once by a chance meeting with Palmerino, but could he survive on his own? He knew Peter had left his good-luck talisman behind and worried his friend was in danger, if not already dead.

Back in England Lynette Anderson suddenly woke up covered in sweat, feeling instinctively that Peter was in dire straits. Quietly, so as not to wake her husband, she put on her dressing gown and went downstairs. In the sitting room, she went to the cabinet to place Peter's leaf at the base of the family jade tree and pray for his safe return. As she prayed tears flowed down her face at the thought that she may never see him again, nor any of the children he would have, in time, produced to keep up the family traditions. It was just all too much to bear, and her tiny frame shook with a sadness that she could not explain. In her mind, she felt that her ancestor who went to China and found love, would look down and help as best he could.

Lynette lit three joss sticks as an offering to her ancestral spirits to protect her son. Then she fasted for a week for her son's life and to help her share his troubles and appease the bad spirits.

'I am glad that you have stopped this fasting nonsense. We need you alive, and well, dear wife.'

'I only did what my ancestors required for the good of our family. I regret, dearest husband, if I have caused offence. Please forgive your silly wife,' Lynette replied.

Both knew that there was far more to her actions than she was prepared to divulge and so nothing was said.

# 11
## A Guest of the Kempei-Tei

*No man is an island, entire of itself.... Any man's death diminishes me, because I am involved in mankind; and therefore never send to know for whom the bells toll, it tolls for thee.*

John Donne (1624) from *Meditations* XVII.

Peter was transported northwards until dusk when they stopped in a compound where the prisoners were pushed onto the dry mud floor of a building and trussed up like chickens awaiting the cooking pot. An hour later the guards untied their hands so they could eat a meal – rice balls and one mug of water between the three of them.

'*Hurio food*. Eat.'

'*Arigato gozuinas* major-san,' the white officer replied.

'*Hurio yazume*,' the guard replied before leaving and locking the door.

Alone, the three watched each other. They took some rice, swallowed it, and sipped the precious water. Each man rubbed his wrists where the ropes had burned their skin in an attempt to get the circulation back into their hands. Soon they could feel and move their fingers.

As it grew darker, they saw through the bottom of the door, the shadows of the guards chatting noisily around a fire, totally uninterested in their prisoners. Now they talked in whispers so that the guards would not hear and come to beat them.

'I am Captain Godfrey of 1st Gurkha Rifles. Six of us were caught on patrol; sadly, we are the only two left alive.'

'I am Squadron Leader Peter Anderson of the RAF who was shot down five days ago over the Arakan.'

'My name is Havildar Temasen of 1st Gurkha Rifles, sir! There were just too many of them. We didn't surrender, shamefully they caught us.'

Peter decided that Captain Godfrey was the talker and Temasen the dutiful sergeant. To look at, they were like Laurel and Hardy, as Godfrey was tall and thin while Temasen short and stocky. Peter felt that though Godfrey had the rank and maybe the brains, Temasen was the sort who could survive anything and still keep on smiling. In fact, Temasen was a bit like Pip's Man – and who better to be with when in a difficult situation than someone like him?

'How long have you two been prisoners?' asked Peter.

'We were caught two weeks ago near Akyab and then moved north. Two of my men died from their wounds, and two were tortured to death,' Godfrey replied.

'Your Japanese seems quite good.'

80

'One secret old chap is to pretend you have no brains and always remember to bow to all Jap officers. Remember *Hurio* means prisoners. *Yazume* means rest or at ease. *Arigato gozainas* means thanks. They like being called major-san.'

'Always remember that *hancho benjo* means permission to go to the toilet. *Hai* is yes; *nei* means no, and *mizu* means water and *tabe* food,' added the Gurkha.

'Also *wakasu-nai* means I do not understand.'

'The basic rules are that you never talk while there is a guard around.'

Peter nodded.

'Never answer a question directly.'

'That seems easy to remember.'

Lastly, you must always bow at the Japanese officers and to the flag.'

'Why should I,' Peter commented angrily.

'To stay alive and not be beaten,' the Gurkha answered.

'If they beat one, they will beat all of us!' Godfrey added.'

Sorry,' whispered Peter, 'I never thought of that.'

'When you get food always slip a small ball of rice into your pockets. Feeding time at our zoo tends to be a bit irregular, as does drinking,' The Gurkha advised.

'Do they starve you?'

'I don't think so, but they do not have enough food for their own needs as they cannot get much from the land or the villages. So they share what little they have. Water is the main problem.'

'What are the officers like?'

'The Japanese officers and men talk about their homeland. Believe it or not they get homesick, just like us. There are few privileges for them, unless they are senior or members of the Kempei-Tei.'

'Is it wise to speak Japanese?'

'Only use the words I have told you. If they find out that you know any more, they will consider you as a spy. Then they will torment and torture your body and your mind to extract any bit of information from you. Mum's the word.'

'I am speeke lille engleesh, no Nippon. That's what I say,' interjected the Havildar. In the morning they usually come and separate us. Then there are the usual questions, and when they learn nothing, the beatings start. Let's pray that the interrogators are from the army, or at least the Kempei-Tei, and not the Burmese Defence Army.'

'Why? I though the Kempei-Tei is worse than the German Gestapo.'

'They are very cruel, but keep you alive to become labourers or to gather information. The vilest is a BDA torturer Bo Ba Tin, who we call the Devil's Helper.'

Peter winced at hearing his cousin's name, maybe there were many Ba Tins.

Perhaps they would never meet.

'A week ago the bastard pulled Temasen's toenails out one by one while a soldier held a knife at his throat. He could not move and had to control his screams otherwise the knife would kill him.'

'Oh, bloody hell!' Peter exclaimed in sheer horror.

'Bloody my feet more like,' Havildar Temasen stated with a grin.

'Now they help me, as me no walkee nowhere!' The cheeky Havildar added. 'The Japanese leaves the crippled slave of the white colonial masters alone and to concentrate on you guys. So I make them carry me to the latrine. However, give me a chance, and I will be away from here as fast as I can, even if I feel like a tiger running over burning coals.'

Everyone grinned at the brave Gurkha who though injured was not broken, down but certainly not out.

'How do you remain sane?'

'I think of all the women I have known, or wish that I had known. Especially a beauty called Carol, a little blonde nurse in Colombo.'

'I think of a woman waiting alone for me to comfort,' said the Havildar with a twinkle in his eye.

'Temasen is a devil with women, a real Don Juan. No woman is safe between the ages of ten to sixty.'

'That is not fair Captain Sahib, only those between fifteen and fifty.'

On that note, they fell asleep on the uncomfortable hard earth floor to await the dawn and a very uncertain future.

The night went by too quickly. It was hot, humid and the ground very uncomfortable. Peter found that the hard earth floor rubbed against his skin making it both sore and itchy. He kept on waking up and thinking. He knew he was caught like a rat in a trap with little chance of escape. He must now face the future with courage and hope. He worried about how he would behave if tortured. Was he going to die and be buried in some unmarked grave or would he just give up?

Then he noticed the little Gurkha Havildar looking at him with an encouraging grin. He did not have to say anything as his expression said it all. You can take me; you can beat me; you can kill me, but you can never take away my soul. Somehow this made Peter feel stronger and more positive about their situation.

Before the cock crowed and the sun rose from the east, the door was flung open and two soldiers took Peter. He was dragged across a clearing to a large thatched hut raised off the ground on stilts. In front of the hut's wooden staircase flew the Japanese flag.

Obviously, there was to be no breakfast today, Peter said to himself that he fancied a couple of eggs and a piece of bacon. The thought made him smile as he was pulled up the stairs and into a large room. Inside there was a desk, chairs and a cool breeze from a bamboo fan powered by a man sitting outside, rhythmically pulling on a string. Behind the desk stood a dark-skinned Burmese dressed in the black uniform of the Kempei-Tei.

'You may sit down,' the man said softly.

'Thank you,' Peter replied.

'May I give you some tea?'

'Yes, thank you Major-san.'

The man poured out two small cups of sweetened green tea and gave one to Peter. Then they both sipped the drink while watching each other. It was a bit like a hungry cat eyeing up a helpless mouse. The only trouble was that Peter was the mouse and the Major the cat.

'Welcome Englishman, It is nice to see you. You are indeed very privileged to have me to interrogate you.'

There was a silence as the interrogator slowly lit a cigarette and inhaled the smoke-filled nicotine.

'Let me tell you about myself. I am not Japanese. I am Burmese from an ancient line of wealthy patriots. Like all famous people, I have many names. The latest I think is the Devil's Helper. You should know me as Bo Ba Tin.'

Peter shuddered as he sat in front of his own cousin. Was this the face of a sadistic torturer? Indeed, he could be the Devil incarnate.

'You should be afraid for I am your worst nightmare. By the time I have finished with you, you will wish that I were Japanese. You may scream but there is no one to hear. You may cry to your precious Lord, but he will not listen. You will beg for anything that I offer. For I and I alone control your life, which I can end just as my fingers put out the light of a candle.'

Ba Tin seemed totally happy as he lay back in his chair, took another puff from his cigarette and leant over towards Peter.

'Now let us start. What is your name?'

'My name is Squadron Leader Peter Anderson number 2946291 sir.'

'Ah so, Squadron Leader number 2946291. What do your friends call you? Is it Pete, or Peter? Oh, I wonder what you are like under that uniform.'

Bo Ba Tin ordered the soldiers to strip him leaving Peter naked facing his tormentor. It was all intended to reduce his self-esteem, and it worked. He remembered his dad had told him not to feel shame as all humans came into this world naked, and as such we must depart.

'You are dark for an Englishman and more like a chichi. Yes, I think you are chichi,' Bo Ba Tin said as he felt Peter's skin.

Peter did not move or make any comment for he knew that the slang term chichi referred to people of mixed race. Perhaps Bo Ba Tin would remember his aunt had married an Anderson. If he did what would happen?

'Was your mother an Oriental? Or was your father?

Bo Ba Tin looked him in the eyes pretending to scratch his head.

Your name is English, so your mother is Oriental. Maybe she is Thai, Malay, Indian, or even Burmese. Am I right?'

'I have nothing to say. I am Squadron Leader Anderson number 2946291, sir.'

'Don't play around with me. Before we are finished, I will know everything there is to know about you. I'll know your father, your mother, your brothers, your sisters, and your cousins and your aunts. You will tell me everything as you can have no secrets from me, as from this day forwards remember I am your God, your priest, your father and your confessor. Without me, you are dead.'

Peter grinned in an attempt to laugh at his tormentor only to receive a slap across the face for his impudence.

'Think carefully, chichi. We are winning this war while your colonialist masters run like cowardly white rats before our mighty armies. In weeks, we have conquered Malaya, Singapore and Burma. Soon we will be in Delhi, and all the Orient will be ours. You and your kind have no courage. When the British ruled Burma, they made us their servants. Telling us to clean this or do that. If we complained, they beat and kicked us. They took our women whenever they felt like it and were so bloody proud. However, now that we are winning it is our turn to make them our servants and use their women.'

'Major-san, what you say is true. However, I demand to be treated as a prisoner of war.'

Bo Ba Tin moved so close that Peter could smell his tobacco-tainted breath.

'How can you be a prisoner of war? You people run; you torture our people and destroy our lands. You are nothing but white vermin! You are the race of rats that is about to become extinct. It is what your Charles Darwin called the survival of the fittest. You are a decadent race that brings disease, corruption and slavery. My people not bow our heads to the white man. Never again will we kiss your dirty, smelly feet. No longer will our women warm your beds; instead, your women will beg for our sexual favours. You do not exist. You cannot demand anything, chichi. Not even to die unless I let you. When I want you to die, you will thank me for it.'

He returned to sit behind his chair and laughed.

Bo Ba Tin was a dangerous man who was enjoying every moment of this interview. In another place at another time, he would be restrained in a straitjacket inside a mental asylum. However, now it was the time when he, and similar vile creatures came out of the shadows to enjoy destroying the unfortunate.

'I take any woman I want, and they thank God that I did not kill them. Indeed, I make them very happy and fulfilled so that they cry out with joy. In Japanese, they say *hippi mai-nichi* – that is, sex every night. I don't care if they are young or old, white or dark, even if they are women or men like you. For me, sex is a sign of power when I can dominate and hurt another person so that they cry out for more. It is the ultimate conquest of the body over mind that I use with great skill to extract everything I want to know from the lucky person.'

He stopped as if remembering some poor creature forced to give him carnal pleasure. It obviously excited him as now, a big smile crept over his face, and his breathing became pronounced.

'I find that women satisfy many of my basic urges, but not all. I find young white men fulfil all the others. You are lucky as you have a good body, but you are too dark for my taste. I like them very pale, and cooperative.'

Yes, thought Peter, his tormentor was another pervert, but felt he could handle that, just like the homosexuals who at school had prowled the dormitories at night.

'I find having sex with a Britisher tells me everything. If they hate it, they are heterosexual, and I have started to break their spirit. If they like it, and many do, they are homosexual, so I play on their feminine side. You see; sex has its uses for all of us. It is all so simple to enter the very being of your white scum and destroy your soul.'

Bo Ba Tin strutted in front of Peter like a toy soldier. His gloved hands were rubbed together in a gesture that had some unknown meaning. He was an actor on this, his stage, revelling in the power it gave him. 'The mountain man is very difficult. You can pull out his toenails, but he will not scream. I cut his skin, but he did not break. I think that I could cut off his head, and you gain nothing. So I must seduce him like a woman until he volunteers to join the ranks of our allies, the Indian National Army, under the command of that magnificent Subhas Chandra Bose.'

There was another pause as the interrogator walked up and down the room puffing at his cigarette. At each measured step, his polished high leather boots hit the boards making a monotonous tune. His eyes always looked at his prisoner checking for any reaction that could be of use, any chink in the victim's armour that could be exploited.

'Captain Godfrey is different. I can break him. I know that soon he will eat out of my hand like a little puppy dog,' Bo Ba Tin laughed in anticipation of what sick and warped joys were to come.

Peter shivered at the thought of what this creature would do to him. Bo Ba Tin did not finish the sentence, as he wanted Peter to be attentive and to worry about what he would have said.

Now Bo Ba Tin was playing with his prisoner like an angler with the fish on a line and enjoying every minute of the contest. There was no hurry as no one was going anywhere. Time was on his side, so he returned and sat down in his chair. Peter shivered at the thought of what this vile creature would enjoy doing to him. He noticed that Ba Tin had little eyes like a rat that darted around the room before staring harshly into his. Bo Ba Tin was worked up, even hyperactive, as the fingers of his left hand played an unknown tune on the surface of the desk. Maybe he was on drugs or was turned on by power. Whatever it was he was an evil man, indeed devilish.

'Yes, let me tell you about your white friend. When I have subjected him to every form of degradation, he will start to die from the inside. He will lose the will to live as he fears what I can do to his proud body. Both, he and I know it.'

He lay back in his chair and pondered a while.

'That is enough talk about your comrades. The question is what shall I do with you?'

He then jumped up to walk over to Peter and spoke into his ear.

'And what shall I do with you? Answer me, chichi boy!'

It took all of Peter's concentration to reply. 'My name is Peter Anderson. Rank Squadron Leader. My serial number is 2946291. My name is Peter Anderson. Squadron Leader...'

A fist hit him so hard in the pit of his stomach that he cried out in pain.

'Ah! You will be easy. Already I hear fear in your voice as your body starts to tremble. You will not give me much sport. You are weaker than a sexually excited schoolgirl pretending to preserve her virginity from her lover. I expected a tiger and found a mouse. I win. You lose.'

It was true. Peter was starting to tremble from feeling cold and embarrassed, standing naked in front of this pervert who probably was his cousin. He started to know that he would not be able to survive long at the hands of this sadist. The pain worried him as he had made up his mind that, death was preferable to living and being tormented by Bo Ba Tin.

Bo Ba Tin saw that the humiliation was working. This one was not afraid to die but did not like exposing himself, and that was his weakness. Then the short razor-sharp knife used for the coup de grace after *hari kari* was placed under Peter's scrotum touching the skin. It was essential to make the patient feel the touch of the cold sharp blade without cutting anything off ... well, not just yet.

'Just think that with one stroke, I can turn you into a woman. I can change your sex, a thing that nobody else has done! In seconds, I can make you my little eunuch dog that must crouch to urinate.'

Peter shuddered as sweat ran down his face and felt the cold of the knife's blade against his manhood knowing that Ba Tin would not hesitate to cut it off if he gained anything by it.

Peter decided that Bo Ba Tin really was a devil and was going to castrate him. So he would never have any children and maybe die from the loss of blood or the pain.

'What is your name?'

'I am Peter Anderson.'

'What is your rank?'

'I am a Squadron Leader.'

'What is your number?'

'My number is 2946291.'

'What were your orders?'

Peter did not reply.

'What is your squadron?'

Peter bit his lip feeling the knife, but he said nothing as his sweat was on his face and hands.

Suddenly, the knife was removed, leaving him still a man.

Bo Ba Tin looked into Peter's face and laughing said. 'Well big fighter pilot, how brave are you now? Oh, mighty warrior of the skies! Oh, the big master! Oh, how small I have made you. I am more destructive than the most ferocious dragon or poisonous snake. I am your worst nightmare. Soon you will do anything that I ask. Believe me, you will do anything.'

Then in a very low seductive voice he whispered in his ear, 'You will sleep with me and caress me. You will tell me about anything, and anybody that I wish to know about. You will be my little puppy. You will bark when I tell you to bark. You will follow me. You will do tricks for me.'

'I'll never serve you!'

'Oh! Yes, you will.'

'Never – you're a monster!'

'Ah. You recognise me as the Devil's Helper. You will soon be mine my little chichi dog. Fear is how I will unlock your heart and spill out your feelings.'

Bo Ba Tin turned and shouted at the guards. 'Take him away and leave me alone.'

Then he reconsidered. 'No, let me think. Bring me the white man. I need some pleasure.'

They dragged Peter naked out of the room to throw him back in the prison hut and took Godfrey away.

Peter must have fallen asleep, or drifted into a state of unconsciousness, as he remembered nothing until being woken by the screams coming from the interrogation hut. They rang out through the still air, sending a chilling message to all who could hear that they were in hell. This made Peter quietly chant his prayers. Maybe he did not realise, it but his chanting drowned out the cries from across the clearing.

'Dear God! I pray to you Holy Mary, blessed above all women, Holy Mother of Christ, to intercede on behalf of Godfrey. Take away the pain, fear, and hatred for only you can save him from the hands of such a monster.'

An hour later Godfrey was back among, with his badly swollen face covered in blood. It was clear that he had been cut many times on his arms and chest. By the grace of God Godfrey must have fallen unconscious and escaped some of the pain. Havildar Temasen gently covered his body and tried to clean his wounds with a piece of cloth.

They were fed before nightfall. This time there were two plates of rice balls in some coconut juice with two mugs of water. They ate and drank before slowly feeding Godfrey.

When it was dark, Godfrey managed to talk slowly and painfully. 'The monster thinks I am his. He has hurt me, humiliated me, and abused my body. However, I hate him, so that he will never get anything out of me.'

'I know, old chap, just rest. We will survive.'

'He raped me like some school pervert. He hurt me where no one else has ever hurt me. Still I refused to give in.'

Peter knew that Godfrey would prefer to die than give in. Hate was keeping him alive, but at the same time it was eating into his soul. Whether they died or were broken no longer mattered, for it seemed that Bo Ba Tin would always win.

Again on the second morning Peter was interrogated. This time they beat the soles of his feet with sticks and cut the palms of his hands with small strokes of a knife. Peter tried in vain not to cry out, but he did. Back in the hut he could not close his hands without being in agony, so Temasen helped him eat and drink. How much more of this punishment could he take before he gave in?

On the third morning, Godfrey was taken to where two wooden posts were erected in the clearing. Here he was spread eagled naked with his arms above his head, and his feet tied so that they did not touch the ground. Peter and Temasen were forced outside to watch as the guards placed a rope around Godfrey's neck that was attached to a wooden bucket. Slowly, the bucket was filled with water so that it pulled down on Godfrey's neck.

All day long, they sat watching their companion struggle against the weight pulling his neck forwards while the rope cut into his neck. Every sinew in Godfrey's body fought against the intolerable weight as he grew weaker yet still defiant. There was no shade from the burning rays of the sun that soon burned their naked bodies. Now the effects of dehydration and fear took over as their mouths dried, their lips cracked, and their eyes became sore. They were slowly cooking in that Devil's cauldron.

At dusk, they were returned to their hut. By then Godfrey was half dead as they tried to tend his wounds. Around his neck were the raw cuts where the rope had burned into his flesh.

That night there was only a bucket of water and no food. It was the same bucket that had hung around Godfrey's neck with blood on it.

'Drink, don't think,' Temasen said. 'We must drink and wash ourselves, otherwise he has won. Don't you see it is one of his vile games?'

Peter looked into the Gurkha's eyes and realised that he was right, so he closed his eyes and slowly started to drink. As he swallowed the water, his body shook and the pores of his skin seemed to explode as they opened to allow sweat to form on his body. It was very cooling, and made him regain some hope that they might live.

Temasen cradled Godfrey's head on his lap as he gave him water and washed his body. Then when Godfrey was sleeping, he washed himself before hiding some water in an old can in the corner of the hut. They realised, that unless a miracle happened, they would all die a slow and ghastly death. Godfrey would be the first to die, as he was rapidly deteriorating under the constant punishment. Then Peter would die and last would be the tough Temasen. Temasen began to meditate as he turned to his gods for assistance to help Godfrey, whom he felt was dying. For it is better to help the dying than glory in life as we all must die as certain as after every day comes night. The gods ordained it and so man must learn to live with this sad but unavoidable truth.

That night sleep was impossible. Godfrey cried out as he drifted in and out of consciousness. The air seemed thick with foreboding. Peter's sunburned skin was sore and red. He was hungry and felt grimly that they had not been fed because food is not wasted on those about to die. He chewed on a ball of rice that they had squirreled away. It tasted foul and probably would do him no good, but it was better than nothing.

At last, sunlight entered the hut heralding the start of a new day. For a moment, Peter thought that they would be left alone, but he was wrong as the door opened, and Peter was taken outside. In front of him were his clothes clean and washed.

'*Hurio*, you dress now. *Speedo, Speedo.*'

So without a second's hesitation he put on his clothes noticing there were no shoes. Then he was taken to the interrogation hut to find Bo Ba Tin sitting at his desk sipping his green tea. He turned as Peter entered, giving an enormous smile that showed all of his teeth, including a large gold one.

'Sit down Squadron Leader Peter. Good to see you.'

Before he could reply, Peter was thrust down into the chair by the two guards.

'You look tired and worried. You have no need to worry. We will have a time together. Your white friend made me very impatient, but now I am tired of beatings. Today we have tea.'

Bo Ba Tin flicked his fingers, and a servant appeared who poured out two cups of tea.

'In Japan to share a cup of tea means that we are friends. I know that we may even be relatives. So tell me about yourself. That is what friends do, eh!'

They eyed each other sipping tea. Peter needed it, but felt that he was supping with the devil.

'My mother's sister trained as a nurse in England where she married an Englishman to give birth to a daughter and then a son, who must be your age.'

'Then he would look just like you,' Peter commented.

'If my cousin was sitting where you are I would kill him very slowly. I would use the old method of a thousand cuts, what you call flaying alive. In the end, weakened by loss of blood and in terrible pain, he would die in my arms. For the existence of this mongrel insults my ancestors.'

Peter did not reply.

'Have you seen a man flayed? I have and found it very exciting. The first cut does not really hurt as I use a very sharp blade usually on the arms. The second cut is not too bad. However, by the time I have cut him a hundred times his whole body is screaming. The trick is to do it slowly so that the person takes two or three days to die. That is – complete ecstasy.'

Peter thought how evil this man is who wants to flay me as he knows, or has guessed, that we are cousins. Otherwise why does the monster play this game with me? He was nice one minute and terrible, the next. Peter felt a mixture of fear, and disgust ran through his body.

He smiled back at Ba Tin, saying. 'If you say so Major-san then so it must be.'

'I'm no Major-san I'm Captain-san.'

'I'm very sorry Captain-san *Hai*!'

'That is good; you learn fast chichi. You make good coolie.'

'Yes Captain-san.'

'You must bow when addressing a Japanese officer. You must bow now!'

Peter swallowed his pride and bowed deeply, as expected.

'Good – very good – but I still know nothing about you. I have not yet entered your soul and got into your mind, but I will. What is your mother?'

'Mum is Malay from Penang where she worked for my father.'

'Pity, I had hoped she was my aunt.'

Then, there was silence as Bo Ba Tin thought before leaning across the table and saying. 'Let me tell you about Captain Godfrey. I have entered him, and he is mine. I made him be the lady while I acted as the man. He did not enjoy making the beast with one back. I think he likes women. It is a pity that he will not be having any more. Well not in this life.'

He coughed on his cigarette before continuing his monologue. 'Godfrey has white skin, but he gave me little pleasure. He resisted me as my stalk plunged into his sacred bottom. If he had made me happy, I would have been kind. He made me feel unsatisfied and sad, so now he will be sadder. Only when he cries out in pain do I enjoy satisfaction. By now, he hates me so that I can take his spirit. Hate is good. The hate will give me his soul so that I can crush it in the palm of my hand. Oh how hatred works! As a nation, we Burmese are weak, preferring a quiet life, believing all those false British promises. We have taken back our lands from the colonialists with the help of our Japanese friends. Soon our armies will sweep through India to free our brothers from the western imperialists, so that we will be ruled by the Rising Sun and the Swastika.'

He lit another cigarette before blowing a puff of smoke into the air, then one directly into Peter's face, before stubbing it out.

'Would you like some more tea?'

Peter did not reply.

'I asked if you would like some more tea. It is rude not to reply. Do you want to make me angry?'

'No I do not wish to annoy you Captain-san Yes, I would like some more of your excellent tea.'

'Ah. That's better. Now say, please!'

'Please may I have some more tea Captain-san.'

'Excellent Peter, of course you may.'

He clapped his hands, and more sweetened tea was poured. Peter sipped the tea slowly waiting for something to unfold. He knew he was being softened up to make the shock still greater when it came.

'You interest me enough to want to I play with you just like in chess game. One wrong move and you are mine. You cooperate. You be happy as my little playful dog. If you do not cooperate with me, you will die very, very slowly.'

By now, Peter was feeling that the meeting was coming to its conclusion.

'You learn fast to caress me and make me feel good.

The idea of caressing this monster disgusted Peter to make him lean over the table as if to kiss his tormenter before spitting into his face.

In a flash, Bo Ba Tin wiped his face with his gloved hand, jumped up and smashed his fist hard into Peter's mouth. Next his fists pounded his face, and stomach. Peter felt his tormenter's uncontrolled rage as another blow fell on his face as blow after blow hit him. He could not move because the guards held him making resistance impossible. He just had to take it and say nothing, even though his face showed the pain. In the end, he cried out.

Suddenly, the beating stopped as Bo Ba Tin ordered the guards to strip off his clothes. They did. Then Ba Tin's knife cut the skin of Peter's arms to make a neat four-inch incision. The knife was cleaned and replaced in its scabbard. Then salt was rubbed into the cut sending his raw nerve endings into instantaneous convulsions. Peter could feel his warm blood slowly running down his arms. He was not going to scream or show fear. He did not, but his teeth cut through his lower lip. Then, unable to bear it any longer, he yelled out cursing his tormenter. 'You're a little bastard! Just let me have a go at you without your guards, and I'll break your scrawny little neck with my bare hands.'

'I am not stupid. I offered you life, and you rejected it. For insulting my people, you will suffer and regret your foolish words. Perhaps I may even cut off your stalk and let you feed upon it. For you, I will choose something special, very special for the proud chichi with no brains.'

Then Peter was taken into the courtyard to be spread eagled between two posts with his right arm and leg on one pole and his left limbs to the other, as if crucified. Opposite was the naked Temasen suspended between another pair of poles. Both were tied so that feet could not touch the ground, putting all of their weight onto their arms. Then a bucket was placed around their necks and slowly filled with water. Peter realised there was a third pair of poles facing the staircase of the interrogation hut.

Time now had no meaning as the two men struggled against the weight of the water against their neck. Peter felt that the flies crawling across his face were a distraction, even a blessing. For a second, the mind tried to focus on the little dipterans feeding off his sweat, so forgetting the forces trying to break off one's neck. Maybe some twenty minutes later – it could have been an hour. No one was counting: the defiant Godfrey was hoisted onto the third pair of poles.

The scenario was complete as all three awaited their execution.

Godfrey tried to hold his body at attention if only to annoy the interrogator. Peter noticed the deep cuts on his arms, the drawn face and the blankness in his eyes. From a distance, it must have appeared as though they were three people being crucified in some pagan amphitheatre in ancient Rome.

They waited naked in the sun, but nothing happened. Gradually, the sun dried out what little moisture they had within their bodies, making them slip in and out of consciousness. Then as the sun set, Japanese flag was lowered to the sound of the evening bugle call. However, still the three men awaited their fate.

The guards removed the buckets to give them some water to drink. It was not enough to quench their thirst, but sufficient to moisten their cracked lips and wet the parched throats. The rest was thrown over them to wake them up. Peter thought that it was all over, and they would be cut down and taken to rest in the hut, may be allowed to have a day with food, water and perhaps a chance to live. Everything was blurred, as if the heat had cooked his brain.

Suddenly, the courtyard sprang to life as searchlights illuminated their naked bodies, like part of some pageant or satanic ritual. They could see each other but little else, as the light was very strong and their eyes so weak. All they could hear was the sound of cicadas and the beating of their own hearts.

Half an hour later they heard the sound of a solitary drum. At each beat Captain Bo Ba Tin descended the steps of the interrogation hut with sword in hand. The noise of the drum and the sound of boots on the wooden steps joined in unison to make a compelling noise that entered the most inner reaches of one's mind and concentrated one's thoughts on the approaching person. Ba Tin looked sinister in his black uniform and little peaked hat. It was the correct dress and appropriate for the evil Devil's Helper.

At the bottom of the steps, the drum stopped and Bo Ba Tin stood with two soldiers on either side of him. It was a series of well-practiced theatrical moves intended to intimidate, and it did just that. Then he yelled in English with a screeching voice that rattled with uncontrollable rage. 'Today is your first day in hell. You insult me, the Emperor of Japan and the Government of Free Burma. For this offence, there can only be one punishment: death.'

Everyone waited as he paused.

'I pronounce the sentence is to be carried out immediately.'

He walked over to Peter and said, 'By the time the sun rises from the east you will be mine or dead. It is all up to you. Think well, little chichi.'

Turning around he strutted across to Temasen and put his hands on his hips. 'You are ignorant little Indiaman, hear me well. You are beneath me. You are just a native mountain man and slave of white captain. Soon you will join your brother Bose and fight the colonial swine to liberate our people. You have two choices, join us and fight or fight us and die. It is all very simple, so that even a mindless mule like you can understand.'

It was all an act. A bit of Shakespeare played out for real in a place with no name where the stage was set but without an audience. As if it was a dress rehearsal, the players waited to start the next scene in this bloody saga.

Bo Ba Tin strutted over to the semi-conscious Captain Godfrey.

'Oh Captain Godfrey, you are brave, but a bloody fool. Your God cannot save you. Why don't you say what he said?; 'Father forgive them for they not know what they do.' You say the words. *Hai*.'

'No. I will never forgive you.'

Then Captain Godfrey gathered up all of his remaining strength to shout in a coarse crackling voice. 'I will never tell you anything. I condemn you, Bo Ba Tin, to burn in the fires of hell and call upon the Lord Jesus to send his Angel of Death to your door, knowing you will pay dearly for your evil ways.'

'You dare to condemn me! Your life is in my hands. You arrogant Engleesh you think you can order me!' yelled Bo Ba Tin.

For a few seconds, Bo Ba Tin was stunned into silence as he tried to control the redness crossing his face as, his blood pressure climbed out of control. He was visibly shaking and strutting about nervously.

Unfortunately, it did not last. 'I make you pay for insulting a Japanese officer and the Japanese flag. No god can stop me for I am indestructible and almighty.'

'You can't kill me twice, you swine' Godfrey replied.

Bo Ba Tin raised his baton and smashed it against Godfrey's face.

'I show you I am a God and know that swine means pig. I am no pig. You are a big white pig. You know we hunt pigs with spears so that they squeal before they die. For you, the game is over; you lost; I won and so it is the time to pay the price!'

He walked back to the foot of the stairs and climbed the veranda from where he issued a stream of orders in Japanese. Then out of the back of a lorry came two Sikh soldiers of Bose's Indian National Army. Their turbans and beards were neatly tied in the traditional fashion with eyes that showed no pity, just their contempt for the prisoners. At the foot of the stairs, they saluted Bo Ba Tin, and turned to face the prisoners with rifles and bayonets held firmly out in front of them.

All Peter heard was something like, 'Let's have sport with the pig and *ichi* (one).'

Then a Sikh charged at Godfrey's body yelling Banzai, Banzai. He stopped a foot in front of Godfrey before thrusting the long, cruel bayonet forward to pierce his victim's right leg.

'Aaah…!' screamed Godfrey.

The soldier pulled out the bayonet and returned to the foot of the stairs.

'*Ni*' (two).

The second Sikh ran forward and bayoneted Godfrey in the left leg. He screamed in pain but defiantly glared back at his tormentors.

Peter prayed harder than ever before, not for himself, but for Godfrey. Lord God be with us as we face death in this our darkest hour and let your angels help us bear the pain so that the transition from this world to the next will be swift. For life no longer has any meaning. We are captives of the devil and there can be no escape. Forgive us penitent sinners and give us peace.

There was a lull as Bo Ba Tin walked slowly towards Captain Godfrey. He said, 'Bow your head to acknowledge me as your superior and I will shoot you. If you do not, you will die many times.'

Godfrey said nothing, but his eyes opened to glare down at his tormentor. His eyes said it all. Go to hell you little bastard. Shocked at this defiance from a broken, dying man, Bo Ba Tin walked back to the stairs and yelled again.

This time both Sikhs charged piercing Godfrey's chest with such force that the wounds should have been fatal. So Bo Ba Tin went to Godfrey with his automatic pistol in his hand to administer the coup de grâce. By sheer determination, the broken Godfrey stared defiantly into the Devil's Helper's face. It stopped Bo Ba Tin dead in his tracks as though this dying man was taking something from him, the tormentor, that could not be replaced. Maybe Godfrey stole part of Bo Ba Tin's spirit. All Bo Ba Tin's superstitions started to gather in his mad mind, so he clenched his fists as he struggled to control his fury, and fear. He knew he must show that he was the master and they, his servants. It was a matter of honour, and essential that no one doubted his authority.

In an eerie silence, Bo Ba Tin walked back towards the stairs and with a wave of his hand sent the Sikhs to the lorry. Then in a voice that quivered and lacked authority, he said, 'The night is young and I can wait.'

Bo Ba Tin had lost his confidence, or was he making their torture last longer? It really did not matter, as Bo Ba Tin had departed. It was clear to all who had eyes to see that Godfrey had physically lost the contest, but won it spiritually.

The three prisoners drifted into that state of oblivion, between life and death. Pain was no more as their minds glided slowly away to ride above all sordid things and live in the land of peace and tranquillity.

# 12
# Help Comes in Many Different Forms

*Qu'est-ce qu'un homme révolté? Un homme qui dit non.*
What is a rebel? A man who says no.

Albert Camus (1951) from *L'homme révolté*.

A few miles away, Major Suki and his men travelled northwards to the camp for his men to rest and the wounded receive medical attention. It was sunrise when Major Suki entered the camp, a time when he normally thought of home, and his loved ones. He enjoyed seeing the beauty of the rising sun coming from the east to bring light unto nations? Just as it had been ordained, and so it was.

Major Suki's happiness was destroyed by the horrific spectacle that lay before him of pairs of wooden poles holding the spread eagled bodies of three naked men. As though hit by a bolt of lightning, he was angry as he hated bullies and cowards as much as torturers. War was bad enough without letting loose maniacs on unprotected prisoners. He was a soldier who fought to the death while striving to follow the path that leads to enlightenment and the hope of everlasting life. Now he surveyed the scene to see an arrogant Sikh INA soldier grinning at him without saluting. This, alone, was enough to justify action, so he ordered his men to occupy the camp.

In a foul mood, with pistol in hand, Major Suki entered the command post to be met by an angry Burmese Kempei-Tei interrogator that tried to send him away. No trumped-up local lieutenant was going to dismiss a career Major of the Imperial Staff. No one knows what was said but Suki had Bo Ba Tin arrested, along with the other Kempei-Tei and INA personnel. Each of them had his shoes removed, and hands tied behind his back before being marched out of the camp to the regional HQ, a hundred miles away. The journey would take a week, and they would suffer from sore feet and numb hands. By then Major Suki's men would be on their way.

Now Major Suki's attention turned to cleaning up this hideous butcher's playground. The three broken bodies were taken down so that their wounds could be tended. A doctor examined them before an orderly cleaned their wounds and gave them water. Still is a state of shock, Peter and Temasen watched the doctor attempting in vain to save poor Godfrey. He never regained consciousness and died to go to a better world where love prevailed and violence was unknown.

Peter heard the noise of trucks, the marching of men entering the clearing, followed by the sight of Bo Ba Tin and his men being arrested. He found it hard to believe that what he saw was happening and not a dream. He hoped he would not wake up to face the Devil's Helper?

Confused Peter looked at Temasen, who shrugged his shoulders knowing all they could do was wait and see what happened. Later, a Japanese officer came to see Godfrey, bowed to what remained of his torn body and shook his head before walking towards Peter and Temasen to say. 'I am Major Suki of the Japanese Imperial Army, and I promise you will be treated as my prisoners. We recently fought your people in the Arakan where they proved worthy adversaries. No warrior should die like your colleague. It is wrong. It is not honourable.'

'May we bury him, Major-san?' Peter ventured.

'We have no priest with us because ours died from his wounds. However, I can arrange for a Burmese pongyi to ooficiate. Would that be all right?'

Yes please Major-san,' Peter and Temasen replied.

Major Suki nodded, turned and left them.

Peter saw tears in the Major's eyes, but surely Japanese did not have western emotions. He was wrong, for Suki felt soiled, and sad at what he had witnessed.

It was so quiet that it was surreal. There were no screams, just the noise of men walking around, the smell of cooking, and a feeling that an angel had been sent to help them. In this frame of mind, they fell into a deep sleep.

They were gently woken by an orderly who brought them newly cleaned clothes, including shoes and socks. Eagerly, they put them on and started to feel human again. They were still under guard but were helped to the latrine, given food and water, and not unduly disturbed.

Before dusk Captain Godfrey of 1st Gurkha Rifles was buried. Peter said a prayer, as did the *pongyi*, before a Japanese guard of honour fired a salute. Major Suki said nothing and left after bowing deeply to the grave. Temasen made a cross out of two bits of stick and placed by the grave. He attached a piece of wood giving Captain Godfrey's name, number, and the date. It was then that they discovered that neither knew his first name, for he had always been just Captain Godfrey.

After the funeral, the two were helped back to their beds and left to rest. They were only disturbed by the orderly arriving to change their dressings, and bring food and drink. They were too ill to travel and needed a great deal of rest if they were to live.

When alone Temasen whispered to Peter, 'Look sick so that they will not know when we are fit. Then when we have a chance, we can escape.'

'Yes, but can we pull it off?'

'There's no harm in trying, sir. Soon these men will move on and leave us in the next camp with the Kempei-Tei. I do not think we would like that.'

'What chance do we have?'

'Have faith in God and his people!'

They said nothing more.

During the following day, more wounded Japanese soldiers arrived to keep the doctor busy though a medical orderly checked their injuries. Then they were given a meal of rice and fish stew together with a pot of tea. After the meal, the orderly gave them quinine tablets still in their British package. They must have been captured during the recent battles.

In the evening, the Major appeared and Temasen asked him if he could pray with a *pongyi*. The Major agreed, so later the *pongyi* appeared and talked to Temasen. Peter wondered what language they spoke as Temasen knew no Burmese and the *pongyi* no Hindi. They spoke briefly in whispers while the pongyi lit some joss sticks in a bowl of sand before both men meditated.

Later, the *pongyi* walked over to Peter's bed and placed a bowl of sand in which he lit two more joss sticks whose fumes smoothed Peter's pain before putting his hand on Peter's forehead and whispering in perfect English. 'Why did you stop following my lights? Tomorrow night you must follow my lights. It is your only chance!'

'Why choose me?'

'Because I, like you, believe in the good of mankind. And I, like you, know that if you stay here as a prisoner, you may die. Not under good Major Suki, but later as he must hand you over as a POW.'

The pongyi placed a small grey ball of, what Peter thought was, opium in his hand. 'Chew on this when you have pain. This opium is a traditional medicine from the white poppy of the Shan people. It is very good in small doses, but very bad if liked too much.

Before Peter could thank him, the pongyi left the room walking slowly like an old man with a broken bent back, painfully shuffling his feet. Peter watched as he shuffled on past the guards. Then as the pongyi entered the jungle, he walked upright like a young man.

Peter wondered who the man was and what did he want of him? Probably more importantly, why should he help two wounded men escape?

Maybe it was a trap.... Still he lay down and looked ill. It was only part acting as his wounds hurt, and it was hard to walk. The soles of his feet were raw and blistered after the beatings. He could now partly close his hand, but it was very painful even after the good doctor had treated them. Peter looked across at Temasen pretending to be asleep and decided that sleep was the only viable option. So he slept as he let tiredness overcome his body.

The next day the Japanese Major asked, 'Can you walk now?'

'We will try Major-san.'

'You can stay here a few days longer to regain your strength, as my men also need rest. Then I am afraid that you must go to prison camp and I to battle. There is nothing that I can do, as soon I expect the Kempei-Tei to return. You will be safer in a real prison camp than remaining here.'

'We understand Major-san and thank you for your kindness.'

'It is how warriors should treat each other. You did not surrender but were captured in battle. Thus as one soldier to another I respect you. It is the Samurai code.'

They parted. Maybe in all armies and in all wars, there is the good as well as the bad. Then they had their bandages changed, were given medicine and ate as much as they could. Both men slept most of the day only waking to eat, wash and hobble outside to the latrine.

'*Hancho, benjo*,' Temasen called out at regular intervals.

The guards appeared to carry Temasen to the latrine. Before sundown, their bandages were changed, and they were given drugs to ease the pain.

Peter noticed that the medicine was British and unopened.

'Doctor-san, is this British medicine?'

'*Hai*. In the battle, we received many packages of medicine, food and ammunition from the air. It is only proper that you should share it. The medicine was not a gift; I remember that three men were killed when a crate of ammunition landed on top of them. Unfortunately, they died for nothing as it was shells for your howitzers, and we had none. So they were no use to us,' said the doctor.

The doctor left and the two set about organizing themselves. It was nearly dark when their food and drink arrived. They ate heartily, putting a few rice balls into their pockets for the journey ahead and waited. Through the window, they watched the flag lowered and the Major and his officers retire with the folded flag to the big hut. By nine, or was it ten, everything was quiet except for the moans of the wounded men from the hospital. Now Temasen watched each sentry patrol the grounds and noted that none went near the latrines. Then Temasen motioned for Peter to follow him out of a window. It was now or never.

'Peter, come here very slowly and quietly,' Temasen whispered.

Peter nodded. First Temasen and then Peter rolled out of the window on to land on the soft ground. They walked quietly towards the jungle only three hundred yards from the hut, but it felt like ten miles. Now it was dark, as the moon was covered by thick clouds, as it started to rain heavily. Then they heard one of the sentries call out.

'*Gumso, taxan ame.*' (Too much rain).

'*Hai, yazume.*' (Yes, rest), another sentry replied.

A soldier walked to a latrine within a hundred yards of where they stood, so they kept absolutely still, hiding in the shadows so that he did not see them. While the guard was answering the call of nature, they moved rapidly into the dark the jungle. Their injured feet make walking difficult, but the pain could not stop them. They felt that it was better to suffer than risk having no head, so they moved as fast as possible. They did not care if they stood on scorpions, snakes, thorns, glass or hot coals as all they wanted was to get away from that terrible place. If they died of fever, of snakebite, or were shot, it was better than going back. They were surprised that the alarm did not sound, so their escape was not discovered.

It was not as it appeared, for Major Suki watched the duo escape and was pleased. He hoped that they would escape and so reduced the guards. Now he must get ready to leave; when the prisoners were found missing he would dispatch a search party in the wrong direction. He felt what he had done was correct, for surely no man should face death by torture more than once. He never forgot the scenes after the rape of Nanking, for they were inhuman and horrific to behold. He doubted if the Japanese nation could ever be forgiven for such atrocities against women, children, and even babies.

The further Peter and Temasen were from the camp the quicker they walked. They had no map, no compass, and did not know in the darkness where they should travel. However, Temasen moved on with the occasional look to see if Peter was with him, or if they were followed. After an hour, they stopped resting against a banyan tree. Here, Temasen said, 'Look at the tree and pray. Focus your mind on your friend the *pongyi*, and he will come to us so that with his help, we will be safe.'

Peter felt such a fool as he wondered why the normally sensible Temasen believed that prayer would help. He didn't have a bloody clue where they were. All he had to guide him was the word of a Buddhist priest and the hopes of a Hindu Gurkha. Still maybe he should have faith and pray for guidance, there seemed no other option. He remembered the pongyi's words: 'Why did you not follow my lights? You must follow my lights. Follow my lights, if I am to help you. You must believe and follow my lights.'

Peter closed his eyes and prayed for help.

When Peter opened his eyes, he felt good. Nothing had changed but somehow he felt better as his feet were guided over the ground, and the pain was gone. It was probably the effect of the opium.

When he had given up hope, it happened.

It was as though all the jungle creatures and spirits, or nats, were on their side and some magician had waved his magic wand. First there appeared a little dim light that flickered like an old lantern high up in a nearby banyan tree. There was nobody there to hold it, and yet it gave forth a warm light. He shook his head in disbelief before looking ahead deeper into the forest to see another lantern come alight, and then another appeared, and another. Soon, there was stretched out in front of them a lantern trail leading from one banyan tree to another. It was a miracle or the answer to their prayers, but it also made them feel uneasy.

'Temasen, are the lights real or am I dreaming?' Peter asked.

'You must be blessed Peter; I have never seen such a sight, and I know the jungle nearly as well as I know my mountain homeland. However, no God has ever lit my way home. It is magic, clean, beautiful, and bringer of hope.'

'No Temasen, I did not bring the lights. It is the *pongyi* coming for us.'

Peter still did not move but strained his eyes to make out the images at the end of the trail of light. He thought he saw people holding lanterns making hand gestures that said, come to us. It must be his imagination for as they walked forward they were no closer to the mysterious lantern carriers.

'You believe in this pongyi, don't you Temasen?'

'Yes. He said that you had a pure of heart, and war has made you old. You have experienced things that make all men go grey, and yet you are not bitter. I think we should follow his lights.'

'For some reason, I do, so what are we waiting for? Let's go.'

So they went towards the magical lights feeling a sense of purpose and hope.

# 13

# The Jungle and the Lights

*And a light shall bring forth hope in a time of darkness*

When exhausted, they slept until dusk, feeling at peace for the first time since their capture. When hungry, they ate jungle fruits and drank water from the leaves. The cool jungle water cleansed their souls and revived their bodies.

'Temasen, what did the *pongyi* tell you?'

'He said that I had a new baby son who awaits my return.'

'I am sure that is true. How many children do you have?'

'I have two girls and now a boy. Indeed, I am blessed.'

'Indeed I envy you the joy of having a child of your own.'

'You need not. Tauk says you will live long and have three children with your wife. Maybe, others as well,' he giggled.

'That's a lot of old baloney. Anyways who is Tauk?'

'Tauk is the *pongyi*. Well, that's the name he gave, but many Burmese has two or three different names. It is what we call alibis.'

'No Temasen an alibi is when you need an excuse for not being somewhere and say that you were in Kathmandu when really you were with the merchant's wife.'

'That could not have been me, sir! I never met a merchant's wife whom I fancied ... Perhaps it was his daughter.'

'You are incorrigible rogue! Damn it, what was I saying?'

'You were explaining to me the differences between aliases and alibis.'

'Oh yes. What you wanted to say was an alias, meaning a false name, not your real one. For instance, a woman asks your name, so you say 'Peter Anderson from Ranchi'. So I get the blame for your naughty deeds.'

'So I was right all time. An alias is the name you use to have an alibi.'

Laughing, Peter gave up. Temasen was a great master at understanding what he wanted to and misunderstanding everything that he did not like.

Would he live long enough to have a wife and a family of his own? He was never very good with the opposite sex. All he knew was the tenderness and the loving Anna gave him, the pleasure and comfort that helped conquer fear and loneliness. Surely, God must care for her and give her happiness, for she above all women deserved to be loved and cared for.

When night came they waited by a banyan tree for the lights to appear, and again, they did. Therefore, they followed the lights, wanting to meet the people behind them. Peter did not care whether they were little devils or angels as they emitted an aura of goodness, and safety filled his heart with joy.

Fate is not always straightforward. Sometimes at joyful times one experiences great sorrow. For instance, while running one falls flat on one's face. It was just such a time when Peter tripped and fell down onto the ground.

In seconds, loyal Temasen was by his side.

'Can you get up Peter, sir?'

'Of course I can; I fell over when something cut my skin. It was probably just a thorn. Stop fussing over me like an old woman.'

Temasen saw a Russell's viper slide away into the distance. If Peter had been bitten and received a full dose of venom, he would die – and quickly.

'Don't move. Just lie still so I can see if your leg is broken.'

Peter's head started to feel dizzy, and his leg ached. Temasen pulled up Peter's trousers to reveal the telltale, double puncture marks of snake bite. Quickly, he placed a tourniquet around his leg before cutting the skin between the puncture marks so that it bled profusely.

'Hell, does everyone have to cut me?'

'Peter please lay still. You have been bitten by a snake, but I will make you better. Don't fear, as I will suck out the venom. You rest and have a cup of tea.'

Every few seconds Temasen stopped sucking out the poison and spat it onto the ground together with some of Peter's blood. Where was the cup of tea? Then Peter remembered that they did not have even a cup of water between them.

'Peter, now I must carry you. Remember a snake bite very rarely kills. The poor snake meant no harm and only bit you because you scared him.'

Peter forced a grin. Temasen was becoming more like Pip's Man every day. So he slept, waking to find to find himself alone to think Temasen had done the wise thing by leaving him. Not so, for soon Temasen gave him some water to sip before mopping his fevered brow.

'Leave me Temasen and save yourself. I'm just another weight for you to carry. I order you to go away.'

'Poor man, the poison makes you confused. Still you are getting better. I will never abandon you. I am a Gurkha who will die before I leave you. Rest now.'

With those comments, Temasen walked a few yards away, shaking his head and muttering. Peter tried to eavesdrop on his private thoughts. Temasen turned around to say. 'Don't treat me like a fool or a coward! I could not die for Captain Godfrey, and now you die for me. It can never be so as the Pongyi says you will have many children. So you better live and start making them.'

'Yes, Temasen, with your help I will live.'

'Good. Now stop acting like a baby and eat the food.'

They found under a large banyan tree a packet of dried meat, some fruits and a container of water with bandages and two small knives. Someone had left the packages for them, and they were certain it was the pongyi or his people. When they left there were no traces of the packages so that no one else could find them. It was not difficult as everything was wrapped in banana leaves that they shred and buried in the fallen leaves that lined the jungle floor. They felt obliged, even their sacred duty, to make certain that no enemy could follow them towards their friends. It was their secret way through the magic jungle, and they wanted no form of evil to pollute its purity.

That night they moved closer to the lights, with Temasen walking as fast as he could on his sore feet with Peter on his back. Just before daybreak they entered a clearing where stood the *pongyi*, Tauk, with several others clad in white and holding lanterns. Peace prevailed, helped by the persistent chanting and soft singing, sounding like angels calling them onwards to safety. They were surrounded by huts raised from the ground by stilts with a small white-painted temple, guarded by a pair of chinthe containing a little golden Lord Buddha.

Just before Peter lost consciousness, he understood the song they sang.

It went:

'Come to us all you wounded soldiers,
Come to us all with a pure heart.
We will tend your wounds,
Heal you and then let you depart.
Come to us for peace and rest,
Come to us, you with a pure heart.'

It had to be a dream, as they sang in Burmese and yet the words were in English. Maybe he was translating his mother's language automatically, as a good linguist should. Such thoughts make happy dreams to help soothe the soul and calm the tormented mind.

# 14
## Peace at Last

*Even in the midst of chaos spring small oasis of peace*
*where the weary traveller may find peace and hope.*

It was four days before Peter fully regained consciousness, having been at death's door from the snake venom and his other wounds. Patiently, the *pongyi* kept him alive with herbal medicines and prayers. It was hard work, as Peter was so weak that he wandered between life and death. They first cut off his clothes, then washed his body, and administered treatment. The snakebite soon healed, but the other wounds were deeper and needed careful attention if the cuts were not to cripple him for life. Each cut had to be cleansed and treated to reduce the formation of scar tissue or the onset of infection.

Peter awoke stark naked on a rattan bed, being washed by a beautiful young girl and watched by the *pongyi*. He felt embarrassed at his nakedness, trying in vain to pull a cloth to cover his body. His efforts were greeted with giggles from the girl and loud laughter from Temasen.

'Dear Sir, this young lady has nursed you, treated your snakebite, and tended to your other injuries for the past four days. Without her, you would have died. She has seen all of you and treated your body with the greatest respect.'

'Sorry, I'm not used to being naked in front of a woman, especially such a beautiful one.'

'I am sure that this will not be the last time you will find yourself in such an unfortunate predicament,' said Tauk, *the pongyi*. 'We have a saying that only the ugly, the unlucky and the pongyis will never find the true happiness that a good woman can give her man.' Then, Tauk dismissed the girl, who obediently left. Peter did not know that she and her sister spoke fluent English.

'I suppose you want to know who we are and where you are, and why?'

'It seems a little ungrateful sir, but I would like to know these things. However, I am surprised that you speak such excellent English.'

'Thank you. However, I cannot take all the credit, for my lecturers at Rangoon College were excellent. They were mostly British, though one was an Irish priest. Later, I went to London to attend a course on government administration.'

'So why are you a priest? Or is it a disguise?'

'It is partly a disguise, though I do obey the priestly rules. I joined the Thankin movement to gain Burma's independence. The movement divided between those who wanted a Dominion, an independent nation but associated with Britain, and those who wanted to side with the Japanese. I supported the group that would have made Burma a Dominion, like Canada and Australia.'

Tauk looks changed from smiling to be sad.

'Sorry if I've opened up old wounds, especially as you have saved us.'

'Thank you Peter! I regret the trust we placed in the Japanese. The desire for power has blinded my people, so they fail to realise that fascism never brings freedom and what the Japanese is doing is unforgivable. Therefore, my daughters and I fight a long way from our Karen homeland to eradicate evil of the Empire of the Rising Sun. We are the Pro-British and Anti-Fascist Freedom League, AFLA in short. We are a mixture of Karen, Shan, Chins, Burman (Bamar)s, and some Naga. In this village, there are no tribes, for we are united in our aim to defeat the enemy.'

'Thank you for telling me about your people, it helps me understand.'

Tauk rose and clapped his hands like people accustomed to power often do.

'Can you walk?'

'Yes I think so, though I would like some clothes.'

'You must wear the longyi by the bed, since I have burned your clothes to hide you from peeping eyes.'

So Peter got up and wearing the longyi went with Tauk to find Temasen in the next hut sitting in front of a banquet laid out on a mat covering the floor. There were slices of fresh fruits, mangoes, bananas, papaya and cooked chicken. Two large dishes full of rice next to one containing steamed fish placed next to small bowls of thick lentil soup in which floated soft noodles. It smelt delicious, indeed the best meal in the world.

'Just eat what you can as there is much more where this comes from. We even have a choice of tea, Indian or Chinese. I recommend the Chinese green tea, because it has great medicinal properties.'

Slowly, Tauk placed his hands together in prayer while they waited impatiently.

'You should start to eat before I take the lot,' Tauk said.

Neither man needed a second invitation as they set about devouring the feast. It was a long time since they had eaten so well, so this meal he would always remember. Later, they sat in the veranda, dressed in Burmese clothing, drinking green tea and smoking Burmese cheroots. The cheroots reminded Peter of Pip Palmarino, dearest Anna, friendship, and good little Tim.

'Our small community is a base used by my elder daughter's Little Pagoda fighters in their war against the Japanese. It is a part of your Force V and gathers information for the British Army, among other things.'

'You mean that this is a kind of guerrilla base run by a woman?'

'You wait until you meet my daughter, Susie. You already know her sister, Maria, who was your nurse. Both girls are Catholics like their mother, but here Susie is known as Myint Suu Kyi and Maria as Myint Ma Hla.'

'Where is their mother?'

'She has passed on to a better life. She died saving the girls when the Burmese Defence Army attacked their Karen village looking for resistance fighters. There was nothing to find, so they raped and killed everyone present. She hid the girls under the hut's floor before taking a rifle and shooting at the intruders. Others joined her in the vain attempt to stop the atrocities.'

Tears formed in Tauk's eyes as he remembered his loss before taking another puff from his cheroot and continuing. 'At nightfall there was a lull in the fighting, so she sent the girls away with a friend to hide in the jungle for two days until all was quiet. When they returned everyone had been shot or mutilated. Even the dogs were killed. They found their mother's torn body still holding her father's old Martini Henry hunting rifle in the remains of our home.'

Tauk stopped to wipe a tear from his face. Then he added, 'I was in Mandalay working for the Japanese when I heard what had happened. Immediately, I asked my Japanese masters' permission to go to Rangoon to find my children. After they agreed for me to travel, I left and, instead of going south to Rangoon, I went east to our home to bury the only true love I have ever known. I swore to bring peace to this land and help others destroy all those who harmed her. So, after a hurried funeral, my daughters and I, together with some friends, travelled westwards to help the British. Everywhere we went; we found burnt villages where the enemy had been until we reached here.'

'So when did you become a *pongyi*?'

'Like all Buddhist men I served my initiation as a monk. So I decided to follow the true path by cleansing myself of all worldly goods, of money, of women, or the lust for power and to preserve life in all of its forms. It is difficult, but it helps me. Still I cannot become a full priest until the war is over as I must feed my people and if necessary, kill to preserve them.'

'Now what can I do?'

'You must regain your strength to be fit enough to travel, meanwhile Temasen will leave us to be taken to Imphal.'

'Why will he travel north?'

'After the Ha-Go campaign failed, it was replaced by the U-Go offensive, whereby three Japanese divisions have been sent north to the Naga Hills.'

'So how do I get back?'

'When you are fit, Suu Kyi will take you when they attack the Japanese in the Kalewa valley before ascending the hills to Kohima.'

'That appears simple. First, I must fight the Japanese Army and then climb some hills.' Peter replied.

'Peter you must stop thinking and rest. Soon you must earn your living like the rest of us, otherwise the Rising Sun will rule forever, and we will be its slaves or have died in vain.'

'Come Peter, we must leave Tauk to meditate,' stated Temasen.

'Yes it is time for me to meditate on all our futures. Since we only survive this world of pain when prepared both spiritually and mentally for the trials to come.'

Tauk bowed before walking to the shrine, where he gently beat the temple brass gong and lit the joss sticks in a bowl of sand before the image of Buddha. A few minutes later, Temasen followed to kneel by the priest's side as they bowed and chanted their prayers. There was the educated Burmese trying to find the true path of peaceful coexistence, praying with the hardened Hindu warrior. However, both believed in honour and goodness, while they prayed that the Japanese would be defeated.

Maria washed and bandaged his wounds placing some leaves on them that she bound firmly with clean bandages. Peter worried about the leaves being placed on his wound. He did not realise that the leaves were dropped in boiling water and dried before being placed on his body as every care was taken to make him well.

'Is it getting better, nurse Maria? May I call you that?'

'You heal well, so soon you will travel with us northwards. You must never call me Maria in public, only by my Burmese name Myint Ma Hla. I will call you Myint Saw Shwe so that no one will know that you are English. We must always be very careful, especially near strangers. Is that understood?'

'I understand Myint Ma Hla.'

How the mighty have fallen! Here he was – a Squadron Leader – taking orders from a fifteen-year-old girl? Oh well, that's life. She was like his sister: beautiful, soft-spoken and a pig-headed bully.

'Now we polish your Burmese so you sound like a bearer.'

'Is my Burmese poor?'

'No, it is classical and old fashioned. Your teacher taught you traditional, polite and accurate Burmese. The ordinary villager talks in shorter sentences with poor grammar, not caring if something is or was, is she or he, or when it was.'

So Peter learnt to speak like an indigenous Chin. He enjoyed his lessons as much as she enjoyed teaching him. When he was too formal, she reprimanded him but on speaking in village Burmese, she beamed with joy.

Tauk said to Temasen, 'Soon Tun Kyi will arrive and a few days later will take you to your people.'

'Thank you, Tauk, but like my ancestors before me, I swore allegiance to the King, and so I must rejoin my regiment to fight the yellow devils.'

'Each of us fights in our own way. I have collected for you a jungle knife, not quite a kukri, but a good weapon, a British pistol and a first-aid kit. The evening before you leave we will give you enough food for five days. Remember, forget where we are as remaining undiscovered is our only protection.'

'I will die before I tell anyone.'

'My Burma is lost as each day the Japanese becomes more arrogant while their Burmans (Bamar) are crueller. I know we shall all meet again in happier times, though I fear Burma may never recover from this war. In Rangoon, the Indian merchants work for the Japanese conquerors by supplying them with everything that they need. It is said that Rangoon receives ships loaded with supplies and munitions that leave with rice, timber, and precious jewels.'

'They seem to feed off the land and travel light. The only things they need are fuel and ammunition,' added Temasen.

'They will soon find it harder as the rice grows in the lowlands not in the north where they must travel. Here the jungle is thick, the slopes steep and muddy, and food scarce. And the villagers will not be helpful as they dislike the Burman (Bamar). This is not southern Burma where the Burman (Bamar) live. This is the land of the minorities such as the Chin, Karen and Naga people.'

'They must be stopped from crossing the Brahmaputra River and entering India where they may get support from those who believe that Japan will give them freedom. They should all be here and see how we are treated,' commented a frustrated Temasen.

They walked across the clearing to see Peter. They found him dressed in a faded cotton *longyi* and a white vest. On his feet, he wore a pair of leather thong sandals. From a distance, he looked like an Arakan labourer. They listened as Peter was coached in Chin and told off by his young teacher whenever he got it wrong.

Tauk smiled, and Temasen grinned at what they saw.

'See the officer taking lessons from a Karen schoolgirl.'

'Your daughter, sir, is a good teacher.'

'Maybe, it is because Maria is young and pretty, and I suspect Peter wants to impress her. Were we all like that when we were younger?'

# 15

# A Little Lady and her Warriors

*Beauty is in the eye of the beholder.*

One night, twenty armed soldiers entered the village. Peter noted that they looked like a motley crew attired in different uniforms, carrying weapons and wearing bandoliers of bullets as if they were a pirate crew scared of nothing. Tauk greeted the one wearing a Japanese cap with hugs and kisses to make Peter wonder if men do this to each other in Burma? Some European and Arab men greet each other by kissing their friends on both cheeks; maybe some Burmese does the same?

Then, Tauk took Peter and Temasen to meet the newcomers.

'Squadron Leader Peter Anderson and Havildar Temasen, let me introduce you to the leader of the Little Pagoda resistance in Force V and the second in command.'

Peter noticed that in front of him stood a man in his early twenties wearing Burmese attire with a British Sten gun on his lap next to the woman wearing a Japanese hat. Assuming the man was the leader, Peter tried to shake his hand. The man ignored it while staring out into space. Peter now sensed the man's hostility.

Why? What had he done wrong?

The woman laughed as she took off her cap to free her long black hair. Peter saw her smile, and it captivated him as she was both very beautiful and brave.

'Tun Kyi you must shake the man's hand as he thinks that you are our leader,' the woman said.

'No my leader, it would not be right to let him think that I am in command as I serve you and trust you with my life.'

'I am told that the British like their women to stay at home to look after their children. They cannot give orders or be soldiers. Poor things, they can't help themselves. It is the way they are.'

Peter was embarrassed by his error feeling that he had insulted her. He felt much better after looking into her round face to see the sparkling brown eyes shining on him.

'Sorry, Peter, I should have told you that my daughter was the leader,' Tauk stated. 'So Peter I want you to meet my eldest daughter, Lieutenant Myint Suu Kyi, my little Susie, of V Force, and our friend, Sergeant Tun Kyi.'

'Pleased to meet you,' Peter managed to say without stammering too much as he could not take his eyes off her. He was mesmerised and suddenly as shy as a young schoolboy.

Shaking Peter's hand, Susie said, 'Forgive my father, but he does not think of me as his daughter when I am in uniform. In the morning, after I have rested, I will be different. When I dress like my little sister, you will see that I really am

107

a woman. The journey has been long and full of many difficulties that have left us all exhausted. So for now, we must leave you to get some sleep, and tomorrow we can discuss how to help take you home. Goodnight.'

Susie turned and walked across to her hut while Peter's eyes followed her until after she closed the hut door. He was smitten and did not realise it.

Tauk walked with Peter and Temasen back to their hut. 'They have been away for twenty days and are very tired. Tomorrow you will see that they are very likeable people. Twenty-two went, but alas only nineteen returned, so I must console the families of those who perished. Sleep well my friends, for soon you return to fight in the war that stains this land with blood.'

At dawn, Peter and Temasen were up, washed and dressed eager to know more about the newcomers. They carried out their allotted chores, had breakfast and waited while noticing that on either side of the village compound, there were sentries concealed among the bushes. It was a reminder that even in this paradise death was all around.

Tauk prayed before the shrine with his hands closed as his ancestors had done for thousands of years. If one was very quiet, you could make out the words of the ancient chant used for thanks, followed by another requesting guidance. Then he placed a garland of flowers around the Buddha and lit the candle in two paper lanterns hanging from the roof. The silence was broken by two women chatting away and laughing as though life was just like it had always been. The giggles came closer as two women dressed in their finest clothes walked towards Peter's hut. On the right was his teacher, Maria, looking radiantly happy, next to her was Susie dressed in a nearly transparent white ingyi and a blue silk longyi. Her long black hair hung down her back, and on top she wore a yellow orchid. Peter felt that she glided towards him with her head held high so that her hair blew freely in the wind. She was 5 feet tall, small with a narrow waist and delicate features. As the women drew closer to where Peter sat in the veranda, he looked into Susie's deep brown eyes and was transfixed. He wanted to keep her safely in his arms and yet was afraid that she would break like a little doll. Maybe she did not find him attractive or had a boyfriend, even a husband. Maria left to walk off holding hands with Tun Kyi into the distance. Now alone, Susie felt Peter's stare that, she responded with a smile before sitting down on the floor next to him. Then for, maybe one minute, or was it ten, both looked into the eyes of the other, lost in their own private world. Nothing was spoken as each tried to understand the other's innermost thoughts.

'Good morning Squadron Leader I trust you slept well,' asked Susie.

'Indeed I did, ma'am. I hope that you are rested from your ordeal.'

She ran her fingers through her long, black hair, which had fallen over her chest.

'Squadron Leader, if you want to understand me, you must realise that there are two people sharing my body. Here I am Susie, a young woman who wants peace and happiness, while at other times, I am Lieutenant Myint Suu Kyi, guerrilla leader. I try to keep the parts separate, but it is very difficult.'

She was uncertain what to say and was surprised as she never had this problem telling people what to do when fighting. So why should this stranger cause her to be unsure of even her innermost feelings? It was not fair.

'Please call me Peter – everyone else does.'

'Only if you call me Susie.'

'That sounds like a good idea.'

Susie looked very serious and asked,' Can you forget those that you have killed?'

'I used to think that being a pilot, I did not see the face of the enemy. However, I remember the face of the first pilot that I shot down, especially as the plane was on fire, and he did not escape. I know that he would have killed me but when I saw him fail to escape; I felt sad for him and his family.'

Susie replied. 'It is like that for me. I hate the Japanese and their allies for what they have done to the Karen people and for my mother's death. I tell myself, that unless they are stopped all of Asia will become their slaves. So either they must die or leave. When the fighting starts it is different because I know that they must die before they kill us. It is a matter of self-preservation.'

'Susie you must do what I do that is when the fighting is over, sit down and pray to Jesus knowing he is always there while your father asks Buddha to protect all of us, and I know it helps.'

'My father is a Buddhist, while my mother practiced the gentleness and caring of a Buddhist though being a devout Catholic. Both Maria and I were raised as good Catholic girls who under different circumstances would now be studying for a career before getting married. However, in the war, all things are turned upside down.'

'Where has my Maria gone?'

'She has gone to walk by the river with the love of her life, Tun Kyi. It is good that they have each other, for life is too short. If war teaches us anything, it is that life is so precious that we must grab all the happiness we can before the next storm comes.'

'You will live for a thousand years to be a mother to all. Since you care for your people and have so much love to give,' Peter stated.

'There speaks the old wise owl. I hope you are right as I thank God for this moment of peace and am glad. Friendship and happiness are only brief incidents in a troubled world. The Buddhists are right – all life is suffering and must be handled with patience and caring.'

Maybe, but nothing as beautiful as you could be sent to earth without some important meaning,' Peter said, and then blushed.

'You are a very romantic Englishman, probably married, or at least have a fiancée. Maybe you like to seduce young, innocent women ... Or you like men!

'I'm none of those things,' Peter stammered. He had not stammered since childhood, nor felt so self-conscious. Yes, he wanted to touch her, to hold her in his arms, but how could he tell her that she was his first love and hold her in his arms. It was love at first sight. Whatever his desires he must not repay the good pongyi by seducing his beloved daughter; it would be unforgivable and could have dire consequences. Why can't life be simple and straightforward? He knew that he was lost and yet would not wish to be anywhere else.

Susie sensing his feelings, held his hand in hers. She too felt an instant attraction to this gentle man but dared not to think of falling in love. She feared anything that would affect her duties, though she wished, the war was over, so they could have time to know each other. Indeed, her whole body wanted to be in his arms to share a few moments of happiness.

Maybe this was just some animal instinct that needed to be satisfied, or controlled before it went too far. Perhaps God had sent him to her to calm her fears by loving her, like Tun Kyi cared for Maria. Neither of them knew what to say nor what to do, so they said nothing. Instead, they just sat there holding hands. Soon the sun shone more brightly giving all around them a special magical glow, while the songs of the birds drove away all thoughts of war so for now, they found peace. It was good. It was just what they needed.

Across the courtyard, Tauk gave Temasen a jungle knife and a Bren gun. Immediately, Temasen sat on the ground to clean the gun so that the bolt moved smoothly up and down, making certain that there was no moisture or dirt in the barrel, and the firing pin was correctly aligned. Then he loaded the bullets one by one into the curved magazines. When one magazine was loaded with thirty rounds, he started on another. Tauk saw that the havildar was again the professional soldier and was glad that he was leaving. The idea of killing was unacceptable to his Buddhist nature, and yet he knew that he would, without the slightest hesitation, kill and die for his people but prayed that it would never be necessary.

Where was Susie? He felt that the war robbed his daughters of their childhood. Then he saw Susie and Peter chatting away and prayed that at least for now they would be good for each other. She needed to be loved both physically and mentally, while Peter needed someone like Susie to care about. Love is a great healer, and true love a gift beyond all others.

Tears formed in his eyes as he remembered when he met his now departed wife. She was lovely, and he so timid. She had controlled him from the first moment they had met, making him putty in her hands, and yet she never misused her power. It was a miracle that they grew to love each other and raise a family. But they did. They argued about silly, unimportant things. He was not a good husband, as he often misbehaved, and she reprimanded him. However, she was always there for him as the very cornerstone of her family. Now she was gone; he must copy her and help the others have a good life, even find true love. He would always be there for his children, for as long as he lived, and they knew it.

Maybe if Susie bore Peter a child, she would stop being a soldier. He feared she would die by the hands of a torturer like the Devil's Helper. However, when he meditated on the subject, he always saw her as an old lady surrounded by her family. He was wise enough to know he could not change their destiny but must wait and pray that Lord Buddha would give everyone the one ingredient that none of them had, time to be young.

Some things cannot be rushed, but must be taken one step at a time. For one cannot make a beehive without bees or honey without flowers.

# 16
## Some Leave While Others Remain

Just before sunset Temasen woke Peter to say. 'Peter it is time for me to return to my unit. Tun Kyi will guide me by night to avoid the Japanese forces. He says that they are moving westwards so we go north for two days and then west to the town of Ukhal.'

Peter put his arms around his friend knowing they had been to hell and back together and yet no words could express how he felt. 'Good luck my friend. If God wishes, then we'll meet again, for I will miss you. Without your courage, I could not have survived imprisonment. I am glad that you are my friend because I would hate to be your enemy.'

'Remember that we have survived meeting the Devil's Helper and will always be friends. My house is your house, though I am only a havildar and you an officer. You have more courage than you know, so just believe and the true path will be shown to you. I hope to see you again.'

Then Temasen saluted, turned around and carrying the heavy Bren gun as though it weighed nothing, started walking away with the group. No one looked back; it was as if they were no longer villagers.

Peter, Susie and Tauk watched them disappear into the distance.

'Where is Maria?' Peter asked. 'I thought that she would wave good-bye to Tun Kyi?'

'I am sure she has said her farewells, so we should leave her alone to cry as her love goes away to war, for she may never see him again. She may be young, but she knows true love and is wiser than most twice her age.'

Then Peter and Susie were alone again.

Tauk left to chant his prayers, worried that Maria could become a widow, without having been married, to mourn her first love. He shook himself, and the feeling went away. Maybe all would end well.

Peter put his arm around her shoulder as she placed her head against his chest.

'If any two people were made for each other to live as husband and wife, then it must be Maria and Tun Kyi. So I think they will be happy forever and ever. We cannot change the future but can pray for them both.'

'Father says that one must grab the moment, for life is too short as it is no rehearsal for anything. It is funny that two days ago all I wanted was to kill the Japanese and safeguard my family. However, since I have met you, everything has changed as I'm a girl again, and you make me feel young and full of hope. '

'I am glad, as you are the most beautiful person, I have ever met, and I want to keep you safe in my arms.'

She said nothing but put her arms around his neck, pulling their bodies close and kissed him. Neither moved away, instead they clung onto each other as though their very existence depended on this kiss. Perhaps it did.

If they were timid before, now they forgot their shyness. If they were afraid, they forgot their fear. If they wanted privacy, they were in the wrong place as they could be seen by the whole village, who were glad for them. If ever two people needed love, they did.

All that night they stayed together in each other's arms. It was all perfectly proper. She awoke to find it was dawn, and she had slept all night in her clothes. So she went off to her hut to wash and change, wondering why he had not tried to make love to her or whether she wanted him to. Maybe he would not like her without her clothes on. She was sure that she would love him even if his body was torn and ugly. She must think for the both of them, for time was not on their side. She was inexperienced in the ways of lovers but knew she must grasp the moment before it flew away.

Peter woke up to find there was not Susie sleeping by his side; was it just a dream? He was surprised that he had slept fully clothed, so he undressed and washed. When he tidied up his sleeping mat, he found the flower that Susie had worn in her hair.

At breakfast, Peter found Tauk and Maria sitting by the low table, but there was no sign of Susie, so he worried at what her father would say.

'You look well today, Peter. Now your wounds have healed, you must practice walking and using your muscles. So Susie will take you into the jungle to stretch your legs because soon you must start the long walk home.'

'Thank you, sir! Have you any news of Temasen?'

'We will hear nothing until the others return. Temasen left with Tun Kyi, Ba Saw and Setcha. Setcha is frail, but he wants to join the British as a translator to help them fight against the Japanese and will take Temasen to Ukhrul while the others return.'

'I pray they get through the Japanese lines without harm.'

'There is no sense in worrying about things that one cannot control, so eat up and grow strong. They will get through as there are no distinct lines in the jungle. Each side moves along different parts of the same front. The Japanese used larger formations to attack pockets of the British soldiers to have numerical superiority. If the British kept together they would survive, instead they leave a few brave men as a rearguard to die; to allow the rest to escape.'

'Don't be cruel father. Peter is not responsible for the generals. Anyhow, I told you the British won a battle at Sinzweya around Okeydokey Pass forcing the Japanese army to move north. We saw thousands of Japanese soldiers crossing the Chindwin river on their way to the valleys and mountains of Nagaland.'

Peter heard Susie telling her father off, politely but firmly, but all he saw was her beautiful firm body through a white silk longyi. He sensed that he could see her nipples pushing unrestricted under her ingyi. Embarrassed, he looked up and noticed in her hair was another flower, which made her eyes even more enchanting.

She kissed Peter then sat by his side. He worried what Tauk would feel, not knowing that he had seen them kissing last night on the veranda.

'Susie, stop tormenting the poor boy. You may be a soldier, but you are also my daughter. In my village, you will treat my friend with respect. So eat up, otherwise I will have two sickly lovers on my hands.'

Maria giggled as they looked at Tauk with a degree of uncertainty. After breakfast, Tauk and Maria left them alone.

'Can you walk?' asked Susie.

'Of course I can walk, but why?'

'It is time you had some exercise, so we shall go for a walk by the river.'

'Can you swim?' Peter asked back.

'Better than you,' Susie replied.

'We will see about that.'

'I bet you have never swum a river carrying a rope to haul your men across. Or waded up to your waist in mud carrying 60 pounds of explosive on your head and a gun in one hand?'

Peter had not, so he changed the subject to say. 'Is it safe to be so near the river?'

'Oh Yes. The Japanese army is to the north, so there is little activity here.'

'But we can still be seen from the air.'

'Yes, of course we can be seen, but who is going to question a woman and a man swimming in the water on a hot day? It is so natural. That is unless you wish to wear a uniform or wave your flag.'

So they walked together into the jungle. For a moment, Peter felt fear when the light of the day was replaced by the gloom of the forest. But then he felt the warmth of her hand and knew that it was just perfect. They arrived at the river where the waters fell between rocks as a small waterfall to form a pool. Here Susie stopped. 'This is my special place where I am part of nature. Let's enjoy the cool water that will wash our bodies clean of our past.'

Peter was mesmerised as Susie took off her *ingyi* to reveal her small but firm breasts with their hard, pointed nipples. Eyes down, she slowly removed the *longyi* from around her waist and stood totally naked. She did not look up at him as she folded her clothes neatly before going into the water. She felt his eyes watching her every move, delighting in her beauty until her body disappeared leaving only her head visible, with the flower still in her hair.

'Come on in to the water, you slow coach! Surely, a big man like you is not afraid of a frail little girl like me,' Susie said trying to get him to join her.

'I somehow don't think the warrior princess is a frail little girl.'

'You are a silly boy. That is the other me, now I am Susie. Come in quickly as I am getting cold, and I need you to warm me before I freeze to death.'

Without hesitation, Peter threw his clothes on the ground before running naked into the water. She watched his body, noticing the scars on his arms where he had been tortured. Maybe he could not love her, but unless she helped him, they would never know their real feelings. She was wise enough for both, for she had seen people become dehumanised by thugs and torturers. So now she intended to remove such memories from his mind, at least, for the time being. They swam and splashed each other. He held her in his arms as they kissed. He felt her warm body moulded against his that made his whole body want to make love to her. She broke away to swim a few yards before splashing water in his face. The noise from the water from the stream above, falling down into the pool; the light reflecting on their bodies and the sun's warmth was like a dream. Perhaps they would have stayed there for ever, except their bliss was disturbed by the sound of a low-flying aircraft that went over, totally ignoring them.

Their dream was gone and they left the water to sunbathe on the rocks in each other's arms. Here, they kissed. Slowly, they grew together, naked as God made them, without embarrassment and knowing that this was a very special part of their lives. It was too precious to waste, as opportunities like this come but once in a lifetime.

Later, they touched each other, revelling in the special sensations that set their bodies tingling and excited beyond expectations. She loved the feel of his lips gently kissing her breasts and the feel of his manhood, which seemed so large. They slowly made love, until confidently they were passionate. Susie found it was painful as he entered her body, but soon it faded as he made her feel so good. It was natural as they cared about each other, sharing the most intimate feelings that only a man, and a woman can know. Afterwards, they swam in the cool waters playing like carefree children.

Peter told Susie about his Burmese mother and the ancient jade tree that was passed on from generation to generation. She in turn informed him about her family, who traded and mined jade and rubies in the mountains to the north and how they looked after the mountain people who helped them. It appeared that good deeds often have unexpected rewards.

They watched the beautiful butterflies flitter from flower to flower so that the sunlight on their iridescent wings formed tiny rainbows around them. They laughed at the sight of the monkeys playing among the trees and marvelled at the birds as they dived into the stream to catch fish or just drink water. It was how God created the world so that all men and women would marvel at his great work.

As the sun started to set, they dressed before slowly walking back. Susie felt very special, loved and deeply content. Peter felt proud to be Susie's man, and that was all he cared about. However, the nearer they were to the village; the more worried Peter became. Surely, he had sinned and had misused the trust his friend Tauk had placed in him? Maybe he had betrayed the love that Anna had shown him. Was he such a rat?

'Peter. Don't worry. My father likes you as a son and knows that I love you. It is only natural that we are lovers. Tonight I will move in with you.'

'No, your father will be offended that I have betrayed his hospitality.'

'He will not, but if you don't want me, I will not come.'

'I want you to come. I just don't want to cause your father any pain after all that he has done for me. For without his help we would have died a terrible death, so don't think that I can ever forget that.'

'I know that, but he is a far greater man than you think. Not only does he have the gift of sending the lights to guide us, but he also reads our minds. He was young once and had many lovers, something that he now denies – but I know he only really loved my mother.'

'I hope that he cannot read mine. From the moment, I first saw you; I wanted you to be mine.'

'Wait and see. Tonight, when I move in, you will see him go to the shrine and light five instead of four joss sticks.'

'Why?'

'He usually lights four joss sticks as he prays, one for each of us and the other for himself. Tonight he will light one extra for you. It is his way of thanking God for the love we have found, even if that love lasts only for a few moments. When I was younger, father would tell me to grasp the moment and hold it firmly in your hand, for time waits for no one, and a missed opportunity is one lost forever.'

At dinner, they chatted about life in general and Tauk behaved towards everyone with his usual good nature. He saw in Susie's eyes her happiness at becoming a woman and her love for Peter. So it was written, so then it would be. No man may change what was written by the ancestors in the sands of time concerning the rules of life and death, of a man and a woman. Anyway, why should he wish to change anything, since it was good and so natural?

Then Susie moved her clothes over to Peter's hut while Marie and Tauk watched, saying nothing. As Susie had predicted, Tauk went to the shrine and lit five joss sticks. What neither Susie nor Peter heard was his prayer. 'Thank you God for now Peter has become a man and Susie a woman. Both have shared each other and in so doing, have blessed their love. Now give her his seed to carry as it grows into their child. Give them time to live, love and let them nourish their child so that together they see him grow to manhood while they grow old. For though you say life is suffering, give them some peace as they have already experienced too much.'

He then meditated for ten minutes and felt something special. So he picked up another joss stick and placed it in the sand and lit it. He bowed his head before Lord Buddha and recited a dedication. 'Lord Buddha I dedicate this offering to you as my request that you care for Maria and the baby who grows inside her womb. This I know from her face and from her spirit that says without sound that it is so.' He then picked up yet another joss stick, placed it in the sand filled jar and then slowly lit it saying, 'Lord Buddha, I light this stick of incense for you to give Peter and Susie happiness and a little child.'

With tears in his eyes, he turned his face to heaven and prayed once more. 'Dear Jesus, I pray that you look after my departed wife and tell her that I am trying to be a good man and will die to protect our children. I am confused, for I know not whether you or Lord Buddha is God. Maybe you both rule in different ways, teaching forgiveness and the sanctity of life. I too need comfort but yet forgo the pleasures of the flesh until my family is safe again. I humbly ask you to hear my prayer.' Then he quietly walked back to his hut in the knowledge that life is controlled by our actions and by the will of God. He never could distinguish between his wife's Christian ways and his own relationship with Buddhism. She always said he was a good pagan, and that she would pray to the Lord Jesus to forgive him for his beliefs. He was troubled deeply by the fact that the Nazis in Germany were Christians and the Japanese were Buddhists, and yet they both killed people for pleasure.

What a terrible thing is fascism, destroying all in its path. No animal could be safe while such evil grows in strength, taking away love and caring and replacing them with fear and hatred. Just where will all this turmoil end?

Must death and destruction always stalk the world and leave mankind wounded and bleeding, with only hope and love to live for?

# 17

# Temassen Travels to Sangshak

After two days of travelling along jungle paths, Temassen and his friends were north of the town of Kiang in a village, not marked on any map, where they met some Chin fishermen. The villagers were friendly, and told Tun Kyi about how the enemy crossed the river at night and by day were exhausted, often sleeping or preparing for the night's work. So the group rested, were fed and slept before sailing at sunrise the Chin across the Chindwin River. They waved as the boats sailed past the enemy to appear as normal villagers, but as usual, the Japanese ignored the indigenous people. Temasen saw through the bushes along the riverside hidden barges waiting to carry the Japanese Imperial army over the river to start the invasion of India.

Once across the river they moved carefully as they were aware of the noises from the trucks, tanks and troops on the move. Sometimes they were so close that they could hear the Japanese marching songs that masked their own movements and let them continue unnoticed. Every time they saw a group of Japanese, Setcha estimated their numbers, recorded how many vehicles and guns, as well as what unit they belonged to.

During the night of 15th March, they watched the Japanese 31st Division infantry moving westwards after crossing the river by ferry boats and barges. It was only the advance party, as most of the Division had not yet arrived. They saw the enemy attacked only twice. Once, two low-flying Beaufighters bombed a supply column and destroyed a ferry boat. Then three Hurricanes strafed the Japanese waiting on the riverbanks.

On leaving the river banks they moved fast through the same jungle as the Japanese and probably towards the identical destination. Now they were in the swampy valleys alive with mosquitoes and leeches. Here everything was wet, including their clothes and boots and making their bodies sore. Simple cuts from the sharp bamboo and thorn trees readily became inflamed and infected. So when they stopped, each cut was treated with iodine. It was tiring cutting through the bamboo thickets or wading waist-deep in mud and water. To make matters worse, at any moment around the next tree could appear a column of enemy soldiers. Then it would be a matter of kill or die. They felt the further they were from the river; the greater was their chance of reaching safety. So no one complained as they walked on throughout that day and the next night. They did not stop for food or water, as all were driven on by the thought that behind them, or in front, were thousands of the Japanese.

At Witok, the Japanese 33rd Division's type 95 tanks were stopped by six British Lee tanks long enough to cover the British retreat to their new defensive positions around the Imphal plains. It was only a small success, but it gave the retreating troops some breathing space.

Tun Kyi let them sleep for two hours before waking them to eat some dried rations and drink water. They were tired but still working as a team. Then he led them north towards the Naga town of Ukhral. Some six miles south of Ukhal Tun Kyi stopped and pointed to a group of Gurkha troops establishing a temporary base besides an abandoned church in a place called Sangshak.

'Temasen! Can you see your people waiting for your return?'

'Yes, Tun Kyi, they are further south than what we expected.'

'We must part, as it is time that Ba Saw and I return, while you and Setcha join the Gurkha Rifles. May God be with you and keep you safe.'

'Thank you. Without your help I would not have made it. If the gods are willing, we will meet again. Go in peace and stay well my friend.'

They shook hands, hugged each other, and parted as Tun Kyi and Ba Saw left to carry on their private war. While Temasen and Setcha went on to join the British lines a few miles ahead of them.

They met up with the British as planned at Sangshak where they were given food and water. Setcha joined the Intelligence Unit while Temasen was given a spare uniform, and allocated to H Company 52 Battalion, 50th Indian Parachute Brigade. Most of his men were young raw Nepalese recruits with only six-weeks basic training. So he showed them how to make defensive positions. It proved difficult, as the trenches were only two feet deep when they struck rock and there was no supply of water. Whoever had decided to defend this position was not experienced in warfare. So they placed rocks and logs in front of the trenches to make them higher before camouflaging the lot.

Meanwhile, Setcha translated documents and acted as an interpreter. Intelligence was disappointed that he only knew about the Japanese 31st Division and nothing about the other two. Setcha explained that he identified the one division by its markings, so he could have missed the others. He did not add that in the dense jungle, you could be a few yards from the enemy without you seeing them. The British urgently needed to know where the Japanese 33rd Division and 15th Division were. All the patrols had reported nothing, except some Naga scouts who said that 33rd Division was going west. It looked like the 31st Division would advance on Kohima while the 33rd marched west from Kalewa, but where would the 15th Division go?

All the documents arriving at intelligence for translations were checked by Setcha. They came from raiding parties operating in the Kabaw valley to gather intelligence about the enemy movements. Most were of little use, but sometimes they showed maps with information that included the dates of rendezvous points. Then they found some papers recovered from the body of a Japanese officer who belonged to Lt General Mutagushi's 15th Division. This was so important that Setcha ran with it to the intelligence officer Captain Allen.

'Captain Allen, I know where 15th Division is, sir.'

'Then tell me what you have found, I haven't got all day.'

'They are coming to Uhkal and will arrive in the next few days.'

'Show me,' Captain Allen replied, and Setcha did.

'My God, the garrison at Uhkal hasn't a snowballs chance in hell with a whole Japanese division descending upon them.'

'Sergeant Wye, inform Uhkal that 15th Division is advancing on them.'

'Yes sir,' replied the sergeant before he left.

'I'll tell the Brigadier that the Japanese 15th Division is in our sector. Log the report and send it to GHQ. Make it damn bloody quick, as time is against us.'

The Brigadier was not concerned, as there was no real proof that a whole division was coming his way. Perhaps just part of it would attack Uhkal and the rest move on to attack Imphal. This idea was reinforced when the Naga scouts from V Force arrived from villages to the east saying that two hundred Japanese had arrived there, so maybe nine hundred Japanese was advancing towards them. This should prove no problem, even though each defensive position from Uhkral to Sangshak was only at company strength.

On 20th March, only twenty survivors from the 120-strong C Company withdrew to Sheldon's Corner, just nine miles away. So GHQ ordered the survivors to regroup at Sangshak, where they arrived, exhausted, after fighting a series of running skirmishes. They were horrified to find no barbed-wire perimeter and inadequate supplies making such a position difficult to defend.

# 18
# A Wedding of Sorts

*If I could write the beauty of your eyes*
*And if fresh numbers number all your graces,*
*The age to come would say 'This poet lies;*
*Such heavenly touches ne'er touched earthly faces.'*

William Shakespeare (1609) *Sonnets,* sonnet 17.

When Peter asked Susie to marry him, she gave him a hug. Then she told him not to be silly, as she loved him and did not care if she was married or not. He was not so easily put off, as his father said that faint heart never won fair lady, and how his mother had at first rejected his father's proposal of marriage. So Peter waited for the right time to approach Tauk.

'Excuse me sir. May I speak with you in private?' Peter spoke firmly, though his body was full of trepidation.

Tauk looked at Peter, reading his thoughts in a sympathetic manner to say. 'Please sit down with me and tell me what the trouble is.'

'Sir I love your daughter, and I think that she loves me.'

'I would think that by now everyone in the village knows that's true. So what do you want me to do about it?'

'I need your help and blessing.'

'You are like a son to me and there is little that I would not do for you.'

'I have asked Susie to marry me.'

'Well I suppose she said no.'

'She did not say no, or yes, but told me not to be silly.'

'So you want me to find out if she wants to be your wife or whether she just wants to be your lover. Is that what you request?' Tauk said as always put his finger on the heart of the matter without giving Peter time to explain things.

Temasen said that Tauk saw into the hearts and minds of people. The thought made him embarrassed as he worried how her father would react to his Susie being seduced by a foreign soldier who may take her away from him – maybe even for good?

'Please find out why she thinks marrying me is a silly idea. I know we love each other. We do not have much time before I go back to war that it would be a sin to waste what little we have.'

'I will talk to Susie, but it will not be easy. She can be very stubborn and thinks I'm a baby, incapable of looking after myself without her fussing over me. She is just like her mother and her sister. She hasn't thought that maybe I want to be free to follow my own chosen path without having to look after two daughters. Perhaps I too wish to find a warm woman and start another family?

Tauk turned his head and looked deeply into Peter's eyes. 'Are you sure that you want to marry such a stubborn woman? She can be a bully, be tender, and be ruthless. If you do, then we must convince her to leave with you and give up soldiering. It is not right for her to kill people when she has to care for her children yet unborn.'

'Please persuade her that I love her and will protect her all the days of my life.'

'That I believe. But how long is that for a fighter pilot in war time? Still it is better to have one minute's true love than never to have loved at all. Stay here while I talk to my difficult daughter. Just promise me that you will never hit her or abandon her in some foreign land without friends or money to return home.'

'Of course I would never hurt her or leave her, unless she wished to leave me. For she is my light, my love, my future.'

Tauk smiled encouragingly as he thought quietly before getting up and leaving the room.

So Peter sat down to wait while Tauk walked to the veranda to sit next to Susie.

'Susie, I must speak with you.'

She arose putting her arms around his neck to give him a hug and a kiss on his lips. Tauk felt her warmth next to him. She was so like her dear mother, warm, tender and yet had to be controlled. She was much too headstrong for her own good, a trait she inherited from him so must be guided to understand her feelings and let her heart overcome any fears she has for the future.

'Father I hope you haven't come to tell me off for making love to Peter?'

'Don't be so childish. When can a parent tell his grown child whom he or she can fall in love with? Who am I to tell the fates how to behave? I can see the signs and tell the nature of you all, but I cannot change what I see. Love is so very special that it must be cherished above all else.'

'Then what makes you so serious?'

'Do you love Peter?'

'Yes. I love him with my heart and body.'

'Do you want to live with him forever and have his children?'

'Dear father I want that more than life itself. But is it possible when this war may kill one or both of us?'

'The gods give us choices, but it is we who decide our fate. However, we must do so in the full knowledge that certain natural things once started, cannot be easily undone. A seed that is planted in fertile soil will grow into a strong tree. For that is the way it is and has always been.'

'You mean it is like making a baby?'

'Starting a baby is the easy part. It is exciting and gives great pleasure. However, the real test is how you raise that little part of you and how you share him or her with the world. For your child will grow up, fall in love, and leave you for someone else. Children are a blessing from God, given to us on the understanding that the relationship is as temporary as life itself. No one owns a child for we only have him or her on loan. Nature demands they grow older and move on. It has always been that way, and nobody should stop it being so. Do you know that Susie?'

'I know that what you say is the ancient truth that no one can change and remember I will always love you. How can I ever forget how carefully you raised us and how you protected us from harm? You and dear mother are a part of my spirit. It is a thing that I cannot change and would not change if I could. But can I marry a foreigner, especially during a war? He may just leave to go home and what do I do then?'

'I know Peter would never just leave you. However, should he do so you will return to me, and I will look after you as always. You have nothing to fear from him or me. You will never lose me as a father but instead will gain a husband. It could prove a very interesting experience for us all.'

'But what if he should return to his country? Should I follow him or stay here with you? Why can't you accept things as they are and not make me choose between the two of you? This is my country, and all that I know. I have never been to England and may find it a terrible place.'

'My darling, you must realise that the Burma we know will never be the same when this war is over. We of the Karen people, and the other tribes will not forgive the Burman (Bamar) for helping the Japanese. I fear Burma is unlikely to become a true democracy and regret that we refused the offer of being a Dominion. Will our people ever trust people like Ba Maw, Aung San, and U Nu for selling us to these barbarians? Fascism and Buddhism are incompatible, as they are two roads that lead to different worlds. One is a creed based on hatred and power, while the other believes in gentleness, and the search for goodness.'

'Don't despair, Father, for the Thirty Comrades will learn their lesson. Though Jesus teaches us to forgive our enemies, I cannot forget they murdered our people and raped my mother. Strangely, it is our people like the BDA who threaten the very existence of a traditional free Burma.'

'That is why you must build a future for yourself. Peter adores you, and you love him so grab the chance while it is offered. If it does not work out, Maria and I will always be here for you. Maria has Tun Kyi's child growing inside her and has requested that they be married in a church. So take Maria with you to the Christian mission at Dimapur, where she will wed Tun Kyi in the Catholic tradition. If you want to do the same, you have my blessing.'

'Father, I want you to give us the full traditional blessing and prayers so that we may live as husband and wife. I ask you to leave with us, as my mother is dead and do not wish to lose you.'

'I will consider your requests. Tomorrow I will bless you and Peter, and you will swear obedience to him and only to him. Then in Dimapur you will resign from Force V to care for him with all your heart and body to have his child.'

'Who am I to disagree with my father? Indeed, I will obey your wishes with joy in my heart and everlasting thanks.'

'Now you run over to my house to ask Peter for forgiveness. For at this moment he paces the floor while waiting for my return to tell of your love or lack of it. You have most cruelly made him wait and now show him you are his forever. You must forgive him his transgressions and by being his spiritual and physical partner in everything grow together as one. Only then can you build a future for my grandchildren.'

Susie kissed her father before running like a schoolgirl to her man.

As she ran her hair blew in the wind and made Tauk saw in her the same grace and beauty that once made him fall in love with her mother. Indeed, God created woman for man, or maybe it was the other way around. He felt happy that now both his daughters had found true love to help them share the hardships and joys of life. They would need his support if they were to survive the difficult road ahead. He felt that Burma would never return to the old ways as killing and violence had become accepted, contrary to all of their Buddhist traditions. Karen fought the Burman (Bamar). Shan worked with the Chinese. Burman (Bamar) worked alongside the Japanese and even with their traditional enemies, the Siamese. The Indians changed sides so quickly that it appeared all they wanted was to make money. The British wanted their Empire back or at least revenge for their losses. But what did the Americans want from Burma? Perhaps they wanted the teak, rice, and the opium – or precious jewels, such as emeralds, rubies and star sapphires from Mongok. Worse still, they craved for power to control the lives of others to build a new American Empire. No one could question their colonial influences in the Americas and parts of the Pacific that could include the Philippines, China and Burma.

Putting such thoughts aside, Tauk arranged for the blessing with the villagers as witnesses. He wanted to prepare a celebration fit for his daughter to include a feast, music, dancing and gifts to be exchanged. He selected an ancient silver dagger from the days of the Burmese Empire for Susie to give Peter as her acknowledgement of him, as her master and protector. Then he selected a ruby necklace for Peter to give Susie as a sign that he treasured her above all wealth. The deep blood red of the ruby would look beautiful on her wedding dress as a sign of the life blood they would give their children.

Yes, that would do fine. Then from his strongbox, he removed two leather pouches similar to those he gave to Marie and Tun Kyi. In each pouch were three rubies, two emeralds, and ten pieces of jade each neatly wrapped in tissue paper. This would ensure that they never go hungry. He would give one to Susie and the other to Peter. This was the dowry he had promised to give their daughters. He took from an old dry leather pouch ten black pearls and placed them in the palm of his hand. He stared down at these rare, large balls that glistened in the sunlight. Each pearl was as wide as his small finger and of considerable worth. They were collected in the days when men dived in the Arakan seas for the blue and black pearls. It was dangerous work, as these pearl oysters were only found in deep water where oceanic sharks were common. His father-in-law had left them for the family as a treasure that could be sold when all else was gone. Tauk hoped that when he died, he would be able to leave them to Susie and Peter.

Maybe after the war he would reopen the ruby mines near Mongok that had belonged to his family for generations. Luckily, before the war started he closed them, as one seam was exhausted and there was no time to start another. Therefore, looters would get nothing without finding the sites and digging new shafts. Until then, their riches would remain safely beneath the ground.

All of that day and the next, the village buzzed with activity. The tailor made the wedding dresses for bride and groom. The cooks prepared a feast while children made red paper lanterns they erected all over the village.

On the wedding day, Peter was taken away to be prepared for the evening's events. The men cut his hair, washed his body, and dressed him in a traditional bridegroom costume. This was a blue silk *longyi* with cotton *ingyi*; a sash wrapped around his waist and a *taiman* (jacket). Then they left him with Tauk to make the marriage agreement.

'Peter, take this parcel that I wish you to give Susie in front of the people. In it are some precious jewels. I especially wish you to place around her neck the ruby necklace as a sign of your love. Will you do this small thing for me?'

'Of course I will, sir. Whatever you think I should do I will try to do. It is my duty as thanks for giving me the most precious gift of all – your daughter.'

'Now you must wait while I make sure the ladies have made Susie respectable.'

Over in Tauk's hut the ladies had bathed and oiled Susie, washed her in a light perfume, and tied her long hair behind her head with a ribbon. They placed some white and red orchids in her hair to signify beauty and love. Susie was dressed in a yellow *longyi* of pure silk with a matching *ingyi* that reached right high up to her chin. On her feet were golden slippers and on each arm a jewelled bangle. In each ear, she wore a brilliant ruby that made her look majestic.

Tauk arrived and handed Susie the ancient silver dagger (dah).

'This is the dah you will give to Peter to say that he is your guardian and master. Keep it safe for it is over two hundred years old and given to me by my uncle when I married your mother.'

'Yes, Father.'

'Now let us join Peter at the shrine before he runs away.'

The village was decorated with many lanterns placed on every house and in the banyan tree. They burned brightly to welcome Peter into their family. All looked so peaceful except for the ever-watchful armed sentries guarding the approaches to the village. Missing was the traditional flying of painted kites, the dancing lion, and the procession led by musicians.

So father and daughter proceeded to the shrine where Peter waited. Prayers were said and a blessing given. Then Tauk placed Susie's right hand in Peter's left hand and tied them together with a silk cord. This done he lifted the joined hands up into the air to say. 'I, Tauk, hereby take Peter Anderson to be my son, and in return, I give him my daughter Susie Myint Suu Kyi to be his wife. See you all that I join these two together as one by this blessed cord, by my wishes they are united, and so I decree that no man or woman ever question their union. I call upon you all to acknowledge them as Peter and Daw Susie. May the Lord Buddha guide them and give them the happiness that they deserve in this world full of pain and sorrow. Remember it is written that life is a struggle to survive, with pain to bear, and with love and fortitude to help us find joy by following the true path.'

The people replied. 'We call upon the Lord Buddha to bless our two children who now are united. From this day forth, they are a part of us as we are of them. May they be happy and live as long as God allows.'

Then it was Peter's turn. 'I Peter Win Anderson, son of Paul Anderson and Daw Lynette Win Maung give this necklace to Susie Myint Suu Kyi as a sign of my love and devotion. I vow before you all that I will protect and look after her all the days of my life. I swear this before God and the souls of my ancestors.'

'I Susie Myint Suu Kyi give this silver dagger to my lord Peter Anderson as a sign of my vows to stay with him forever and ever.'

Tauk now undid the silk cord around Peter's hand but left it on Susie's hand as a sign that she was now a married woman.

'Well, now that is over; we can enjoy ourselves. Let us make music, dance, and feast. I have so much to celebrate, as at last I have got rid of my daughter and gained a son. He may not be Burmese, but his seed will merge with my daughter's seed to grow strong, and happy grandchildren. What more can an old widower like me want?

He lit a larger golden lantern and placed it high up in the banyan tree. Instantly lights appeared all over the surrounding jungle as each village in turn lit their lanterns of joy. Indeed, the jungle spirits many hundreds of miles away would see the relay of lights and give thanks for the continuance of life.

The villagers threw flower petals over the bride and her groom and presented them with gifts of cloth, or some food. Nothing was of great worth, but an expression of their love for the couple and hopes for their future. Peter sat on the mat besides his bride as she fed him. It was nearly too beautiful to be true, but it was. It was a moment that they wanted to last forever. Of course, in their memories, it would.

To the north on a hill near Sangshak, Major Suki saw the lights to the south that illuminated the jungle while coming from nowhere.

What are those lights in the forest?' he asked his Burmese interpreter.

'Major-san, it is just a native tradition to tell everyone that someone has died; a couple have married, or it is part of a festival. It is hard to know which, but there is nothing to worry about.'

Major Suki said no more but looked in wonder at the little magical lights that seemed to talk to each other. They were like fairies dancing for joy in the night sky, yet it was deeply spiritual to make a feeling of goodness surround him, dimming the effects of war. It was a celebration of life as nature cried out through fire and brimstone that goodness will survive to make a better world. Major Suki was so moved that he prayed to the Lord Buddha to be allowed to live in peace with his fellow men and for this war to end. Certainly, he would never be the same again; grateful that he was not a sadistic monster. How could they crucify, bayonet, and torture unarmed men? It was not correct. It was not part of the Buddhist code and yet everyone in Japan seemed to have forgotten the rules. Even the Emperor as the Sun God seemed to lose his Buddhist origins and become more like an ancient warlord. It did not bode well for a nation when it forgot the roots of its past and the rules of the gods.

Maybe he would return to his father's home to be with his wife and family. Now he longed to feel her warm body next to his and know that special comfort that a good wife gives her man. If this was to happen, he must try to follow the true path that leads to enlightenment. He wondered where the two British prisoners had gone. He hoped that they were safe and found a sanctuary where their wounds could heal. He knew that the Kempei-Tei would not be pleased with him but would do nothing. Even they would not dare to take the word of a Burmese officer over that of a highly decorated Major of the Imperial Staff. He knew that if the Devil's Helper found him wounded and helpless, he would suffer. But then it would only be the will of the gods if he were to die in the place of the two British he had saved. His father said that it was better to die with honour than live in disgrace.

In Sangshak, Temasen saw the lights to remember the pongyi and his people.

Captain Allen asked, 'Havildar Temasen! Do you know what the distant lights are we can see?'

'They are the spirits of the people celebrating life, or death, or just guiding friends to safety. It is their way.'

'Do you believe in the lights?'

'Yes sir, I believe in them as they bring comfort to all who truly believe.'

'My brain says that it cannot be true, but my soul says it is. I feel the lights are telling me of some happiness that I should be sharing.'

'When I was captured, a local priest helped two of us escape and lit our way through the jungle to his village by such a pathway of lights. For when we reached one banyan tree, the lights went out, but there were always other lights ahead to mark our way. His lanterns guided us to his village and from there I came here.'

'It sounds impossible, but I believe you.'

'Well, we have a saying, sir. Follow what makes your soul feel good, for you are hearing the jungle spirits. For me, the lights say that my friends in the village are safe and celebrating an important event that they want the whole world, and especially me, to know. It makes me feel warm and good inside.'

He began to leave to carry on his duties, but before he departed, he took his leave of Captain Allen, he said. 'I must go and check on my men, sir. However, keep that good feeling for moments like these are few and far between. It is written that even with death comes life to fulfil the cycle that had been ours since the world began.'

'Goodnight, Havildar and thank you.'

# 19

# A Brief Honeymoon

The beginning of the rest of their lives.

Peter woke as the cock crowed and the sun rose over the jungle from the east. He turned over on the sleeping mat to feel his bride Susie sleeping by his side. This was not the perfect honeymoon, but it was as good as it could be. He only wished that his parents could have been at the wedding, but that was impossible. After the war, he would have their marriage blessed in front of his family, but only if Susie agreed. He hoped Susie would resign her commission as he would be happier knowing she was safe. He wanted them to remain husband and wife for the rest of their days on earth; however, long that would prove to be.

Out of the window Peter looked out over the scene of the previous night's festivities and was disappointed to see the villagers take away the last of the lanterns, sweep up the debris and turn the village back to normal. In fact, the village looked like all Burmese villages had from time immemorial, tidy, and neat. He smiled at the shrine still adorned with flowers. So the wedding was not forgotten; it was just that another day had dawned, and life went on. A noise broke his train of thought as Susie came close to look over his shoulder at the dawn.

He felt her warmth as she placed her head on his chest and spoke quietly. 'I wish that time could stand still and that the sun would stop rising. It is so beautiful and very good. Soon the coolness of dawn will be lost as the sun's heat builds up again and with it, another day. There is so much to do in preparation for our journey to the Naga Hills. There I will leave you to go to Dimapur, while you must return to your people.'

'I am well enough to return to my squadron but don't want to leave you.'

'In Dimapur, Father Pinto will marry Maria and Tun Kyi in the Roman Catholic chapel. Later, we will travel to Colombo and Tun Kyi will return to continue the fighting.'

'I haven't said you can go to Colombo. Does our wedding mean nothing to you?'

'It means everything and so I have resigned my commission to train as a nurse. They agreed probably because they don't like having a woman warrior within their ranks, especially a married one. Then Maria and I will attend the Nurse training school in Colombo. I never told you earlier as I wanted it all arranged before agreeing to marry you. However, yesterday, I received my orders over the radio to locate and destroy a Japanese supply route taking fuel and munitions to the Naga Hills before I can resign my commission in Dimapur. Afterwards, Tun Kyi will command of our group.'

'Did you tell them about me?'

'Of course I did, my love. I said that you were fit to travel so I would take you to Dimapur. I don't want you accused of being a deserter.'

'Did they agree, just like that?'

'They were glad you are alive and will be returning to your squadron. Someone named Jim said that you must pay for losing a plane. How can he be so horrid after all you have been through?'

'My best friend, Jim Ashton is joking! When we started in Rangoon, we were told not to return without our aircraft, as the RAF had lots of pilots but too few planes. It's his way of saying, welcome back; all is forgiven.'

'That is good news, my dearest, for within the week we leave to go to war. We will travel by day as the enemy moves at night. Then we move north to find the supply routes.'

He marvelled at how brave she was, and yet how beautiful. What a contradiction! By his side, she was the jungle warrior, but in his arms, his beautiful princess. She was so right. He dreaded her dying in the jungle and knew she would be safer in a hospital away from the dogs of war.

'When we get to Dimapur, we will get married in the church.'

'I would love to, but you are ordered to Kohima and me to Dimapur. Later, we can be married in church. I can wait, but can you?'

'I can and will, if you are sure that's all right. However, I must inform the RAF that you are my wife so that you are treated properly. In fact, I need to ask my CO for permission to get married.'

'You must do what you think is right. However, be aware that people will say you have gone native or the sun affected your brain. One sleeps with wogs – one does not marry them.'

'Never say that word wog again! You are the most beautiful thing that I have ever seen, and I love you. Now come here.' She obeyed as he put his arms around her and pulled her onto the bed.

'Stop it Peter. I have a lot to do.'

'You said we have all day.'

'You are just a sex maniac. Haven't you had enough loving for now?'

'Of course I have not. This is supposed to be our honeymoon.'

'No stop it! I demand that you stop being silly.'

'You demand? You swore total obedience to me, and now you break your oath. Your father will be very angry when I tell him how disobedient you are.'

'I am deeply sorry, my lord and master. Well, I do have things to do, but they can wait for a little while longer.' Susie giggled and snug up against him, purring like a small cat, and he was deliriously lost in her arms. They were living in a beautiful place where for that brief moment time stood still. It was a perfect place and time to be in and make love. And so they did.

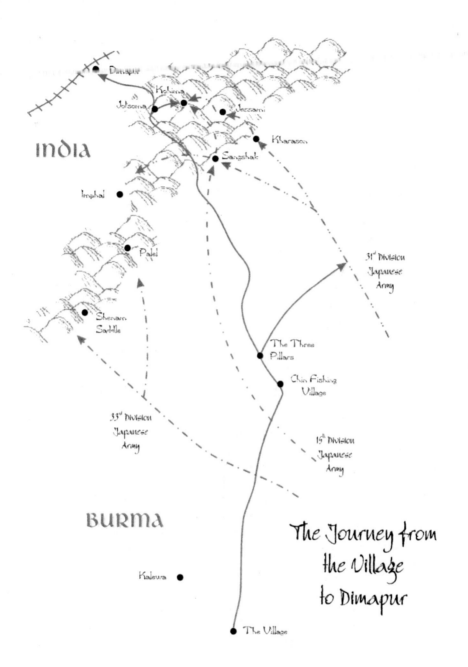

Dimapur

Kohima

Jotsoma

Jessami

INDIA

Kharason

Sangshak

Imphal

Palel

31st Division
Japanese
Army

Shenam
Saddle

The Three
Pillars

Chin Fishing
Village

33rd Division
Japanese
Army

15th Division
Japanese
Army

BURMA

The Journey from
the Village
to Dimapur

Kalewa

The Village

# 20

# When the Trousseau is Replaced by the Battledress

On the evening of 21st March, the Little Pagoda group consisting of twenty-five people left the village after quickly saying good-bye. They knew they might not see each other again in this world, but everyone smiled while holding back their tears. Sons and daughters left parents, husbands their wives and children, and all left part of themselves in the village they called home. The dangers ahead showed in their faces as they lost their joyful expressions, for now, they looked much older and very determined. Most of them wore uniforms; Peter was given a battle tunic, jungle trousers, and jungle boots. All had clothing that protected their bodies from the jungle. Women lit lanterns in the banyan tree to burn until their men returned, or they died, whatever came first. Death was a constant visitor to all villages like this, and acknowledged as such, for it was the way things have always been. It is written that all life from the cradle to the grave is a struggle against pain and sorrow that must be born with fortitude and caring. Everyone must inevitably die. It is in the manner and way of dying that we prove our faith.

The group was armed with every weapon known to man; one had a Naga crossbow, two others short blowpipes with poisoned darts, and the rest rifles. Susie kept them walking at a steady pace, holding a Sten gun in her arms with her finger on the trigger. By her side walked Peter, and a young Chin called Hla Tun with a Lee Enfield rifle in his arms. No one spoke, smoked, or lagged behind as everyone helped carry the mortar, Bren gun, or supplies. One man carried the heavy radio in his haversack followed by Maria and some women with more supplies on their heads. They were a mini army, travelling north-west to bring death and destruction to the Japanese. The odds of them surviving were, to say the least, not good. However, they felt it their duty to destroy the Rising Sun, and all who supported it.

They fought against Japan rather than for Britain. All had their personal reasons for hating the invaders. Mostly, they wanted to return to old days of a prosperous Burma where everyone had food, where war did not happen, and where the laws of Buddha ruled supreme. None of them realised, as Tauk did, that such times would never return.

At first, the journey was easy as they moved along well-used paths. They saw no signs of the enemy, but every finger rested on the trigger, in case they ran into a Japanese patrol. Then, only the group that shot first could live, so scouts were sent ahead to look out for danger, but it did not come. After walking for five hours, they rested for twenty minutes, drank water, ate dried food, and talked as the rays of the rising sun in the east heralded in a new day. It was now the 22nd March, and they had to reach Dimapur by 30th March.

'Now we must cut our way through the jungle to the river north of Kiang. Somewhere near here is the Japanese supply route that the British wants us to destroy.'

'When shall we make camp?'

'Not yet, we carry on further towards the Chindwin before we can camp and eat. Once by the river we will rest until nightfall when the Japanese lorries start to move from their hidden positions. The noise will help us locate their positions without being discovered, and we can use our radio to call in the British bombers before retiring to a safe place.'

'What happens if they find us first?'

'We kill them as silently as possible and move on to the other side of the supply route. We must destroy as much of their supplies as we can. Further to the north, the British Chindits are destroying the supply routes around the towns of Myitkyina and Indaw. We will attack those coming from Shwebo, Meiktila and Mandalay.'

They now cut their way through the bush with its thick bamboo thickets. Their hands and feet were cut from sharp thorns and bushes while the half-light strained the eyes that always looked out for the enemy. It was so slow that it took three hours to travel five miles. They stopped to have their last supper before the inevitable conflict. Everyone ate well, knowing that it could be days before they ate another cooked meal, and only then if they were alive. After the meal they tidied up, cleaned and oiled their weapons, before taking turns at sleeping. Peter found a place to rest next to Susie between the large buttress-type roots of a big ironwood tree.

At dusk, they went nearer to the noise of vehicles moving by the river crossing. Soon they found the Japanese had linked a number of barges to form a bridge to carry the transports. It was tempting to call in the bombers and just leave. However, Susie wanted to locate where the Japanese vehicles and the barges were hidden. Only then would she call in the bombers. She looked at her compass to take a bearing while Hla Tun made a simple map. They must have unknowingly crossed the supply route and were only two miles north of the crossing point. This was ideal for their purposes. Therefore, Susie divided her men into groups. Two men and all the women with the radio operator went to the top of the hill with a small white pagoda near its peak. It would be the observation post as well as the assembly point after the attacks. The others set out to place explosives in the enemy's supplies. If it went according to plan, they would explode at the same time as the bombs fell.

Susie discovered that the supply dump contained hundreds of petrol drums and ammunition boxes. Peter waited with another man armed with a Bren gun on its tripod to cover their retreat, while Susie with two men crawled towards the dump carrying explosives inside small satchels. Peter watched anxiously as they drew closer to the target and nearer to the sentries who patrolled the outer area. He was certain they would be discovered. Time stood still, as Peter heard every little creature that moved. His heart nearly stopped when a bat flew low towards the dump, but no one noticed the small mammal hunting some insects.

What in hell are they waiting for? Peter wanted to yell to Susie to get it over and done with. She said the secret was speed, but failed to add that timing was the essence of a successful operation. Seconds seemed like hours as he watched sweating profusely while the sentries walked up and down, rifles on their shoulders. When two met they chatted before continuing to patrol the area like clockwork toys. Then some lorries arrived, so the sentries helped unload the supplies on the far side of the dump. Susie and her men slithered across the open ground to disappear under the camouflage nets covering the dump. She opened a large, metal, ammunition box containing rows of shells where she placed some plastic explosive with a pencil fuse. She bent the fuse to break the seal setting it to explode in three hours. The timing of these fuses was never very accurate, but with luck, when they exploded, they should be safely away in the hills. She closed the lid, replaced the lock, and crawled over to a pile of oil drums. Here she placed a limpet mine on the side of one of the drums to be hidden from all but the most careful scrutiny. Then she placed explosives into the breech of a type 94 75mm mountain gun and set the fuse. If it only broke the firing system, the gun would not function. She had taken fifteen minutes, and now it was time to leave. She reached the edge of the camouflage net, looked around and seeing nobody, ran across the open ground without being observed, as did one of her men. However, a Japanese guard suddenly appeared out of the bush to run into the last saboteur. The guard was as surprised to see the Karen as he was to see the guard. For a second, both men stood there looking at each other. The guard raised his rifle to open fire at the same moment that the Karen did, but neither fired. For in a flash another Karen slit the guard's throat before carrying the body into the undergrowth. It was over in a few seconds so no one raised the alarm. Susie searched the body for documents before they buried him beneath some fallen leaves.

It was a race against time for soon the dead guard would be missed. So everyone retreated to the pagoda where the radio operator had signalled the position of the dump and awaited the bombers.

By the river's bank, the second group planted explosives on the machinery used to build the barges and construct prefabricated bridges. There were no guards, only workers busy loading materials onto a stream of trucks. A third group placed their explosives on a patrol boat and two limpet mines on a river ferry. All left unseen for the assembly point, but unfortunately, war is not so simple. On their way back, they placed the remaining explosives under a small bridge over a stream. It should have been easy but just as the last satchel was placed and the fuse broken a Japanese lorry full of soldiers arrived. The driver slammed on the brakes as he saw people running from the bridge. Then out of the lorry poured twenty soldiers who looked around and saw nothing in the dim light from the lorry's headlights. They fired into the nearby jungle, and on getting no response returned to the lorry.

'Did you see that?' the driver asked his officer.

'I saw nothing! You see shadows where there are none. Anyway if there had been people hiding in the jungle they are now injured,' said the officer.

'Ah so, we must move on before the sun comes up.'

And so they departed.

By the road, two of Susie's men lay injured not daring to speak or cry out. Instead, they kept quiet by biting hard on a piece of leather as their colleagues carried them on their backs to the rendezvous point. They should leave them but could not bring themselves to do so. One was shot through the leg while the other had received a ricochet in the arm. Both could be saved.

At the pagoda, most left to join their Chin friends, while Susie and Maria with her women, and the radio operator remained. Then the last men arrived carrying the wounded; Peter saw the damage a rifle bullet did to a human body. He was shocked but kept silent, as unlike the others, he had never before seen such wounds.

Maria removed the field bandages from the injured man to clean the wounds. The shoulder wound was not deep, but the bullet was still inside. It would remain there until she had time to remove it. The other man was luckier as the bullet went straight through his legs without hitting anything important. Then Maria injected both men with morphine before sewing up their wounds with catgut and bandaging them.

'Why do they carry a short leather strap?' Peter asked Maria.

She gave him that smile that said you don't know much.

'The leather straps are what we use to stop bleeding or to bite on when one is in pain. It is very simple but very effective. Did you know that before people discovered anaesthetics, the wounded in your army had similar things? Surgeons placed a piece of leather in the patient's mouth to stop him biting through his lips and to help alleviate the pain. It is simple, but it works.'

'Oh! Sorry. I just did not think.'

'That's fine. Living in a jungle one improvises.'

'Will you leave the wounded?'

'They can fight, so we carry one while the other walks until tomorrow when we meet Tun Kyi.'

'How do you know that?'

'Tun Kyi promised he would be there and will be.'

So they carried the wounded north to liaise with the others.

'Now what do we do? Peter asked Susie.

'We must wait to see what happens, my darling. War is a waiting game when those with the greatest patience and most courage usually win,' Susie replied touching his hand.

Soon they heard the distant alarm bell ring out from the depot.

'They must have found the dead guard.'

'I hope the bombers arrive soon.'

'Have faith in your own people, for I believe that they will come.'

'I know you're right, but this is not my sort of war. I never get this close to the enemy nor feel so vulnerable.'

'It doesn't get any easier the more you do it. The first time was an adventure, as I had not killed before. Afterwards, I felt guilty for killing a fellow human being. Then I remembered my mother, and the guilt vanished. Now I worry about what can go wrong more than how simple it will be.'

As dawn came, they lay on the damp earth listening to the radio and to the noises in the air. Surely, the bombers would come soon! Then they would fire a mortar shell to illuminate the targets.

The waiting was over when the radio burst into life to announce, 'Eagle One calling Little Pagoda.'

'This is Little Pagoda calling Eagle One, receiving you loud and clear. Over,' the radio operator replied.

'Eagle One to Little Pagoda we will arrive in about ten minutes. Over.'

'Thank you Eagle One, here the visibility is good, and we will mark the targets on your order. Over!'

'I will tell you when to mark them, Good-luck Little Pagoda.'

They waited as Susie prepared the 2-inch mortar with the blue smoke charge.

Then they heard the drone of the Mitchell bombers' engines long before they appeared flying low in the sky, followed by their Spitfire escorts.

'Eagle One calling Little Pagoda, send up the markers and get out.'

'Roger. We will do, over and out.'

'Do they want the markers now?'

Susie nodded as she dropped the first shell into the mortar and watched as it streaked over the jungle, exploding in a luminescent blue cloud over the dump. She checked the settings on the mortar before firing a second shell over the crossing point.

Then the squadron leader issued his orders, 'Eagle One to Squadron, bomb in pairs on the two blue targets. Thank you, Little Pagoda. God speed, over and out.'

'Let's get the hell out of here!' Peter yelled.

'Yes. Let's disappear,' Susie ordered. So they rapidly left the hill, knowing it was 23rd of March, and they only had two days to reach the Chin village by 25th and meet up with the rest of her men.

Overhead the bombers lined up in pairs each one aiming for a blue smoke marked target. While the bombers discharged their fatal loads onto the dump, the fighter escort strafed the nearby roads. The Japanese army waited, hoping that their positions had not been located. Normally, most bombs missed their targets but today would prove different. The bombs and the planted explosives destroyed the depot and the assembly point along with tons of supplies.

When the bombing stopped and the fires extinguished, the Japanese engineers started to repair the damage. It was severe, as the barge-building plant was destroyed along with two riverboats. So they salvaged what was useful before building new equipment to reopen the crossing within days rather than weeks. With hard work and great efficiency, they made everything serviceable in six days, so that in the end, it was just another of those unfortunate delays so common in conflict.

As they ran through the jungle trails leading north, Susie and Peter heard the explosions and briefly stopped to see the sky filled with black smoke and red with fire. They now knew that the attack was successful but must vanish before the enemy found them. Now they were the hunted surrounded by many more hunters.

In the Chin village by the Chindwin river, the others waited. When Susie arrived, everyone was greeted warmly, before settling down in small groups to prepare for the river crossing. Some slept, some rested, while others lay awake guarding their friends.

Peter walked around the little village noticing children swimming while nearby mothers washed their clothes. It looked so peaceful with the wide river water only occasionally crossed by a fishing boat. Peter found it strange that just a few miles south were a Japanese army hiding among the bushes preparing to cross the same river. The sounds of laughter from the children mingled with the noise of the river water lapping against the jetty produced a comforting music to his ears. It was a blissful change from the sound of explosions and the noises of the jungle. He sat beside the little wooden jetty next to two fishing boats.

A hand touched his shoulder to say, 'Peter you must stay in the shadows as here you can be seen. One report there is something happening, will result in them attacking our Chin friends.'

'Sorry.'

Peter felt an idiot. How could he endanger the villagers who risked their lives to help them? So he quickly moved under a nearby tree next to a sentry.

'It is quiet now because it is day, but at night, it will be busy. We will cross the river in the early afternoon when the Japanese sleep or are preparing for the night's work. Now we must watch the skies for spotter planes and the occasional motor launch that patrol the river banks looking for the British or groups like us.'

# 21
# The Battle of Sangshak

*I am dying for you, and you are dying for another.*

Rudyard Kipling (1888) Punjab proverb from *Plain Tales from the Hills*.


For reasons that only GHQ knew, it was decided to defend the unimportant hamlet of Sangshak against the expected Japanese attack. It was a tragic mistake, for it lacked all the necessities such as, a water supply, and barbed wire fencing while the shallow soil prevented the trenches being deep enough to protect the soldiers. In an area of only 800 yards long and 400 yards wide one thousand eight hundred and fifty men waited armed with mountain guns and 3-inch mortars to stop any attacking force. Then the rain came down as if to tell the commander about the need for water, but he did not take the hint. He informed GHQ of the need for aerial supplies when the battle started against the 15th division. Little did he realise that the 31st division, after overrunning nearby Uhkrak, would also attack Sangshak.

The Japanese advanced rapidly across the waterlogged land. Small rivers were crossed as Major Suki's men produced prefabricated bridges based on measurements provided by their scouts. Each bridge was long enough to cross the obstacle and no longer. Nothing was wasted following the British saying, 'Waste not, want not. In war, it was probably more important than in peacetime. So the advance continued unabated just like the well-oiled machine that indeed it was. Engineers and advance troops worked in unison to keep U-Go on schedule.

Major Suki's men were more successful than their predecessors had been, probably more by chance than by ability. In February while they were working by the Chindwin River, they were bombed so that the 15th division lost four thousand men. To avoid such attacks all activities were conducted at night. It did not work, as the RAF Beaufighter, Mitchell and Hurricanes caused havoc by destroying bridges as well as disrupting supply routes and the lines of communication. It was a very different war compared with the one they fought in Lower Burma when they had air supremacy. Now they did not. The constant enemy air activity was inflicting serious casualties and causing dangerous delays.

And time was precious if they were to cross the Naga Hills into India before the monsoon came bringing so much rain that turned roads into rivers and mountainsides into mudslides. Their advance was meticulously planned and expected to run on a timetable to avoid the rains. All they had to defeat were men fighting behind shallow trenches with few supplies, no barbed wire, and maybe a tank or mountain gun. So the Japanese decided to capture Ukhul before descending upon Sangshak.

Everyone in the Japanese army was happy as they were ahead of schedule having met little resistance.

'Major Suki-san!'

'Hai Captain, what is the news?'

'We attack Ukhul where we expect only light resistance. The town is defended by the lightly equipped, 50th Indian Parachute Regiment with no tanks. Then we join up with the 31st Division to take Sangshak. Though by the time we get there, I believe 11th Battalion will have captured it.'

In Sangshak, Havildar Temasen set about organising the men as best he could. He carefully rationed the water, divided the ammunition and food supplies between them, sufficient for their needs during the initial attack. He established a position in front of the abandoned church. The 3-inch mortars covered the western approaches. During the night of 22nd March, they were ready for the enemy to arrive.

'Havildar, why do we fight here where the trenches are too shallow?' asked a soldier.

'Be quiet, you are a Gurkha paid to die. Watch but do not fire unless ordered to as the enemy will try to creep up on us like a thief in the night.'

'Yes, Havildar.'

So all along the perimeter the Nepalese soldiers waited while tried to see through the darkness. Every shadow appeared to be an advancing soldier, but none were. No one fired, when something was seen a message was sent to Temasen, who checked it out. They lay there for hours waiting for the shouts of *Banzai* or the sound of their silly bugles that did not came.

Then Temasen saw the first wave of one hundred men running towards them. They came on with fixed bayonets led by an officer holding his sword in the air. He really hated Japanese swords.

'Sir, one hundred Japs at 10 o'clock, range is about three hundred yards.'

'Well spotted, Havildar. Order rapid fire at one hundred yards,' the officer commented.

'Yes sir!'

Temasen turned to his runner to order, 'Open fire at hundred yards.'

Then he placed his Bren gun selector to fire one shot at a time and waited ready to fire. The enemy came nearer to where he lay as he checked the gun's magazines with the palms of his hands damp with sweat. He noted with satisfaction that none of his men moved, or spoke. Each moved the bolt of his Lee Enfield rifle forward to place a round in the barrel and took off their safety catch ready to fire. Some said a silent prayer or touched a lucky charm, but most just waited patiently.

The enemy advanced two hundred yards and was still closing as Temasen took aim at the officer carrying his sword. When the officer was one hundred yards away he fired one shot.

The officer went down.

Immediately, the Gurkhas opened fire with deadly accuracy. Each man aimed at a specific target, and having hit him fired at the next. The enemy was cut down as they moved over the open ground. A few survived to return fire, but most were dead or wounded; none reached the Gurkha positions. Of the one hundred attackers only twenty escaped.

It lasted less than ten minutes. They had won the first round, but now the enemy knew where their positions were, so the next attack would be more difficult to repulse.

Now was the time to get ready. 'You, you and you come here.' Temasen said, pointing towards three Gurkhas. 'Go forward and collect their water bottles and supplies.'

'Yes, Havildar.'

So the three crept forward to collect what they could before returning to their lines with some water that helped satiate their thirst.

Then the waiting started all over again.

This time the air was filled with the noise of the wounded Japanese crying out for help. No one could risk helping them in the middle of the battlefield. It was terrible to hear men cry out in pain. Some cries were genuine, but many were not. It was a trick to lure them out of their positions to kill them.

Nothing happened until ten minutes later when a second wave of attackers appeared. This time they were more cautious and managed to get closer to the British lines. Again, the attackers were cut down, leaving none alive to retreat. All died falling, where they stood. This time some of the defenders were injured.

'Check ammunition and take the wounded to the medics.'

'Yes sir!'

Casualties were few, as so far there had been no mortar or artillery bombardment. Temasen prayed that the Japanese did not have such equipment, as they were not effectively protected in the shallow trenches from bomb blasts or shrapnel.

That night there were two more attacks, with one getting up to the British lines and ending with hand-to-hand combat. The last was the worst. As the Japanese came ten yards from the trenches, Temasen gave the order. 'Gurkha draw kukris.....attack!' His men responded in seconds, slashing and parrying the enemy bayonets with deadly efficiency. In the turmoil, it was hard to make out who was the enemy and who a friend. The flashing kukri was the only way of identifying these mountain men as they cut and thrust through the attackers. The Gurkhas won each round but took serious casualties with bullet or bayonet wounds.

When the enemy had withdrawn, the Gurkhas returned to their positions to prepare for the next round. The wounded were removed; ammunition checked, and kukris cleaned and replaced in their sheaths. They opened the boxes of ammunition so that each man collected his own requirements before loading them into magazines of their rifles while the Bren gunners did the same. The Bren guns were set to rapid fire that in a minute use up a full magazine, but it took five to reload. Each rifle, Bren gun and Vickers machine gun were cleaned, oiled and made ready. It was important because one piece of dirt would jam the gun making it useless. Only then did they drink and eat before taking turns in trying to sleep. This was difficult, when at any moment, the enemy could appear. To make matters worse the Japanese jitter men were calling out for their surrender and taunting them. Luckily, it was in English, which many Gurkhas did not understand.

Nearby, Major Suki and his men employed elephants to pull the heavy guns on top of a hill overlooking Sangshak. It was hard work as the ground was too slippery for the lorries and the elephants were slow. The native oozies controlled the animals as they moved their enormous bodies to climb the slopes. It took a great deal of time and care. Each elephant was first fitted with a leather harness attached to long metal chains. At the end of the chain was either an artillery piece or boxes of ammunition weighing over a ton. So in one journey an elephant moved more than any lorry could, without needing petrol.

One elephant spooked by gunfire ran amok, destroying a gun with its supplies. However, two days later, by the 23rd two mountain guns with their ammunition was in place, and the bombardment of Sangshak began.

Without cover, the defenders protected themselves as best they could; however, it was the start of a massacre. Men and mules were blown apart, and their bodies strewn all over the ground as the shells rained down on them. There was not enough ammunition, food or water to survive – and yet they did. They held their ground surrounded by the smell of rotting bodies, cordite and the sweat of unwashed men.

Their requests for help were answered from the air as low flying Dakotas dropped supplies while fighters strafed and bombed the Japanese lines. Above them, precious supplies attached to different coloured parachutes floated down. Red was for ammunition, blue for rations and white for water. Some landed safely; others went straight to the enemy, while others ended in between. When the RAF fighters attacked the enemy with 250lb bombs, the field guns opened fire, and the counter attack began. Then they collected the supplies to find only a few contained water; enough four days. So water was rationed to try to make it last longer.

'Water is rationed to one bottle a day', Temasen told his men.

The defenders felt let down and irritable through lack of sleep, with no shelter while under continuous attack. In one attack, Temasen was shot in the head but carried on fighting after a medic applied a field bandage.

At last, there was a lull in the fighting, so they searched the dead for rations, water and documents. On the body of one Japanese officer, Temasen found a dossier full of what looked like battle plans, which he took it to his officer.

'Sir, what shall I do with these documents?'

'Are you badly injured Havildar?'

'It is not too bad.'

'Good. Havildar, take the documents to our Intelligence unit and get your head attended to by the medics. You're no good to me injured.'

'Thank you, sir!' said Temassen as he went to the HQ tent to meet Setcha.

'I have some documents for you guys.'

'Temasen get your head treated while we look at it the documents.'

What Setcha found stretched across the table were the detailed enemy battle plans for the Japanese 31st and 15th Divisions with dates and routes to be taken.

'Captain Allen, sir I think you will want to see this!' Setcha said firmly.

'Setcha what have you got for me?' replied Captain Allen.

'I think they are the battle plans for the Japanese advance on Kohima and the railway at Dimapur.'

When Captain Allen saw the name U-Go and the battle plans, he rushed off to return a few minutes later with the commander.

'Let me see these so-called battle plans,' questioned the commander, who had seen a lot of things but never a complete plan. He knew that often senior officers carried document cases with such plans, but capturing one was unusual. Then he recognised they were the outlines of the U-GO campaign to capture the Naga Hills and enter India.

'My God, this is dynamite! Bloody well done, chaps; it details everything. When Slim sees this, he can strengthen the defences and stop them before they reach Dimapur and India. Captain Allen you must send a soldier to take Setcha to GHQ in Imphal as soon as possible.'

'Yes sir! May I send a wounded man with him as we can't send able-bodied soldiers in our present position?

At that moment Havildar Temasen came in with his head bandaged and looking worse for wear.

'Havildar, can you take Setcha to GHQ in Imphal?'

'Yes sir, but my duty is here,' Temasen replied.

'No Havildar your duty is to obey orders, and you must take Setcha safely to Imphal.'

'Yes sir!'

'Captain Allen, make a copy of the plans and proceed to Imphal by a different route. It is vital that General Slim knows that two Japanese divisions are advancing on Kohima. We will hold Sangshak for a few days.'

'What supplies do we need, sir?'

'We need everything from gallons of water, reinforcements and more firepower. This is not the best place to fight. By tomorrow, we may fall back to a smaller perimeter, but I hope we do not.'

At dusk Temasen, Setcha and Captain Allen left for Imphal, passing through the enemy lines unseen, before parting. Captain Allen took the direct route to Imphal while Temasen and Setcha went on a longer northern loop. They delivered their precious messages to GHQ in Imphal on 25th March. However, no one knows if the U-Go battle plans reached General Slim.

What happened next suggests that General Slim did not know of the planned attack on Kohima, or just did not care. In Imphal, Temasen had the shrapnel removed from his forehead and was transferred to the Gurkha Rifles at Dimapur.

At Sangshak many escaped, carrying their wounded to Kohima thanks to the Mahrattas rearguard action. When the position was finally taken, the Japanese were shocked to find less than a hundred wounded from the gallant rear guard. Here Major Suki found the carnage of war, where bodies of men and donkeys lay together on the bloody ground. It smelt worse than an abattoir on a hot summer's day. The Japanese only found a few packets of cigarettes, a radio and some tinned food, a rifle and less ammunition. All the artillery pieces were useless. So the attack on Kohima was delayed for four days, and men lost to capture an insignificant hill, making Major Suki wonder why two divisions had to attack such a small position. Had it been worth it?

Now U-Go was a week behind the dates on the timetable making everything harder. Since leaving Kalewa the Japanese lost five thousand men, leaving only three-quarters of 31st Division, fifteen thousand men, to advance to Kohima. Suki noted that most of the dead were Indian and Gurkha soldiers and was left to wonder why they fought for the ungrateful British and not for the Japanese. The defenders held the 31st Division from a position without water, proper trenches, barbed wire, or tanks. Surely such bravery would cause the Japanese problems, especially as the long supply route was disrupted by both air and ground attack. Had they wasted the chances of capturing Kohima and the railhead at Dimapur by attacking this useless enemy outpost? Such losses were not acceptable to his trained military mind, and not for the first time he considered that the idea of capturing India was over-optimistic.

In Imphal, Temasen requested to be sent to join his men in Kohima under Captain Charles Brighton. Neither knew that the other was a friend of Peter Anderson, though if they had it would have made no difference.

The journey to Kohima was chaotic. There was no transport for the Gurkhas so they marched in small groups, getting a lift whenever possible. While the British sent most of their resources to reinforce the Imphal-Shenam Saddle enclave while ignoring the garrison at Kohima.

# 22

# Across the Chindwin into the Kalewa Valley

*Sometimes the gods talk to us in our dreams,*
*And then it is only wise to heed the message.*

At noon on 24th March, Susie's Little Pagoda group left the Chin village in three boats at ten minute intervals. She and Peter sailed in the first boat with seven others to catch the afternoon breeze that blew gently making the crossing both swift and safe. Once across, they signalled to the others to set sail. They knew as dusk fell the river would be busy with Japanese craft, which would intercept any vessel. However, by then, the Chin fishermen would have returned safely to their village to resume their traditional way of life.

Each group disappeared into the jungle to follow a well-worn path towards the sign of the three pillars. The ground was soft and the vegetation easy to pass. Two scouts went ahead to check the way was clear; when it was, they left behind them pieces of linen that Susie picked up.

'When do we meet up with Tun Kyi?' Peter asked.

'He and Ba Saw should be at the three pillars having met up with the Naga warriors of V Force.'

'When will we get there?'

'Dearest, you ask too many questions. We will arrive before dawn, if we are not distracted.'

Every few miles the men carrying their wounded friend changed places so that one held the man on his back while the other looked after the equipment. The change over was quick and the injured man remained silent, even though every movement hurt. Peter hoped that if he was shot, he too could be quiet and protect his friends. Maybe the morphine deadened the pain; he hoped so.

Now they were in the swamplands with soft mud and water everywhere, so that they were in a steam bath. The deep mud clung to and tugged at their feet, causing a problem for all, especially the man carrying his wounded friend. The extra weight of a man on his back forced him to sink further into the mud making every step a major effort.

'Susie. Stop a minute.'

Susie stopped to look impatiently at him. 'Peter there's no time to waste. We must move on.'

'I think we should wait while I make a stretcher for the wounded man. He's too heavy to travel on another's back through this mud.'

'All right, but you only have ten minutes.'

Quickly, Peter pulled two long thick bamboo poles from a thicket to make a stretcher. Suddenly, Susie pulled him backwards as her dah slashed into the bamboo above his hands to cut off the head off a small green snake.

'I said to be quick darling, not foolish. This bamboo snake is deadly. Now cut the bamboo to make the stretcher. I didn't marry you to become a widow.'

He gave her a big hug before cutting the poles. Then using webbing army belts he made a primitive but effective stretcher. Within ten minutes, they were on the move again and more quickly. The wounded man was carried horizontally on the stretcher by two friends, who found walking this way much faster and less tiring.

One hour after dusk the scouts returned to say ahead were the three pillars where Tun Kyi waited. With this news everyone, especially Maria, started to race towards their friends. In a clearing, they were welcomed by Tun Kyi, Ba Saw and some Naga tribesmen. The site had a ceiling formed from bent-over branches interlaced with wild plants by three large stone monuments encrusted with vines. It was the perfect hiding place, being cool and invisible from the air. The three pillars were long forgotten ancient monoliths where the Naga placed offerings, just as they left them in banyan trees. Peter was pondering the age and origin of the prehistoric stone pillars when they were addressed by Tun Kyi. He said, 'No one leaves here until they know where the mantraps are. If you fall into one, you will die. This place is safe only because we have made it so. You must remain in the covered area and never go into the open. Remember that low-flying aircraft patrol the skies looking for us and will tell the soldiers where we are. So there will be no cooking, just eat the fruits and dried meat.' Susie spoke. 'It is the evening of 24th March, so we can eat, rest for four hours and then climb the hills. The Naga will lead us as it is too dangerous to follow the paths that the Japanese may be using. Remember that Tun Kyi said not to leave the area as the paths to the north are crisscrossed with camouflaged traps that, if you fall in, will kill you. Each trap is five feet deep containing many sharp bamboo spikes that will pierce your body. If they do not kill you, the poison on their tips will.'

The fear of being impaled on sharpened bamboo spikes was more than enough to keep them all together. People sat down and ate the food provided. Others went to the bush latrines away from the paths. Some washed while most just rested. Maria placed her head on Tun Kyi's lap as he sat upon the ground with his Sten gun at the ready. Her long black hair fell down like a scarf that reached the ground below. She fell into a deep sleep smiling as Tun Kyi stroked her hair with his left hand as he guarded them. His eyes showed the determination that makes most opponents think twice before trying anything. Maria was content as like a small child or a cat she rested on her master's lap. Yes, thought Peter, they made a good couple. Surely, God will preserve them through the dangers to come.... He prayed for them until, overcome by tiredness he drifted off to sleep.

Normally, Peter did not dream, but tonight was different. He dreamt of a battle between a giant, blood-red snake with long curved fangs and a smaller, fire throwing golden dragon. The dragon made Peter feel good while the snake filled him with fear and loathing. In a jungle clearing surrounded by every type of animal, the two adversaries eyed each up and down looking for an advantage. Behind the dragon was a jungle lit by thousands of magical lanterns. Behind the snake were burning villages, smoke filled skies and the cries of the damned. It was an unequal contest between the wounded dragon and the fast, uninjured snake. The golden dragon's red eyes and long tongue saw and tasted the position of his enemy. The gigantic snake watched the dragon through jet-black eyes while his forked tongue darted in and out, trying to taste the dragon's scent. The dragon was slow, held back by the weight of its wings and the severity of his wounds. The huge red snake was streamlined and very fast making it difficult for the beautiful dragon to avoid the snake's fangs as they struck. Each time the deadly teeth only hit the thick scales covering the feet of the dragon as the dragon struck back with his long curved talons that tore bits from the snake's skin.

The snake rose to its full height above the dragon and threw its long muscular body into coils around the hapless victim to tighten his hold on the ensnared dragon. The dragon responded by using his talons to cut the skin of the snake to cause bleeding, but not enough to stop it contracting its fearsome coils. As the dragon fought for air, Peter felt himself being suffocated and his ribs starting to give in. The contest was all but over as the dragon lay in the mud, totally immobilised by the rope-like coils that held him. Indeed, the dragon was dying.

Peter willed the dragon to get up and fight on. He tried to shout 'Don't give in!', but could not. He could watch helplessly as the friendly dragon lay dying. Then the half-dead golden dragon seemed to hear Peter's pleas to inhale large amounts of air, expanding its lungs to fight the ever-tightening coils. Afterwards, the dragon exhaled a stream of flame from his mouth onto the dreadful snake's head so that Peter thought he could smell burning snake's skin. The snake relaxed its coils in order to strike the dragon – but too late, for the dragon struck first, raking his talons over the snake's face. No one won, as the wounded red snake slithered away into the jungle, severely hurt but not dead. The golden dragon was covered in blood, but alive and able to fight another day. Slowly, he licked his wounds to regain his magnificent self, ready for the next encounter with the snake.

Peter must have cried out in his sleep because Susie quickly placed her hand over his mouth to whisper. 'Darling, be silent otherwise the Japanese and their reptilian allies may hear. There's nothing to fear, you've been dreaming.'

He saw her looking at him with the way women give their lovers or children. It felt good, so he started to forget his nightmare. Then Susie asked him what was wrong, he told her. She listened intently to every detail before trying to explain it. 'Dreams are God's way of communicating with us. I can interpret your dream. The golden dragon is a Burmese symbol of goodness and represents us, while the red snake is the Japanese whose vileness roams this land. Red is the colour of the Rising Sun that promised to free us from the colonialists but enslaved us. It is a case of 'out of the frying pan into the fire'. So it is telling you, my love, that we may be wounded, but we will survive.'

'Yes that makes sense. It's strange, because I rarely dream.'

She placed her arms around him, kissed his eyes, so he felt good. He just wanted to stay like that forever and ever. It was simple all he had to do was to freeze time, and they would remain, maybe, cast into rock as two eternal lovers in each other's embrace.

'You are starting to dream for now you know true love and my need for you. Soon you may even discover how to interpret your dreams and look into the hearts and minds of others.'

'No one can do that my love.'

'Oh yes they can! Father does it all the time. He reads our innermost thoughts and feelings, and responds accordingly. It works most of the time, unless he's angry or sees something that he does not know about a person. He says that a person who charms others is often more dangerous than the tiger, or in your case, the snake. This is, as he puts it, because one tends to trust the charmer while distrusting the snake. So we were taught to avoid snakes and beware of charmers with silky but deadly tongues.'

'Am I a charmer?'

'You are so silly. If father thought that he wouldn't have helped you or allowed us to become lovers. No, you are too straightforward to be the sly fox. You are more like the little mongoose, quick to attack the snake and without fear of the mortal danger held within those poisonous fangs.'

'Thank you my sweet, but why a mongoose?'

'The mongoose kills or defeats the snake because it has a brave little heart. It looks in the eye of the evil snake yet does not get mesmerised by it. It taunts the snake to strike out while jumping away to avoid the fangs. When it attacks it bites the snake behind the neck, severing the spinal cord. It is the art of the complete warrior. The attack is quick, clean and deadly.'

'Do you like mongooses!'

'As a child Maria and I had mongooses as pets – they are great fun but not tameable. They will eat out of your hand, especially if you hold out a chicken's egg and will come back for more. However, they are not pets that come when you call. Instead, they always go away but returning for eggs. When they eat an egg, their sharp teeth gently cut a ring at the top of the shell, lifts it off then suck out its contents. Afterwards, the shell is empty having been licked clean.'

'If they ate so many eggs, then why did your parents let you feed them?'

'When a house has mongooses, it never has snakes. Is it not better to pay nature a small fee in eggs to keep one's family safe from danger? They are like the night watchman looking after their friends or those who pay them.'

'When the war is over, we will have a mongoose in our house to protect our children from snakes.'

'And place a Madonna over the fireplace with a chinthe by the door to guard the temple of our hearts. Then it is home.'

To Peter's annoyance, Susie got up to wake her group. Some were already awake. Others shook themselves, wiped their eyes and were ready for the next stage of their saga. Tun Kyi and Susie led one group westwards while Ba Saw left with ten of her men, and two Naga warriors went to attack the Japanese bridges along the road to Kohima. They parted with silent hugs and a wave.

Travel was slow in the Kabaw valley criss-crossed by the Yu River as the swamplands were covered by bush that was nearly impossible to penetrate. So they walked in the river until finding another tributary running west that they followed. They moved close to mangroves aware that at any moment, an enemy patrol could appear. However, they and the Japanese were travelling in the same direction only a few miles apart, neither knowing that the other was there. They crossed the valley before climbing the foothills until at daybreak on 25th March, they rested. Their legs ached, and hands were sore from cutting the undergrowth. They made a temporary camp inside the dense vegetation away from the riverbank, hidden from both the river and the air to sleep. There were no fires as everyone slept or took turns watching for danger. The peaceful silence was broken by the lights from a small patrol boat and the sounds of the chug… chug… from the outboard motor. It was a shock to hear the enemy so close by and watch the beams of light cutting through the dense vegetation. They wondered if they were discovered being too near the river? Fingers tightened on the triggers as they waited hardly daring to breathe.

Peter saw a small flat river craft with three Japanese pass only a few yards away. Apparently, the enemy was oblivious to their presence, and he hoped that they would stay so. For on the bow of the small river patrol boat was a machine gun that could cut them to pieces. As they passed by Peter heard every word and smelt their cigarette smoke. He mentally translated their conversation as the craft past them to go on downstream towards the Yu River.

'*Dii-sana taxan malaria. Ashita mati mati.*'(There is lots of malaria. So tomorrow you may die.)

'*Hai gunzo. Yazume ashita mati mati.*'(Yes old man. Rest for tomorrow you may die.)

'*Ah so ka! Ah so ka!*' (Is that so? Is that so?)

Peter heard no more as their voices trailed out while the patrol boat disappeared downstream. Now awake, they ate their dried rations and drank a mouthful of precious water before moving on. Susie looked at her watch to see it was four pm to realise that sunset would come within a few hours. Sometimes they heard artillery fire coming from the north as people fought for their lives. Then, there was silence as columns of black smoke rose to darken the sky. It reminded them of their predicament. It was lucky they did not know they were travelling in a line that crossed the path of the 31st Division moving from Sangshak south towards the British position at Imphal. It is one of life's little miracles that what one does not know about, does not worry sensible people. For example, in life, there is always that strange thing we call fate, which affects all sometimes for the better or for the worse. If Susie had known that a few miles north were ten thousand Japanese soldiers, it would not have changed her plans. They had no choice, as the only way to safety was via Laisen and Maram to Kohima and Dimapur.

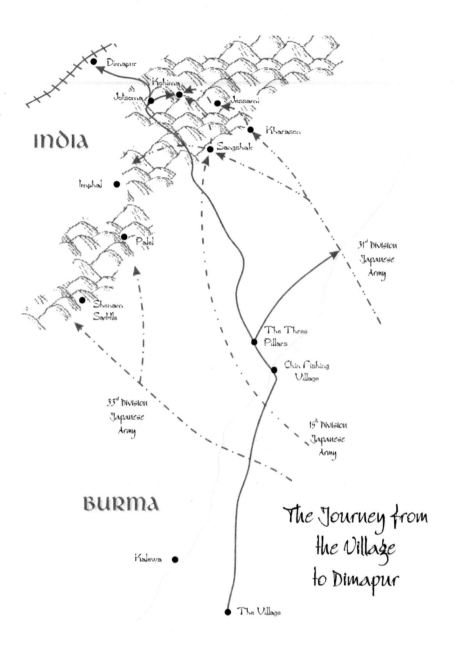

Dimapur

Kohima

Jotsoma · · Jessami

INDIA

Kharasom

Sangshak

Imphal

Palel

31st Division
Japanese
Army

Shenam
Saddle

The Three
Pillars

Chin Fishing
Village

35th Division
Japanese
Army

15th Division
Japanese
Army

BURMA

The Journey from
the Village
to Dimapur

Kalewa

The Village

# 23
# The Way to Dimapur

West of the Kabaw valley, they left the jungle to move through woodlands with thick undergrowth. Here the ground was as slippery as ice as they climbed the foothills leading to the mountain pass 5000 feet above sea level. By now, everyone used some sort of walking stick and helped each other by forming a human chain when the slopes were too dangerous. They were a team that helped each other without having to be asked.

They travelled knowing the British would fiercely defend Dimapur, as it was the railhead for the trains to and from India. If the British failed to stop the Japanese, the road to India was wide open. People worried that the Indians may rise up in support of the Japanese against the British as happened in Burma. In the early morning of the 26th, they were awoken by the scouts reporting that something was wrong.

'Myint Suu Kyi, the Japanese are in Sangshak having killed too many Indian soldiers. It looks like they have become two columns, one going north and the other moving across our path to Imphal. What should we do?'

'We go towards their column, locate the weakest link, and cross. We may have to fight but with God's help, we will get through. There is no other alternative. To stay would mean either we starve to death or surrender.'

'If we fight it must be by stealth,' stated Tun Kyi. 'The noise of gunfire will attract more Japanese and then surely we shall all perish.'

Susie thought for a moment and knew that Tun Kyi, like always, was right. It is funny that a successful general is often only as good as his wise assistant. She remembered her father saying that a great king needed a trusted advisor, and a happy man a devoted woman. I suppose a content wife needs a loving husband as an officer needs a loyal sergeant.

'We must try to cross their lines without a fight or take out an isolated group using crossbows and knives. If we are quick, we will succeed. If we are attacked, Tun Kyi will take you to Dimapur while Peter and I will form a rearguard to keep the enemy at bay.'

People mumbled while others shook their heads in disbelief as no one wanted the newly weds to die for them. They couldn't change Susie's mind, even Peter felt that if he was to die, it would be with Susie by his side. They faced combat, consoling each other with the thought that they would die among friends. Weapons at the ready, they stealthily moved forwards like hunters towards the enemy lines. All knew that things had changed, as the jungle stayed silent indicating that the enemy was not far away, even the chatter of the cheeky monkeys had ceased.

They heard nearby rumblings like distant thunder, the shuffling of feet, the noise of mules and the smell of cigarettes. A Japanese column was near them.

Was it just a few men or part of a much larger formation?

Half bending they moved slowly through the undergrowth until above a stream, they saw the enemy below. The Japanese soldiers were moving fast in tight columns of twenty men followed by bearers pulling heavily loaded mules through the shallow waters. They did not look up in their rush to get out of the water and into the jungle. Peter likened them to a trail of ants moving as one, towards their target with little in sight except for the one in front. A sort of follow my leader.

At sunrise, they found a gap in the enemy column, so they could cross the stream without opposition. As each group crossed the others stood by with their rifles ready to give covering fire if the enemy should appear. Then they climbed to Maram where they parted. Susie went to Zubza and Dimapur, Peter with a Naga guide towards Kohima.

By evening, Peter arrived with his Naga guide at the Kohima garrison to be escorted by a suspicious British sentry to the military police. The red caps took them to the bungalow where the Nagaland Deputy Commissioner resided. When the Japanese invaded Burma, he formed Force V with Ursula Bowers as a resistance movement. He liked the Nagas, and they trusted and loved him. He gave his word not leave Kohima alive until the Japanese were defeated, and he was not the sort to break a promise. It was not for the money as the salary was poor; he just felt duty-bound to share their suffering, even if it meant he was tortured and died.

The DC's bungalow had a large veranda that overlooked the valley below and the Naga village across the road. On the terrace above was his tennis court that led up the hill towards the Ridge. The area was terraced with rings of small tracks linking each building in the camp. In peacetime this was an idyllic setting where people gathered to escape the heat.

Peter was greeted by the DC sitting at a big teak desk, wearing an open-necked shirt and shorts. The DC's eyes showed a sense of understanding that put Peter at ease.

'Squadron Leader Peter Anderson number 2946291 reporting sir,' Peter stated, while saluting as smartly as possible.'

'Squadron Leader Anderson, welcome to Kohima. Don't salute me, for I am a civilian. I had you brought here because we need an airman to help us guide in the air support if – heaven forbid – the Japanese attack.'

'I'll do what I can sir. However, I have little experience of ground combat except with some Burmese and Naga warriors.'

'The Naga is totally loyal to the crown. Sometimes they get so excited that their reports are hard to interpret. I expect our Intelligence boys will be eager to have a word with you.'

'The news is not good – there's a Japanese column only a few miles away.'

'Sadly, what you say confirms what I have heard.'

At this point, in came an old Naga servant carrying a tray that he placed carefully on the table. He was well dressed with shirt and a *longyi*, but still wore the pierced ear lobes through which was held a small tusk. The old Naga poured two cups of Assam tea each with milk and one spoonful of sugar. By the side of each cup, he placed two biscuits. It was the way he always served tea that varied very little from day to day or from visitor to visitor. Perhaps at sundown the tea was replaced with a glass of whisky, or a gin and tonic, but never during the daytime or while on duty.

'Enjoy the tea while I inform HQ of your arrival. I hope you like the biscuits; they're Huntley and Palmer's gingerbread.'

The biscuits melted in his mouth as Peter sipped the warm, sweet tea and felt it slowly warm up his whole body. There is nothing in this world like a fresh cup of tea to make an Englishman feel good. The strong Assam tea's aroma seemed to fill his nostrils as its taste washed away the journey's grime that covered his body. Sitting there in such luxury, he became aware that he had not had a bath for days. In fact, he probably smelt like a dirty old tramp.

'The biscuits were delicious. May I take a bath, and shave. To be truthful I feel decidedly scruffy.'

'That's no problem. I was about to suggest that you may want some clean clothing, and a long soak in the bath. You do smell a bit rural, but after years among the mountains I tend not to notice such things. I enjoy the special fragrance of the frangipani while not responding to unpleasant odours. Selective responses – what that Russian Pavlov, called conditioned responses. You know what I mean. The smell of good food cooking makes one feel hungry, and that sort of mumbo-jumbo.'

Peter first showered off the excessive mud from his hands, face and feet. Then he slowly climbed into the warm bath while his discarded clothes were discretely removed. He lay back in the water feeling its warmth relax his tired limbs. The bath water turned a reddish colour as the ingrained dirt was washed from his body. All he needed was a gin and tonic, and it would be bliss. Perhaps, on second thoughts, a bath with Susie would be much better. Then in came the old Naga bringing a gin and tonic and some clean clothes.

After bathing, Peter shaved the stubble from his face and dressed in a British Army uniform with the long-sleeved shirt worn by most officers. Next to the clothes were three pairs of boots one size eight one size nine and one ten. He selected the size nine shoes and was relieved to find that they were a good fit. It was the wrong uniform, and rank, but it was the right nationality, so that would do quite nicely. Now he felt ready to face his future, little realising, that in the coming weeks, he would see war at its rawest.

# British Defensive Positions
## Kohima, April 5th, 1944

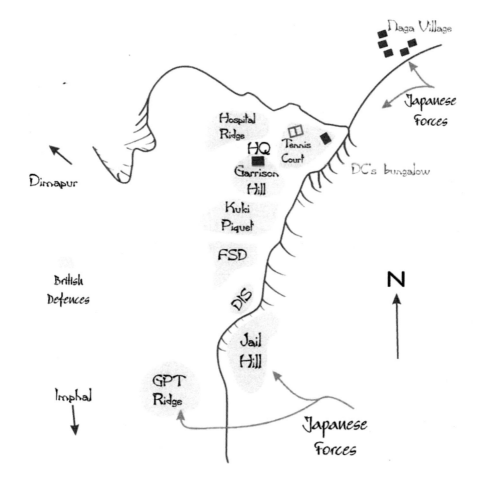

Naga Village

Japanese Forces

Dimapur

Hospital Ridge

HQ

Tennis Court

Garrison Hill

DC's bungalow

Kuki Piquet

FSD

British Defences

DIS

N

Jail Hill

Imphal

GPT Ridge

Japanese Forces

# 24
# The Hill Station at Kohima, March 1944

*When the earth was sick and the skies grey*
*And the woods were rotted with rain,*
*The Dead Man rode through the autumn day*
*to visit his love again.*

Rudyard Kipling (1888) 'The Other Man' from *Plain Tales from the Hills.*

The Kohima camp was everything that Peter expected to find in a storage depot consisting of a collection of warehouses, basha huts and bungalows laid out around a series of hills. When he arrived at the camp, everyone was busy so that few noticed him. So he sat in the Officers' mess to devour a large lamb chop with mint sauce and mashed potato washed down with lime juice and tea. Afterwards, he reported to the officers in the Intelligence hut where he found two pale and very English men looking over a series of maps of the area. Peter wondered if either had ever been in the jungle or seen war at first hand. It was of no importance as he was ushered politely into a chair and then repeatedly asked similar questions. They listened to Peter's every word trying to establish what he knew and whether he was the genuine article or an impostor.

Did you leave Burma with the Little Pagoda group led by the Karen woman, Myint Suu Kyi?'

'Yes that is correct. Otherwise how could I get out of the jungle without either a compass or being helped?'

'By the Chindwin you met the V Force Naga scouts who led you here.'

'Yes.'

'What enemy positions did you see and where were they going.'

'There are some thousand men moving west with tanks, trucks, artillery pieces and mule trains. Furthermore, by the Chindwin River, there were ten thousand Japanese troops with INA and Burmese nationalists moving north. They had what I believe you call mountain guns, trucks, tanks and mule trains. At dusk, they assemble pontoon bridges that are pulled out of hiding by elephants for their army to cross the river.'

'Do you think that they will attack Kohima or bypass us to go to Dimapur?'

'My guess is that they will take this hill station first as it controls the road to Imphal as well as the way to Dimapur.

'Why do you say that?'

'Getting here from the Chindwin is difficult, as the slopes are steep and the altitude tiring. However, I could easily be wrong as they could go to Maram then bypass Kohima to move on to Dimapur. I believe they usually overrun each defensive position before attacking the next.'

'I tend to agree with you. However, GHQ thinks that they will bypass us to cross in strength into India to meet up with Indian Nationalists and end the Empire.'

'I find that hard to believe for Kohima Ridge dominates the area.'

'I agree. Would you like a cigarette or some tea?'

'No thanks,' Peter replied, being suddenly reminded of Bo Ba Tin. He was trying very hard to control the icy feeling that started to swell in his veins and kept smiling. He wondered when these fools would let him get on with the war.

'One worries, whether the Indian and Nepalese soldiers will fight for us when the Japanese is winning every round. What do you think?' asked Lt Smithers.

'Well I was captured and tortured by a Burmese of the Kempei-Tei with another British Officer and his Gurkha havildar. Though severely beaten, Havildar Temasen refused to turn against us and would have died with me, if we had not been rescued. I trust a man like that with my life.'

'Well, that's interesting, very interesting indeed. Isn't it Smithers?' replied Lt Jones.

Smithers grinned. 'There can't be many havildars called Temasen, who recently escaped from captivity.'

'Well, old chap, I have news for you. Havildar Temasen is serving here with a company of Gurkha Rifles under Captain Brighton,' continued Lieutenant Jones.

'Captain Charles Brighton?'

'Do you know him?'

'I should as he is my brother-in-law.'

'Well, that settles the matter of who you are nicely. Sorry about all the fuss but nowadays we can never be too careful, bloody infiltrators everywhere. Now that we have two people who can vouch for you, there is no problem. What do you know about football?'

'Not much as I played rugby.'

'Well, that's a bit of luck as we ask questions like who plays centre forward for Manchester United.'

'Frankly, I haven't a clue.'

'Don't let it worry you, if I didn't have the answers in front of me, I wouldn't know. Whoever invented these questions didn't play rugby.'

'That's good, since I rarely saw a newspaper or read a book since coming here. It was one endless cycle of flying, sleeping and surviving another day.'

'Well let's look at the maps while I send for Captain Brighton and Havildar Temasen. Is there anything that we can get you?'

'I would like a cup of tea if that's at all possible?'

'Of course, someone somewhere is always brewing tea.' The Intelligence officer paused before calling out, 'Corporal Edwards.'

'Sir!' the elderly Corporal Edwards replied.

'Try to scrounge up a pot of tea and plenty of cups with a lot of sugar. We are expecting visitors.'

'No problem sir, one pot of tea coming up in a jiffy.'

A jiffy must be ten minutes; Peter thought, as it took that long for the tea to arrive. No sooner had they sat down to drink the warm Assam tea than in walked Charles Brighton followed by the small, indestructible figure of Temasen.

Charles gave Peter a great bear hug before standing back to look at him, noting he was well but had lost forever his schoolboy charm.

'Well, what is my pilot brother-in-law doing in an army uniform at Kohima? I heard you were shot down and missing in action, so I'm delighted that you're here and in one piece. I was just thinking about you, when you turn up from nowhere.'

'It's a very long story involving a bit of luck and the help of true friends. I would like to know if my friends arrived safely at Dimapur.'

'I'm sure that can be arranged as we are always in touch with HQ in Dimapur. Though they are not very good at giving us what we want.'

Peter saw his old friend Temasen staying in the background being very much the sergeant when among officers.

'Havildar Temasen! By the grace of God, it's good to see you. I trust you are well. It seems years since we were in that dreadful camp with the Devil's Helper.'

'Squadron Leader Anderson, it is good to see that you have recovered.'

'Indeed I have, but like you, I have the scars to remind me. Susie and her people I hope are in Dimapur, while Ba Saw has set out to attack the Japanese lines east of here.'

The intelligence boffins were satisfied as obviously, the three men knew each other and were overjoyed to be reunited.

'Well, Squadron Leader Anderson, we will hand you over to Captain Brighton to look after you while we work out how best to use your services. There's no real danger as the Royal West Kents will arrive today to reinforce the CO's Assam Regiment to be followed by the rest of 6th Brigade from Dimapur. They should give the Japanese the biggest surprise of their lives.'

That night Peter slept on Garrison Hill among the Gurkha Rifles with his brother-in-law. For the first time in weeks, he dreamt of home and his family and worried as to how Susie would fit in. There would be no trouble from his family – but what about other people? He shrugged his shoulders when he thought that his father had overcome those difficulties and so would he. Only time would tell if there was any left for them in this godforsaken war.

At home in England, Lynette Anderson slept peacefully for the first time in weeks and dreamt of Peter and Charles together safely on a hilltop. When she awoke she went to sit in front of the jade tree and lit joss sticks for them. Somehow she knew that they needed all the spiritual protection her ancestors could provide.

Next morning everything was quiet so Peter was given a map of the positions and shown the layout of the land. The base at the Kohima Ridge was above the hill station town of Kohima, nestling between a series of high mountains. It was the main junction of the mountain road from Dimapur to Imphal. To the north were wooded ridges that ran from the road to the Naga village; to the east was the town of Kohima and to the west was Mount Pulebadze rising to 10,000 feet. To the south, either side of the road was a series of defensive positions guarding the hospital, petrol supplies, ammunition dump, and garrison command post.

From the top of Garrison Hill, Peter could see below the terraced slopes to the Kohima garrison clubhouse, over the tennis courts, past the DC's bungalow, down to the road to Kohima town and beyond to the Naga village. The whole place was an idyllic refuge in peacetime, cradled in the mountains where the air was cool and the mosquitoes few and far between. It was where the rich and famous came to escape the summer heat in the valleys below. The layout of the land was simple. To the east of the Imphal road was a very steep slope that acted as a natural barrier to any attack, then the road reached Jail Hill and Transport Ridge some 1,000 yards away. The whole camp probably measured no more than 1,700 yards by 750 yards and was too small to be worthy of a major battle.

Everybody was confident when the Royal West Kents (RWK) arrived and started to dig in. However, within days, the RWK was ordered back to Dimapur with all of their supplies and equipment. So the lorries that should have evacuated the civilians only carried a few to safety. The remaining one thousand clerks and non-combatants had no choice but to wait to be evacuated.

Now the situation appeared to be impossible making the DC furious that Kohima was left to be defended by five hundred soldiers and one thousand non-combatants. The loss of the eight hundred soldiers of the RWK and their artillery was disastrous. At Jessami, some twenty-five miles away, the Assam Rifles were fighting the 138th Regiment of General Sato's 31st division. Outnumbered, the Assam Rifles survived for three days before being defeated to allow the enemy to advance to Kohima.

Urgent requests were sent to Dimapur for coils of barbed wire to establish defensive perimeters, but there was no reply, and none arrived. They were left as lambs to the slaughter, while elsewhere better defensive positions were established. The CO accepted the hand of cards that fate dealt him. So he set out to reinforce the defences around the road junction near the DC's bungalow.

The garrison now consisted of the Shere Regiment of raw Gurkha soldiers, the Assam Regiment and a few platoons of 3rd Naga Hills Batallion. Then there were the cooks, drivers, mechanics, clerks, secretaries, hospital orderlies and medics. All were issued with weapons, except the padre, who politely refused them. Experienced soldiers taught them to fire a rifle, dig a trench and how to avoid being hurt when shelled. Most of them wore their metal helmets for the first time. A few found it exciting, though for the majority, it was a time of great fear and trepidation.

Rumours circulated that the Japanese were invincible making the garrison feel that they had been left there to die. Others were that the Japanese took no prisoners so one must keep one's head down and wait until there was a chance to escape. Then the CO decided to improve the morale by a bit of bravado. The garrison was cheered up by the sight of the CO and the DC having tea served by the tennis court as they had done many times before.

Surely, the DC and the CO would not take unnecessary risks? The effect was magical. If the DC and the CO were not afraid, then why should they be?

The remaining defenders deepened the trenches started by the RWKs, built bunkers for the Bren guns and distributed ammunition, rations and water. When the enemy attacked it would be difficult to supply everyone as they were stretched out from Jail Hill to Garrison Hill. In the hurry, they forgot to establish a reliable supply of water. It was probably because it was cool and damp. In this way, they prepared against an attack by the elite of the Japanese Imperial Army. They knew the enemy was nearby as the distant sound of gunfire from Jessami had ceased days before.

On 3rd April, two hundred and fifty survivors from the original six hundred strong Assam Regiment arrived in dribs and drabs from Jessami. The news was shocking. The Assam Regiment had fought General Sato's 31st Division of twenty thousand men with mortars, tanks and mountain guns that were now advancing on Kohima. Then a few survivors from the 5/7th Rajputs from Jotsoma arrived. Now the GHQ ordered the eight hundred men of the Royal West Kents back to Kohima. On the 5th April, only five hundred RWK troops returned to Kohima having fought their way back through the Japanese troops already encircling the base. In the confusion, many men died while others were forced back to Dimapur, so that many supplies and equipment never arrived. So now the garrison consisted of two thousand five hundred men, of whom one thousand were civilians, with a battery of mountain guns but no tanks or barbed wire.

Peter was sent to the artillery observation position to work under a cool-headed Major, who guided artillery fire onto the Japanese attackers. By radio, he gave the grid references and acted as the spotter for the artillery situated two miles west at Jotsoma. Peter's job was to assist the Major to direct any RAF aircraft, when and if they came. All supplies would be parachuted onto the small dropping zone (DZ) that was a few hundred yards wide in a mountainous valley. The DZ was not ideal though it was the only one possible. Maybe supplying ground troops from the air between the mountains was not a good idea.

Communications both within the garrison and with the outside world were vital as the thickly wooded slopes made finding the enemy difficult. Worse still, thick morning mists covered the slopes, reducing visibility to a few yards while making everything cold and wet. So they looked for the occasional movement of undergrowth or the flash from a rifle to locate the enemy.

Before dawn on the 6th April, the Japanese quietly captured the Naga village and Kohima town to the north-east of the garrison. Later, that morning a few civilians and soldiers were captured as they went into the village to get breakfast. After a brief respite to consolidate their newly captured positions against a counterattack, the Japanese restarted their advances. With a mixture of quick ferocious attacks and stealth, they soon descended in force against the allies holding Jail Hill and captured it. The battle for Kohima Ridge had begun The Japanese suffered so many casualties while capturing Jail Hill that they halted the attack until reinforcements arrived. The Kohima garrison was about to feel the full effect of a Japanese division of fifteen thousand highly experienced men.

On Jail Hill, the enemy established defensive positions before starting their next offensive. It was a well-oiled war machine used only to victory and run a watch. Everything was planned so that nothing or nobody could stop it from running on time. The plans for the assault on Imphal and Dimapur were made weeks before, and the dates set as if in stone. All they had to do was capture a small depot protected by a thousand soldiers before the road to India was theirs. Victory was certain. Defeat was not a possibility. So they attacked the defences in the DIS and FSD. On confirming that the Japanese held Jail Hill, and all British troops had withdrawn; the Major directed the brigade artillery at Jotsoma to fire on Jail Hill. Then the enemy replied by bombarding Kohima Ridge with artillery and mortar fire.

The Japanese completed their pincer movement to isolate the garrison from Dimapur by capturing the roads and surrounding wooded high ground. The besieged garrison were about to be put to the sword. No person would escape alive as the undefeated Japanese army took no prisoners. Prisoners would slow down their progress and were not planned for in their strict timetable. Whatever the cost, the hills must be theirs before the monsoon came. Now the battle became the siege of Kohima Ridge.

It should have been easy, as all the Japanese had to do was squeeze the perimeter tighter. The more the allied soldiers fell back to Garrison Hill; the smaller was the area they had to defend. Then a few well-placed shells followed by waves of infantry attacks would cut them to pieces. They successfully used similar tactics at Sangshak and Jessami, so why not at Kohima?

However, cracks were forming in their plans. For the Japanese generals had, in their unquestionable wisdom, decreed that the men should not rely on supplies being sent to them but should live off what they could capture or local food like the British Chindits had done. They limited the amount of ammunition supplied to their troops to what was considered adequate for the task and as in many cases in war, the figures proved to be too low. They had never planned for any fierce resistance from a defeated and retreating rabble that only the British would dare to call an army. It was no contest – the mighty samurai warriors versus the lazy British.

Inside the Kohima garrison, the water supplies were getting low as the defenders slowly lost ground. In the next few weeks, this hill station would see the bloodiest battle of the whole war as each yard was fought over, often in hand-to-hand combat.

# 25
# The Royal West Kents at the Daily Issue Store

By dusk of the 6th April, the soldiers of the Royal West Kent Regiment were dug in on what was the Daily Issue Store, known as the DIS. They were quietly confident having survived the fierce fighting of the previous night when they repelled a series of ferocious attacks from Jail Hill. They understood their enemy, having fought them at Sinzweya in the Arakan campaign. So they watched for the enemy jitter parties that would try to infiltrate their positions.

In the trenches, men drank the tea and ate their rations from their cold metal canteens. They all wanted to smoke a cigarette or two, but waited for permission from their sergeant. It did not come. The sergeant was a great believer in giving the enemy as little help as possible, and that meant no smoking, no lights and no noise.

'Eat up, you lot, and no bloody smoking,' Corporal Joe Brown told his men.

'We understand, Corp. No need to get rattled as even the yellow buggers need some rest.'

'Don't be silly Spike,' Corporal Brown replied. 'The little buggers never stop and there are more of them than there are of us, so one lot rests while the others keep us awake.'

'You are an old worrier, I only want forty winks to dream of Jennie with the long brown hair.'

'The only Jennie you are bloody going to see, Alf, is a little yellow man blowing a trumpet and coming to kill you.'

'He will have no chance of killing me, as I will be ready for him. However, where women are concerned, Alfie has all the luck,' someone added.

'Quiet you lot. The only gift he'll get is a bloody great bayonet in the ribs or a bullet. Remember anything that moves is the enemy, so shoot it.'

'Even if it is you, Corp?'

'If I'm so daft to be on the wrong side of the trench, you can.'

'Hear that Alfie, I can shoot the corporal.'

'Shut up Spike and keep that bloody Bren gun pointed at the bastards. They shoot men for hurting NCOs.'

They were quietly waiting as on the breeze was that smell of cordite and death that lingers over battlefields. Corporal Joe Brown wiped his eyes with a tattered handkerchief, adjusted the strap of his helmet and stared out across the dark and now misty slope towards Jail Hill. It was getting cold and damp. Fingers were getting chilled and a bit numb. Joe fancied a pair of his mum's knitted mittens and a scarf to keep the cold off his neck. Joe was certainly not a sissy, but he knew from the 1930s depression that it was always wise to make the best of a bad situation. Moaning was never any good; better to use your head and work something out. He remembered seeing a destitute middle-aged man settling down to sleep on the cold pavement with old newspapers stuffed inside his trousers and in his jacket to keep him warm. Today he was probably dead or fighting for King and Country where at least he would get clothes, food and shelter.

Joe's thoughts were not allowed to remain undisturbed for long. His men rubbed their hands together or moved their feet in the vain attempt to keep the chill out of their bodies. Otherwise, it was as still as a graveyard just before the witching hour. Until the silence was broken by someone shouting out in poor English and running towards them. 'Heya Tommy! Quick let me through as the Japs are after me.'

Nice try, thought Joe Brown, you did this before in the Arakan using the same words. I may be stupid, but I won't fall for that old trick twice.

'There is another Jap attack coming, fire at will!'

'Thanks Corporal, there's nothing like a bit of action to keep one warm.'

Out of the mist appeared two Japanese infantrymen with bayonets in front. They did not make another yard before their bodies were riddled with bullets. As they fell to the ground, the defenders saw that behind them in the shadows were another fifty.

'There are more of them coming in. Wait for it.... Ignore the noise and fire when ordered to. Make every shot count.'

The shadows came closer but still nothing happened.

'You lot stay calm and only fire at my command.'

Then, there was the sound of bugles muffled in the mist, the noise of rushing feet, and the shouts of 'Banzai!' as out of the mist came fifty men racing towards the trenches. Still they waited.

The enemy came closer with their long, cruel, steel bayonets glinting in the half-light. The very thought of that metal piercing one's hide was enough to put the fear of God into any man. Some prayed; others just vowed to get the slit-eyed monsters before they arrived.

Thirty yards and they came on like an express train. It seemed that nothing could stop them.

Twenty yards....Closer they came until you could make out their faces and still nothing happened as everyone waited for the order.

Then the order was given loud and clear.

'Fire!' commanded the sergeant.

Immediately, a blaze of lead screamed down into the attackers. Only a few Japanese survived the first volley and retreat. However, most of them died less than ten yards from the trenches. The firing continued until the remaining attackers were repulsed or killed.

Afterwards, there was the strange, sudden, stillness as the noise of gunfire was replaced by the cries of the dying. No one moved forward to help the injured enemy, as they knew from bitter memories of Sinzweya that the enemy wounded often killed the medics that came to help them.

Corporal Brown checked that his men were all alive. The Welshman Dowey Evans had cut his face, but it was only superficial. Still, the extent of a facial wound was hard to determine; a small cut often caused a lot of bleeding.

'Dowey, do you need to see a medic?'

'I don't need one at the moment, Corporal! It's only a little scratch, so I'll put a field dressing on it. Mind you, if they have a glass of brandy, then I wouldn't say no. You know that we from the valleys are much harder than the coal we mine. Ta, all the same.'

Typical Welshman, Corporal Brown thought, looks small and a bit fragile, but as good a man as one could ask for when the gauntlet was down. But what were they fighting for? A few square yards of a supply dump. The reason didn't matter, as his job was to fight when ordered, and he was good at it. He could not understand why there was no barbed-wire perimeter or some concrete bunkers. Furthermore, a few tanks would help. The more he thought of it the more disgusted he felt. Surely, they were worth the price of a few rolls of barbed-wire?

'While it's quiet, take it in turns to sleep as the other watch out for jitter parties. Reload and keep the guns dry and clean,' the Corporal told his men.

Half of them tried to sleep while the others loaded .303 bullets into the empty magazines of their guns. It was strange that in the dark one could clean one's weapon and push each round into the magazine without being able to see a thing. Still they practiced stripping their guns down, cleaning and reloading them so often that it was nearly a knee-jerk reaction.

Alfie cleaned the inside of his rifle before lightly oiling the bolt. He moved the bolt a number of times to make certain the action was smooth and replaced the magazine ready for firing. During the Great War, his dad said they had to keep their feet dry and their rifles sparkling. He was proud of his father and his Lee Enfield. It was heavy rifle and even when held tightly to the shoulder it gave a hell of a kick when fired. However, at the end of the day a .303 bullet would stop anything, and that was all that mattered.

Every now and then, the silence was broken by a few shots as one enemy intruder after another was located and killed. The Japanese jitter parties never stopped attempting to infiltrate, becoming more of an annoyance than a danger. If a field mouse had dared venture onto the slopes below the DIS the men of the Royal West Kents would have obliterated it. It was the sort of night when all wise owls and mice stayed at home away from the noise and carnage of battle. Even the movement of the wind through the trees attracted a few bullets, sometimes followed by a cry as it hit someone. Occasionally mortar shells landed on or near their positions usually followed by a few shots from a well-hidden sniper. They watched for the flash from the sniper's gun before riddling the area with bullets. It usually worked, and the sniper was dead or moved elsewhere. The average soldier hated snipers, as they indiscriminately killed anything in their sights, often shooting the medics and stretcher-bearers.

The Japanese occupied some basha huts at the base of the DIS slope to use as a staging post for their next attack, as it concealed them from the British eyes. This could not be left unchallenged. Either the huts must be destroyed or the Japanese displaced from them. So before dawn when the mist was thick and visibility only a few yards the order came to recapture the huts. It was just a few hundred yards and would not be necessary if they had a tank or a flamethrower. However, they did not, so it was a matter of fixing bayonets and up and at them.

'Get ready, lads! We're ordered to flush the enemy out of the basha huts and hold the position. So bring all your gear, water, food, ammo and the radio.'

'What If we can't hold it?'

'Then we bloody set fire to the huts and scamper back to our warm, comfortable trenches. Is that clear Spike?'

'Yes, Corporal.'

They knew the drill. Fix their bayonets, put one round up the spout with safety catch on and climb out of the trench onto one's belly. Slowly crawl down towards the huts making as little noise as possible. No one spoke as they made no noise. They had done this before. It was always the same but now the ground was damp from the early-morning mist and the air cold. Luckily, no one saw them before they stood up and charged the huts. Spike and Alfie took the first hut, killing three Japanese soldiers where they stood. Quickly, they checked for documents. Corporal Brown and Dowey Evans rushed the next hut to be met by a hail of bullets. Dowey was again cut on his face, but otherwise, they were not hurt. Corporal Brown gestured to Dowey to fall on the ground as he pulled the pin out of a grenade, counted to three and threw it inside the hut. There was one blinding flash as the hut and its defenders were blown into oblivion. Rapidly, Brown and his men captured and destroyed the other huts before falling back to the first one and prepare for the inevitable counter-attack. By now, the sun had risen, and they could see the Japanese above them on Jail Hill.

Then they came.

First, the defenders heard the distant sounds of bugles and waited to see the soldiers advance. They were hard to find because they had grass and twigs on their helmets to look like small shrubs. However, Corporal Brown knew of no shrub that moved. He would not call himself an educated man, but he knew his Shakespeare and Bible.

'Men watch out for moving shrubs. Unless it is something from Macbeth or a special Indian tree, I think our yellow friends have all returned to nature.'

Someone giggled at his poor joke as they all watched the slowly moving bushes with apprehension.

'Who's bloody Macbeth when he's at home?'

'He's a Scottish king in a Shakespeare play. You read it at school.'

'I didn't know the Scots had kings.'

'Yes, you do! He had a wife who killed kids and owned a dog named Spot.'

'Don't remember a dog named Spot.'

'Aye, you do. "Out damned Spot," says Lady Macbeth, and the good doggie leaves the room!'

Corporal Brown smiled at the old joke. Now they must wait. He had been there many times before, but it never became easier. He set the firing regulator on his Bren gun to the automatic position so that it would send a stream of lead with such effect that it stopped all comers.

'Be quiet you ignoramuses.'

'Sorry, Corporal forgot you got an education.'

Maybe the noise the men were making did not matter since the Japanese knew exactly where they were. So all they could do was wait in the lull before the storm.

Brown's mind raced twenty to the dozen. His training had taught him that timing was of the essence. They must not open fire until they saw the whites of their eyes or their yellow faces. Keep calm, he told himself. He had been in this situation many times before, but it never became any easier. He checked that his Bren gun had its curved magazine in place with one bullet in the barrel. Then he made sure he had three loaded spare magazines and some loose ammunition within his reach. Finally, he set the fire control of the Bren gun to the automatic position so that it would send a stream of lead capable of stopping the enemy.

Then Corporal Brown saw the enemy advance towards them to say. 'Take your time, lads. Wait for it. Fire!'

The attackers fell to the ground revealing a second group behind them who rushed forward to be met by the roar of Bren guns so that only a few reached the basha hut. Spike bayoneted the first intruder with one powerful thrust to the chest. While Alfie shot the second at such close range that the dead man fell on top of him.

'Hey, someone, please take this body off me!'

Quickly, Corporal Brown pulled the dead man off Alfie.

The attack ended as quickly as it had started, leaving behind the dead and dying.

During the lull, the sergeant appeared with another twenty men.

'Well done Corporal Brown. Let's see how long we can keep them at bay.'

'It will not be for long, Sergeant. They hold the high ground and outnumber us ten to one. We will hold out for most of the day but at night, we haven't a chance with no effective cover and no trenches. By nightfall, we'll be low on ammo and bloody hungry.'

'I think that sums up the situation, Joe. Still, we must do as we are told to 'old 'em, and orders are orders. Let's see if we can keep them at bay for a few more 'ours, then back up to our trenches. So, lads, keep your eyes skinned, fingers on the trigger and a round up the spout.'

'Yes, Sergeant.'

'Are any of our men wounded?'

'Two of us were hit, Appleby and Smithers, Sergeant.'

'Send 'em back to the medics. No sense in sending for stretcher bearers when our lads can take them there.'

'No need to send Appleby, Sarge – he died. Still, Andy Smithers has a chance.'

'Dowey Evans carry Andy Smithers to the medics and have them look at your face. It was never a lovely sight, but covered in red stuff you're enough to frighten even me.'

'Thanks Sarge! I won't be long,' Dowey replied with a grin.

Dowey liked the sergeant's sense of humour and for always being there when things got tough. He was a Hampshire Hog: hard as nails and dropped his h's when he was excited. He was a decent sort, though. Of course, he was, wasn't his mother a Welsh lassie from Swansea – or was it from the valleys. He couldn't remember. It didn't matter, just made the sergeant kind of kith and kin.

The Welshman put Smithers over his shoulder and ran up the hill to the trenches by the DIS position. He did not stop or look back but ran like a bat out of hell expecting to feel the burning sensation of a bullet in the back; however, it did not happen. He was lucky, being half-hidden by the mist. Soon he was running to his trenches shouting, 'Don't bloody fire! It's Dowey Evans with a wounded boyo coming in.'

'I would recognise that Welsh voice anywhere. No Japanese jitter man could copy the sound of the valleys. Let him in, lads.'

As Dowey cleared the trenches, the men cheered, telling Corporal Brown, Dowey had arrived safely. The thought gave them a sense of achievement. Now, two of them were safely back in the trenches. So maybe there was a chance for all of them. It may be slim. However, any chance was better than none.

A few hours later Corporal Brown decided to retreat as the attackers came closer and his men were getting injured. So he ordered the men back to the trenches while giving covering fire before blowing up the last hut. Then, taking one final look at the enemy, he ran as fast as his feet would carry him until he was pulled into the trenches.

'Well-done laddie, you did all you could,' said the sergeant.

'We stopped them three times, Sarge, but we were all getting shot up.'

'Go up to the medics and get a bite to eat. One advantage of having so many cooks, the food is always good and available.'

'We lost four men in the last charge. They were cut to pieces and most no older than me.'

'You did your best lad, write the names down and give them to the officer. When it's over, they'll send their mums the dreaded telegram.'

Only a hundred yards away, nineteen year old Lance Corporal Harman won his Victoria Cross. During the 7th April, the Japanese captured the bakery in the FSD and hid in the ovens endangering the RWK position. Harman single-handedly attacked the ten large ovens throwing a hand grenade into each of them. The action resulted in over forty Japanese dead. The next day the Lance Corporal destroyed a Japanese machine gun post but died on his way back. His sacrifice was not in vain as his actions blunted the Japanese onslaught. The bravery and sheer determination of those few defenders of that lowly hill were to prove significant in starting the defeat of the Japanese in Asia.

# 26
# The Battle of the Tennis Court

*When grenades and bullets replace rackets and tennis balls...*

The CO ordered Charles Brighton to make his men to dig trenches to the west of the DC's tennis court as a fallback position. It would prove vital if, heaven forbid, the Japanese captured the DC's bungalow on the terrace below. He knew his garrison was greatly outnumbered and needed every bit of help they could muster. Now both soldiers and civilians, using spades and any implement, they could get their hands on, dug into the earth. They started to feel safer as the trenches became deeper. These were not regulation trenches, nor deep enough to protect the occupants from shelling, but they did stretch along the edge of the tennis court. The thought of the advancing Japanese drove the men to dig faster. So when a shell fell nearby, the rate of digging increased to a fever pitch.

'Temasen where is the nearest water supply?'

'It is not too far away, sir! The only trouble is that it is in no-man's-land.'

'Do we have enough for now?'

'Yes, but when the trenches are deep enough they will need more food, water and ammunition.'

Charles nodded his agreement as he went to the HQ, wondering if the CO realised just how terrible things were. He thought that the bad feeling between some of the RWK officers, and the CO could only bring disaster. He felt obliged to pour oil on those troubled waters before they reached the boiling point. At times like these petty differences must be forgotten.

Inside the HQ, the CO greeted Charles in his usual warm way.

'Well, Charles, how are your lads shaping up?'

'Fine, sir, soon the trenches will be deep enough to make a good fall-back position.'

'That is excellent news. Are there any other problems?'

'There is no reliable supply of water. Is that true for the whole garrison?'

'Yes. At the moment, that's the picture. However, we are working on it.'

'Let's hope so. I fear that we must expect heavy casualties now the enemy has started an assault on the terraces below the DC's bungalow.'

'I know, but I have some good news! We have one more doctor. The Colonel here just walked in from Jotsoma to give us a hand.'

Charles turned to the Colonel and shook his hand.

'Well done sir! With a few more people like you and we'll have a fighting chance.' He then asked the CO, 'Is there any hope of reinforcements?'

'I do not think so. GHQ doesn't respond, and the RAF is nowhere to be seen.'

'How many Japanese soldiers do you think are coming this way?'

'We think most of General Sato's 31st Division or what's left of them. Our men at Jessami really hurt their 138th Regiment while at Sangshak, the 50th Paras destroyed much of their 58th Regiment. Sato has fifteen thousand men with artillery and has sent five thousand of them to attack Jotsoma. I think that we have ten thousand enemy soldiers waiting to knock on our door. Isn't that right?' the CO asked his intelligence officers.

'Yes sir! Though we believe General Sato is still bringing up more troops.'

Then the DC spoke for the first time. He looked at the officers gathered together and pointed to the map on the wall. 'My Naga report the enemy is using elephants to take artillery onto the mountain slopes to the north and east of us. If that is true, and they are rarely wrong, we must prepare for a heavy bombardment. I think everyone should realise that there is no way out. The road to Dimapur is cut. Sato's men hold the Naga village, Kohima town and Jail Hill. So we must agree on what areas will be defended to the end and make certain our fallback positions are ready.'

'We must hold as much ground as possible while safeguarding the men. When it is necessary, we will retire in stages to Garrison Hill. Is that clear to everyone?' The CO stated.

'Sounds to me a bit like defeatist talk,' remarked a RWK officer.

'Nonsense, we must plan an inner defence to fall back to if we are not relieved or receive no more support. As far as I'm concerned, I'm here to stay and nobody, and I mean nobody, is going to budge me from this position. We have our duty to hold out as long as possible. General Sato is unlikely to let us retreat or allow us to surrender. He wants a victory, and to control the road.'

'How long before we retreat or are relieved?'

'We hold the positions until ordered to make a break out, if that is indeed possible, or until we are relieved.'

'Or we're dead.'

'If it is ordained, then so be it. I will not debate the issue with anyone, as no one knows what GHQ wants except that we are ordered to stay and fight. Any other thoughts are defeatist. You all know what to do. Whatever happens, we must delay the Japanese advance. That is all for now, gentlemen; good luck.'

Charles left the meeting to walk through the wooded hillside pockmarked with holes from enemy mortar fire to go by the cooks calmly preparing the endless stream of tea and food. Maybe by keeping busy, they had no time to be afraid. The shelling would increase as the artillery on the nearby hills joined the mortars to wreak devastation among the defenders.

Charles commanded the tennis court trenches knowing the Japanese held the bungalow below. A shell burst illuminated the scene to reveal a hundred Japanese soldiers advancing only some forty yards away. The attackers fell to the ground as the sky lit up but continued crawling forward.

'Gurkhas do not allow any Japanese to cross the trenches either dead or alive!' ordered Havildar Temasen.

'Yes, Havildar! They shall not cross,' his men replied.

Then the RWK sergeant told his men, 'Hear them, men! Fix bayonets and wait. Steady lads, be quiet and listen for the noise of them coming.'

Someone fumbled in the darkness and then there was total silence. The cold night air was filled with a freezing mist that shrouded everyone so that neither side could see the other. As they waited, they could hear the dripping of water from helmets formed by the condensation of the mist. It was a deadly game of chess where each yard was fought over and changed sides throughout the day. As they waited, they felt the cold on the fingers from the metal of the rifle's trigger.

Charles heard the scuffling noise of men getting off the ground. It must be the enemy or a band of elephants. So he ordered, 'Gurkhas! First platoon open fire.'

The guns roared into the mist where the cries of pain from the attackers came from. The return of fire showed where they were. At twenty yards, the Japanese emerged out of the mist like some phantom army, rifles in front and closing fast.

'All units fire at will.'

By the DC's bungalow, things were rapidly moving towards a climax. The Japanese easily captured the houses on the terrace below. Then they attacked the next terrace to be confronted by the Assam Rifles who kept them at bay for hours. However, like the incoming tide on the seashore, the sheer weight of numbers made the Japanese advance unstoppable. So by nightfall, they held the DC's bungalow and started to advance towards the HQ on Garrison Hill as the Assam Rifles retreated across the tennis court to join the others in the trenches. So the remnants of the Assam Regiment, 3rd Naga, Royal West Kents, and Gurkhas waited in the new defence positions. Each platoon was from the same outfit but often a RWK platoon stood side by side with a soldier from a different regiment.

All at once, there were bodies running, people falling down, and a ghostly mist covering the ground. The sound of gunfire mingled with the cries of the wounded filled the night with a crescendo of noise and death. Some of the attackers were shot many times, even after they had died. Therefore, for the men in the trenches, there was no way of telling who among the attackers was alive or who was dead as the mist again covered their bodies. All they could see was an outline of a man who at any moment could kill them.

Then as suddenly as it had begun, it stopped and all was quiet.

Temasen nodded to Charles then crawled over the edge of the slit trench followed by one platoon to check the tennis court. It was littered with dead or dying Japanese. The others must have retreated to the DC's bungalow and the buildings nearby. Rapidly, they searched the dead for water, documents, or anything useful. After a few minutes, they returned to the trench.

'Well, Havildar! What did you find?'

'Captain we found forty dead; unfortunately, the others must have escaped.'

'That is not too bad, in fact very good.'

Then the usual post-skirmish checks were made.

Was anyone missing? There was none.

Then Temasen checked that the wounded were taken to the first-aid station.

'Do you know what day tomorrow is Temasen?'

'It is Sunday 9th April, sir!'

'Well this is a very special Sunday for us Christians. Do you know it?'

'It's Easter Day, sir, a time for coloured eggs and extra rations.'

'Yes, at home my family will go to church to pray for us and celebrate the holiest day.'

'Well, sir, all of their prayers will be gratefully received.'

'What do you do during your festivals?'

'We, light candles or a lantern during Diwalli, what you call the Festival of Lights, give to the poor and sacrifice an animal. It all depends. However, usually we dance, sing and have lots of fun.'

'I wonder why your people smile even when fighting for your life.'

'Oh that's simple, sir! We believe that life from the cradle to the grave is a struggle against pain and hardship shown to us by our fathers. We grin in the face of danger as to look sad denies the fact of life. For in life all are born and all die. It is only the circumstances and time that change. Some die in their beds or die from disease. The Gurkha soldiers are taught that it is better to die with honour than live to old age in shame. To die by your side would be an honour, sir! Surrender is no option.'

'Why did you become a soldier in a foreign army?'

'My grandfather fought with the British in the Afghan wars. My father fought in the Great War, so now I carry on the family tradition. We only fight for Nepal or Queen Victoria and her children, but never fight for anyone else. It is our tradition, and it serves us well.'

'It is funny because my grandfather was an officer in the Second Afghan war, and father was in the Great War. So I suppose we both fight out of duty.'

They both felt a kind of unspoken relationship that had been forged over the last hundred years by their forebears. Now, like their ancestors before them, they shared the damp trenches and the dangers of war. Charles had never heard Temasen say so much. Either he was ready for the inevitable end of this life, or declaring his loyalty even unto death.

The RWK sergeant crawled over to Charles.

'Can the men take turns in getting a short rest, sir?'

'Yes, of course, Sergeant, usual drill. Half rest while half keeps watch. Change watches every hour. They might as well get some sleep.'

The nightly bombardment began.

'Thank you sir, though I doubt if they'll get much sleep. Can the men smoke?'

'I don't see why not, if the Japanese don't know where we are after this lot, they'll never find us. Keep the men busy, as it's getting damn cold.'

'It's as cold as brass monkeys, sir!'

Charles never understood the term 'brass monkeys' when talking about the cold. It must have had a meaning sometime as every sergeant he had ever met talked about them. He sometimes wondered if military academies should have courses on how to interact with the other ranks. The stiff upper lip or being distant from your men didn't work in the jungle and here on the mountain slopes.

'Captain Charles, sir,' Havildar Temasen said. 'Isn't it time to report to HQ? We will survive without you.'

'I will go in a moment, Temasen, but be sure you're here when I come back.'

'I am not going anywhere, sir!'

Charles smiled, put his hand on the havildar's shoulder, then walked away up the hill. He wondered why sergeants sent their officers back to HQ at times like these. Maybe they wanted to smoke or tell dirty jokes. If the havildar did he would not have known as Charles' Gurkhali was only rudimentary. He would send tea down to the men in the trenches as he felt that was the least he could do.

The CO told Charles that they had located a water supply and were busy collecting as much as possible during the night. Then Charles left to arrange for supplies, including tea and food to be sent to his men before sitting down with Peter to eat their corned beef stew.

'Did you hear about the new doctor who took four lads out across the lines to collect two hundred blankets?'

'Peter surely you don't believe that! Where could he get that many blankets?'

'It seems he heard that one of the captured stores contained blankets. So he went and brought them back.'

'That's a tall story, if I ever heard one. Surely, the Japs guard the stores. Anyway how on earth do you walk through both the enemy and our lines and still be in one piece?'

A cook overheard them and butted in.

'I know, gentlemen; it's unbelievable, but it happened 'cos I was with him. The doctor seemed to feel the way through their lines. He even killed the Japanese guard with his bare hands. Then he loaded us up with blankets and led us back. We got two hundred blankets and not a scratch. That's what I call the luck of the devil.'

'And then what did you do?'

'We handed out the blankets to the wounded while he returned to be a doctor. Blokes like that are not human. He must be mad or blessed with an angel on his shoulder.'

As the cook disappeared Charles and Peter laughed. They both thought it funny that to the cook, any hero must be mad or blessed. Such ideas were common among the civilians like the cook or some NCOs. They believed that you never volunteered for anything, and above all did not take any avoidable risk. However, even the most hardened NCO admired the valiant; brave and foolhardy.

'Charles, was the doctor a hero or just foolhardy?' Peter asked.

'If they had died, the men would say he was foolhardy or even mentally deranged. However, as he survived then he's a bloody great hero. You know all things are subjective.'

'Like they used to say, one man's hero is another man's fool. It is a bit cynical, as I think, anyone who risks his life for others is a hero.'

'I agree. Remember the naval officer, Oates, on Captain Scott's last expedition. When he knew he was dying, he walked out into the freezing night so not be a burden to the others. What a man! I just hope when my time comes I can be as brave.'

'I think we all feel that. We hope to live, but hope to die well, and quickly. During the Battle of Britain, we called pilots aces when they shot down five or more enemy aircraft. Now I wonder as my men in Burma each destroyed that many aircraft in a week. Some of the best pilots were the older Sergeant Pilots, who the brass ignored.'

'I know but don't say it too loud. Let's face it, we are happier fighting alongside Temasen than some officers. I suppose that's treason. Don't know and I really don't care.'

'In the Army and I think in the Navy good sergeants and petty officers are promoted to officers. It may not be the acceptable thing in certain circles, but it happens. That is true, isn't it, Charles?'

'I suppose you're correct. Sometimes in combat the Army gives field commissions that later can be confirmed. It seems the only fair thing to do.'

'Then why do so few sergeant pilots get a field commission? It seems a bloody disgrace. Even if they get a gong, it is different to that given to officers.'

'Take care Peter as neither of us can demolish the snobbery and stupidity that rule the services. Please don't talk about such things among our fellow officers. They'll think you're a red revolutionary and make your life hell. Though I know of some Sergeant Pilots in the RAF who were promoted to officers.'

'You're right; one must not rock the boat in case it sinks.'

'Well I must go back to my men to await the Japanese. They hate each other with equal ferocity. It is a parody of the animals in Kipling's Just So Stories, Nepalese mountain tigers versus the Japanese wolves. Happy Easter!'

'Happy Easter,' Peter replied as Charles disappeared into the morning mist.

Back in the observation post, the major was guiding artillery fire on to the Japanese positions below the DC's bungalow. Peter marvelled as the major radioed Jotsoma the coordinates followed a minute later by shells that rained down on the enemy. So throughout the siege they helped keep the enemy at bay.

Peter's work was less effective. Whenever he contacted the RAF for support he received a typical nonsense reply. Sometimes it was that they had no spare aircraft, or they were too busy to assist Kohima. He felt ashamed when the radio operator would say, 'It'll be better tomorrow sir.'

No one in the observation post blamed him for the lack of air support. Maybe the RAF ceased to exist in this sector! The only planes they saw were Japanese Oscars and Sally bombers. It was the Fall of Rangoon all over again. Only a miracle could help any of them if it was another rematch on those terms.

At dawn on that Easter Day, the men in the trenches had a surprise when the padre visited every man he could find bringing warm food and tea, including those in the front line. He wished them a happy Easter and apologised that there were no pink painted eggs. The men mumbled their thanks and hurriedly tucked into the gifts. His actions remained with the men all that day and for years to come. For this Man of God warmed their hearts as much as the food and drink warmed their cold bodies. They say the way to a man's heart is through his stomach, and that day the padre found their hearts by his unusual Easter blessing.

Up the hill under the cover of the trees the surgeons carried out their grizzly duty while the wounded survived the shelling, partly protected by the deep trenches. The orderlies removed the dead while assessing who would be treated first.

It was a horror story, indeed a scene from Dante's Inferno. During one bombardment, the operating table received a direct hit. It killed the surgeon, his assistants and the patient. Often stretcher-bearers, cooks and other non-combatants were shot by enemy snipers or blasted by shrapnel from an incoming shell. It was total war, where the Grim Reaper rode among all ranks claiming his victims wherever he found them. Shelter became more restricted as the defenders were forced back. Even the air they breathed smelt of death, and they struggled on, apparently oblivious to the grotesque surroundings. The battle became the same routine of attack and counterattack that continued for days. Patches of land were fought over in hand-to-hand combat while the number of dead and injured grew. Few of the defenders were untouched, though most only had cuts and abrasions. Two hundred of the RWK soldiers were so severely injured that they could no longer fight, while only one hundred of The Assam Regiment men remained free from serious injuries.

Without any chance of escape, or hope of rescue, the defenders fought on against endless infantry attacks followed by shelling. Supplies of ammunition, water, and medicine were being exhausted at an alarming rate. And yet, there were still no signs of any relief column or air support.

Surely, someone somewhere cared whether they lived or died?

They did, but they were slow in coming. To quote one survivor, they were coming like the old tortoise when they should have been running like the bloody hare.

Now, when it was nearly too late, GHQ realised the significance of holding Kohima and the road junctions. So supplies earmarked for the Chinese in the north were redirected to Kohima and the artillery at Jotsoma. The Americans and Chinese protested – but to no avail, as the Dakotas and the fighter escorts went to support the Kohima – Imphal positions. The first priority was to keep the airfield at Imphal operational and hold the positions around it. Even now the survival of the garrison on Kohima Ridge was a minor consideration.

Then a Dakota squadron went to Kohima and Jotsoma to drop water, medicine, ammunition, and food. It was not a moment too soon, as on Kohima Ridge, the defenders were in a desperate situation with everything severely rationed. The situation was deteriorating so fast that few expected to survive the next few days. Without more supplies, the hungry, thirsty men knew that soon their ammunition would run out. Then all they could do was to fight the Japanese with bayonets.

# 27
# The RAF Responds

*Supplying a besieged garrison from the air is difficult especially among mountains.*

Before dawn on 10th April, Peter was woken up by a radio operator with a cup of tea in one hand and a grin on his face saying. 'Good news, sir! Our air force has signalled that they're coming to our aid.'

'That is marvellous news, what time is it?'

'It's around six, sir!'

'Wait for me and then we'll get down to guide in our supplies.'

Peter looked up at the clouds that were low over the valley knowing he would fly in these conditions, but would the others risk it? He doubted if any sane man sent an unarmed aircraft to fly over enemy territory to dispatch supplies by parachute on a minute Dropping Zone (DZ) from five thousand feet and encircled by mountains. In peacetime, Peter would never agree to such a foolhardy venture. Unfortunately, parachutes don't fall in a straight line but are blown by the prevailing wind that changed direction four or five times a day.

The airdrop system supplied Orderly Wingate's Chindits in the jungle, but it was different. The Chindits cleared areas large enough for gliders to land and were where the planes could fly low. Here in the mountains the planes must be above six thousand feet, find the small DZ and drop the chutes, before climbing sharply upwards to avoid hitting the mountains. The cloud base was around ten thousand feet, giving five thousand feet over Kohima but only a few thousand over the mountains. The normal ground mist hanging over the position should not affect the aircraft. So he now had to guide them safely through the mountains to drop their cargo into the DZ.

Peter calculated the direction and speed of the wind in an effort to maximise the chance of a parachute landing in the DZ. Any change in circumstances or bad timing would send the supplies over to the enemy. He sat down by the radio with notepad, and maps then spoke into the mike.

'This is Kohima calling incoming flight! Respond. Over,' Peter called out over the radio.

He received no response and tried a second, third and fourth time. Then, there was a distant voice intermingled with static. It was faint but clear.

'This is White Leader calling Kohima! White Leader to Kohima...'

Peter responded. 'This is Kohima to White Leader! I am receiving your weak signal. Over.'

'I hope you can now hear me. This is White Leader to Kohima, will arrive around 1000 hours. Repeat ETA 1000 hours. Confirm. Over.'

'This is Kohima hearing you loud and clear to confirm you are expected here at 1000 hours.'

'White Leader to Kohima what are the conditions like? The static is bad up here, slight cross winds, and poor visibility.'

'Kohima to White Leader we advise you to approach from the east. The wind speed is 10 knots with good visibility.'

'Will do, can we see you through the cloud?'

'Not yet as the clouds are down to eight thousand. Approach from east, descend to six thousand, drop the chutes, and climb rapidly to starboard. It should be straightforward.'

'That's what you think. Flying is not like driving a car, you can't stop or reverse. Still we will do our best.'

'Hope so, otherwise I'll come up and give you a hand.'

'Why does everyone think they can fly better than us.'

'I can fly as well as you.'

'That's a joke I have been flying for six months.'

'I am not joking! I am Squadron Leader Peter Anderson, and I have flown for over two years.'

'Are you the Hurricane ace who was shot down over the Arakan a few months back?'

'Yes, that's me.'

'Well that's one for the books! Whatever happens, I will come in as I can't leave a fellow pilot in the lurch. I just hope the other aircraft will follow me.'

'Thanks, Kohima is ready for you.'

'Great! Wait until you see us. Over and out.'

Peter said to the major. 'There are six Dakotas coming to us that will arrive at 1000 hours.'

'That's good news. I'll tell the DZ men to be ready for parachutes.'

On time, the droning of the Dakota's engines reverberated around the valley and yet there was no visual contact.

The radio burst into action ending the waiting to hear the pilot say. 'White Leader to Kohima sorry I am the only one coming in; other pilots think it's too risky. I'm starting my run now and dropping to six thousand feet so wish me luck!'

'Thanks White Leader, I'm with you all the way. Good luck.'

Out of the air slowly came the silver Dakota. At first, the enemy did not fire as they thought it was one of theirs. The aircraft flew from the east in the same direction that the Oscar and Sally bombers usually came. When they identified the aircraft as a Dakota, it was too late. They opened sporadic fire that failed to stop the eagle of the skies, but on returning to base the plane had minor damage to one wing.

The silver bird descended through a series of jerks like a ship riding a storm. One moment it was up, next down, as she flew towards them. The pilot kept her steady as she flew through the thermals found in mountains and warmer climates, and the bursting shells. Everyone on the ground was afraid that she would disappear in a burst of flames. She did not.

Corporal Joe Brown pointed at the lone Dakota in the sky above them.

'Bet you a fiver that you are safer down here than up there. The whole Japanese army is firing at the poor aircraft!'

'I wouldn't bet a farthing. She's the hungry greyhound racing towards us, and we're the bloody rabbit,' said Alfie.

'Nah, she's more like a little Welsh pit pony, small, alone and totally reliable. I bet anyone a shilling that he makes it,' dared Dowey Evans.

'No, she's a bloody Father Christmas, if not, she should be. For anything that he sends will be gratefully received.'

No one dared to take up Dowey's bet as they all hoped that he was right

Meanwhile, Peter watched the aircraft as he guided it in.

'White Leader you are six miles out and expect you in two minutes. Wind is north-easterly at five knots, so drop the chutes before the road. If my calculations are right, we will receive your cargo near the DZ. Over.'

'Here we come. I can see the DZ. Pretty small isn't it? Over.'

'Yes a bit tight. Over.'

'Dispatchers on the red light dispatch cargo. I can't see the road but can see DZ. Over.'

When the plane was near the road, Peter radioed.

'White Leader to dispatchers, drop the cargo now.'

'Roger sir, parcels going now.'

The red light went on, and the cargo streamed out. Then the Dakota climbed and turned starboard to clear the mountain tops with lots of clear air.

'Good-luck Kohima, This is White Leader leaving.'

The pilot turned to the navigator and pointed out of the windscreen.

'Let's join the rest to supply Jotsoma. Hope the DZ is bigger there. The DZ at Kohima was a bit like trying to bomb a car at ten thousand feet. I hope they get something.'

'You did your best. No sane person could expect us to drop twenty chutes on a DZ that is a few hundred yards long at 200 mph.'

As the parachutes descended the RWK's 3-inch mortars opened up bombarding the Japanese positions. Hopefully, it would keep the enemy heads down while the recovery teams ran across the open ground to drag the precious cargo back to their lines. The first parachute fell short near Jail Hill to land behind the Japanese lines. The next ten landed on or near the DZ before the wind changed direction to blow the others away to the enemy.

'Some of our chutes are going to the nips. Some bloody Father Christmas,' said Spike.

'He's got no reindeers 'cos it's Easter. That is if you forgot,' Alfie replied.

'Let's go and get 'em,' ordered the sergeant.

'Mortars and Bren guns give them covering fire,' a lieutenant ordered.

It was like the Charge of the Light Brigade as men ran towards the enemy to retrieve large crates with different coloured parachutes. They ran as fast as their feet could carry them, cut loose the chutes before dragging the boxes back to the lines. Within twenty minutes, ten boxes were recovered and rapidly opened to identify the goods. Two boxes had medicines, especially morphine, that was sent to the field hospitals. Next was a box full of biscuits, sugar and most importantly tea. Another box contained tins of corned beef. Lastly, there were six boxes of ammunition, but no water. Inside each crate were smaller ammunition boxes marked with their calibre 0.303 and sent to the supply points.

173

One extremely heavy ammunition box contained shells destined for howitzers. Corporal Brown knew the only howitzers were at Jotsoma, not in Kohima.

'Sergeant, what do we do with the shells?' asked Joe Brown.

'Send it to the artillery. You know what to do Joe, so why ask?'

'They are 3.7-inch shells for howitzers. We don't have any howitzers.'

'Stop being silly Joe and let me have a look.'

The sergeant looked inside the crate to find they were 3.7-inch shells.

'Bloody 'ell Joe what next? We have Jotsoma's ammo, and I expect they have ours.

'So what do we do?'

'Send them to the artillery, so they can roll the bloody shells down the hill onto the enemy when the final assault comes.'

'Thanks, Sarge!'

'It's bloody SNAFU again so if we lose it's because someone let us down.'

The sergeant was right, Situation Normal All Fouled Up (SNAFU), or words to that effect. What bright spark thought up the idea of dropping twenty parachutes on a DZ less than three hundred yards long between the Garrison Hill and the Kuki Piquet? Bloody miracle that we got anything, thought Corporal Brown as he watched the enemy collecting some parachutes. He walked between battered trees to sit in a trench preparing for the next bombardment that would be followed by another attack from the Japanese infantry.

Peter sensed the mood change from jubilation when the Dakota came into sight, to despair when parachutes blew over to the other side. He felt a hand touch his shoulder.

'It was not bad for a first attempt, Peter! The weather was no bloody good. It'll be better next time,' said the Major.

'That is if they come again,' Peter replied sullenly.

'From experience I know that when the Top Brass remembers we're still around and sends a plane to drop supplies for us; they will keep on sending more of them. It's just how things work. My mum would say, the poor dears can only think about one thing at a time.'

'I suppose you're right. However, only one came; the others wouldn't even try. What do they think is going on here – a bloody picnic?'

'Peter, never waste your energy on what you can't change. Save it for later. Mark my words before the week is out we'll need all the strength we can muster. You must never blame the workman, always the tools. They've probably had not flown so low before. They'll learn.'

'I'm sure you're right, but I wanted to do my bit.'

'You did. Now we have more supplies, so that's an improvement.'

At the HQ, Peter was surprised to be warmly greeted.

'Well done, sir!' said an NCO.

'Bloody good show Peter,' said the CO.

'Better luck next time eh,' said a grumpy captain.

'Fifty percent is pretty good,' said Charles.

'Gentlemen due to Peter's help we have an air supply route. It may not be much, but it's a hell of a lot better than nothing.' the CO stated.

Then those in the room shouted, 'Hear, hear!'

'I am glad they came as it means GHQ has not forgotten us.'

Everyone laughed because the CO was right. Now they had all lost that awful feeling of being abandoned.

'We recovered ten parachutes. I never expected it to work, so I'm delighted to be proved wrong. The pilot was bloody marvellous, as it must have been like placing a ball in a cup at five hundred yards while riding a polo pony.'

No one was quite sure what a polo pony had to do with it, but all smiled.

'Importantly we now have enough morphine for at least a week that will please the medics and the wounded. I am sure that the Brigade is on its way to relieve us, so let's make history by holding the hill until they arrive. Every day, we hold the enemy at bay is a day longer for our people to attack and defeat them. Good luck and God be with you.'

The airdrops helped the defenders but also supplied the enemy. Rumours circulated that they were shelled by British mortars dropped by the RAF. It was impossible to prove, but it was probably true.

Peter hoped to see RAF fighter aircraft strafe the enemy, but none came.

After the briefing, Peter and Charles talked.

'The airdrop was important because it showed that someone cared whether we lived or died. Today's drop, even if it's the last, has brought us all just what we needed: hope.'

'Why should it be the last?'

'I'm sure the RAF will return. The question is can we can hold the DZ long enough to receive more supplies? Of course, there is the wind, will it allow the chutes to drop on us or be blown to the enemy.'

'Anyhow the CO says the Brigade is on its way to relieve us.'

'I wouldn't bet on it. The CO said what we wanted to hear. He knows that the odds of holding out long enough to be relieved are getting shorter by the day. Count the men and note how many are wounded. Each day we lose more and have no replacements. There's walking wounded refusing medical assistance to fight. The odds are poor, as the enemy replaces their dead with fresh troops.'

'Well, you really dampen one's spirit.'

'Don't mean to, but forewarned is forearmed. Keep your revolver loaded at all times and get a rifle. At the end, we will be fighting for our very survival. See over by the kitchens how the cooks have rifles by their side while they prepare the food? They're no fools, and prepared to take an enemy with them. It's only wise for us to do the same.'

'We are like the long yellow haired, General Custer, and his last stand against the Redskins.'

'Yes I suppose so. However, I hope it will be different as I don't fancy dying.'

'What happened to Custer, can't remember that bit?'

'The Red Indians killed General George Armstrong Custer, and his men in a place called the Little Big Horn. There were no survivors.'

'Whoops! I chose a bad example; I'm an idiot.'

'Still that was a long time ago, since then things have changed. You heard the CO; we're going to make history and survive.'

Peter told Charles about his Susie as they sat beneath the remains of a tree. Charles was pleased that he, and Peter had found true love and affection. Now they both had someone to live for and that always made a man more careful. They shared a brief meal together before returning to their posts. Both now understood and respected each other in a way that only those who face death can understand. From out of adversity comes strength, and with it comes courage and tolerance.

No one fighting in those hills questioned the man next to him, for he was his pal, even if he wore a turban or carried a kukri. They were brothers fighting for their lives at a place from which there was no escape. Nearby the wounded lay in deep trenches near the first aid posts with no hope of evacuation. This was total war, and they all knew it. The Japanese promised no quarter; the defenders gave them none.

# 28

# Even the Japanese have Difficulties

After endless delays, the CO was informed that the Brigade was on its way to their rescue. Next he heard that it may take longer as they first had to capture the road block at Zubza. That was not too bad as it meant maybe a day or two delay. Then the next message was that the Brigade would relieve the artillery at Jotsoma before coming to Kohima. So maybe it would take three days.

It took longer.

The CO brushed his hair away from his eyes and felt the stubble on his unshaven chin. There was too little water to spare for shaving or washing properly. Every drop was precious and must be saved for cooking, drinking and the wounded. He looked at the map to see how close the Brigade was and wondered if they would arrive in time. Was it possible that his men could hold the line against such overwhelming odds? Even if they were ordered to retreat, he would not obey because there were too many wounded to leave behind to be butchered. He was determined to make a stand and to hold the enemy as long as possible. Likewise, the DC refused to leave his loyal Naga as did most officers. The few supplies were rationed and fairly distributed. Guns were issued to the wounded for self-defence or to use on themselves. No one wanted the sick to commit suicide or be mutilated where they lay helpless on the ground.

The Japanese commanders were angry as their advance into India slowed down to a crawl. Too many men and munitions were wasted capturing insignificant targets such as Sangshak, Jessami and now Kohima. Everywhere the enemy surprisingly fought like devils, so that places where the enemy should have been crushed in hours, they took days to capture. The Japanese plan stated that they would obtain supplies from the enemy stores they captured. It did not happen that way as in most places they captured, there were few usable supplies. So now the ammunition and food supplies were low and the men both hungry and thirsty.

Subhas Chandra Bose had promised that the Indian and Nepalese troops would not fight, preferring to surrender or join the INA to liberate India. He was wrong on all counts. At Jessami and Sangshak, they refused to hand over their British officers, choosing to die by their side. Why were the Asian victims of British colonialism now fighting so hard and even dying for the British? The Japanese thought their behaviour was illogical!

Even the British soldiers changed; they no longer ran but faced their attackers like Bulldogs to defend their territory. According to the timetable for the campaign, they should be in Dimapur, but they were not. Things were going wrong in an army where failure was not tolerated.

Meanwhile in Rangoon, the delays and losses disturbed Generals Kawabe and Mutaguchi of 15th Army. The Imperial Staff and the Emperor Hirohito expected all to succeed or die in the attempt. So in desperation they ordered their armies to attack with all force necessary to win. They must die for the Emperor and the Rising Sun. The Sun rose in the east and must never set until victory is assured; now was the time for Japan to rule the world. General Sato in command of 31st Division worried about the impatience of his masters and the problems his men faced. Things worked together to run swiftly like an ebbing tide against him, yet failure was unacceptable. He had noticed that since the Ha-Go campaign in the Arakan, the British soldiers found the courage to stand up and fight. It was as if someone, or something, had woken a sleeping dragon, that once angry, would prove difficult to destroy or even tame. His troops hated the little Nepalese with their curved swords. They were a thorn in his side for they fought with such ferocity that it unnerved his men. These mountain people knew no fear but seemingly enjoyed the perils of war. He now understood why the British had never captured, or even tried to capture, Nepal. Maybe they were not human but mountain creatures, who could only be killed by magic. He knew of such a creature, the yeti, which roamed their lands and maybe protected them. He had defeated them at Sittang and would do so again. They were an irritation to Japan's global ambitions and no more than a flea bite on a dog's back.

He never considered that defeat was possible. Why should he? He had never suffered a defeat and had no wish to start now. Why have the white, cowardly rabbits turned into brave tigers? His men had always defeated the British in Burma from the first battles in Moulmein, until now. Their large garrison surrendered in Singapore when attacked by a smaller army. They had changed, and he was starting to respect an enemy that up until then he had despised.

The U-Go plans demanded the capture of the mountain passes before the monsoon struck. It was too late for this to happen so he must face the consequences. He had been told that the heavy monsoon rains would disrupt the long supply lines when the rivers trebled in size, and the roads became mudslides. Then the only way to move their supplies and equipment would be on mules and elephants. When the monsoon started, ten inches of rain fell every day for weeks on end totally saturating clothes, food, and munitions. Even in the deepest jungle the water ran like a river over the forest floor or continually dripped from the leaves onto the ground beneath. The wooded slopes leading to India became a quagmire of sticky mud that clung to boots and engulfed the vehicles. Even tanks and bulldozers had problems. Diseases increased so that many men died from malaria and pneumonia. Only the unlucky and the foolish would fight through the monsoon. The Japanese generals in Rangoon decided that the invasion of India was less important than the security of the new Burma. Therefore, after capturing the Chin and Naga Hills their armies would go north to destroy the American run Chinese Army. It was a slow campaign, but they had surrounded Kohima and Imphal as well as attacked some airstrips.

On the other side, things were changing for the better. The Allied Air forces flew supplies from India to China and to the beleaguered garrisons in the mountains. The new priority was to supply the important mountain base at Imphal. They transported to the defenders thousands of 44-gallon petrol drums for vehicles, and the Imphal based Spitfires and sent by parachute over a hundred of tons of food and water. Other planes landed on the short airstrip around Imphal bringing in ammunition, medicine, and reinforcements, while leaving with the wounded.

At the British GHQ, the hypothetical penny dropped about Kohima, that the garrison had no way to escape with so many wounded. If Kohima was captured, Imphal would fall, and the road would be open for the enemy to advance into India; so they sent more reinforcements. Cynics later said Kohima was abandoned as a lost cause and the defenders were just casualties of war. Others said GHQ was unaware of Kohima's plight, but how, as Kohima's CO sent daily messages asking for help.

At last, the Allied Air Command sent Hurricane and Vengeance aircraft to attack the enemy around Imphal and supported the Brigade as their tanks advanced towards Kohima from Dimapur. The men fought their way through narrow mountain paths arriving at Jotsoma on 14th April. Then they waited until 17th to destroy the Japanese artillery on the Merema Ridge that endangered their advance, and for 2nd Division to join them before going on to relieve Kohima.

Now all the guns at Jotsoma were directed on the Japanese around Kohima rather than defending their position. Still the Brigadier failed to appreciate the seriousness of the situation in Kohima, though he knew that were at least three hundred casualties awaiting evacuation.

The Japanese knew the Brigade was in Jotsoma but could do little about it. They were low on food and ammunition while getting no help from the Naga or Chin. The few captured supplies were not enough to feed fifteen thousand men as even the oxen had been eaten. That old killer we call hunger now stalked both sides at Kohima.

General Sato ordered his engineers to build bunkers and other defensive measures while increasing the attacks on the Kohima Ridge. When complete he would be better prepared for the inevitable counter-attacks from the advancing Brigade.

'Defeat is not acceptable,' General Sato told his staff. 'There are food and munitions awaiting us in Kohima. Your Emperor demands your obedience, loyalty and victory unto death. We shall never surrender but attack in force, even if it means we die. Kohima must fall and quickly.'

The Japanese officers bowed deeply and left. The adrenaline rush from the thought of victory was no longer driving their tired legs. Now it was clear that for the first time they faced an expensive victory or, worse still, defeat.

# 29

# Ba Saw Settles a Few Old Scores

The Little Pagoda group under Ba Saw continued fighting even though the going was tough, but they were used to that. They cut new paths leaving few signs of their passing that made some think they were a ghost army that flew through the jungle to attack the invaders. Ba Saw carefully planned his last action. First locate the nearest Japanese assembly point, before placing limpet mines in the fuel and ammunition dumps to cause enough damage and commotion to cover their escape; then attack all the bridges and vehicles until their explosives were used up before making for the hills. He did not expect to live, but hoped his men would.

After a cooked meal, they doused the fire before darkening their faces with black charcoal. They looked at each other and gave that characteristic giggle that is so common in the Orient saying 'You look funny' as well as expressing tension. Each man placed a joss stick by a small offering of food near a Banyan tree. Then, in complete silence, a lit lantern was placed in the tree to guide them home and tell the spirits of their intentions. Ba Saw knew that back in the village Tauk would see the light and pray for them. Tauk saw the image and was tense as he shared their perils. His soul went out to them as he prayed for all creatures and spirits to guide his friends safely home or if not, to a quick, painless end. In front of the shrine, he lit joss sticks and knelt before Lord Buddha. Then he took a large paper lantern, lit the candle inside and placed it high up in the Banyan tree before chanting a prayer for purity of mind as well as a request for the jungle to take good care of his friends. Not for the first time did he wonder if he should abandon the village and move to safety. Maybe he should have left with Susie and Marie, but he had no wish to be a burden. In his heart, they would always be his little girls and a living memorial to his late, beloved wife. Tears wet his eyes as he missed them, but then he remembered what his father had told him: Children are a gift from God that we must nurture, but they must become adults and lead their own lives. He believed that he would see them again, if not in this world, it would be in the next.

When Ba Saw found the Japanese bridgehead across the Chindwin River, he divided his men into groups before setting off on their separate tasks. Two men went into the fuel depot where they set three limpet mines on the drums to explode in one hour and rapidly left. Another group set charges in an ammunition dump. It was relatively easy as the sites were in darkness to avoid being seen by the RAF. It was nearly too simple. Both groups met at the pre-arranged assembly point and hugged each other, waiting for the others to return.

Ba Saw discovered there were two large wooden animal crushes, each holding ten fully grown elephants waiting to be taken out and harnessed by their oozies. Then they would be linked to the steel hawsers, and made to pull the barge bridge across the river. He watched this every night for three days to learn what to do. The crushes were made of bamboo woven between existing trees with a gate at one end. They were tough enough to restrain the elephants and prevent them from stampeding at the sound of gunfire. These strong, intelligent beasts became nervous over the sight of fire and the sound of explosions. Ba Saw knew that frightened elephants will go on the rampage causing more damage than any enemy bomb. He hoped that their training had not controlled their natural instincts to run from a fire.

Therefore, he placed three sets of explosives under the landing stage, and by the hawsers that pulled the barges across the river. Swimming in the river, he laid wires underwater from the charges to a firing site on the bank. Then Ba Saw connected the wires to the small box that was on the river bank where the grass was tall. Ba Saw withdrew the plunger to prime the detonator. Now ready, he sent his men to the assembly point to wait for three hours, but if he failed to arrive, they should travel to Dimapur. They reluctantly left their leader as they had an uncomfortable feeling that their friend had no intention of returning but wished to die among his enemies. Ba Saw tied two hand grenades together on a lanyard around his waist to be hidden between his legs under his *longyi*. It was an old dacoit trick that more often than not escaped most body searches.

On the riverbank, things started to happen. The Burmese oozies, elephant handlers, released the elephants from the crushes one at a time. A huge leather harness was placed around the neck and under the forelimbs of each beast. Under the chest, the straps were joined together and attached to the metal chains that were linked to the steel hawsers holding the barges. Thus, the elephants would pull the barges across the river to form a bridge. Ba Saw waited as the elephants pulled the hawsers to drag the linked barges towards them across the river. It took time, but Ba Saw waited as he wanted to destroy everything, for this was to be his last chance to harm the hated enemy. Calmly, he faced the inevitability of death that he no longer feared. Now he breathed slowly while meditating on the goodness of Lord Buddha and the true path.

When each barge was in place, the engineers fixed the securing bolts to link the bridge. It was fifteen minutes before the first trucks started to drive across the bridge of barges now spanning the river. Ba Saw would have waited longer, but a Japanese soldier noticed something in the river and was pointing to what looked like his firing wire. There was a lot of yelling, and someone rushed onto the landing stage.

There was no more time. So, Ba Saw plunged the ignition lever hard into the detonator to set off the explosives. It worked. With a series of deafening blasts, the hawsers were blown into tiny pieces of steel that flew in all directions, followed by the landing stage and the first barge, which just disappeared behind a cloud of smoke. The other barges making up the bridge were carried by the river current towards the other bank as men and vehicles struggled to survive before they toppled into the fast-running water. On the land, all hell broke out as the hail of shrapnel pierced the elephants' thick hides, causing them to run amok. Tons of angry charging elephants damaged everything within their paths. These huge feet crushed tents, supplies, buildings and vehicles as the elephants stampeded away from the river. Chaos rained throughout the riverbank as everyone ran for their lives.

Now Ba Saw could have escaped, but instead he was so delighted that his plan had worked that he stood up to survey the scene and for a moment forgot the danger. It was a second too long.

A bullet hit his right arm followed by another that hit his leg knocking him back onto the wet ground. His war and his life were over as he was surrounded by the enemy who searched him, removing a knife and gun before hitting him on the head. They failed to look under his *longyi* and so did not find the grenades. Then they dragged him to the Kempei-Tei, who handed him over to Aung San's dreaded Burma Defence Army. Ba Saw immediately recognised them as the betrayers of Burma and everything Lord Buddha meant to him. He felt contempt rise up in his body and the foul taste of bile in his mouth, as he saw the men who sold his people to the Japanese. He knew they were insignificant puppets of an evil regime whose Emperor was a god, while pretending to believe in Buddha. What living man could be a god? Only fools or the insane could believe such a thing.

'Now old man you will wish that you had never been born. For you are lucky to be interrogated by the Devil's Helper,' said one of the Burmese.

'It is good,' Ba Saw replied, thinking that maybe he could still cause some damage. He knew from Peter, who the Devil's Helper was and started to look forward to his own death. In the next life, he would be rewarded for dying for his people. Perhaps he would rid the world of this evil Burmese traitor.

The bleeding Ba Saw now faced the infamous Devil's Helper. Bo Ba Tin was dressed as a Japanese Kempei-Tei lieutenant; that is, open white shirt, black cap and jacket. The latter greeted his latest victim by blowing cigarette smoke into his face but Ba Saw did not blink.

'I think you are another silly Burmese rebel? You tell me everything, and you live. Okay?'

'Honourable sir, I know nothing. I'm a fisherman trying to get to my village near Meitkila.'

'Then why do you carry a rifle?'

'It is to protect me from headhunting Naga and the evil British that linger in the forest.'

'Maybe you tell the truth or just a bloody great liar. No matter. Before night comes you tell all. You are my slave and must obey me in everything.'

'Be merciful great Major-san, and give me a chance. Anything you wish to know I tell you.'

The Devil's Helper smiled. It would be good if the captive gave him some useful information before he died. So to gain the prisoner's trust he brought in a doctor to treat his wounds.

He then clapped his hands for some tea to do the same ritual done he had performed so many times before by drinking fine green tea before starting work. Bo Ba Tin did not fear this dirty peasant bleeding from a series of wounds. Soon this son of the soil would bleed even more as Bo Ba Tin tasted the sense of excitement that inflicting pain on helpless people gave him. It was so much better, and more profitable, than sleeping with a woman. He loved his work to the point of being complacent. Few prisoners ever resisted his charms, and many talked so much that he was tempted to cut out their tongues. There were always a few who preferred to die. He thought that the tired, wounded wretch in front of him was helpless. So Bo Ba Tin turned away to take another cigarette from a silver cigarette box and lit it with a silver lighter taken from another dead victim. It was all part of the game played a hundred times before, it puts prisoners at ease before they knew hell for the little time left in their lives.

Ba Saw seized the moment to take from beneath his *longyi* a hand grenade and lanyard. He pulled out the pin before slipping the lanyard over the Devil's Helper's head. The surprised torturer underestimated the strength left in his victim's body. He struggled only to feel Ba Saw's left fist hit his chin with such force that it sent him flying backwards in his chair. The grenade and its lanyard was a necklace of death primed to explode in seconds.

'I send you to hell!' Ba Saw said as he tried to crawl away from the grenade. Each movement was painful, but he moved a few yards before it exploded. Then Bo Ba Tin disappeared behind a cloud of smoke. As the dust settled Ba Saw held the other grenade and waited for the door to open. When it did, he removed the pin from the second grenade and rolled it across the floor into the doorway. In rushed the two guards, who first saw the bleeding figure of Ba Saw before noticing the grenade rolling towards them. It was too late; the grenade blew them into oblivion and destroyed the hut so that the roof and walls collapsed on all inside. From outside it appeared that no one could be alive in the ruins.

People ran around in aimless circles searching for the attackers, never thinking that a half-dead prisoner had caused such damage. They must be under attack from an enemy hidden among the bushes! Maybe it was from those ghost-like Burmese bandits still lurking nearby, waiting for a chance to sweep down and suck their blood. It was common knowledge that these creatures were guided by spirits who flew silently through the jungle to cut off their enemy's head and eat their brains, others who sucked one's blood and ate human flesh.

Ye-Htut watched everything with great concern feeling that Ba Saw intended to die, and he was not going to allow this to happen. At first, he did not know how to rescue his friend, but somehow he was going to save him or die in the attempt. Then a BDA soldier solved the dilemma by walking to the forest to have his last cigarette. Therefore, Ye-Htut simply slid behind the soldier, put a hand over his enemy's mouth and broke his neck. Reluctantly, he undressed the dead man before putting on the dreaded uniform. If he kept a distance from the others, no one could tell that he was the enemy, as the dead man was Burmese and so was he. Then, mustering up all the courage and bravado that he could, he simply walked from the trees into the camp.

People ran around in circles, shouting at each other in Burmese and Japanese. The language barrier made the scene quite comical as one side never totally understood the other. In the end, everyone went off into the jungle to find the assailants. It was the moment Ye-Htut was waiting for to search the remains of the hut. Here he found the wounded, but still breathing Ba Saw. With one great heave, he threw his friend's frail body over his shoulder and walked off into the jungle. He expected to be hit by a bullet or someone stopped them to question his actions. But nothing happened. Then, in the jungle, he ran.

Unknown to Ye-Htut or Ba Saw, Bo Ba Tin was alive, having removed the grenade from his neck before it exploded. He had lost half of his face and an arm, but would live to wreck havoc upon the innocent. For the rest of his life, he would feel the terrible pain, similar to what he had inflicted on others. Morphine and opium replaced cigarettes making him often enter the realms of madness.

At the assembly point, the men were stunned to see Ba Saw being carried like a sack of rice by an enemy. Khin-Lin carefully aimed his rifle to shoot the man in the dreaded uniform without hitting Ba Saw. Only an act of God stopped him from doing so. As his finger tightened on the trigger Khin-Lin wondered why the enemy would carry Ba Saw back to them. So he concentrated hard to see the face that he now recognised as Ye-Htut.

'It's Ye-Htut carrying Ba Saw!'

Then they raced to treat their wounded friend before making a rapid exit. Some guarded the trail while two men made a hammock to carry their leader. Khin-Lin U Thant stitched Ba Saw's wounds after injecting enough morphine to deaden an elephant's toothache.

'Will he survive the journey?' Ye-Htut asked Khin-Lin U Thant.

'Maybe.... He's a tough old tyrant.'

'Yes, tough and bloody-minded.'

So they carried Ba Saw to Dimapur. At the military hospital, the doctors noted that Ba Saw was just hanging onto life by a thread, but hang on he did. The doctors and nurses successfully used their skills on their new patient. Little did they realise as they removed bits of metal and wood from his body, that he was a man of destiny who would encourage others to make the world a better place.

# 30
## Defeat is Inevitable

*Oh! Where would I be when my froat was dry?*
*Oh! Where would I be when the bullets fly?*
*Oh! Where would I be when I come to die?*
*Why somewhere anigh my chum,*
*If 'e's liquor 'e'll give me some,*
*If I'm dyin' 'e'll 'old my 'ead'*
*And 'e'll write 'em 'ome when I'm dead.*
*Gawd send us a trusty chum!*

Rudyard Kipling (1888) Barrack-Room Ballad from
*Plain Tales from the Hills.*

By 13th April, the survivors of the badly mauled defenders of Kohima Ridge were down to their last supplies. They were tired and hungry having fought for every yard, but still the perimeter shrank. They were too exhausted to complain or joke but shared the ration of corned beef and biscuits before washing it down with a mug of tea. All they could do was fight to the bitter end as relief seemed impossible. Somehow, three days later, the Assam and Gurkha soldiers crossed the tennis court to attack the Japanese holding the DC's bungalow. Their brave efforts failed but kept the enemy at bay. Meanwhile in the FSD, the Royal West Kent soldiers were driven back to the Kuki Piquet in hand–to-hand fighting. Every yard was precious, and won with the sweat and blood of the loyal garrison. Next day, the RWK soldiers were moved to Garrison Hill after the Assam Regiment replaced them. After surviving a heavy bombardment followed by attacks from waves of enemy infantry, the Assam soldiers were also forced to retreat. The Japanese position on Kuki Piquet was attacked by mortar fire directed by a severely wounded RWK sergeant as the whole defence consisted of able men and the walking wounded who refused to leave their positions or had nowhere to go. Nobody wanted to wait for medical treatment or be bayoneted to death by the triumphant Japanese.

'I thought we would be relieved by the 15th or was it the 17th. It's the 18th and our race is run,' Peter said to Charles.

'It is now too late. Where are the planes, tanks and 2nd division?'

'Making tea while we die,' Corporal Brown said.

'No way to talk to an officer,' Havildar Temasen stated.

'Sorry, I don't think we can last much longer,' Brown stated.

'Don't know what's come over the corporal, sir!'

'It's all right, Sergeant. Corporal Brown is only saying what we all think. If the buggers don't get a move on, we'll all be dead. I am certain God doesn't have special places for officers and other ranks in heaven! That's correct?'

'Yes, Captain!'

'Heads down, everyone, here they come again. Looks like the enemy are keen on finishing us off. So let's make it difficult for them. Hold your fire until you can see the whites of their eyes. Then fire on my command.'

All the guns of the valiant defenders were aimed across the area littered with rotting bodies to await the enemy. If Dante or Blake wanted to paint a picture of hell, then this was it. They were a mixture of British; Indian, Gurkha, and Burmese troops prepared to die. Each man hoped for a quick death but privately expected a slow and painful one. They all looked identical, encased with deep layers of mud, gunpowder, and unwashed clothing as their tired eyes looked out from unshaven faces often with bandages darkened with dried blood. All that was left of Kohima Ridge was smashed down trees, dead bodies or parts of them, coloured parachutes lying like spilled laundry in the mud or from the remains of trees, broken buildings and piles of brass spent-shell-cases.

'Captain Brighton, do you hear them, sir? The guns are not from Jotsoma – they're the 2nd division's 25-pounders,' Corporal Brown pointed out as a bullet cut through his exposed arm.

'By God you're right! Better go to the first-aid station. You can't die now as it appears that the relief column is coming.'

'No need, sir, it's just a scratch. I'll put on a field dressing and be ready for any attack before the lazy bastards from division get here.'

At that moment, as if by a miracle, the sky came alive as three RAF Hurricanes swept down towards them and low over Garrison Hill to strafe the Japanese on GPT ridge and dropped bombs onto the other Japanese positions to the north. Within the hour, another RAF aircraft bombed the enemy to the west, clearing the way for the relief column to advance into Kohima Ridge. The next thing they saw, as if in a dream, was coming out of the mist, the advanced columns of 2nd division coming towards them. They could make out the tanks followed by the infantry fighting their way through an enemy resolved to stop them.

The sight of the RAF and the advancing columns cheered everyone and think that they would survive. A dying man on hearing that the relief column was near told his doctor, 'I am dying, so please look after those who have a chance. God bless you.' The doctor with tears in his eyes knew his patient had no chance and though not a religious man, mumbled back quietly, 'May God receive you in heaven, my son.' Moments later the man died with a smile on his face. He had done as much as any man could have done and died as he had lived – another unsung hero.

'Where have you been you bloody beauties?' Peter yelled at the RAF.

Peter had difficulty in moving, having been shot in the waist and the leg, while Charles didn't have a scratch and was as strong as an ox.

'Heads down everyone here they come again,' Charles yelled.

'Draw Kukris!' Temasen ordered his men knowing the sight of the curved blade always upset the Japanese.

'Fix bayonets,' Corporal Brown ordered his platoon.

'What a life Spike! One moment we fix bayonets, use them and then take them off our rifles. A bit of a palaver, eh, boyo,' Dowey Evans responded.

'Just do it Evans me lad to keep me happy for a change,' Spike replied.

'Well if it's for you, Spike, boyo, then fix bayonets it is,' Dowey replied.

'Bayonets ready! Line up on the devils. Men 'old your fire until the officer says fire, and 'eaven 'elp the blighter that doesn't wait for the command. Steady lads!' the sergeant cried out.

Charles waited until the Japanese soldiers were a hundred yards away to order, 'Fire!' However, through the mass of lead, the attackers still advanced over the bodies of their comrades.

'Up and at 'em, lads and give 'em a taste of Sheffield steel!' the sergeant ordered as he led his men into combat.

'Kukris in front! Kill them. Kill them!' ordered Havildar Temasen as he charged the enemy.

The sergeant and the havildar were in the middle of the fighting, slashing and cutting the enemy. Then the inevitable happened: the sergeant was bayoneted, fell to the ground to be beheaded by a sword yielding Japanese officer. This enraged Temasen so much so that he single-handedly charged six Japanese, crying out as he went. The Japanese stood petrified as he charged at them waving his kukri, and with a single stroke, cut the head off the officer who killed his friend. Not stopping, he turned to slash another soldier. Then a bullet struck his face knocking him backwards. He stood up, wiped the blood from his eyes and yelled for his men to come to him. They did. He was a fearful sight with blood streaming down his face as they killed the enemy. Finally, they retreated, exhausted, with one man carrying Temasen on his back.

This last encounter was terrible, but Charles kept the men together until he was shot in the face by a sniper's bullet. An orderly bandaged his wound and gave him some morphine. Then Peter and Corporal Brown carried Temasen and Captain Charles to the first aid post.

The relief forces took over the front line while their tanks provided the firepower needed to keep the enemy at bay. So at last the siege was over – yet the battle had only just begun. The Royal Berkshire Regiment and the rest of 2nd Division now controlled Kohima Ridge and started to evacuate the survivors. The uninjured survivors helped their wounded colleagues down the hillside to the waiting lorries. They looked like tramps, but inside each man was a heart that beats with pride at having the Japanese. Never before, or since, had fifteen hundred men, including civilians, fought and held at bay fifteen thousand enemy combatants for such a long time or so effectively. As the CO said, they had made history. For without tanks, barbed-wire or deep trenches and bunkers, they bloodied the enemy's nose and inflicted a wound that started the end of the war. Alone, cold, miserable, low on supplies, and without shelter, they survived, to win by sheer courage.

Back in England, Mai woke up screaming, having dreamt that Charles had been injured. Calming herself, she went downstairs to find her mother, Lynette, in front of the jade tree with tears streaming down her eyes. Sensing Mai's anguish, Lynette said, 'I saw Peter and Charles shot, but they are alive and will live. Around them lay many dead bodies on a small hill with only broken trees and deep bomb craters. I saw men smiling, even those with bloodied bandages over their faces as they walked to some lorries.'

'Mama, what does it mean?'

'It means, my dearest, that our men are safe and will come home to us. They must have been through hell, so we must be strong for them.'

Then both women lit joss sticks by the jade tree and prayed.

'You mustn't tell your father as he will worry.'

'I will not say a word to dad or anyone as I don't want him to worry.'

Little did they realise that Paul had heard every word and as usual remained silent. He prayed to Jesus in thanks, and in the hope that they would return in one piece. Whenever Lynette left their bed in the middle of the night, he silently followed to hide in an alcove. He knew that she could see things thousands of miles away and wanted to share her visions. A smile crossed his face as he lay in bed pretending to be asleep when she returned.

Lynette was gifted with what the Buddhists call the third eye, but she could never tell how much Paul knew. In fact, she would often admit that she did not know when Paul proposed to her. She blamed her failure to understand him on the fact that she had no jade tree to communicate with during her meditation, until after they were married. However, even now she never really understood her husband, and he was glad she didn't. He loved Lynette more than life itself but did not want her to know some of the secrets he learnt in his new job in Military Intelligence, especially what he knew about the fierce fighting occurring around Imphal and Kohima.

# 31
# The Way Out

The three-ton Bedford lorries bumped down the narrow mountain tracks carrying the remains of the Kohima Hill garrison to Dimapur. At first, snipers fired at them, with little effect. Inside the lorries, they were cramped together like cattle on the way to market, the walking wounded painfully lurching against each other. Officers rubbed shoulders with enlisted men with little notice of rank. They needed medical attention and some well-earned sleep. Everyone was glad to be alive and proud of being undefeated. The men's tired eyes sparkled with pride having for stopping The Japanese where all others had failed.

They were a pathetic bundle of dirty men with unshaven faces and sunken eyes through lack of sleep; whose clothes were encrusted with dirt, blood, cordite, and all the smells of war. Their faces had a greyish tinge mixed with mud and unwashed beards. It was impossible to see who was a Briton, an Indian, a Gurkha, a Naga, or a Burmese. All looked like tramps who had seen hell and wearing torn uniforms. Dried bloodstained and dirt impregnated bandages covered their wounds that took on a dull appearance from the dust and smoke. During the journey, some wounds started to bleed again and others just hurt like hell.

In one of the lorries were Peter, Charles, Temasen and a mixture of Gurkha Rifles and Royal West Kents soldiers; all were injured but could be transported without taking up stretcher space. Ahead of them drove the lighter vehicles taking the urgent stretcher cases to a hospital. Corporal Brown and his men shared their last cigarettes while leaning out of the back of the lorry. Strangely, they were forged in the heat of combat into a brotherhood of heroes. If they had a pot of tea, they would share it. They were a family forged from pain and suffering – the Kohima Ridge survivors.

'Havildar, would you like a fag?' Corporal Joe Brown asked Temasen.

'No thank you, Corporal,' Temasen replied. 'I don't smoke but thank you for asking.

'No bother, Havildar, it leaves more fags for the lads. After that lot, we all deserve a gong from the King at Buck House, especially your lot. Your men fought like bloody tigers!'

'Thank you, I think we all fought and died like brothers. One day our children will be proud that we fought at Khohima.'

'But why do your people fight even harder against the Japanese than anyone else. The Japanese, pardon me saying it, is a similar in race to you people.'

'We are a different race and culture. Isn't your King of German descent?'

'Cor, yes, I never thought of it like that,' Brown replied.

It was always after the fight that one shook and felt afraid. Like in the early hours of the morning nightmares relive the horrors of one's life. So Peter remembered when as a prisoner fear had taken over his body. His cousin had destroyed his youthful confidence for now he had seen the Devil and all his works. First, there was the Devil's Helper and then the carnage at Kohima. He felt suddenly cold as his body shook while the palms of his hands were wet with sweat. He told himself that it was the after-effects of being shot, but somehow his brain did not agree with his statement. So he held tightly on to the tailboard with such force that his knuckles went white. Only those who have suffered the humiliation, pain and terror induced by torturers can understand. Bo Ba Tin broke his body and mind reducing him to a plaything that, when fed up with is thrown away like a broken child's toy. Of course, Temasen was right; one must forget this memory, but how?

His mother must never know that her nephew was his torturer. He could not hide the scars, but she must not know who made them. The shame would kill her. How could he tell her that every nation has their Devil Helpers? Such thoughts and ideas are best left alone.

Then Temasen said. 'I see a little chapel in Dimapur where Susie and Maria pray for us and light the candles to guide us home.'

'Thanks, I can imagine that as if I were there,' Peter commented.

Charles interrupted the conversation in an attempt to cheer them up.

'There you are Peter. What is better than going to the warm arms of your woman? I tell you there is nothing more satisfying. You may be a very dirty, unshaven, beggar-like, smelly creature with bandages and holes all over you, but you still are her man. Never underestimate the power of a woman. When they give you their love without question then you have the greatest gift that any man can ever require.'

'Yes indeed, though I'm sorry Mai will not be in Dimapur to give you some TLC.'

'I admit that as an older man, I still like a bit of tender loving care. It is much better than a bottle of beer or a double gin and tonic.'

Charles turned towards the men and addressed Corporal Brown.

'Corporal Brown! What do you want – a drink or a good woman?'

'I do not want to cause offence, sir! I would like a good woman or, better still, a loving woman to feel in paradise. A cool beer would be nice, but different.'

'Well said Brown! You're like me who believes God created Eve for Adam. For a man without a woman is as useless as a cart without a willing horse.'

'I am not so sure that Mai would like the idea of you two being a horse or cart,' Peter joked.

'So don't tell her,' replied Charles.

'They say women are a different species to men. You can't live with them, but you can't live without them. So life is a confusing paradox.'

'I don't believe you; you made that up.'

'The second no-no is to ignore her. Wasn't it Shakespeare, who said nothing is more terrible than the wrath of a woman scorned?'

'You win point two.'

'Then be grateful to be alive and think of tomorrow.'

Peter started to smile at his friends who though badly injured, worried about him.

'How's the head Temasen?' Peter inquired.

'It is still in one-piece Peter, sir!'

'Your head hurts like hell, but you won't say so. It is like your bloody feet used to feel.'

'Remember the Buddhist teaching that all life is suffering that must be endured with patience and understanding.'

'How can I forget how we first met? If I remember you were all beaten up, bleeding, and had a few toenails missing.'

'Bad things are best forgotten. Think good thoughts like a loving a willing woman, warm bed, fine food and friends. My memory is not so clear since I was shot in the bloody face. Now I cannot remember anything before Kohima. To tell the truth I know little only, all I remember is good and nothing bad. I think it is best if you also forget the horrid things.'

'I know how you feel. I pray that we will find peace of mind with only the scars to remind us. It is easier to understand getting shot in battle. Like you, my wounds hurt, but I never saw who shot me. However, the wounds inflicted by Bo Ba Tin poisoned my soul to remain forever in my mind.'

'Nonsense, you must forget such things. I see your Susie and the pongyi and feel good. You do too. Remember only the good, forget evil.'

'I feel the pongyi's path of light and pray that they are safe.'

The conversation was overheard by Charles, who leant against Peter as he was weak and his head hurt like hell. It was much worse than having one's teeth pulled without an anaesthetic.

'See Peter, Temasen has it all worked out. Always trust the sergeant to know what is best. As my grandmother said we must always look on the bright side of life,' Charles urged his brother-in-law.

'Cheer up; we will soon be in Dimapur and out of this madness,' Charles added. He worried that Peter and Temesen were becoming morose and troubled whenever they referred to their imprisonment. It was like some fatal disease that never left their bodies.

'Captain Charles is right Peter. The past has gone, and the future is yet to come. God knows our futures are a clean sheet on which we will write our lives without too many concerns over the events of yesteryear. Today is better than yesterday and tomorrow will be even more so. Soon you and Susie will be together making babies and laughing like the good people you are.'

'What do you really believe Temasen?'

'Simply that life is a process of good and bad. When a child you adored your mother and trusted and loved your father. For that is correct. Then one day you meet that someone special and there were fireworks when she makes you feel alive, safe, happy, even unsure, and you know you are in love. It happens to old men like me. I remember that when a child, I saw beautiful butterflies flying over the grass blown by the mountain breeze. At other times, I felt the warmth of the sun even on the darkest days when snow covers the mountains. So you, like all of us, are called to your love in the same manner that a moth is attracted to the light. There can be no escape for us men because women are both lovely and delicious while driving us poor men insane.'

Nothing else was said.

Peter saw the smile on Charles's face and the longing in Temasen's eye. He indeed was the lucky one. He felt close to his friends who, though injured, still had time to encourage him.

'If God wishes, we will reach safety, be healed, and again enjoy our families and friends,' Charles spoke totally oblivious to the fact that all around him were listening.

'We all say Amen to that, sir! If God is just, and I'm sure he is, we will soon know the songs of the valleys and the love of our women,' Dowey said for all of them.

Charles felt embarrassed at having expressed his private thoughts in front of the men. Looking around he saw them as a bunch of ruffians, capable of scaring any pirate into surrender, while giving him that look of respect.

'Let's have a singsong – how about singing Bread of Heaven?' Dowey suggested.

'You can always trust a Welshman to get all religious! I think we ought to sing about the Grand Old Duke of York – who took his men to the top of the hill and marched them down again! Bit like us moving between Dimapur to Kohima to Dimapur, then to Kohima, and now back to Dimapur,' Joe Brown commented.

So they sang as many songs as they could remember. Many would make the padre blush, but he did not as he knew they were celebrating being alive. They didn't look much but had the hearts of lions, that is except for Dowey, who had a heart of his beloved Welsh dragon. As they sang out, others in the following trucks joined in, making the journey seem shorter and less bumpy.

# 32
## Dimapur at Last

It was dark when they arrived in Dimapur. The last few miles of the journey were too much for some of the stretcher cases; so they died. In a lorry, a nurse held back her tears as a young man, no older than she, died under her care. She had done everything to keep him alive but the bleeding never stopped. Then she heard the weak voice of another patient addressing her. She moved closer to hear what he was trying so hard to say. 'Cheer up lassie. Frankie wanted to die with his boots on among friends and not shot in his bed by a Japanese bastard. He was my brother, so I know how he felt. We both thank God for sending you to save us. You're our Angel of Mercy- like a dream come true -if I live to be a hundred I will never forget you. It is a pleasure to die in such lovely company. May God bless you and keep you safe.'

His words opened the floodgate of her emotions, letting tears run down her face. She bent over and kissed him on the forehead. Whether she realised it or not, the young man decided that she was worth living for and vowed to marry her and did. It just proves that a little loving goes a long way.

Peter and Corporal Brown watched the lines of trucks; tanks and supplies passing by as they travel to Kohima. They looked at each other, and dare not say what was passing through their minds. Why, oh why couldn't they have come a week earlier, before so many died? It was a question that seventy years later has not been answered.

'Who said we didn't have any reserves left?' Corporal Brown said.

'Now the division will finish the job and get all the glory,' Peter replied.

'It's not the why that matters; it's the Welsh and all of you that counts for holding the bloody line. It's in our blood, just as we held the Zulus at the Battle of Rorke's Drift in the South Africa. We showed the Japanese that they can lose, and we won.'

'Were we really up against a whole Japanese division?' Joe asked.

'Yes, we survived even when the whole 31st Japanese Division attacked us. I reckon there were fifteen hundred of us against fifteen thousand of them like at Dowey's Rorke's Drift.'

'No wonder they kept on coming,' Alfie groaned.

'I reckon we made history and taught the Japanese Army a lesson they will never forget. We probably saved the whole of bloody India.'

Then they were quiet, savouring being alive and hoping their wounds would not kill them. Many like Charles, were too weak to talk and looked a ghastly white through loss of blood.

The trucks halted beside a row of tents that were erected in front of the military hospital. In the darkness, the lighting revealed that all around them the place buzzed with activity. People appeared and disappeared as they attended to the needs of the wounded and the dying as others quietly removed the dead for burial.

As the tailboard was lowered, they were helped down from the lorry by the orderlies and nurses. Stretcher cases were rushed through the hospital doors to the awaiting operating theatres, though others went to the mortuary. The doctors, nurses, and medical orderlies at Kohima did such sterling work that many men were saved. The non-urgent cases were taken into a triage tent to be evaluated as to the urgency of their condition. The triage staff expected to find wounded and worn-out men but were shocked at what they saw: men covered in dirt and blood, some hardly able to walk, being helped along by a friend. All were pale, weak, and exhausted, but had a smile that said, thank you God for saving me. Luckily, it was dark so the horror was not as visible as it would have been in the daylight. It was a scene too terrible to record on film as men of all ages, some with limbs missing, all with blood and grime encrusted clothes, waited patiently for help.

Outside the hospital, a young doctor shared a cigarette with a nurse to try to overcome the shock at seeing a long line of bedraggled men helping each other walk to the hospital. In the half-light and with the encrusted dirt, it was impossible to tell who was a civilian or a soldier.

'They're like one closely-knit group of brothers where rank, colour and nationality are lost in a brotherhood forged by war.'

'That is very romantic, Sister, sadly it is not true. They all should be treated equally and with respect, whatever their race or creed. Maybe one-day people will forget their differences to become equal.'

Each man was separated according to his needs and ranks. Peter and Charles felt a great loss as Temasen was rushed off to the operating theatre and Corporal Brown, and his men were ushered elsewhere. It was the way of the Empire and yet, whether they liked it or not, they were part of it.

They were examined, given a badge with name, rank, serial number, and told where to go. Once labelled, orderlies helped them make their stumbling way to ward 10A, that to their amusement had written in large letters over the door:

Woman's Maternity Unit
Strictly, No Men Allowed
By Order – Matron.

'Hey Charles, read the sign. Someone thinks we're women.'

'No Peter, they think we lost our manhood and not just our senses.'

Once inside the ward a dictatorial-looking sister took charge. Charles had to be helped to bath and have his bandages replaced. Peter, on the other hand, was given a towel and soap and sent to the showers. An orderly helped him undress and then removed his clothes, which would be burnt along with the rest of the tattered uniforms. Peter thought that the Sister was trying too hard to keep her hospital sheets clean. What he fancied was a hot bath with Susie and a gin and tonic. However, the Top Brass had not ordained such frivolities, instead it was carbolic soap, and cold showers.

Under the shower, Peter felt the joy of clean water running through his hair and over his face. As he washed, the water around him turned a dirty brown in colour. Slowly, he washed away the grime, smell, and horror of Kohima. After his allotted five minutes in the shower an orderly dried him and with a towel around his waist, he was helped to another room where there were ten identical hand basins each with some shaving soap, a brush, and a safety razor. After this Peter was placed on a chair to be shaved by an orderly who removed Peter's scraggy beard. Peter thought that surely the man had better things to do. Maybe they thought they would try to commit suicide when they were celebrating being alive. He understood the reasons when a nearby officer, who was too weak to stand, stumbled and was caught by the orderly. They were like tired children, needing help to wash and brush their teeth before going to bed.

Soon, rows of nearly sweet- smelling officers wearing hospital gowns were lying in bed. Peter was delighted to have Charles in the bed next to his, but was alarmed at how much older he looked.

A doctor examined Peter, felt his pulse, and stitched his wounds.

'You're fine – we'll change the bandages and watch for signs of infection.'

So that was that, Peter thought, as he felt a jab of morphine in one buttock and a jab of what the nurse called 'a wonder drug' in the other. He was falling asleep when they took Charles away. He prayed that Charles would live, for Mai's sake and for his own. He must not lose Charles, not now. He tried to say the Lord's Prayer, but the words got jumbled up. He felt that, power and ability without compassion were like a world without God or without love. With that thought he fell into the deepest sleep possible that even the bells of hell could not disturb.

In the operating theatres, surgeons and nurses worked without respite for days removing bits of bent metal from torn bodies. They amputated mutilated limbs with horrific regularity. Some patients died on the operating table unable to survive the anaesthetic, or were too severely injured to live. In theatre seven, Temasen lay unconscious as a surgeon worked desperately to remove the shrapnel embedded near his left eye. With great care, patience, and a steady hand, the surgeon eased out the ragged bit of metal from just below the eye without damaging it or its nerves. Once removed the evil piece of shrapnel was thrown into a bucket to join the rest removed during the day. The surgeon cleaned the wound, tied the sutures and smiled at his theatre nurse showing his satisfaction. For though there would be a scar, the patient would have full use of his eye.

As Temasen was wheeled away the surgeon hurriedly sipped cold tea before scrubbing up for the next patient. Many years later, as a consultant surgeon, he told his students in the London Hospital Medical School that he learnt more about surgery at Dimapur in a few weeks than anywhere else in his whole life. They, being medical students, had no clue what he was talking about.

Nearby a surgeon was facing a dilemma as whether to operate or not. It was the type of wound that a year ago he would never have been able to deal with. However, since then he operated on similar cases. All presented serious risks, but if he did not operate, the patient was facing a long and painful death because a bullet after hitting the cheekbone was deflected towards the brain.

'What do we do about this case?' the surgeon asked his assistant.

'The bullet's too close to the brain so it may be better to leave it in and send him home.'

'That is one option. However, if we leave the bullet inside the head, it will move as he talks, breathes and eats to be painful, even fatal. So I will locate the bullet, and remove it. Only if that is impossible, we will leave it in.'

'I'm sure you're right, but it's risky. So let's start and with God's help, we will succeed.'

'Amen to that,' said the surgeon as he started to explore the wound.

Carefully, he probed and enlarged the entry point to get more access to the inner tissues. Moving slowly, he felt the hard metal embedded in the jawbone.

'He's lucky – the bullet is wedged in the maxilla. I can remove it without causing more damage.'

It was not easy to locate the bent lead from around the jaw and remove it. Still, it was done, and the lead was ceremoniously cast into the bucket; the wound cleaned and sutured. The surgeon made the suture tidy so that the scar would be minimal. He was proud of his neat suturing. A nurse once said that when he was older, he could make a good living sewing, as his technique was worthy of the finest seamstress.

'Well he's certainly a lucky son of a gun. What's his name?'

'Captain Charles Brighton, Gurkha Rifles.'

'Remind me to check how well he does when I do my rounds.'

'Now I intend to urinate to make myself more comfortable before drinking another hot, milky, sugar-laced cup of what they dare call tea. Why must we drink such awful tea when all around us are some of the world's finest tea plantations?'

'It's army life,' said a nurse as she removed his blood-stained gown.

Charles recovered with only a headache, a sore jaw and a neat scar across his cheek that was hidden by the clean bandages.

As Charles was wheeled out the next patient came in. The theatre sister read that he was a Sergeant Jeffries, aged twenty-two, with severe head and body wounds. The anaesthetics soon made him unconscious so that the surgeon could start the examination. The right eye was beyond saving and the other wounds extensive. It seemed that his injuries were days old and covered only with field dressings. Clearly, he was never examined by a doctor in Kohima but was another who had injected himself with morphine from his first-aid kit to carry on fighting. The surgeon felt sick as he wondered for how much more could he stomach of this mutilation of young men. It took an hour before the surgeon removed four bullets and one twisted piece of shrapnel. The young man was alive having lost an eye, with limited movement in his left arm, and a definite limp. Back in England his patient would be near his loved ones as surely his war was over.

# 33
# A Time for Secrecy

*Careless talk costs lives.*

A slogan from World War Two.

Throughout Dimapur, the news of the arrival of the bedraggled survivors from Kohima caused a sensation with everyone talking about the shadows of men who came from the mountains in the middle of the night. Rumours circulated the bars and marketplaces of civilians caught up in a battle with nowhere to hide, but nobody believed such a wild yarn.

All around the town stories were told, over drinks, about cooks who to survive were forced to fight single-handed against the Japanese. Others talked of hand-to-hand combat and trench warfare. The old hands told those who spread rumours to stop being silly because there would never be another Somme, and such stories were circulated by the Japanese to reduce the morale of the British troops and disgrace General Slim for abandoning his men. If the full details were published no one would have believed it. It sounded like a schoolboy's novel of the few brave soldiers against the many foes. For most people, what happened on the Kohima Ridge would always prove hard to believable.

When people asked questions, a finger was pointed to the Ministry of Information poster that said 'Careless Talk Cost Lives.' It was true as all around the Assam hills Japanese spies listened to casual talk or learnt from the soldiers when drinking beer, or sleeping with a call girl.

It was always that way in war and probably will continue to be so.

GHQ when unable to find a good excuse for having abandoned their men at Sangshak, Jessami, and Kohima, chose to forget what happened. Instead, they publicised the successes in the Imphal plains and 2nd division's advance on Kohima town. Any mention of civilians caught up in a battle would spread panic like the wild fire through the streets of Dimapur. Anyway, who would believe that some men of the Royal West Kent Regiment along with Indian and Burmese soldiers, held fifteen thousand Japanese across a tennis court?

To keep the truth secret, the authorities ordered that all the defenders of Kohima Ridge were dispersed to remote areas where there were no reporters to record their stories. Therefore, all the wounded were sent for rest and recuperation in Ceylon. There, it did not matter what they said as they would be miles from the front. History is written by the victors, so the Siege of Kohima Ridge became a minor part of the battles in the Imphal region. Even the most honourable generals re-write history when it suits them, and Slim was no exception.

The commander of the garrison at Kohima sat down at a large teak desk to write his report determined to describe the gallantry of his men without criticising anyone as it was the gentlemanly thing to do. He thanked GHQ for the privilege of commanding the gallant men who held Kohima Ridge from 4th April until 18th April 1944. He recorded the events, recommending awards for bravery for many more than actually received them. However, that is the army way. The report told of a surgeon who walked through enemy lines to help them, the padre that kept the men's spirits high as he blessed their Easter and the major who directed the artillery from Jotsoma to fire on to the enemy.

He stopped, re-read what he wrote, and sipped some Assam tea. He recommended that they strike a special medal for his men – the Kohima Cross – for they had made history by holding the enemy for fourteen days without tanks or barbed wire. He then told of a Deputy Commissioner and his Naga tribesmen that stayed to carry the wounded to the medics, ran messages, and fought. Of a blinded sergeant who remained by his Bren gun so his men would not be afraid and the corporal who single-handed destroyed the Japanese in the ovens. Of the cooks and medics that worked nonstop and the Indian Army survivors from Jessami, who stood their ground to fight alongside regular soldiers.

Again, he paused to inhale the nicotine from his cheroot to feel invigorated. Then he continued to describe the courage and fighting spirit among his men who outnumbered ten to one, held Garrison Hill. Now he remembered with anger, but it didn't show in his report, about the lack of air support. He finished by recommending that all attacks on the Japanese positions should be preceded by intense artillery and aerial bombardment. He noted that after the Japanese captured a position, their engineers built bunkers and fortified defences on all vital points.

When finished, he gave the report to his secretary to type and mark it 'Top Secret'.

'Please type this with a copy for me. When you have finished I expect both copies and the carbon paper. I hope you understand that nothing you read can be repeated. For what is in this report did not happen until someone someday says it did. Is that clear?' the tired CO told his secretary.

'Yes sir! I will make only two copies, one for GHQ and one for you. The carbon paper is to be given to you. Don't worry, my lips are sealed, sir!' the startled secretary stated.

'Good. I don't want you to be shot for treason. This story is too sensitive to leak out,' the CO replied before putting on his hat and calling for his driver. 'The hospital, if you please.'

Once in the hospital compound he wondered how his visit would be received by the men. Here he was in a clean uniform and uninjured, whilst they lay wounded in bed. It would take years, or an eternity, to forget the lines of tired men, the sight and smell of the dead and the petrified civilians.

On the veranda, he found the less seriously injured sitting in chairs or lying on beds. He put his shoulders back and walked up the stairs to where his men were. Each step took him nearer to them and closer to how they felt.

They were all delighted to see their old man and greeted him with smiles. Each man addressed him correctly, and many thanked him for helping them survive. It was rapidly becoming the most emotional day of his life.

'And how are you doing?' the CO asked Dowey.

'I'm much better than I was a few days ago, sir.'

'Indeed you all look and may I add, smell better than before.'

Everyone laughed at his weak joke, and that made him feel proud.

'So do you sir,' said Spike.

'Now watch it you lot,' Corporal Brown ordered.

'It's all right. It feels strange without my stubble and wearing clean clothes,' the smiling CO replied. The ice was broken as they all shared their common bond as survivors of the Siege of Kohima Ridge. The CO accompanied by the padre, continued visiting each ward. They started to enjoy the men's company as if they all wore a special badge of courage. Their faces said, never defeated or broken, just worn out and in need of an overhaul with a bit of rest and recuperation.

Peter was getting stronger but worried about Charles and Temasen. To make matters worse he heard nothing from Susie. So he was feeling particularly maudlin when the ward sister announced. 'Squadron Leader Anderson! I am pleased to tell you that Captain Charles Brighton and Havildar Temasen are recovering from their injuries.'

'Oh, thank you, sister. Thank you very much indeed. Do you know when I can see them?'

'Captain Charles is coming soon, but is still weak, so let him sleep until tomorrow.'

'Thanks again, sister.'

The sister stayed by his side before asking, 'Are you up to receive some visitors?'

'Do you mean that I'm allowed visitors?'

'It's not a prison you know! It's a hospital and be bloody grateful that you made it, sir!' sister reprimanded him with a seductive smile.

Before he could apologise for appearing ungrateful, she had left him. Maybe she wasn't so bad after all, just fed up like the rest of us, Peter thought before wondering who would visit him.

'Come in, he's as decent as I can make him,' the sister told his visitors.

Peter heard the laugh of Jim Ashton, who came in sight followed by two others.

As they drew near he smiled, and tears blocked his eyes, for standing in front of him were Susie and Maria. He felt Susie's hand in his and blushed as Jim spoke. 'Well Peter, you old rogue! I find you here among the beautiful nurses and such a kind sister! So after all of their efforts the little yellow fellows still could not keep you. Tonight the squadron will drink to your health and that of your good lady. I always hoped that you would make it.'

'Thanks Jim it's super to see you again! How's the Squadron?'

'A bit depleted but still flying. As soon as we heard that Kohima was relieved, and you were down here, the Wing Commander sent me to tell you that all was forgiven and welcome home. In fact, he's put you in for another medal to brighten up your uniform. When I reached the hospital, I met these two smashing married ladies who knew you. I must say that you have all the luck.'

'Well I deserve some compensation.'

'That reminds me,' Jim said, as he took a small object wrapped in a clean handkerchief from his pocket. 'You left this behind.'

There inside the handkerchief was Peter's jade leaf talisman.

'Thanks a million. I've missed my ancestral good-luck charm.'

'No problem! Remember a good-luck charm only works if you wear it. So put it on, old chap, and come back to us with all your famous luck and charm.'

After that comment, Jim left Peter with the ladies. Maria gave him a gentle kiss on the cheek and left to join Jim. Susie stood there holding his hand and smiling, making her eyes sparkle like diamonds. Both said nothing. Words could not express the unbreakable love felt by those joined together by the silk. They did not notice the sister pull a screen around the couple isolating them from everything and everybody. Then she took Jim and Maria to her office for a cup of tea. Maria was quite impressed by Jim's conversation, as he was obviously attracted to Sister Louise as much as she was to him.

Maybe Cupid would bring them happiness like he had done for her and Tun Kyi. If not, they should have some nights filled with that much-needed duo of love and unbridled passion.

'You look very tired my love. I hope that you have not suffered too much,' Susie said while squeezing his hand.

'Oh I'm alright just caught one in the waist and another in my thigh. Both went straight through. It was so quick that I hardly noticed them at the time.'

'Sister says you will be as good as new in a few months.'

'Even sooner, now I have you.'

'I have prayed for you every day since we parted. Marie and I go down to the chapel and light candles for you every morning and every night. I think Father Pinto feels we have many sins for God to forgive. Maybe he thinks we are scarlet women making our money from the sex-starved soldiers. He never says anything critical, but welcomes us and hears our confessions.'

'Have you been naughty since I left? You know that while the cat's away the mice will play.'

'Don't say such things! Remember I tied the cord of silk that joins us to be loyal to you until my very end. Only if you no longer want me as your wife shall I leave you or until God calls me to his side.'

'I will never want to leave you Susie even when you are old, grey and wrinkled with six children and a limp. I prayed for this moment.'

She kissed him carefully on his lips making sure that she did not lean on his leg or waist.

Then she sat down, and they talked.

'You look more radiant than ever. In fact, you've put on a little weight.'

'You are so horrid! Don't you like how I look?

'Yes I do. I like what I see very much indeed as your breasts are getting bigger and cuddly.'

'Well it is only natural for a woman to get bigger when her man's seed grows inside her waiting to be born.'

'Are you saying that you are pregnant?'

'Yes.... I hope that is alright.'

Heavens above – I am going to be a father.'

'God has answered my prayers, for your child grows in me, and you have returned.'

Peter's face shone with joy as pain was forgotten and fears abated. He silently thanked God for Susie and their baby she was nurturing in her womb. His mind raced nineteen times to the dozen as what he should do first. They must get their marriage registered and blessed in a church, as a traditional Burmese wedding would be unacceptable to the British Military, or even, the civilian authorities. He must contact his parents to say that he was alive and tell them about Susie. They would be shocked to hear that the overgrown schoolboy they saw off to Burma was now married. How could he know that his mother Lynette had followed his adventures in her dreams and already knew that she was going to have a grandchild, and that it would be a boy? It was just how she was; she was gifted with having great insight and understanding of all her family.

Susie and Peter must have held hands and looked into each other's eyes for over thirty minutes, only saying the occasional nonsense remarks that lovers utter after being away from each other. For them, time had no meaning, as they had totally forgotten about Maria and Jim. However, like all good things, it had to come to an end when the curtains parted, and in came sister with the doctor. The doctor looked at Peter's chart, briefly examined him and said something to sister before turning to address the couple.

'Well, Squadron Leader you may leave the hospital to stay with your wife. However, you must return every day to have the dressings changed. You are on the mend and will be fine, as long as there is no violent exercise for at least one week. If you develop any problems come back immediately.'

'Thanks, but I need some clothes.'

'Sister will collect a uniform for you, but I doubt if it's an RAF one. Good luck, and come to see me in three days time at 10 a.m. sharp.'

'Thank you for everything.'

'Just part of the deal you made when you signed up! You fight the enemy, and we patch you up,' said the doctor before leaving to continue his rounds.

Miraculously, sister returned with a Flying Officer's uniform, underpants, socks, pale blue shirt, shoes and an RAF officer's hat. Susie helped him get dressed. The trousers, were too short and the jacket rather large, but the shoes fitted and that was all that mattered.

After thanking sister, the four friends left the hospital. As they passed by the wounded, they were met with the usual British comments and wolf whistles.

'Ruddy Officers always get the beautiful women.'

'Now you must mind your Ps and Qs boyo. Sir Peter deserves a break after being our only fly boy. He's our lucky mascot; and bloody good luck to him, I say,' Dowey added.

'That's enough from you, Dowey! He's an officer, so treat him with respect. As for you, Spike, shut up, or I'll put you on a charge,' Corporal Joe Brown barked.

Peter turned and smiled before saying: 'Good luck you lot. Joe let Spike off this once as he certainly knows a beautiful woman when he sees one. Sorry,

Spike, she's my wife. All of you come and say hello when you are up, and Dowey, I would like you to sing at our church wedding.'

'I would be honoured to sing for you sir,' Dowey replied, feeling very glad that someone appreciated his marvellous Welsh tenor voice.

The Royal West Kent men gave a great cheer and wished them well.

They left to walk at a snail's pace to the waiting car that carried them the mile home. Home was a large bungalow on the edge of the compound with a newly painted sign that read:

**Private Officers Quarters**
**Military Personnel Only**
**Keep Out.**

It was a wooden teak bungalow with a veranda screened against mosquitoes; a corrugated metal roof painted red, and a thick teak door. Just outside was a large jacaranda tree and a few yards away the magnificent red-flowered flame-of-the forest. It was the perfect place for their first home. Peter was too tired to see the paper lantern high in the banyan tree that was lit every night to guide Susie's love home. That night after dinner with Jim, Maria, and Tun Kyi, Susie and Peter retired gracefully to their bedroom and slept in each other's arms. To be more accurate, Peter slept with his head between Susie's breasts. Susie as always said her prayers content to be holding her man. All she wanted now was for her father to come and join them.

# 34
# A Mother's Dreams and Traditions Upheld

The dreaded telegram arrived at the Anderson's home in England addressed to Paul Anderson about Peter. With fear and trepidation, Paul opened the yellow envelope and read the words he had so often heard others say.

**TO MR P. ANDERSON**

**WE REGRET TO INFORM YOU THAT YOUR SON SQN LDR PETER WIN ANDERSON IS REPORTED AS MISSING IN ACTION AND BELIEVED DEAD.**

**MINISTRY OF WAR. RAF DIVISION.**

Paul fell back into a chair as tears masked his eyesight and sorrow blocked his throat. Now he was confused and sad, so he put his head in his hands as the yellow letter dropped on to the floor. Paul felt that his life was over as the boy, he taught to play cricket and loved was no more. It was an expected but horrible blow that was too hard to live with, for life suddenly lost its meaning. Later, Lynette came downstairs to find whether Paul had made the usual morning pot of tea. She took one look at her husband bent over in his chair and knew that something was wrong. Seeing the telegram on the floor she picked it up, read it, and then hugged her man.

'Dearest, Peter is alive! I have followed his life in Burma through my meditation and in my dreams. I know he is well, but in hospital recovering from his wounds.'

'Are you sure?'

'In my dreams I saw him shot down, captured, tortured, and carried to safety by a little soldier. In a Burmese village, a *pongyi* says the prayers that I do and see me as I see him. I know you can't understand, but I believe it to be true.'

'I cannot say why, but I believe you. For months, I have watched you toss and turn in your sleep. I have heard you cry out in pain as your spirit fought some foul fiend. I followed you downstairs to watch you pray in front of the jade tree.'

'I can't be that psychic, as I never realised you watched me pray for our loved ones. Though I knew you were not deeply asleep when I slid back into our bed.'

'Why?'

'Because your snoring was not as loud as usual!
You make me sound like a fat snoring hippopotamus!'

'No you are not my darling, just a happy, cuddly, snoring father.'

During the weeks that followed, both husband and wife kept themselves busy. Lynette kept Mai happy by helping with her baby daughter and visiting people in need. She read to the patients in the nearby hospital and worked part-time as a nurse. Paul carried on working in Military Intelligence and when he returned home started spending longer in the garden than was usual. When asked why he worked so hard gardening, he replied that he was digging for victory, but really it was his way of keeping sane. The physical effort seemed to sap his energy while taking his mind from the thought of having lost Peter. He checked with his colleagues to find that Peter had not returned to his squadron or shipped out as one of the wounded. However, he was aware that during the war in Burma communications were totally unreliable.

One-night Lynette woke up and shouted out with joy.

'I saw Peter in a bungalow with his beautiful Karen wife. He and Charles were shot, but both are well again. I also saw him wed her, dressed in gold, in a village surrounded by lights and love. I have seen the *pongyi* tie the silk cord around their hands.'

'Steady darling, and take it slowly.... as I want to know where they are.'

'They are in northern India at a town called Dimapur. I sensed inside her womb was growing our grandson, and that they will live to see him become a man.'

'I hope it is true, now go to sleep.'

'I thanked Jesus and my ancestors for caring for them. Now I can sleep.'

She put her head back on the pillow to sleep peacefully for the first time for many weeks. Meanwhile, Paul was wide awake and not knowing what to think, kissed her on the forehead before going downstairs to make a cup of tea. He carefully selected a special Assam tea that he had kept since before the war and supped its delicate flavour slowly.

Next morning Lynette came downstairs to find Paul asleep on the sitting room floor in front of the old chinthe and the jade tree. To her surprise, he had placed Peter's jade leaf back on the tree to indicate that he believed what she told him. She set about correcting his good works by placing two new jade leaves from the tray below. One leaf was for Peter's wife and another for his unborn son. So she now included all of them in her family and felt warm, even glowing, and jealous that she was a bit too old for another child – or was she. When she watched her young granddaughter, Jade, sucking at Mai's full breasts, she remembered that feeling as her body yearned for such a sensation. It was both thrilling and tender making her feel broody. She knew what it was like to give birth to a helpless bundle of flesh who fed happily on her breast, the sensitivity of her enlarged nipples, and the way that the milk formed like a never emptying bottle that once sucked refilled itself. She forgot all the less pleasing aspects of motherhood, but everyone remembers the good parts and leaves out the unpleasant and mundane.

Maybe she should try to conceive again, perhaps without telling Paul. He always liked children and was an excellent father and grandfather. So she lit the joss sticks: two for Paul and herself, three for Mai, Charles, and her baby daughter Jade, then three for Peter his new wife and unborn son, and with a sense of naughtiness one for the baby whom Paul may give her. Perhaps she was being silly, even selfish, but she left the outcome in the hands of God. Anyhow, she vowed to make herself, especially attractive to Paul. She would wear a sexy see-through lace nightie and some sensuous perfume. That might just do the trick and put life back in the old dog yet, she thought. Maybe she should give him a nice bath followed by an Oriental massage. Yes, in such delicate matters, there was no sense in not trying everything.

A few days later a colleague informed Paul that Peter and Charles were alive in Dimapur, having survived a battle at Kohima Ridge. It made his day as it confirmed what Lynette had told him.

# 35

# A Happy, Overcrowded Bungalow

Each day Peter grew stronger as he walked around the bungalow while Susie cared for him. He had never been so happy as everything was just perfect. He was eating well-cooked food surrounded by love. Susie left him twice a day to visit the chapel to light candles for father and in gratitude for the safe return of her man. Even then he was never alone for long, as Tun Kyi and Setcha would visit between shifts at Military Intelligence. He asked Setcha to send a telegram to his parents saying that he, and Charles were alive after a battle and soon would be fully recovered. The censors deleted 'after a battle', but it still made enough sense for his parents to be overjoyed when they received it.

On the third day, Peter saw the doctor in the hospital, as arranged, and then visited his friends. He walked with a distinct limp that the doctor said would be less visible as he grew stronger. Now in a new Squadron Leader's uniform he could go anywhere, even the Military Policemen saluted and never asked for ID. He did not salute back, as to do so hurt his healing wounds.

Inside the ward, Charles lay in bed covered in bandages with his jaw wired together. Now it was his turn to be apprehensive wondering how ill was his brother-in-law?

As Peter approached, Charles smiled. Peter talked while Charles nodded or made a gesture with his free hand. Now and then Charles tried to speak so that Peter could just hear his words. It seemed painfully slow and yet with each gesture the two men grew even closer together. Every day for the next few weeks Peter visited Charles. Soon Charles regained his strength well enough to be discharged into their care. They tried to trace Temasen but without any luck.

In the bungalow, the old study became Charles' bedroom; the master bedroom was for Peter and Susie and the second for Maria and Tun Kyi. A third bedroom Susie reserved for her father, insisting that he would come. Routinely, at dusk, the women lit the lantern in the Banyan tree, calling their father to come to them, in what Peter thought was a futile gesture. The light could never penetrate the solid rock barrier of the Naga Hills. He said nothing, as his mother had always told him that faith moves mountains; however, he did pray that their beloved father would join them.

Nothing really happened until the second monsoon came to bring a season of flowers and rapid regeneration when the trees visibly grew inches in a day.

On one such day, when the water cascaded down the streets and the rainfall flowed from the sky in sheets; Temasen came. At first, no one heard the gentle, polite knock at the door, as the noise from the rain hitting the metal roof was deafening. They were not expecting visitors as few people ventured out in the rain preferring to shelter until the rain stopped. Now the roads became streams, which turned into fast running rivers. Everything stopped awaiting the lull in the storm.

Peter heard the faint tapping of a polite woodpecker on the front door that paused and a minute later restarted. Then, as suddenly as it had started, the rain stopped and the only noise was the knocking at the door. When Peter opened the door, there was sheltering on the veranda a small figure covered in a waterproof cape with an Australian style bush hat over his head. He looked again and saw through the disguise Temasen.

'Sorry to bother you, sir, but I have come to say good-bye,' Havildar Temasen said in an unusually shy voice.

Unlike Peter, Temasen knew the rules used by sergeants when dealing with officers. He knew his visit was unorthodox, but made the excuse that he must report to Captain Charles Brighton.

'Come in out of the rain, old friend, and join us. I think you know everyone.'

'I will – but only for a minute sir!' I'm a havildar and you an officer, so I must not disturb you.'

'Nonsense you're family! Give me your wet cape and hat,' said Susie helping him off with the sodden cloak.

'You're too kind to me, memsahib.'

Susie did not like being thought of as a Memsahib, especially by the man who saved her lover. Deciding that actions were better than words, she kissed Temasen on the cheek before leading him by the hand into the sitting room as he blushed from head to toe. As Temasen sat down, Peter remembered what a good friend he was, a man who never took liberties, always knew his place, and would die defending his comrades. His small stature and reliable nature proved that the best things often come in tiny packages.

Tun Kyi and Maria chatted to Temasen until he felt relaxed and part of the family. Susie brought beer for the men and freshly lime juice for the women. Then Maria served her latest effort at baking in a gas oven. It was a fruitcake had failed to rise properly so it was lopsided but tasted good. Susie, being the eldest sister, could not resist making an inappropriate comment.

'Well Maria my dear, it tastes much better than it looks. You'll need more practice before you can sell any.'

'Oh!' a downtrodden Maria replied. 'It's so difficult.'

'It tastes damn good! Best cake I've had in years,' intervened Peter.

'A lovely cake cooked by a beautiful woman – what more could any man want?' Charles added.

'Baking during the monsoon is difficult due to the high humidity. I never succeed at making cakes during the rains, so I always bake scones,' Temasen added.

'You men think that because my pretty sister cooks the cake, you must tell her, it is good,' Susie started trying to regain the high ground in a discussion that she wished she had not started. Of course, Temasen was – as always – correct as the dampness had made the dough rise slowly.

Peter decided to change the subject. 'I forgot Gurkhas are not only good at fighting, but also excel at hunting, fishing, cooking, and singing.'

'I do not excel at anything, but a havildar must look after his men for he is their parent, cook and disciplinarian. It is better to deal with any problems without bothering the officers.' Temasen nearly bit his tongue remembering that he was surrounded by officers. If he could he would have hidden in a corner, for a good sergeant never let his officers know how little they understood the men's problems.

Good old Temasen,' Charles laughed. 'Always suspected you kept the scandal from me. That's why it is better to have a good sergeant by your side than a lieutenant with a long unpronounceable double-barrelled name.'

The atmosphere between the two sisters was still too tense for comfort. Maria looked at her sister with anger at her ingratitude about her cooking over that awful hot oven. Temasen wanted to leave while the others could not find a way of keeping him as suddenly everything was terribly wrong. Damn that stiff upper lip ways of officers and public schoolboys making them feel awkward and yet needing each other's friendship but not daring to say so.

Luckily, the atmosphere was broken by the sound of a distant grumbling that gradually grew closer. Peter saw through the window an army Humber saloon car coming through the rain towards them. It was strange, as they were not expecting any visitors. It stopped at their front stairs to let out five men who ran through the rain to knock at the door.

'Are we expecting guests?' Peter asked

No one replied but all eyes turned toward the door.

Now the brass knocker tapped at the door in a manner that it sent a shiver down Susie's spine as the coded taps went: Tap... tap... tap, a pause of four seconds, then Tap, tap...tap. There followed yet another pause before the knocking continued. Tap... tap, tap, tap, tap. Then, there was an eerie silence that seemed to last forever.

Gradually, the penny dropped, making both Tun Kyi and Susie run to open the door. It was a long time since they had heard their group's coded knock that said 'Let us in; we are friends.' One extra tap would mean to prepare for danger. Peter noticed the revolver tucked in the back of Susie's skirt. Even in this haven of peace she was prepared for an attack from her enemies or their agents.

Susie opened the door with one hand while the other held the pistol to give a shout of joy, and fling her arms around a man's neck while all got even wetter. Now Maria joined them to cover the man's face with loving kisses.

It made Peter wonder who was it that brought such joy and tenderness.

A very wet Susie came in holding her father's hand and followed by his companions. Soon the door was closed to keep out the rain to reveal the bedraggled travellers. Though wet, but smiling, there stood Setcha, Khin-Lin U Thant, Ye-Htut, Ba Saw, and the pongyi Tauk. Now, at last, the band of friends was complete. For as it was written, so it turned out, that the lantern had brought them safely home to share food and the comforts of family.

All looked well except for Ba Saw, who was on crutches, who Ye-Htut helped to find a straight-backed chair to sit on and take the weight off his heavily plastered leg. As was his Karen way, he quietly sat down and smiled at everyone. He believed that a real man shows no pain and thanks the Lord for his safety in perilous times. So he silently recited a prayer for this reunion and to be among friends. Ba Saw never expected or wanted to live, only to destroy those who had invaded his lands and killed his people. Normally, he was unemotional but this was the exception. When he buried his wife along with his child next to Susie's mother, he had not cried, so why should he cry now? It was not tears of sadness or tears of pain, but a celebration of love and friendship. He noisily blew his nose with a handkerchief, while secretly wiping his eyes dry.

'Please excuse me, I always get a cold in monsoon season,' Ba Saw said in an effort to prevent his emotions marring this God-given moment.

'I hope you've all come to stay.' Peter ventured.

'Well, we didn't come just for the beer?' Tauk replied.

'I knew that space may be limited so the army issued us, on a special loan, with camp beds, bedding, and food. They're being delivered by a Corporal Joe Brown and a Squadron Leader Jim Ashton. I think that you know them?'

'And when should we expect them?' enquired Susie.

'They said for us to allow for a few of hours, so they can pick the right time to avoid the red tape.'

'Well Maria and Tun Kyi will move in with Peter and I...' Susie tried to say before being stopped in her tracks by her father saying. 'I will allow no such thing. If we stay, and that depends on you, we'll sleep on camp beds in your sitting room. I would like a mattress for Ba Saw as he is not well. If you or your sister dare to defy me, I will either spank your bottoms or stay somewhere else. It is enough, for I have spoken.'

Everyone laughed as Tauk stated his terms both as the father, *the pongyi*, and their friend. This man was the centre of their lives, their spiritual leader, guide, and the person they all loved and admired. To Peter, he was the lantern lighter, *pongyi*, father, sage, but above all a man whom war could not destroy. He had kept his people united while never taking to killing anything, though he helped those who did. He prayed for peace and understanding to the Lord Buddha while keeping the Theravada traditions. For Tauk brought together the Burmese people of Christian, Buddhist, and animist beliefs into one family to resist the Japanese invaders and their accomplices. Now everyone was talking at the same time, laughing and being happy. Even Temasen decided to stay for a few days to sleep in the sitting room.

They all did their bit by moving furniture or going into town to buy more fresh fruits and vegetables. During the commotion, Jim and Joe arrived with the beds that they assembled before quietly leaving. Temasen helped Maria bake scones while Peter and Tauk cooked a fish and vegetable curry. Susie managed to burn the bottom of the rice, but no one seemed to notice; though Maria gave Susie the look of a wise old owl, as if to say, 'No one is perfect, even you, sister dear!'

Every scrap of food was eaten by an appreciative clientele; mind you, they would have eaten anything and enjoyed it just to keep each other happy. They talked about insignificant things and made jokes about each other as only true friends can do before tactfully retiring early to bed. Then, when everyone was in bed, Tauk went to the veranda to place his small statue of the Lord Buddha in one corner with the bowl of sand in front. Ceremoniously, he placed three joss sticks into the sand, lit them, and as the fragrant incense rose he prayed. One candle was an offering for his family, another in praise of the Lord Buddha, and the third for his dead wife. He did not realise that his daughters were listening to these, his most sacred prayers. Both women knew they should not be listening but could not help themselves. So, like little schoolgirls, they stood behind him holding hands while he prayed, so that his beloved wife knew he had fulfilled his duty by keeping their daughters safe and married. He wanted her to know how much he missed her and how their children had grown into women just like her.

He stopped and looked out into the sky to see that the clouds had parted so that the moon and stars shone clearly. It was always at night that he missed her. He often reprimanded himself for all the time he had wasted in arguments over silly, unimportant matters, and hoped that they would be united in the Christian heaven to live together for eternity. Though the girls did not realise it, he was aware of their presence and added for their benefit a prayer that was simple and yet full of wisdom.

'Dear Lord, who rules the land, sea and air, I asked you to help Susie and Maria to learn the true paths such as wisdom, patience, the joy of love, and the importance of forgiveness. If they gain these virtues, they will become like their mother and make their husbands truly lucky men. Give them the understanding to guide their children in the ways of peace that they grow up to keep our ancestral line everlasting. Above all, let us love each other, for in your sight; we are all equal and part of your grand plan. For none of us is worth more than a grain of rice without following the paths of pain that leads from life unto death. However, by patience, understanding, tolerance and love, life can be a beautiful adventure, where many doors open to reveal worlds and emotions previously unknown.' He prostrated himself on the floor, pretending to be in deep meditation until he heard the little footsteps dutifully return to their husbands' rooms, and the doors close. He extinguished every smouldering joss stick, packed his small Buddha in his box; and only then took his exhausted body to bed.

Next morning the rain stopped, so Tauk opened the shuttered windows to let in the fresh air. The sweet fragrance of the frangipani and other flowers entered the house, blessing all within. Then he quietly brewed the green tea for everyone before giving Ba Saw his morphine injection, noting with pleasure that his patient was better.

Tauk and Temasen sipped their tea on the veranda and chatted as the cool morning breeze comforted them. Both were early risers and enjoyed the natural beauty of the flowering trees and plants that surrounded them. The birds hovered around the trees and all around them, many silent, though some very noisy.

The monsoon rains are something that one must personally experience in order to believe them. For though they are heavy and turn the roads into mudslides, they wash the land clean and turn dry lands into beautiful, fruitful gardens. The water transformed the landscape so quickly that it was nearly miraculous. The accumulated rotting waste in the pungent smelling *nullahs* (open drains) were washed away. Dimapur smelt of flowers in the clean streets, and market places, instead of that horrid odour associated with poverty and poor sanitation. Somehow the smell of stale curries that impregnated the very framework of the town was less obvious. For the poor people living in leaky, makeshift huts, the rain drove away the mess but brought malaria, fevers, colds, dysentery, typhoid, and the dreaded cholera, The water became so polluted that it had to be boiled and filtered before it was safe to use. Though in many traditional houses such as this bungalow, there were water butts that collected the pure, sweet-tasting rainwater for drinking.

After dinner, they settled down to talk of their adventures since parting, Tun Kyi told about the journey from the three pillars westwards until they reached Dimapur. Once in town, they found that nobody wished to train two pregnant women as full-time nurses, especially when both suffered from morning sickness. So Susie was demobilised, while being given part-time work as a translator. Maria helped in the hospital while Tun Kyi and Setcha worked in Military Intelligence. Luckily, they had the use of the bungalow owned by Tauk's brother Tun Tin, to live in while he was away fighting with the Chindits. It was a large but basic weekend retreat where before the war, Tun Tin entertained his friends when on a break from his tea plantation. The bungalow was raised from the ground on wooden stilts and surrounded by a large well-planted garden. On a clear day, you could see the Brahmaputra River and the lands beyond.

Then Peter, Charles, and Temasen told of the Siege of Kohima. They gave only the bare facts. It was pointless telling of the carnage and butchery, feelings of betrayal, and friendships fashioned together in that living Hell. Temasen briefly summed up his feelings by saying, 'Kohima was a battle of the trained and raw recruits, in fact, what you call the Tommies, Dicks and Harrys. How do you say that?'

'Tom, Dick and Harry,' Peter offered.

It was we soldiers, and the Tom, Dick and Harry's of civilian life against a Japanese division. We were totally outnumbered and forgotten, but we survived to tell the tale. We didn't win, but importantly, we didn't lose.'

'Yes Temasen, we held the line when left as cannon fodder to give the others time to respond. It was fifteen hundred British, Indian, Burmese, and Gurkha soldiers against fifteen thousand front line Japanese infantry. In the end, we bloodied the noses of the Emperor and his generals,' Charles added with pride.

Reluctantly, Ba Saw briefly told the story of the attack on the crossing and how the elephants rampaged through the enemy lines. Then he could say no more leaving Ye-Htut to tell the rest. So Ye-Htut told of how Ba Saw was captured and killed the Devil's Helper. Then in the mountains, they met Tauk with the villagers escaping westwards to travel to Dimapur. Here Ba Saw was admitted into the hospital as a Chindit Major, arranged for by Setcha, and recovered. The other villagers went to live with friends or acquaintances while they looked for Susie at Tun Tin's home.

Peter and Temasen were delighted to hear that their Devil had been blown up. Now the world had one less evil man to contend with, and their own secret fears were demolished by Bo Ba Tin's ignoble death. Both doubted that the Devil's Helper was so easily killed, and they were right. For on leaving hospital

Bo Ba Tin learnt to live with one eye and one arm while his heart grew even darker as he vowed revenge on all who opposed him.

Tauk told how the British wanted to give Ba Saw a medal for nearly single-handedly blowing up the Japanese barge bridge. He refused unless they were all honoured. So there was no medal, but he accepted a release from active duty and the salary of a liaison officer.

Later, Tauk explained that they came to attend Susie and Peter's impending wedding in the Catholic Chapel. Maria and Tun Kyi were married in church, and now it was Susie and Peter's turn. He arranged for the priest, Father Pinto, to carry out the ceremony the following Saturday.

'This time, Father, you have gone too far. How could you do this without our agreement?' Susie reprimanded him.

'No, he's right, the sooner we're married the better. If I am quick, I can get a fabulous Welsh tenor, Private Dowey Evans, to sing for us,' Peter exclaimed.

'And a Gurkha, RWK, and RAF guard of honour,' Charles added.

'Sadly I can't marry without written permission from my CO.'

'That is not a problem. I talked to your CO so the RAF has given the required permissions. It is all in this letter addressed to you,' stated Tauk, as he handed Peter the official letter, duly signed by the right people. Peter was glad that his marriage would soon be legal, which was lucky, for everyone.

# 36
## A Church Wedding

Peter and Susie were married at Dimapur in a chapel filled with flowers where every pew was occupied. On the groom's side of the aisle sat members of Peter's squadron, the CO, Jim Ashton, Temasen, Joe Brown, Spike and Alfie of the Royal West Kent Regiment, the Commander of Kohima Ridge and the Deputy District Commissioner. On the bride's side were Tun Kyi, Ba Saw, and others from her Little Pagoda group and from the village. Distant relatives and friends of the family filled every seat wearing their best clothes to make a colourful spectacle of Burmese silk clothing, military uniforms, and Indian saris. The old, but newly tuned, piano accompanied the choir and the congregation in singing 'All Things Bright and Beautiful' so that the joyful song filled the air as they waited for the bride.

Susie entered on her father's arm. Tauk wore Burmese traditional dress, including silk hat, *longyi* and taiman. Susie looked magnificent in a white silk dress with a simple veil and long lace train to look regal as she walked with her father. A band of orchids sat in her black hair that was pinned up high to show the nape of her neck. She did not hesitate as she walked towards her man to be united before Mother Church in the sight of God. On approaching the altar to stand beside Peter, his best man, Charles, stepped back to stand behind them with her father and Maria. When the time came, with clear voices, both bride and groom made their vows before God and their friends to love and honour each other until death did them part, and this promise they intended to keep.

The scene was worthy of a great artist. For the colour of the bride's dress and the blue of the bridegroom's uniform blended with the gold decorations of the church. While the red flame-of-the forest, the yellow and pink blossom of the frangipani and bougainvillea, the roses and of course, many sprays of different brightly-coloured orchids radiated a mystic display of fragrance, colour, shape and light all around the room. The scene was made beautiful by the sun shining during the wedding service warming the congregation in what was a cool morning. It cast rainbow-like colours as it broke through the stained-glass windows adding a magical effect that all remembered for years to come.

When Father Pinto announced that Peter could kiss the bride, he carried out his orders without delay to the joy of all present. People smiled, some shed a tear, and all approved of this marriage. The choir, led by Dowey Evans, sang 'Bread of Heaven' and 'Abide with Me' as the couple and their witnesses signed the registers; one register was for the Church and the other for State Register of Births, Marriages and Deaths making them officially husband and wife.

As the newlyweds left the chapel, they passed beneath a ceremonial arch formed by the swords of Peter's Squadron, Royal West Kent Regiment, and Gurkha Rifles. It was totally unorthodox, but it signified the unity of all present in saluting two very special comrades-in-arms. Afterwards, there was a small reception at the bungalow where there was food, drink, and dancing. The Burmese played their musical instruments ranging from the bamboo-type xylophone known as a pwe to the booming of gongs, and the special six-reed oboe that carries the main tune known as a hne. The soldiers sang some songs of home as a tribute to the couple with never an improper word or a note out of tune.

Nearly as soon as it began, the reception came to an end. For like all things in wartime, everything was done in a hurry. The serving military men returned to their duties and the men of the Royal West Kent's to their well-earned leave, and the others to prepare for their next assignment. Then the band of friends parted as Charles was flown home to receive further medical treatment and to be reunited with his wife and daughter. On the following Monday morning, Temasen reported back to his unit to be duly assigned to a training brigade in India, after having a month's leave in Nepal. A week later Peter and Susie were sent to Ceylon for rest and recuperation.

In England, Lynette saw the wedding as she knelt in deep meditation before the jade tree. She wept for joy at seeing her son and his beautiful wife among their friends. The man who led Susie to the altar must be her father, though she recognised him as Tauk the *pongyi* from her dreams. Later, when Charles' aircraft took off from Cox's bazaar to bring him home, Lynette saw him coming and prepared the household to give him a warm welcome. She told Mai, who just smiled, knowing that mother had the gift of second sight the Buddhists call the third eye.

The ancestral jade tree held the ancestors' spirits as it looked down upon their world and made it safe. Daily Lynette lit three joss sticks for love, protection, and for thanks. Now the family was growing and in this time of darkness, the light of the jade tree would guide them like a beacon home. Tauk summed it all up saying, 'The tide has turned against fascism. However, I fear in my bones that Burma will never be an innocent and happy nation for years to come. For when brother fights brother and their blood flows like rivers, only a miracle can cleanse this nation so that it can grow again safe in peace. I fear that Burma may indeed be for a long time to come, a paradise lost.'

Besides the remains of the tennis court on Kohima Ridge, someone wrote upon a piece of wood the following memorial to all those who fought there. Its words say it all. In fact, they are known as the Kohima epitaph. After the war, the wooden sign was replaced with a permanent metal one that still remains there for all to see.

The poignant words read:

**When you go home,**
**Tell them of us, and say:**
**For your tomorrow,**
**We gave our today.**

Shortly after the wedding Peter and Susie were repatriated to England to live with Peter's parents.

# Part Three

# 37

# England

*Mid pleasures and palaces though we may roam,*
*Be it ever so humble, there's no place like home.*

J H Payne (1823). The song 'Home, Sweet Home.'

It was in May 1944 when Peter and Susie arrived in England to be met at Blackbushe Airport by Peter's parents Paul Anderson and his Burmese wife Lynette and driven to their large family house near Lancing in West Sussex. Now the family was complete as they joined Peter's sister Mai and her wounded husband Captain Charles Brighton of the Gurkha Rifles already living in the house. The house was full of laughter as the family enjoyed the long warm summer days away from the sounds and fears of war. Lynette was delighted to have Susie in their home to speak Burmese with and talk about her country as they awaited the birth of Peter and Susie's child.

It was about this time that Lynette received three of the jade trees from the executors of the estates of her dead relatives. She gave one of the trees to her daughter Mai and the second to her son Peter's wife, Susie and taught both how to meditate to enter the spiritual world. Susie learnt fast and soon could see her father Tauk and her friends in Burma. While Tauk followed his daughter's life through his prayers and meditation to know everything that happened. When Susie gave birth to a boy, they baptised him Paul Peter Anderson and added his jade leaf to her tree that already held a leaf for herself and Peter.

Everyone was kept busy helping run the house and gardens. The three-acre garden consisted of an extensive orchard of apple; cherry and pear trees next to a vegetable patch complete with greenhouses. The produce from the garden kept the household nearly self-sufficient, but it needed a lot of attention. Every morning they collected the eggs from their thirty chickens and six geese before picking the ripe vegetables. Afterwards, they collected the fresh gooseberries and strawberries before digging up some potatoes and selecting a cabbage and lettuce for dinner. It sounds like an idyllic place to live; it was, except that the war was never far away. At night, the whole countryside was completely dark except for the moonlight, since all lights were hidden behind shutters as the blackout was obeyed. It was deemed necessary even though the enemy bomber raids were less frequent, but they had been replaced by the deadly V1 and V2 missile attacks. It was a time, when though the Allies were marching through France, the Germans still fought back with great determination. Peter was aware that everywhere he went; there were so many women and too few young men. War was a dreadful thing that took so many men and made thousands widows. Even the land had changed as playing fields were ploughed up to plant crops.

Often Peter and his mother went to the local farmer's market to sell some of their produce and buy meat. Of course, everything was rationed; however, they always received the best meat from the farmers, who purchased their vegetables. They had to travel by bus as they did not have enough petrol to run the car. What they had was reserved for special occasions such as taking Susie to the hospital to deliver her baby.

After two months of rest and recuperation, Peter and Charles were ordered to attend a series of medical evaluations and extensive physiotherapy. Afterwards, the evaluation team decided that Charles was only fit for clerical duties and Peter unfit for combat, but could be a flying instructor. This meant that Peter was posted to the nearby RAF station in Shoreham commanded by his uncle, Wing Commander Jeremy Anderson. Here he was impressed by the latest fighter aircraft that had more power and better performance. The new Supermarine Spitfire was a joy to fly, and the two seater trainer version made his work as an instructor easier. It was like old times so much so that he loved flying again over the green Sussex downs and along the coast, though he found that the trainee pilots were younger than he remembered, but they learnt fast. They had to, as their lives depended on a combination of ability, quick reflexes and a lot of luck.

However, his mind often returned to think about his friends back in Burma who risked their lives every day fighting for Britain. He knew that there was nothing he could do, except try to get fit enough for combat. He doubted if they needed him now that the war in Europe was ending, and the war in the Far East was moving very fast with the capture of Mandalay. So he was happy enough teaching flying and living with Susie and their baby son who made his love for Susie greater than before. Peter saw in his son, his wife's beauty and all his hopes for a better world where war was unthinkable. Now he had much more to live for and felt especially blessed. He understood the spiritual importance of a mother suckling her child as personified by the images of the Madonna holding Jesus. They were all content as his parents doted on their grandchildren and cherished Susie as a much-loved daughter.

A Spitfire two-seat trainer at Shoreham Airport.

# 38
## Force 136

*When you give to the needy let not thy left hand know what thy right hand doeth.*

The Bible. St Mathew chapter 6 verse 3.

Peter and Susie remained in touch with their friends in Burma through Paul's contacts at his office in the Special Operations Executive (SOE) branch, simply known as Force 136 and Susie's visions using the jade tree. At the beginning of 1945, the London office of the SOE recruited Peter to work in Force 136 as a liaison officer. Here he assessed the reports they received from Tun Kyi, who was still running the Little Pagoda group. From this, he learnt that the Japanese forces were being slowly driven back, but still inflicting serious casualties among the Allies. It was apparent to all concerned that the Allies found the advance into southern Burma much easier in the places where they had reliable information and support from the local population. Therefore, it was decided to help Force 136 recruit and arm friendly ethnic groups. They also sent more people with Burmese connections, such as Peter, to assist South-East Asia Command (SEAC) under Admiral Lord Mountbatten working in Kandy, Ceylon.

Two weeks later, Peter travelled by Sandringham flying boat to the island of Ceylon. Even after a very long journey Peter was enchanted by the colours of the trees and the smells of the spice islands that reminded him of Burma. Within hours of landing in the calm waters off Colombo, Peter was driven to Kandy and accommodated in the SEAC Officers' Mess that was equipped with a pleasant bar and a veranda. It provided a magnificent view of the green valleys and some of the city while serving throughout the day good British and Indian food. Often when alone at night, Peter sat on a chair on the veranda looking over the countryside as a cool breeze brushed his face, and the intoxicating smells of the spices seduced his senses making him feel revived and relaxed. During his first day, he met people of many different nationalities, including a newly promoted Jemadar (Lieutenant) Temasen, who was recruited for his knowledge of Burma. Seeing Temasen again, made Peter feel that he was going to enjoy his new post. Early next morning he was taken to SEAC headquarters to be introduced to other members of Force 136 and allocated a small office. Everywhere he looked people were busy organising the British forces in Burma and making certain that they had adequate supplies.

The situation changed a month before Peter arrived at SEAC with the end of the war in Europe. Now the British sent more troops and equipment to India and Ceylon to hasten the defeat of the Japanese. By then the Japanese were in retreat having lost northern Burma while being harassed by attacks from local tribesmen who sabotaged many of their supplies. However, the Japanese's ferocious defence of Mandalay shocked the SEAC command and slowed down the campaign. Clearly, the Allies needed more support from the local people similar to that given by the Naga and Chin of V Force. So Force 136 was expanded, to prove particularly successful in areas where there was resistance to the Japanese. Of these, The Karen people proved most useful. Since 1943, they fought with Major Hugh Seagrim in the eastern areas near Siam (Thailand), and were severely punished by the Japanese for being pro-British. Later in that year, Seagrim together with some of his Karen men was caught and executed. However, Force 136 supplied the Karen people with military equipment to have a force of eight thousand men actively harassing the Japanese.

Force 136 was commanded by Lt Colonel John Ritchie Gardiner, who before the war had served in Burma as a manager of a forestry company and sat on the Municipal Council of Rangoon. The last message from Seagrim informed Force 136 that he believed Aung San was disillusioned with the Japanese and wanted to talk to the Allies. He said this was because the Japanese had reduced Aung San's Burma Defence Army to the less powerful Burma National Army (BNA) whose role was limited to supporting the Japanese forces.

Peter kept a picture of his Susie holding baby Paul in her arms next to his bed. It reminded him that God permitting they would soon be together. Every week, he wrote to her describing Ceylon and telling her how much he missed her. Then he received a letter from her saying how Paul was growing and how much they both missed Peter. She reminded him to wear his jade leaf for guidance and protection.

When off-duty Peter wandered around Kandy to visit the area around Kandy Lake where the royal palace, and the famous Buddhist Temple of the Tooth (*Sri Dalada Malgawa*) is situated. He found walking around the city tiring until he became acclimatised to the altitude of one thousand five hundred feet above sea level. Outside the city, he discovered that the hills covered with tea plantations producing some of the finest teas such as the fragrant *Nuwara Eliya* that is best served with lemon. Peter also discovered the expensive white tea as well as many better-known forms. Suddenly, tea became much more interesting.

One morning while trying to interpret different accounts of the Japanese military strengths, Peter was called into Colonel Gardiner's office.

'Welcome to Kandy. You must find this island in many ways similar to Burma,' said the colonel shaking Peter's hand.

'Thank you, sir. Yes, they are similar,' Peter replied, glad to meet his commander.

'I want to ask you, what do you know about the reliability of Setcha, who was in The Little Pagoda group?' asked Colonel Gardiner.

'Sir, I know him well and can say he is reliable. He gathered information for us since the battle of Sangshak,' a puzzled Peter replied.

'Good,' replied to the officer before adding. 'What do you think of his report that certain elements of the Burma National Army (BNA) are joining the Burmese communists to form the Anti-Fascist Organisation (AFO) against the Japanese?'

'It is great news as they would help us advance more swiftly to Rangoon,' Peter replied.

'That is what we think. First, we must secretly contact Aung San and the AFO so that neither the Japanese nor our government knows what we are doing,' continued the colonel.

'Why should our people be worried if we shorten the war,' Peter replied.

'Churchill does not want any agreement with Aung San that could undermine the colonial status of Burma when the war is over. However, Slim and Lord Mountbatten feel that we should get as much local support as possible to end this carnage. Our losses taking Mandalay were unacceptably high,' Gardiner replied.

'Then I suggest you send people into Burma to meet with Aung San and his colleagues to find out if the rumours are true and make a tentative agreement,' Peter suggested.

'Are you willing to join Setcha in the Irrawaddy Basin to meet with the AFO negotiators and try to make a settlement?' asked the smiling colonel.

'I would do anything to defeat the Japanese,' replied Peter.

'That is excellent. I suggest we will drop you by parachute tomorrow night after we have informed Setcha that you are coming,' ordered the colonel.

'May I suggest that Jemadar Temasen is allowed to come with me. We have fought together and both of us know Setcha,' requested Peter.

Two days later Peter and Temasen with three others from Force 136 were parachuted from a Dakota into Burma near the riverside town of Bassein. Peter found the jump straight forward, as they were attached by a static line to the aircraft to wait for the dispatcher to tell them when to jump. Then, there were a few seconds of rapid descent followed by a click as the line pulled open his parachute, and he started to glide more slowly towards the signal fires in the centre of a rice field. On landing they were met by a smiling Setcha and his men who collected their parachutes. Minutes later, they rapidly moved through wet paddy fields to an old house situated in the outskirts of the town. Here Setcha made the new arrivals wear Burmese clothes and hid their uniforms.

'This house is an ideal base as it is near the road with no neighbours. You will find that Bassein is a safe place to be as it is a busy port on the Irrawaddy with few Japanese. Everything is run by liberal elements of the Burma National Army using little force. The BNA in this region is very popular as they even pay the people to work at the docks. However, to avoid unwanted attention we must look like Burmese traders visiting the docks to buy whatever is available in order. One must never forget that the Japanese have informers who check on both the BNA and the local population,' Setcha stated.

'I must inform Kandy that we have arrived,' Peter added. '

Inside the small house, they drank cups of sweet tea while others kept watch to warn of danger. During the discussions, two young men left to go to the town. Then a third man left to transmit Peter's message to SEAC from a radio hidden by the paddy fields.

Kywe Myint and Htet Maung will try to find a friend in the BNA to arrange a meeting,' Setcha explained.

'Thank you, everything must be done secretly so not to arouse any suspicion of what we are doing.'

'I expect the BNA will want us to meet them in a quiet place upriver. Will that be alright?'

'Yes as this meeting was always going to be a dangerous affair for all of us.'

'We have twenty men on guard around the house and in the town as well as many friends in the BNA. So we are safe unless the Japanese decides to send troops down here.'

'Is that likely?'

'I don't think so. However, Peter I think it wise to keep you fully informed of the current situation,' explained Setcha. Then they sat down and waited while a coded message was transmitted to Force 136 to say it was safe for the others to come. That night Kywe Myint and Htet Maung returned with two uniformed members of the BNA who wanted to make agreeable arrangements for the very secret meeting. It was agreed that they would meet in three days at a fishing village ten miles north of the town that was run by the BNA. Then the BNA men left saying they, and their leader would be at the village waiting for the British representatives to arrive.

Three days later Peter and Temasen travelled with three others from Force 136 and Setcha, Kywe Myint and Htet Maung to the fishing village. It was remote with most of the huts built on stilts on the edge of the river. On arriving, they waited cautiously outside the village watching for any signs of a trap knowing one mistake could be fatal. At midnight, they entered the village to find the villagers walking around among their animals; others were preparing to go out fishing in the river using lanterns to attract the fish. It was very beautiful, but where were the members of the BNA? In the darkness, they heard feet running towards them and held their pistols ready to fire until they found it was just a pig. Then an old man who stopped them and invited them to go inside a large hut where they found uniformed BNA officers waiting for them. After a series of brief introductions, they sat down at a table opposite members of the AFO, the political wing of the BNA. Their leader then spoke.

'I am Bogyoke Aung San and wish to start negotiations with the British as to how we can work together to drive the Japanese out of Burma and bring peace to this land,' Aung San stated.

'It is an honour to meet you Bogyoke. I am only authorised to listen to your proposals, and if they are agreeable, you must meet with General Slim,' Peter stated.

For a moment, there was silence, before a series of nods and smiles indicating this was acceptable. This was followed by the AFO leadership talking very fast to each other before deciding what they should offer.

'Well I suggest that I will lead the BNA in an uprising against the Japanese in return for allowing the British recognising us as their allies. In exchange, we expect that Burma is granted independence after we defeat the Japanese and drive them out of Burma,' stated Aung San.

'Sir I will inform my superiors of your terms. If they are acceptable, my superiors will arrange for an agreement to be formalised at a meeting between yourselves and General Slim,' Peter replied.

After much discussion, it was decided that Aung San should meet General Slim to formalise an agreement. The Burmese leader agreed but only when his safety was guaranteed. Then they parted. Peter returned to Bassein with Setcha and the others from Force 136. They were isolated and living under the shadows for the British advance, but Peter still risked sending the terms for an agreement to SEAC.

'Peter, we are ordered north to meet General Slim at his new HQ,' said an excited Setcha.

'Then I suggest we move fast before we are captured,' Peter replied. He was worried their radio signals might give away their position to the enemy.

Within the hour, they were moving north through paddy fields and hiding under trees at any noise. The first night they stopped only to eat their rations and met no enemy forces. The area was quiet until nearing Meiktila when they had to crawl upon their bellies to go through the Japanese lines. The town had changed since Peter was stationed there in 1943 as most buildings were damaged with many in ruins and others pock-marked with bullet holes. At dawn, they entered the town to be met by British soldiers guarding the main road. Luckily, Setcha knew the password that allowed them to be escorted to the HQ complex. Here they were taken to meet the Intelligence officers to be questioned.

'So you are Peter Anderson,' asked Lt Andy Smith.

Yes,' Peter replied.

'As a formality, please tell me your rank?'

'I am a squadron leader.'

'What is your serial number?'

'My serial number is 2946291.'

'What is your unit?'

'I am part of Force 136 under the command of Colonel John Ritchie Gardiner.'

'That is enough questions for now. Welcome to Meiktila,' Lt Smith said shaking Peter's hand.

'It feels good to be safely inside our lines,' Peter replied.

'I must warn you that your negotiations with Aung San have stirred up a hornet's nest both here and in London.'

'Why, we only did as commanded,' answered a shocked Peter.

'Well someone in London does not approve of us talking to Aung San. However, Lord Mountbatten and General Slim think you have started an important agreement that may help end this war. Therefore, the general wants to meet Aung San in person to agree to the terms for his men joining us in the fight against the Japanese.'

'So what do I do,' asked Peter.

'You will fly out tonight for Kandy to inform Force 136 about the current situation. At the moment, we are finding it costly defeating the Japanese in their well-made defences,' Lt Smith replied.

So Peter returned to Kandy to spend the next year sorting out hundreds of reports. He felt frustrated at not being allowed to do anything more while Slim and Mountbatten decided what they should do. Everyday SEAC received reports from the Allied armies who were rapidly moving south towards Rangoon, under a shield of fighter aircraft. The increased numbers of bombers greatly helped, by attacking the Japanese positions throughout both the day and night. It was so effective that they destroyed Rangoon docks and numerous Japanese stores in the city along with six months' worth of essential goods. With few supplies and little food, the Japanese forces quietly left Rangoon to retreat eastwards. Unaware of the Japanese departure the Allies launched both an airborne and sea borne attack on Rangoon. Then a RAF recognisance mosquito flew over Rangoon to photograph a newly painted sign on the roof of Rangoon prison saying, 'British Here, Japs Gone.' This was good news, but still SEAC thought it could be a ruse and ordered the attack upon the city to continue. On 1st May 1945, Gurkha paratroopers landed in force on Elephant Point to advance the few miles into Rangoon. They met only light resistance, so that on 3rd May; they joined the Indian 26th Division to enter Rangoon. They found the devastated city deserted and empty except for a few snipers. Once in control of the city they set up camp and established road blocks before liberating the POWs in Rangoon Prison. They were shocked at the sight of so many thin, starving men in need of urgent medical treatment and food. In hours, they were serving the POWs with nourishing soup while the doctors and nurses treated as many as they could.

Then Aung San was promised safe conduct to and from the British Headquarters in Meiktila. In response, he and Thakin Soe crossed the Irrawaddy at Allanmyo. On 16th May 1945 dressed in the uniform of a Japanese major-general, Aung San met General Slim and after much discussion agreed to join forces against their mutual enemy, the Japanese. The two men understood each other well enough to sign an agreement for Aung San and his men to fight the Japanese alongside the Allies in exchange for Burmese independence when the war ended. On 27th March, Aung San kept his promise when his forces attacked the Japanese. After more fighting, part of the Japanese army surrendered on 13th September as ordered by the Emperor, following the atomic bomb attacks on Japan. Importantly, General Honda did not surrender his forces until the Emperor's orders were confirmed on 25th October. By 6th November, nearly seventy-two thousand had surrendered, and the major fighting ceased; however, there remained some small pockets of Japanese resistance. The Burma National Army was renamed the Patriotic Burmese Forces (PBF) and gradually disarmed by the British as the Japanese forces were driven out of Burma. All members of the PBF were offered positions in the new Burma Army that was under British command as agreed during the Kandy conference with Mountbatten in September 1945. Aung San was offered a senior position in the Burma Army but declined preferring to lead the new Anti-Fascist People's Freedom League (AFPFL).

Peter was shocked by the reports from Burma stating that though the fighting was mostly over, and the military was disarming the PBF; the situation was not getting any better. Food was scarce and starvation spreading from the cities into the countryside. The rice harvest yielded only a fifth of what was expected so that life was harsh even in the best villages. This situation was made more tragic by the lack of transport so it was nearly impossible to transport any crops to the cities. Then the British Military Administration (BMA) was established on 6th June to bring law and order; it lasted until 16th October. The military was successful in arresting many accused of war crimes but also made many bad decisions such as unwisely issuing Proclamation Number 6, declaring Japanese currency invalid without any offer of compensation or exchange. It was a badly conceived plan designed to remove the wealth accumulated by those who collaborated with the Japanese; unfortunately, it hurt everyone. This provoked widespread rioting as no one had any useable money for food and other essentials. Matters became worse because some of the British forces took whatever they found without payment. However, as soon as the new official rupees came into circulation things slowly started to improve. Peter thought that the British had learnt little about Burma and were repeating the same-old mistakes.

When Peter heard that Major Suki was in Rangoon Jail waiting investigation for war crimes, he decided to make a declaration on the Major's behalf. So he was flown to Rangoon to attend Major Suki's War Crimes tribunal. He found the city in ruins with thousands living in temporary shelters along the banks of Victoria Lake. His driver said many Burmese caught the few fish in the lake as their only source of food. Eventually, Peter arrived at the grim Rangoon Jail and was escorted to the War Crimes Tribunal interrogation room. There he sat across a table from the handcuffed Major Suki next to the young interrogator, and in the corner was a secretary taking notes. Everywhere, there were armed Military Police making sure there were no disruptions. Peter was shocked at seeing Major Suki, who looked tired and bruised from being brutally interrogated. It made Peter very angry, but he concealed his feelings knowing that he was here to help the Major.

'This is the third interrogation for war crimes of Major Denjiro Suki of 31st Division of the Japanese Army in Burma. Squadron Leader Peter Anderson is in attendance at his request as a witness,' the Lieutenant said loudly for all to hear and the secretary to record.

'Major Suki what was your role the 31st division?'

'I have told you twice before that I was a logistics officer in charge of arranging supplies and building bridges for 31st Division,' Suki replied quietly.

'Was your unit involved in the torture of Allied prisoners by Bo Ba Tin and others?'

''No, I dislike the use of torture for whatever reason and consider it barbaric even when carried out by your men. I stopped the evil Ba Tin and ordered that he was arrested and marched on foot to the divisional HQ,' a shocked Suki replied looking at Peter.

'May I make a comment?' Peter asked.

'Of course, we must be seen to be fair,' the Lieutenant replied.

'I wish it recorded that Major Suki rescued me and Havildar Temasen from the hands of Bo Ba Tin. Then the good Major sent his own doctor to treat our wounds and when we were better allowed us to escape,' added Peter forcefully watching Suki smile.

'Are you absolutely sure that this is the same man?'

'Of course I am, though he looks as though he has recently been through the mill,' stated Peter vehemently. He added, 'Major Suki should be treated with respect, or I will report this matter to Lord Mountbatten on my return to SEAC. We must not act like the Kempei-Tei.'

The Lieutenant was now worried about his future as the Squadron Leader was serious. He knew the prisoner had been beaten, kept in a small dark cell and fed only scraps of food. This was partly because the prison officers included many who had seen what the Japanese did to their prisoners in Rangoon Jail. It was understandable, but against the Geneva Convention that Britain claimed to honour.

'On account of this new information I recommend that all charges against Major Denjiro Suki be dropped. The Major will be moved to a POW camp to await repatriation to his family with his sword,' the Lieutenant ordered.

Immediately, the guard removed the handcuffs binding the Major's hands before opening the door for his prisoner to leave. Before leaving the room, the Major bowed deeply to Peter before saying, 'Thank you Peter-san, you show that the British can be men of honour,' stated Major Suki.

'Please inform me at SEAC when Major Suki is repatriated and where he is sent. I intend to make certain that he is treated as well as he treated me. So heaven help anyone who hurts this good man,' Peter added getting up from his chair.

'Of course I will, sir. May I arrange transport for you to Mingaladon Airport?'

'Thanks, I must get back to Kandy as soon as possible.'

Once in Kandy, Peter informed Lord Mountbatten's aide-de-camp what he had seen and the chaos in Rangoon. He then ordered that more supplies be sent to the city and distributed among the people. So it was ordered that the many ships arriving to take the troops and the Prisoners of War home, would also bring food and medical supplies to the city.

On 16th October, Prime Minister Churchill, re-instated the government in exile under the former Governor Sir Reginald Dorman-Smith. It was a grave mistake as the Governor returned to take up his pre-war position with many of his old civil servants to re-establish a colonial administration. Many of them were bitter from having lost so much when they fled to India and distrusted Aung San and the other Thankins. The returning civil servants recovered their houses by force and any of their lost property they could find. They also initiated searches for Burmese and Indians, who had helped the Japanese. Dorman-Smith authorised an investigation of a report that in 1942, Aung San stabbed to death a village headman in front of a large crowd. Officially, the Governor did not act, only because he was ordered by his superiors not to arrest Aung San. However, years later Ne Win commented that he and his colleagues were imprisoned in Rangoon Jail and tortured. In fact, he showed the author the scars on his back caused by the canes that had cut through his skin. This cannot be either confirmed or denied as the official records are incomplete and no one wished to accept that British interrogators resorted to torture. All Burma waited impatiently for change that did not happen. Dorman-Smith would not discuss independence but focused his efforts on the vital work of physical reconstruction of the nation. His one great success was to encourage British businesses to return to Burma, especially the Burmah Shell Oil Company which started to open some of the damaged oil wells. Within months, Burma had a reliable, cheap supply of petrol that was refined within the country.

When the newly elected Labour government in London heard of the deteriorating situation in Burma, they replaced Dorman-Smith with Major General Hubert Rance. General Rance immediately appointed Aung San as the Deputy Chairman of the Executive Council of Burma responsible for defence and external affairs. He hoped that this would help stop the growing confusion caused by the many strikes instigated by Aung San and his followers. It worked, and the country became relatively peaceful. However, Rance carried on re-building Burma under very difficult circumstances while forming an interim Burmese government and slowly started to repair the city and make the harbour functional. The remaining British troops now helped repair roads, enforce law and get the buses and trucks moving. It was a Herculean task considering the limited financial resources and the reliance on the cooperation of the Burmese political parties, especially the AFPFL (Aung San's Anti-Fascist People's Freedom League). Many ex-Japanese lorries were handed over to local traders for transporting food into the cities, and others converted into buses.

In January 1947, Aung San visited London to sign an agreement with Prime Minister Atlee granting Burma Independence. Two weeks later Aung San met the leaders of the ethnic groups in Burma at a conference at Panglong to form a united Burma. A treaty forming the new Union of Burma was signed on 12th February 1947, though two groups, the Karen and Mon refused to be part of the agreement. In the general elections held in April 1947; Aung San's AFPL won 176 out of 210 seats, while the Karen won 24, the Communists 6 and the Anglo-Burmese 4. As the elected representative of the people, Aung San established an Executive Council that met in the Secretariat Building.

During a Council meeting, held on 19th July 1947, five men dressed in the uniforms of the British 12th Army entered the building armed with Bren and Sten guns. They broke into the meeting and opened fire killing Aung San and six of his ministers. Interestingly both Ne Win and U Nu were absent from the meeting, and the attack blamed on the former conservative Prime Minister Saw. An investigation found the jeep, and some uniforms used in the assassination in Victoria Lake near Saw's house. Later, Saw was tried, found guilty and hanged. Aung San's death shocked Burma and left a vacuum taken up by an unprepared U Nu as Prime Minister with Sao Shwe Taik as provisional President. As the elected new leader of the AFPFL, Thankin (U) U Nu signed the U Nu-Atlee Treaty in October 1947 giving Burma full independence outside the British Commonwealth.

At this time, it was decided to discontinue SEAC and repatriate their staff. However, they recruited training officers and other staff for the new Union of Burma Air Force and Army and guaranteed the Britain government would pay their salaries for the next few years.

# 39
# The Road to Independence

*Sadly most wars do not end after the ceasefire.*

One day Peter read a notice at SEAC asking for volunteers to work in Burma to help establish a new Burma Air Force. Within minutes, he was talking to the officer in charge about when he could start. After passing a simple medical, Peter was appointed as Wing Commander responsible for training pilots for the Burma Air Force (BAF) to be based at Mingaladon Airport. In the end, Peter was one of a hundred personnel sent to support the Burmese forces after their official formation on 16th January 1947 while still under British rule.

On arriving at Mingaladon Airport Peter was delighted to find the BAF already had many experienced ex-RAF Burmese pilots together with well-trained engineers. The new air force was small consisting of sixteen de Havilland Tiger Moth trainers, forty Airspeed Oxfords, four Auster light aircraft and three Spitfires transferred from the RAF. The Airspeed Oxfords were used as trainers and transports as most were unarmed and slow. Eventually, some were modified as bombers to carry eight 11.5 pound bombs under each wing. The only real fire power came from the three Spitfires, but they were not enough to meet all the requirements of supporting the army in conflicts with dissidents.

Peter was commanded by the Anglo-Burmese former RAF Squadron Leader now Major Tommy Clift. Both men exerted pressure on the British administration to provide more aircraft to help Burma protect her long borders. However, all their requests were firmly rejected so that they could only look on as the last RAF Spitfires left Burma to fly to Hong Kong and Singapore. The interim government promised the BAF that other aircraft would soon be delivered. Peter felt that the British did not want the emerging independent Burma to have an effective Air Force. Later, this was confirmed as rumours emerged of the RAF burying crates of unassembled Spitfire in Burma to prevent them reaching the Burmese government. The British never gave Burma a fair chance of becoming a free, united nation.

While living at the BAF camp at Mingaladon Airport, Peter was visited by Tauk, who presented him with the keys to a large house in Golden Valley next door to his own home. At the house, Tauk and Peter talked for hours while drinking iced tea.

'Thanks for the house. Do you know anything of my neighbours?' asked Peter.

'The five houses around you belong to me and another to Tun Kyi. They were being sold so cheaply that I purchased them as an investment,' added a proud Tauk.

'You have been busy,' Peter replied, surprised at how good a businessman his father-in-law was.

'I wanted to buy some of the houses being sold near Victoria Lake, but they were much too expensive. I think they ended up being owned by government officials and embassies.'

'Well it just shows that even you, cannot always win.'

'I suppose it does. Now tell me when can I expect to see my Susie again and meet my grandson?' asked Tauk.

'I hope they will come here very soon, as I miss them as much as Susie misses you. I am trying to arrange for her and our son to come here on the next available flight. The new British Overseas Airways Corporation (BOAC) has started flying to Rangoon from Southampton using the Short Hythe flying boats,' the smiling Peter added. He missed his family and with luck, they would soon be re-united.

'That is good news,' Tauk commented. 'Do you have a date or need help to buy the tickets?'

'Three days ago, I brought the tickets from the BOAC office for the next available flight on a Hythe flying boat and then started looking for a house. Thanks to your generosity, all I now need to do is buy a suitable family car and furniture,' Peter stated as they could not rely on Tauk to drive them around in his Willys Jeep.

'Buying a vehicle is simple as the British Army is selling ex-military vehicles at their supply depot near Mingaladon. There are hundreds of lorries, cars and jeeps available for sale at very low prices,' stated Tauk. 'Unfortunately they are not selling armoured cars as I could do with one to transport my gems.'

'Are your mines proving profitable?'

'I am delighted to say we are producing high-quality pigeon blood red rubies and fine jade that we sell in our shop on Sule Pagoda road near the Strand Hotel. Many of the richer British officers and officials buy them as fast as I can obtain them to sell in London for much more than they pay me,' replied Tauk. He understood the minds of most people and saw the greed in the eyes of many of his customers.

'How do you bring your gemstones safely from your mines to Rangoon?'

'That Peter is my biggest problem. At present, I employ trusted friends like Tun Kyi to bring them down by road in small amounts. It is costly but the only way to take them through the dangerous countryside to Rangoon.'

'Why not fly them out from the old airport near Mongok?'

'I have considered that option, but first I must find a reliable pilot and a small aircraft.'

'If you buy one of the small Auster aircraft, the RAF is selling; I will fly your gems when I am not on duty,' Peter replied.

'Then you must help me select an Auster that is in good condition for you to fly.'

'We could go tomorrow to the depot at Mingaladon to examine what the RAF is selling.'

'I will meet you there at noon,' Tauk said as he walked away.

The next day Peter examined four Auster planes and selected the newest one for Tauk to buy. The whole deal only took a few hours, and then the aircraft was registered in Tauk's name and taken to the commercial side of the airfield. Peter arranged for one of his engineers to overhaul the aircraft before he took it up for a brief flight. Meanwhile, Tauk paid the fees required for Peter to get a Burmese commercial pilot's licence to fly the Auster and Dakotas. It took five days for him to find a civil servant willing to bend the rules in return for a small ruby. It was the only way to get things done in a country afraid of independence.

The fact was that many rich people wanted to buy the best rubies and emeralds as a method of transferring their funds out of Burma to banks in Europe and America. This was in preparation for their leaving Burma before the Independent Burma was created. Nearly everyone feared what would happen as the Executive Council was not strong enough to control the rebellious minorities while the council contained many who fought with the Japanese. In fact, most of the country was not under the control of the central government as regional groups fought for self-rule. The forces of the Karen National Defence Organisation (KNDO), the Shan militia and the Chinese Koumintang (KMDT) controlled much of the north and east of the country. Elsewhere armed gangs roamed the countryside unopposed, taking what they wanted. The minorities were supported by the profits from the opium trade with Thailand and the USA. Effectively, during the 1950's the American CIA controlled much of northern Burma, Laos and Thailand to run the lucrative opium trade using their own airline of unmarked aircraft based in Vietiane, Laos and Bangkok, Thailand.

With Tauk's help, Peter purchased an American Willys Jeep and a larger Humber Heavy Utility Staff car. Then he employed a carpenter to make the furniture for his house to be ready when Susie, and his son Paul arrived. Occasionally, Peter flew the Auster aircraft to Mogok to return with precious stones. On arriving at Mingaladon, he was always met by Tauk waiting to collect his merchandise. In just one flight Peter transported enough gems to keep his father-in-law's shop well stocked for about a year and ten times what Tun Kyi moved in a year. This kept many skilled men in work cutting and polishing the stones to make them look more appealing.

When not working, Peter met Tauk at the Strand Hotel to be introduced to the people who would help him live happily in Rangoon. At the time, it was the only place where the powerful could meet in a relaxed atmosphere. Though most men had their wives with them, the suspicious Burmese men always came alone.

One evening while waiting for Tauk to lock up his shop, Peter felt a hand gently touch his shoulder. 'Hello Peter. It is nice to see you have survived and look so well,' said the man.

Peter turned his head to see Pip Palmerino standing there holding a glass of whiskey.

'Sir, it is good to see you looking so relaxed here in Rangoon,' Peter replied vigorously shaking the old elephant hunter's hand.

'I returned during the chaos after the war to repossess my bungalow on the Prome Road and be an intermediary between the various administrations and the Burmese. I came back with others from our group, including the civil servant James Barrington and Doctor Lusk,' Pip replied.

'Is there a communication problem with the Burmese?' Peter asked.

'In Burma most people are suspicious of everyone and can be quite hostile and devious, especially if they think you do not respect them,' came the reply.

'Why have the Burmese changed so much?'

'There were always some corrupt officials. However, it is much worse now. After the war, most were penniless and had to endure more hardships than under the Japanese. Then they learnt to get what they needed by bribery and other means to feed their families,' the sympathetic Pip replied.

'This explains why I often have problems buying even the simplest things.'

'I expect it does. Remember most Burmese regard the military as overpaid and dangerous to be seen with. Like most Buddhists, they regard them as a necessary evil.'

'Will it change?'

Perhaps it will. It all depends on how the new rulers and foreigners treat the Burmese people.'

'Maybe life will be easier when Susie arrives. I hope so because I want our life here to be perfect.'

'Dear Peter you must remember that nowhere is perfect as too many people are greedy and never appreciate what others do for them. Simply thanking people always helps; however, the arrogant forgets the simplest niceties. A smile and gratitude are expected by the Burmese.'

'Sadly few diplomats and businessmen understand the rules of Buddhism and treat the waiters and their servants badly. I dislike the bad manners of some customers here at the bar. I must admit that many of the British soldiers are badly behaved, especially after a few drinks.'

When Tauk arrived, they sat down to dinner. It was clear that Tauk knew Pip and were relaxed in each other's company.

'I have just heard that Independence day will be on January 4th when the new Union of Burma flag will replace the British Union Flag,' stated Tauk.

'That is sooner than expected, but nothing will change until U Nu gains experience,' Pip commented.

'Then what will happen?' Peter asked.

'Only time will tell. In Burma, changes come slowly and are influenced by external factors or internal strife,' said Tauk.

'U Nu is a complex character who changes sides depending on circumstances who worked with the Japanese administration under Aung San, but he was never respected. I doubt that he will ever unite the nation as he has too many enemies,' added the well-informed Pip.

Then Tauk brought a Burmese gentleman to meet Peter.

'Peter let me introduce you to Maung Maung Myint, who is both a senior government official and a good friend,' said Tauk.

'It is a pleasure to meet you sir,' Peter said shaking Maung Maung Myint's hand.

'The pleasure is mine as it is good to meet a pilot, especially now that we are considering establishing an internal airline. Any advice you can give me will be greatly appreciated,' replied the immaculately dressed Myint.

'I will help you, but remember I am an air force pilot who has not flown any aircraft larger than a Dakota,' Peter answered.

'I expect we will start the airline using the Dakotas still in Burma as they can easily be fitted out with seats,' Maung Maung Myint continued.

Then the three older men discussed reopening the old social amenities such as the Pegu Club, the Kokine Swimming Club and the Rangoon Sailing Club on Victoria Lake. They agreed to reopen them, but with membership open to all nationalities who could afford the fees. Within a year, the clubs were running with many senior Burmese members. Then it was possible for Burmese and expatriates to socialise. It was a move in the right direction.

Flag of the Union of Burma

At midnight on 4th January, the British Union flag was ceremoniously lowered and the flag of the Union of Burma raised, accompanied by military music and the cheers from the onlookers. The new President Sao Shwe Taik briefly announced that an independent Burma would be administered by the Burmese for all ethnic groups. He promised an honest, peaceful state where everyone would be respected and allowed to prosper. Then U Nu, speaking as Prime Minister, told the crowd that the nation would follow socialistic and Buddhist principles for the benefit of all. At the same time, Burma would abandon the rupee and replace it with a unique Burmese currency called the Kyat. However, for the time being, one rupee could be exchanged at the banks for one Kyat, but only the Kyat was legal currency. There was a murmur of disbelief among the people present who feared this change could impoverish them further.

Peter heard no more about the creation of an airline until after the BAF was renamed the Union of Burma Air Force (UBAF). Meanwhile, the small UBAF was kept busy flying sorties against anti-government forces who regularly attacked the Burmese army. Not a day passed without the Spitfires firing on militants attacking government positions. It was clear that one war was replaced with another as the ravished nation still suffered. It was soon apparent that without more fighter aircraft, the insurgents could defeat the government forces.

On 15th September 1948, the government created Union of Burma Airways (UBA) to be based at Mingaladon Airport. Initially, it was equipped with ex-military C-47s, known as Douglas DC3 Dakotas. It operated commercial flights to all the major cities until in, 1950, it started international flights to neighbouring countries. In 1948, UBA purchased ten new De Havilland DH104 Doves to carry government officials around the nation. This was necessary because the railways were unreliable due to broken bridges and track that had not been repaired since the war. In December 1945, the railway system consisted of only twelve railway carriages, together with fifty locomotives and eight hundred miles of usable track. The lack of reliable communications forced the central government to give extraordinary powers to local administrators. Sadly, many of them misused their authority to enrich themselves. Where this happened, local militants reacted by attacking government outposts and establishing their own 'independent' homelands. So it was that chaos ruled the nation.

# 40
# A Happy Reunion

When the flying boat bringing Susie and young Paul to Rangoon landed in the harbour, Peter and Tauk were on the jetty to greet them. They arrived an hour early being excited at the thought of seeing Susie again. In the small passenger reception area at the flying boat terminal, they were met by the young BOAC station manager.

'Gentlemen, our flight from Southampton will arrive on time. So why not sit down and have a drink as you have fifty minutes to wait,' stated the station manager. 'The river is calm, so we expect a textbook landing.'

So Peter and Tauk sat down to drink glasses of refreshing iced tea and watched the ships at anchor unloading their cargo into the smaller vessels surrounding them. By the airline jetty, were two motor launches, one was for the transfer of the passengers and the other contained petrol drums to refill the aircraft. Nearby the BOAC ground engineer, in white overalls, and an airline hostess walked down to the launch ready to welcome the incoming flight. It was a well rehearsed routine that ran like clockwork to keep their paying passengers happy. Then the refuelling launch moved towards the mooring buoy to refuel the aircraft's nearly empty tanks when she stopped. It was a complex operation involving three men, in which one had to climb onto the wing to insert the fuel lead while another kept the line tight and the third operated the fuel pump.

Suddenly the small office became busy as passengers checked their luggage in for the flight to Bangkok. Some of the passengers objected to being weighed, but stopped complaining when it was explained that for the safety of the aircraft, the pilot had to know the exact weight of the loaded aircraft. This was especially important when taking off from water, because the heavier the aircraft the greater was the power needed to lift her off the water. Peter noticed that most of the passengers were wealthy diplomats and local people eager to leave Burma before life became too difficult. Tauk recognised many as customers who purchased very expensive rubies that were probably carefully hidden inside their clothing.

At last, they saw the white painted flying boat approaching from the west. She slowly came closer until they could hear the roar of the engines as she landed gracefully in the river. After landing, this majestic craft taxied to be attached to the buoy as a launch drew up to the doorway. In seconds, the door was open to let the ground engineer on board while a stewardess waited in the launch.

'Why are they so slow?' asked Peter.

'You must be patient. They have been travelling for five days and are making sure the passengers leave safely with their luggage,' the wiser Tauk replied.

Nothing more was said as through the aircraft's door appeared the first passenger who gingerly walked down the few steps into the launch. Next came a tired Susie carrying young Paul and helped by an attentive stewardess. Having seen Susie safely get into the launch, the two men jumped up and down with joy while waiting for the launch full of passengers and the crew to travel to the pier.

As soon as Susie passed customs and immigration, Peter rushed up to her with tears of joy running down his face. She put her arms around his neck and kissed him so hard as if her very life depended on being with her love. Meanwhile, Tauk lifted young Paul in his arms and kissed the child as he silently thanked Lord Buddha for this blessed moment. At last, they were on their way to the house in Golden Valley where Tun Kyi, Maria and Temasen waited with refreshments.

'It is such a beautiful house. Is it really ours?' asked a happy Susie.

'It is ours my love to do with as we please. I know we will be happy here surrounded by your family and friends,' answered Peter delighted that Susie loved the house.

'Darling, you have forgotten a few essential things,' Susie added.

'Such as?'

'At least one mongoose and a Chinthe to guard us all.'

'Then my dear daughter you can soon put that right,' Tauk intervened.

Susie then entered the large sitting room to be greeted with cheers from all those waiting for her. Maria kissed her sister while putting an orchid in her hair, while Tun Kyi lit a joss stick in front of a small gold statue of Buddha by a window. For the next hour, everyone gave Susie presents for her home; these included a pair of large stone Chinthes to guard the front door, flowers for the garden and bowls of fresh fruit. For a moment, Peter felt that it was all too much for the tired Susie as he sadly watched the tears stream down her face. Tauk then told everyone that it was time for Susie and young Paul to sleep off the effects of a five-day flight, and they did. As soon as Susie's head touched the pillow, she was soundly asleep dreaming of a lake in the forest where she, and Peter were surrounded by beautiful butterflies and birds. Good memories never go away but stay with us forever.

Susie was up at dawn to wash and feed Paul. Afterwards, she walked in the garden to notice that the grass was too long and that there were not as many flowers as she wanted. On entering the house, she found Peter had eaten breakfast and was dressed in his uniform ready to go to work. She kissed him goodbye before sitting down to play with Paul while waiting for her father. She was dressed in her finest Burmese clothes to honour her father as she was sure he would wish to take her to a nearby pagoda to give thanks for his family being reunited.

Tauk arrived in his jeep with Maria sitting by his side. On entering the house, he kissed his daughter and hugged his grandson.

'I am sorry that I am late, but I had to open the shop. Now we must hurry if we are to visit the Sule Pagoda before the sun makes everywhere too hot,' Tauk said.

In minutes, they were driving down Sule Pagoda road to the bottom of the temple stupa.

'Father, this temple is huge and so beautiful,' Susie commented in amazement.

'Just wait until you see inside to appreciate its beauty. It is not the most impressive temple but much easier to enter compared with the mighty Shwe Dagon,' replied Tauk.

'You know that this is my first visit to Rangoon. I am amazed at the wide streets and the thousands of people. It is far bigger than I expected,' explained Susie.

'It is a magnificent city where the good, the bad, rich and poor walk together being equal in the sight of God,' added a proud Tauk. He had forgotten that Susie had not visited the city before now.

Before entering the temple they stopped to buy joss sticks and fresh flowers to donate to the *pongyis*. Then they left their shoes by the entrance to walk barefooted into this holy place. The brilliant morning light reflecting off the gold statues transformed the temple into a colourful, mystical place full of peace and hope. Young Paul was overwhelmed with the beauty and the noise of chanting and the sounding of gongs. So Susie held him tightly by the hand as they moved towards the large room where the gold image of Lord Buddha was located. Inside the room, people were kneeling and praying, while others burned joss sticks or placed flowers near the statue. They knelt down as Tauk lit ten joss sticks for his family and friends before deeply chanting his prayers. After half an hour, Susie remembered that Paul was by her side and must be bored. When she turned to look for her child to find he was gone. In panic, she searched until she found him sitting on the stairs with other children watching the birds flying around the temple and listening to the temple chimes blowing in the wind. When she walked to pick up her child, she noticed that the children were being watched over by a young *pongyi*. The priest was very aware of the danger that lurked outside the temple, especially for children, from the traffic around the Sule Pagoda roundabout.

The Sule Pagoda

235

After leaving the Pagoda, Tauk took them to visit his shop that was full of people buying his exquisite collection of fine gems. They were greeted by the manager, Ba Saw, who ushered them into the backroom where there were comfortable seats reserved for selected customers and close friends. Here Susie saw that the salon opened into a small courtyard full of flowers with a central statue of Lord Buddha. Now they were served iced tea with freshly cooked cakes from a nearby bakery. When Susie was relaxed, she started asking about many things she wanted to know.

'Father, what did you do after we left Dimapur?' Susie enquired.

'We remained in the bungalow until Ba Saw could travel, and it was safe to drive south. By then the British had driven the Japanese out of Mogok, so I purchased a jeep to travel with Ye-Hut down to my mines. It was an arduous journey travelling by river and driving over poor roads. As you know, Mogok is a lakeside town two hundred miles from Mandalay, and at an altitude of four thousand feet surrounded by higher hills. On arriving, we visited the villages of the local Lisu and Palaung hill people to ask them to help me reopen my richest mines. They treated us well, but still it took a few days of feasting and bargaining before we agreed to their terms for working in the mines. Each man would receive one rupee plus food for each day worked in the mines, together with ten per cent of the value of all stones he or she recovered. That was after they had been washed and separated from the gem bearing gravel. It was what they received before the war and much more than they could earn elsewhere,' Tauk answered.

'Within a month the hidden shafts to Tauk's best ruby mine were working, and the open pits expanded in the search for jade boulders. We paid the headman four hundred rupees as a down payment for future work and placed Ye-Hut in command of the mines. He recruited some Lisu and a few local Burmese of Gurkha extraction to guard the mines,' added Ba Saw with pride.

'Then we drove to Rangoon where we purchased a vacant shop near the old Strand Hotel to sell our produce,' continued Tauk.

'Dear father you really have done well,' stated Susie.

'Dear sister, father has not explained how hard he worked searching Rangoon for property for the family and places to convert into workshops,' Maria added with pride.

'Then he made it known around the city that he would employ all skilled gem stone cutters, gold smiths and carvers that proved up to his high standards. Within two months, he had craftsmen polishing cheap star sapphires and cutting jade statues,' stated Maria.

'I hope you donate some of your wealth to the *pongyis* and the poor,' commented Susie hoping her father had not forgotten his Buddhist ways.

'I have given more than money by employing as many honest people as I need and paying them a fair wage,' Tauk replied.

'He has even housed for free the visitors from Britain who came to build the new War Memorial in remembrance of those allied soldiers who died during the war,' stated Ba Saw.

'I only housed the senior men, as I could not accommodate all of them. Anyway, it was the least I could do to honour our fallen comrades.'

Then a lady served them with the traditional Burmese *mohinka* for lunch, which consisted of thin rice noodles in a fish soup with boiled eggs on top. The soup was seasoned with onions, ginger, garlic and lime grass. It was an ideal meal to welcome Susie home. Afterwards, they drove back to Susie's house for Paul and Susie to sleep during the heat of the day. On arriving home, Susie noticed a Naga cutting the grass and a young Burman that opened the door.

'Susie I asked a friend to get you help running your home. He sent a houseboy, his wife as an amah to look after Paul, a gardener, a cook and a night guard. If they prove unsatisfactory, I will get you others,' announced Tauk.

'Thank you father. I hope Peter accepts the idea of having servants about the house.'

'I do not see why he should not. Surely, his parents have domestic help.'

'They only have an elderly gardener to help dig the garden, but no servants.'

'Oh I thought all the British with large houses had at least a butler and a cook.'

'The very rich may, but Peter's family does not.'

'Well I will leave you now. Remember that if you want anything, then send me a message as my house is only next door,' Tauk stated getting into his jeep.

'I will, but please come tonight when Peter is home as I know he enjoys your company nearly as much as I do.'

'I will come after seven, if that's alright. Then I can check if your night watchman is any good.'

When Susie inspected the kitchen, she found the cook carefully washing the fresh lettuce in boiling water to prepare a large salad. He was cooking a mild lamb curry to be served with boiled rice.

'Madam, I hope a mild curry meets with your approval. If it does not, I will boil some fresh fish?' asked the anxious cook.

'A curry will be fine. What may I call you?' said Susie.

'I am usually called cook, and that suits me.'

'Well cook, may we eat at eight?'

'Yes mam, everything will be ready.'

That evening Susie and her father together with Peter dined on an excellent lamb curry complete with Bombay duck and mango chutney accompanied with a fresh salad covered by an oil and vinegar dressing. This was accompanied by freshly crushed lime juice and a dish full of yogurt. For desert, the cook produced individual portions of sliced mango with his own homemade ice cream. It was delicious and appreciated by all.

After dinner, they relaxed under the whirling ceiling fan to drink coffee and talk.

'Well that was a fabulous dinner. Congratulations Susie on finding a superb cook,' commented Peter.

'I must say it was very good, tasty but not too hot,' added Tauk.

'I am always pleased when my men are happy,' replied Susie.

'Peter, have you heard that the government is changing the armed forces?' asked Tauk.

'Yes I have heard the rumours that Prime Minister U Nu places the blames for the failure of his military to defeat the Karen insurgents on the fact that many of his senior staff are Karen. So he issued a decree sacking the Karen General Dun as Head of the Armed Forces and replaced him with his war time colleague General Ne Win. The order removes Chief of the Army Staff Brigadier General Saw Kyar Doe and Chief of Air Staff Colonel Saw Shi Sho. Then he promoted their Burman assistants to fill the empty posts,' Peter informed them.

'Oh dear, will the changes cause you problems because you have a Karen wife,' Susie asked.

'Luckily, U Nu's neurosis does not extend to people's family. I will miss Colonel Saw Shi Sho, who knew how to run a small air force efficiently. However, his deputy is very competent.'

'I wonder what General Ne Win will do now he is in command. Whether you like him or not, he is a talented tactician experienced in dealing with insurgency,' Tauk informed his family.

'Will he do exactly what U Nu wants?' asked Peter.

'I don't think so as Ne Win does not trust U Nu because he refused to join Aung San's revolt and stayed with the Japanese until their final defeat. I find it very strange that the AFPFL elected him as their leader after Aung San was murdered. I feel that had Aung San lived; he would never have given U Nu a position in government other than a seat on the Council,' Tauk stated with certainty. He, like many other businessmen, distrusted Prime Minister U Nu's policies of mixing Marxism with Buddhism to give him nearly absolute power.

'To change the subject, I have reserved and paid for one of the latest American refrigerators and two air conditioners. They are waiting in Steele Brothers warehouse to be delivered whenever you say. I thought it would be a good idea if you had a cool bedroom to sleep in, and keep your food fresh in this new cooling machine.'

'Oh, thanks father. I hope you also purchased one for yourself and for Maria,' Susie said wondering how generous her father had been.

'Yes I purchased half the shipment and will have an air conditioner fitted to my shop to make the customers feel cool even at midday.'

'Father, Peter must stop calling you sir or Tauk. I know you were given a Christian name when mother had you baptised.'

'You may call me *pi* or grandfather. I do not like my baptismal name of George as I am not a dragon slayer.'

They all laughed at the thought of the former pongyi slaying anything.

'I suppose you can call me George in private, but not in my shop,' Tauk suggested.

'I will call you George as I can't call you *pi* as it sounds like our word for the vegetable or even worse the slang word for urination,' added Peter.

'Then I am George the old retired dragon slayer,' George Tauk said with a big grin. He added, 'Today I met James Barrington who is going to New York as Burma's new ambassador to the USA and Canada as well as her representative at the United Nations. It appears that U Nu is changing all his ambassadors in the hope of getting more international support. James is an excellent choice having degrees from Rangoon University and Oxford University before entering the colonial civil services. Peter you must remember him as a member of Pip Palmarino's group you walked with to Nagaland.

Afterwards, James served as a captain in the British Army. Not only is he highly intelligent, but also a decent, hard-working honest man. That is why U Nu chose him, even though he dislikes most Anglo Burmese. U Nu also appointed Aung San's widow, Daw Khin Kyi, as ambassador to India so that she will not be in Rangoon to criticise his actions.'

'Why is the government against the Anglo-Burmese. From what I see they make Burma run and occupy many senior positions with efficiency and without favour?'

'Peter it is simply that they are too good at their work, and few are Buddhists. The government needs them until they have trained their Burmans replacements. Then they will be sacked, that is if my interpretation of U Nu's policy of Buddhists first is correct,' George Tauk replied looking worried.

Soon Susie became accustomed to life in Rangoon, often spending hot afternoons swimming at the Kokine Swimming Club or chatting to the other women. She was delighted to find that Paul rapidly learnt to swim and loved being in the water. Every day before going to bed, she would give Paul a dose of Paludrine in a syrup to prevent malaria and made sure that she and Peter took the daily Paludrine pill. Malaria in Rangoon was very common and a cause for alarm. The best treatment for the disease was quinine, but that was often difficult to obtain. At night, she lit coils of pyrethrum whose fumes killed off the mosquitoes that still came to the house even though all the doors and windows were covered with mosquito proof netting. She organised the garden so that the Naga gardener knew what to plant and where it was to be. After asking the gardener if he could find a pair of mongooses for the garden, the gardener presented her with two young pairs in a bamboo cage. It took weeks for Susie and the gardener to get them to come and feed on some chicken eggs, but though they stayed, they never were tame enough to be regarded as pets. However, they kept snakes away from their home.

# 41

# Peter Joins Union of Burma Airways

*The safest way to travel in dangerous places is by air.*

At the end of 1949, Peter was recruited by Maung Maung Myint to fly and train pilots for his new airline. Initially, the work was straightforward as the DC-3 was easy to fly and ideal for the short, poor runways found in most of Burma. It was an aircraft that Peter knew from the war to be tough, reliable and economical to fly. The Union of Burma Airways (UBA) after one year of operations was accepted as the safest and quickest way to travel in Burma. The DC-3s were noisy, uncomfortable and not pressurised so the passengers felt the changes in altitude, especially when flying over the mountains. The cabin had seats for twenty-eight passengers with a basic toilet in the rear behind which was a luggage compartment. The twin-engine aircraft was cheap to buy, easy to maintain and readily converted to carry both passengers and freight.

UBA flew regularly to most cities in Burma from Tavoy in the south to Rangoon, to Mandalay in the centre and right up to Myitkina in the north. In fact, they had a network that covered nearly two thousand miles bringing essential supplies to the farthest corners of the land. There still were many problems caused by having to fly through tropical storms, land on flooded airstrips and sometimes getting fired upon by insurgents. They employed local staff to run the airstrips and obtain fuel. At each strip, they built a passenger terminal next to a radio transmitter to maintain contact with the aircraft. When there were no flights due to land, the manager arranged for the runway to be maintained, the surrounding vegetation kept short, and all animals kept away. In some cases high trees were cut down to give the aircraft a clear approach. Soldiers were stationed at every airstrip to protect both the passengers and the facilities from attack. Unfortunately, the insurgents often attacked the airstrips, destroying the facilities and stealing the valued radio transmitters. This meant that UBA had problems keeping the airline functioning, especially where the insurgents were powerful. In time, the growing Burmese Army established strong defensive positions around both cities and their airstrips. These logistic problems meant that often some destinations could not be visited by the airliners for months on end. This meant that the air force had to send by parachute urgent medical supplies and ammunition down to their men to keep up the fight. To save money many airport terminals were simple thatched huts that were easily replaced.

UBA Dakota taking off from a rural airstrip.

The airline was based in Mingaladon Airport, and the aircraft maintained in the nearby hangers. They opened offices in most cities as well as placed an engineer and station manager at thirty airfields. It was a huge operation for a small nation to run with little outside assistance. One of Peter's jobs was to visit all the airstrips to recommend improvements. During his first year, Peter flew in all weathers around Burma.

On one traumatic flight, Peter flew north during the monsoon season. The DC3 was full, with people wanting to fly home as a time when the rains made the roads and rivers impassable. As a precaution Peter loaded four drums of aviation fuel in the luggage compartment. This was necessary as though the aircraft had a range of fifteen hundred miles, during the monsoons many airstrips ran out of fuel. Peter and his co-pilot Aung Gyi took off in a cross wind to climb to five thousand feet through thick rain clouds that rocked the aircraft until they were above the clouds. Then the passengers had a more comfortable flight, but Peter had to navigate by dead reckoning and using his instruments as they could not see the land. Luckily, the rain cleared as they approached Mandalay so that they could see the city and locate the airport.

'UBA flight 24 calling Mandalay tower, requesting permission to land. Over,' Peter radioed the airport.

'Flight 24 this is Mandalay receiving you loud and clear. The weather is clearing with a cross wind of twenty knots with excellent visibility. We await your arrival, good luck,' came the reply.

Twenty minutes later, the Dakota was landing on the runway to taxi to the airport terminal. Then the stewardess opened the doors as the steps were wheeled up to the door for the passengers to disembark. They rushed down onto the runway to walk the three hundred yards into the terminal, while the station manager came aboard to brief Peter about the journey ahead and the number of passengers joining the flight. Peter and his co-pilot Aung Gyi went inside the terminal to eat while the ground engineers checked the aircraft and refuelled her in preparation for the long flight to Myitkyina. The two pilots decided on the best route to fly to avoid the rain and places held by insurgents. This was necessary as some aircraft had been fired upon from the ground, but luckily, none seriously damaged.

Once aboard the aircraft, Peter noticed the cabin was full of people together with some pigs and chickens kept in bamboo baskets. It made him realise that for many of his passengers, this flight was their only way home through a war-torn country. Taking off proved difficult as the heavily loaded aircraft needed full power and most of the runway to take off. As soon as they were airborne, they climbed as fast as they could to be well clear of any unfriendly gun fire. The old Pratt and Whitney engines roared at full revs to pull her upwards while shaking everyone on board. Typically, no one complained though a few appeared to pray or smoke their cheroots. When at twenty thousand feet, Peter changed the flaps, to fly in a straight line before reducing the engine revs. This would save fuel and lessen the noise as well as pleasing the passengers. They flew north-west to land between the mountains at Mogok at four thousand feet. It was an easy landing because Peter had flown there before in his father-in-law's small Auster. Most of the disembarking passengers were well dressed suggesting they were businessmen come to trade in gemstones. A few passengers embarked carrying little luggage and looking like people desperate to go home. The fighting around Myitkyina was very intense as the Burmese tried unsuccessfully to defeat the better-equipped Koumintang and their Shan allies.

After refuelling, they flew north along the Irrawaddy River to Bhamo but did not land because of reports that insurgents were operating nearby. So they continued to follow the river north to Myitkyina that lay between the mountains and had an excellent runway. At the border town, they entered the airport building to find Burmese soldiers searching all the baggage and checking everyone's identity looking for illicit supplies destined for the Koumintang. When the soldiers found nothing suspicious, they were better mannered, but still looked formidable. The station manager explained to Peter that the KMT recently overran an army outpost east of the city killing everyone they found. The city was still in shock fearing the return of the ruthless Chinese soldiers who controlled most of the mountains.

When they took off for Mandalay, they came under heavy anti-aircraft fire that destroyed the starboard engine. Suddenly, a routine flight turned into a desperate fight to keep the aircraft in the air. Peter struggled with the controls to maintain altitude while flying from exploding shells. Now he realised how dangerous it was to be an airline pilot in a civil war. Rapidly, Aung Gyi plotted their course to the nearest airstrip that was in Bhamo. This riverside town had a long runway and was at a low altitude. It was exactly what they needed.

The propeller of the ruined engine still rotated while bits from fell from it while emitting oil and fuel that streamed back along the wing and part of the fuselage. Peter saw a fire start in the dead engine that could spread down the wing. He switched on the fire extinguisher to cool the starboard engine with little or no effect. When the engine temperature gauge showed that it was dangerously hot, Peter started to panic. He remembered being in his burning Hurricane and fighting to escape. As sweat fell from his brow, he touched his jade leaf asking for help. However, he remembered to cut the fuel supply to the starboard engine and increased the power in the remaining port engine. With luck, it would keep her airborne long enough for Peter to find a place to land. So he locked his hands on the steering column as he tried to keep the aircraft level. This was very difficult because all the power came from the port engine, so the aircraft tried to move right.

In Rangoon, Susie woke up with a start from her afternoon rest. She dreamt that Peter was piloting a burning plane and was terrified. In sheer panic, she rushed downstairs to light three joss sticks in front of the statue of Lord Buddha before praying, with her body prostrate upon the ground in front of her jade tree. In seconds, she was deeply in a trance that carried her spirit through the ether to be with her Peter. She found herself helping Peter keep his aircraft airborne while desperately calling upon her ancestors for assistance. Her impassioned cries could be heard throughout the house causing the houseboy and his wife to come running. When they found her shaking on the floor, they were frightened and sent the Naga gardener to her father's house to get help.

As always, the spirits of Susie's ancestors heard her pleas and sent a violent rainstorm to cascade water over the burning plane. In minutes, there were no more flames and both pilots could smile as the torrential rain battered the windscreen making the small windscreen wipers work hard to clear the water for them to see ahead. The violent storm was problematic to fly through, but it extinguished the flames and cooled the engines. For the first time since the engine was damaged, both pilots knew they had a chance of surviving this disaster.

'This is UB24 calling Bhamo airport to declare an emergency. We are seriously damaged with only one engine working, so we must approach from across the river. How are the runway conditions? Over,' Peter transmitted while letting the plane slowly descend to three thousand feet over the river.

'UBA 24, this is Bhamo airport; you have permission to land. There is light rain with a slight cross-wind. Be careful as we have a two-inch layer of water on the runway that is slowly rising,' Bhamo radioed.

'Roger, Bhamo. Two inches of water are not a problem for a tough old bird like this, so I am starting my descent. I expect to land in fifteen minutes. Over and out,' Peter replied.

As they descended through a gap between the mountains to fly west over the river, the rain miraculously cleared so the pilots could see ahead. It was a difficult landing as Peter fought to keep the aircraft level as his co-pilot called out the altitude. There was no room for error, as the wings were feet away from the mountains and the wind threw them up and down. Already the overworked port engine was overheating and losing power giving them only a few minutes to land. As soon as they crossed the Irrawaddy River, they descended to five hundred feet and warned the passengers to prepare for a crash landing. Then the aircraft was suddenly full of people chanting their prayers and crying, while the stewardess told them to face forward with their head in their arms. Quickly, she removed anything that was not firmly attached to the floor to avoid injuries from flying objects. Peter saw the airport beacon and lights as he gently guided the aircraft into the flight path on to the runway. Seconds later the Dakota's wheels touched the tarmac, bounced, skidded a few yards, before stopping five hundred feet from the air terminal.

In minutes, the aircraft was surrounded by firefighters and soldiers. Rapidly, the worried ground staff evacuated the frightened passengers to the safety of the terminal while the firemen sprayed water on to the hot engines. It took ten minutes for a doctor and Aung Gyi to ease Peter's fingers from the steering column because they were locked tight due to the effort of trying to steer the aircraft. The muscles in his fingers were so fatigued that they contracted to become claws that were difficult to move without causing further injury. Then the doctor took Peter to the First Aid Post where his bent fingers were massaged until they straightened and were bandaged.

At home in Rangoon, the houseboy and his wife gently lifted the unconscious Susie onto the settee. Then they washed her forehead with cool water believing she had a fever. By the time her father and sister arrived, Susie was sitting up and smiling knowing her prayers were answered as she had seen Peter with a doctor in a building in Bhamo. After telling her father what she saw, they decided to find out for themselves what had happened and drove the ten miles to the airport.

An hour later, they were in Maung Maung Myint's office at Mingaladon Airport.

'Welcome Tauk and Daw Anderson, please sit down,' said the chairman of UBA. 'How may I be of assistance?'

'Sir, we want to know what happened to your flight 24 and Peter Anderson?' Tauk replied.

'I am sorry that someone has not told you, but I am delighted to say Peter is safe in Bhamo and will be back here by noon tomorrow. His aircraft suffered a serious problem, but luckily Peter landed her safely with no casualties. I have sent my personal De Havilland Dove aircraft to pick him up and fly him home.'

'Is he seriously hurt?' Susie asked.

'He is very tired and will need a few weeks to recover from his ordeal that will be hastened by your good nursing and lots of love.'

'Thank you sir, I promise you that he will get both. Now we must leave because we have taken up too much of your valuable time,' a tearful Susie replied.

'You are both welcome to visit my office at any time. I hold your Peter in high esteem both as a pilot and friend,' replied Maung Maung Myint.

Meanwhile, Peter found himself under a mosquito net being attended to by a Shan nurse.

'Nurse, where am I?'

'Sir you are in Bhamo Hospital where you must rest before going to Rangoon in the morning.'

Then the building shook as shells fell nearby.

'What on earth is that noise?'

'It is the usual shelling of the town by the Shan United Army when attacked by the government soldiers. It will be over in an hour, so sleep well knowing they never attack the hospital, and you are safer here than anywhere else in Bhamo.'

So Peter slept as the sedative the doctor gave him took over, and he dreamt of being in bed with Susie while their son crawled between them. It was where he wanted to be holding his loved ones in his arms.

Next morning, Peter and his co-pilot Aung Gyi were flown from Bhamo to Rangoon in the UBA Dove used for government officials and VIPs. As they took off, they passed the remains of Peter's DC-3 that was under repair. The sight of the black streaks on the wing and fuselage reminded both pilots how close to death they had been. If the fire had lasted a few minutes more they would have lost part of the starboard wing or the fuselage would have caught fire. Whatever happened it would have destroyed the aircraft and everyone on board. It would take a month to replace the engine and repair the aircraft before it was again flying passengers around the country. During the flight, the pilots were served with sandwiches and a beer by an attentive stewardess who treated them as heroes for saving their aircraft and passengers. Aung Gyi fed Peter as his hands were bandaged so that he could not hold anything.

At Mingaladon Airport, Susie and her father stood on the runway next to a UBA manager waiting for Peter to arrive. When Peter was helped out of the small Dove, they were shocked to see his hands were bandaged, and how exhausted he looked. For the next two months, Peter rested at home while his fingers gradually straightened and started to move without pain so that his confidence as a pilot returned. Now he had to do all the things he planned to do before fate intervened. So that night he buried his head between Susie's breasts before sucking them like a hungry baby. When she was aroused Peter slowly entered her in an effort to make another baby. This was to fulfil both his sexual desire and to give her someone to remember him by and a playmate for Paul. A very surprised Susie responded eagerly to his body as she wanted to please him and needed to feel his child growing inside her. While convalescing Peter was very passionate both in bed and when walking in the house.

The smallest thing would bring tears to his eyes as he accepted that he was alive and getting better. He had time to play with and teach Paul, who now spoke Burmese much better than Peter. Together they spent hours encouraging the shy mongooses to come to them to feed on chicken's eggs. First, the older female came creeping towards the eggs and sniffed the ground. She stopped when she saw Peter and Paul before cautiously moving towards an egg. Then she cleanly cut open the top off the egg with her sharp teeth before eating the contents and leaving the eggshell clean. When the watchers did not move, she became braver to eat two more eggs before disappearing into the undergrowth. The next day she returned with the larger male mongoose to eat more eggs. A week later, all four mongooses came to feed on the eggs without fear of Peter and Paul. Eventually, they accepted Peter and even allowed him to stroke them.

Two months later, Dr Lusk confirmed that Susie was very healthy and her morning sickness was because she was pregnant. She left Dr Lusk's clinic beaming with joy to touch her tummy hoping to feel the baby inside, but of course, it was much too early. That night she told Peter their good news and was delighted at his response. They decided she would deliver the baby at Dr Lusk's lakeside clinic where she would get the best attention possible.

Meanwhile, the government in response to the attacks on their bases and aircraft enlarged the military. The army was increased from forty thousand to over two hundred thousand and supplied with modern equipment. New defensible barracks were built in all five states and around most cities. At the same time, the Air Force received five De Havilland Vampire mark T55 jet trainers and fifty fighter aircraft. These consisted of twenty second-hand Spitfires from Israel and thirty ex-naval mark XV Seafires from Britain modified so their wings did not fold to make them suitable as land-based aircraft. The new fighters were strategically placed at three air bases, Mingaladon, Hmawbi and Meiktila. While a transport division was created from nine Dakotas to give the army more manoeuvrability. They also purchased six Kawasaki Bell 47G three-seater helicopters for recognisance purposes. With this increased air power, the army pushed the rebels away from the cities. Importantly, there were fewer attacks on civilian aircraft as the nation started to be united.

# 42

# UBA Starts International Flights

*After the war, aircraft replaced ships as the best way to travel as they flew to most nations.*

While Peter was on leave, Maung Maung Myint decided to expand UBA routes to include regular flights to nearby countries. So the government authorised their Embassy in London to approach the Crown Agents to supply suitable aircraft. This was because the British Crown Agents had supplied the excellent De Havilland Doves. Sadly, this time Burma was let down and sold the last three production Handley Page HPR1 Marathon aircraft with an operational range of over a thousand miles and seating for twenty passengers. It was powered by four turboprop Armstrong Siddeley Mamba engines to cruise at 200 mph. Nobody told the Burmese that it had a poorly designed undercarriage, rejected by BEA and the only other airline flying this aircraft was the British owned West African Airways. The Marathon was designed by the bankrupt Miles Aviation before being built by Handley Page. Each of the Burmese aircraft was fitted with extra fuel tanks to increase their range and flown to Burma in stages.

Once in Rangoon, the three aircraft inaugurated the UBA international flights to nearby Bangkok, Dhaka, and Calcutta. The four-engine aircraft operated a weekly service to the three cities for many years until the last surviving one was replaced by the faster and more reliable Vickers Viscounts in 1959. The Marathons in UBA suffered a number of accidents due to their landing gear being too weak to sustain heavy landings on poor runways. In 1953, one Marathon crashed at Myamaungmya when its undercarriage collapsed on landing and had to be written off as irreparable.

Though the Marathons were slow for a four-engine aircraft, they were popular with people wishing to travel to the nearby countries. Premier U Nu flew in one when he visited India to meet Nehru and to Bangkok to meet the Thai leadership. On longer journeys such as to Israel, he flew on other commercial airlines. With the civil war costing most of the government budget, U Nu attempted to get assistance from both the United Nations and the Colombo Plan. During his visits, he helped create the Non-aligned Movement as protection for small nations against the growing threat from both American and Soviet expansionism. Unfortunately, he proved to be a poor manager spending much more money than the country earned resulting in the Kyat becoming nearly worthless.

Prime Minister U Nu's diplomacy was rewarded with assistance from the Colombo Plan to build a much-needed dam on the Irrawaddy to generate cheap electricity. He also received staff from the British Council to teach at Rangoon University and from Japan, the promise of reparations for war damages, initially worth around fifty million US dollars. This was used to build the Balachuang

Hydroelectric dam and four large industrial plants. The plants were run by Japanese companies such as Matsuda, who built small vehicles; Hino that produced heavy construction machines like bulldozers; Kibuta made agricultural machines, and National who assembled electrical goods such as radios. Though the new factories were welcome, the reparations did little to help Burma's cash shortages. The Japanese managers were reluctant to train Burmese staff, relying on importing Japanese labour. It took years before Japan agreed to supply essential materials needed to rebuild the railways and train local staff to run their factories. The best help he received was from the WHO who sent doctors, nurses, technicians and medicines to modernise the rundown Rangoon Central Hospital.

U Nu believed that Burma should be run by Burmans as a socialist Buddhist state. However, he was not powerful enough to make the change as he feared the other religious communities such as the Muslims, Christians and Animists. He became attracted to the Kalama Sutta Buddhist doctrine that challenges believers to question their beliefs saying, 'You must not believe anything which you cannot test yourself.' Though he passed laws governing foreign exchange by restricting the amount residents could send or take out of the country to one hundred pounds sterling a year. Then, he decreed that all international business transactions had to be carried out through the Central Bank after submission of detailed invoices or receipts. This action upset the frustrated business community by making it difficult to import even the most essential goods. Following this he banned the commercial export of gemstones except through his new state marketing company. U Nu hoped these measures would help control his stagnant economy to conserve his limited reserves of foreign capital.

The strict financial restrictions were accepted by most people, until he built a huge conference centre near Rangoon to celebrate the two thousand and five hundredth anniversary of Gotama Buddha's Enlightenment. He spent millions on a complex to house the delegates from the region who would attend the 6th Buddhist Council held from 1954 to 1956. It was fifteen miles north of Rangoon consisting of a Kuba Aye Pagoda (World Peace Pagoda) covered with gold leaf and the Maha Pissana Guhu (Great Stone Cave). The latter was 455 feet long and 370 feet wide with the Pagoda reaching 117 feet. During the Council, 2500 *pongyis* recited the words of Buddha in Pali, including those of the Tipitake (the Three Canons of Buddhism). On hearing of the widespread criticism of his new religious complex, U Nu announced that Buddhism was the official State Religion, and abolished the death penalty. Following this he passed laws banning the slaughter of animals and the selling of meat as being against Buddha's edicts. All schools were forced to teach the Buddhist scriptures, while alcohol was banned from being sold in public places. Like so many things he did, the adaptable Burmese ignored many of the new laws. Therefore, they developed a thriving black market in alcohol and beef, the latter being known as *todo tha* or hush hush meat. When food became more difficult to buy, he declared that true Buddhists did not eat fish. This statement upset everyone in the land, including the Buddhist priests, the pongyis, who relied on fish and beans to keep healthy. Unable to stop the Christian Sunday from being a holiday, U Nu declared it the *Uposatha* or Buddhist Sabbath and reinstated the

Buddhist lunar calendar. It only confused everyone as to the date, so airlines and many businesses used both the western and lunar dates. Again, U Nu did not understand the mechanisms necessary to make a country work.

# 43
## Lynette Plans to Visit Burma

After the war when life was easier, Lynette asked her husband Paul Anderson if they could visit their son Peter in Burma. Luckily, Paul had just inherited five thousand pounds and an estate from his deceased unmarried aunt and could afford paying for their flight to Rangoon. First Paul applied for British passports for himself and his wife to receive them a month later. Then Lynette visited the Burmese Embassy in London to get a visitor's visa or failing this to apply for a Burmese passport in her maiden name of Maung Win Lynette. There she was advised to obtain a visitor's visa as all passport applications were dealt with in Rangoon and could take years to complete. She was shocked to find that the visas for herself and her husband cost one hundred pounds, but would allow them to stay for up to six months.

While they waited for the visas to be granted, Paul found out how they could best travel to Rangoon. It proved easier than he expected as BOAC flew twice weekly to Hong Kong stopping at Rangoon. The cheapest return airfare for both was eight hundred pounds, the cost of a small house, but this did not deter Paul. He was determined to take his wife home after an absence of over forty years. Now Lynette experienced mixed emotions about returning to Burma. She longed to visit the Shwe Dagon to feel Buddha's love while fearing to discover how her surviving relatives would receive her. Her fears grew after she received the compulsory injections against diseases such as smallpox, yellow fever, typhoid, cholera and tetanus. She heard from the airline doctor that Burma had a poor medical service so that many rare diseases were now rampant. The airline clinic sold Paludrine tablets to prevent malaria and two courses of chloroquine to treat any undulating fever.

They eventually managed to phone Peter at his home to tell him of their plans. When Peter answered the phone, Lynette was so happy that she could not speak.

'Hello Peter, this is your father. How are you?'

'I'm much better hearing your voice. The line is bad, so please speak up so that I can hear what you say. Susie and I want to invite you to come to stay here with us, if that is possible,' replied Peter.

'Fantastic, we are calling to ask if we may visit you next month.'

'The sooner the better as Susie is expecting to have another baby within two weeks and will like having all her loved ones here to welcome our new child.'

'Tell us what we can bring for you, especially things that you cannot get locally.'

'Susie would like a nursing bra and some baby clothes.'

'Consider them brought as next week we are going to London to collect our airline tickets.'

'I can recommend that you fly on the new BOAC Super Constellation flight that continues to Hong Kong. I will try to get a friend to get your tickets upgraded to first class. It should be easy as they owe me many favours for helping them deal with the Burmese authorities.'

'If you can do that it will make the long journey more comfortable.'

'You had better ring off before this phone call costs you too much. Susie and Paul send their love. Tell us the date and time of arrival, so we can be at the airport to meet you. God bless you all.'

Then Peter put down the phone and hugged Susie. She cried with joy on hearing that Peter's parents were to visit them. That evening she prayed in front of the jade tree to tell Lynette how much she looked forward to their visit and inform their ancestors to protect them.

When Peter told Maung Maung Myint of his parent's visit, he was ordered to fly to Hong Kong to examine the engine overhaul facilities at Kai Tak Airport. Maung Maung Myint suggested Peter stayed there for a week to buy what he wanted and meet the staff of Jardine Matheson's Hong Kong Airways that was to be expanded with help from BOAC. They proposed to operate the new Vickers Viscount aircraft that he was also interested in buying to replace the two surviving Marathons. When Peter asked Tauk, he learnt that Maung Maung Myint belonged to the powerful Maung family that included General Ne Win and other ministers. These family connections helped Maung Maung Myint to use some of UBA's foreign exchange to purchase necessary supplies and even aircraft. The cost of Peter's airfare to Hong Kong would be purchased using an inter-airline concessionary ticket that was only ten percent of the normal fare and sometimes free. Before he left, Peter received his tickets and paid hotel reservations in the best hotel in Hong Kong, the Penninsular Hotel overlooking Hong Kong Harbour together with a hundred pounds sterling in cash.

George Tauk gave Peter three large rubies set in gold necklaces for him to sell to a James Li who owned an exclusive bespoke tailor's shop on Nathan Road. Peter was instructed to bank half the proceeds from the sale into George's account in the main branch of the Hong Kong Shanghai Bank situated on Hong Kong Island and used the remainder to buy things for himself and the family. It was just another example of George's generosity even though it meant smuggling the rubies out of Burma. Peter decided the safest way to take them out of Burma was to wear the necklaces around his neck next to his jade leaf.

Peter flew first-class in a BOAC Lockheed Super Constellation leaving Mingaladon at night and stopping at Bangkok for an hour. He was told the aircraft could only land during daylight at Hong Kong because the airport had to be approached with extreme caution. After a very pleasant flight, the Captain announced they were approaching Kai Tak Airport in Hong Kong. Peter looked out of the window to be amazed at how low they were flying, only feet above the roof tops. To the right, he saw many large ships in the harbour surrounded by small sampans, while larger ocean-going junks with typically Chinese-type sails crossed the bay. Then he heard the noise of the undercarriage being lowered as they rapidly descended. There followed a single bump and the roar from the engines being reversed to slow the aircraft before it parked by the terminal building to allow the passengers to disembark. Outside the plane, Peter noticed they had landed on a very short runway surrounded by buildings with the sea on one side and the huge Lion Rock at the end. Landing any aircraft on such a runway in a city required superb skill making him understand why there were no flights into Hong Kong at night.

After passing through customs and immigration, Peter was met by a driver who drove him in a green Rolls Royce limousine to the Penninsular Hotel. The short journey took a long time as they had to drive through busy streets where cars, trams and rickshaws vied with each other for lanes to drive in. Unlike Rangoon, Hong Kong was full of brightly painted signs above shop windows displaying a multitude of goods for sale. The choice of goods for sale was tremendous, varying from cheap toys to expensive watches and radios. It was a fairyland, especially for the hundreds of shoppers who filled the pavements. At every road junction, there were traffic policemen standing on pedestals and conducting the traffic with their hands and a whistle. This scheme worked because everyone obeyed the signals, probably because all who broke the traffic code was severely punished. Eventually, the Rolls Royce parked in the courtyard of the huge Penninsular hotel overlooking Victoria Harbour and Peter was taken to his luxurious room.

After a superb dinner, Peter was given a map of the main streets of Hong Kong Island and Kowloon. At the same time, he picked up a leaflet listing all the recommended tailors. He was relieved to find among those listed was James Li, High-Class Shanghai Tailor for Discerning Men whose shop was on Nathan Road together with the telephone number and directions on how to get there. Peter felt the sooner he met James Li and sold him the rubies, the safer he would feel.

After breakfast, Peter took a taxi to James Li's tailor shop on Nathan Road. From the outside, it looked like any other expensive tailor's shop with the window full of fine fabrics and a suit on a tailor's model. Once inside he found rows of high-quality fabric on shelves lining one wall, opposite was a counter and at the back stood a tailor.

'Good morning, I have come to see Mr. James Li,' Peter stated.

'Good morning sir, may I ask why you wish to see Mr. Li?' the tailor replied.

'I have come from Burma with a parcel from George Tauk that I may only hand over to Mr. Li in person.'

Then a curtain opened, and Peter was ushered into a larger room where a middle-aged man sat behind his desk.

'Welcome, you must be Captain Peter Anderson that George said would visit me. I am James Li,' said the man shaking Peter's hand.

'George told me to allow you to examine the rubies that you may buy with sterling.'

'Of course, cash is the only way we do business. However, I first must examine the rubies to see they have no flaws and weigh them. As you know, the quality, colour and weight greatly influence their value.'

So Peter gave James Li one of the ruby necklaces. He then examined the stone very carefully making chucking noises before removing the stone from the necklace and weighing the ruby. It weighed 3 carats or 600 milligrams. Then he started to make rapid calculations on his wooden abacus. 'This is an excellent stone that is very valuable. I will give you two thousand pounds in cash for it. However, George promised me three rubies. Do you have the others?'

'Yes I have them and will give them to you when you have paid for the first one,' Peter replied watching anxiously the tailor's face.

'Of course, I will buy this one, and then examine the others. It is always wise when dealing with such rare items to be cautious,' replied Mr. Li while opening a safe hidden behind a picture. Then he counted out two thousand pounds in new ten-pound notes that he handed to Peter in an envelope.

When Mr. Li examined the other two rubies, he told his assistant to measure Peter for a fine light weight suit. Afterwards, he paid Peter a further six thousand pounds for the other rubies. Peter left to travel by taxi to Ferry Point to take the ferryboat across Victoria Harbour to the island. Then he walked to the massive Hong Kong and Shanghai Banking Corporation building and once inside went directly to a cashier. There he deposited six thousand pounds into George Tauk's account and safely kept the receipt. The whole transaction took only five minutes leaving Peter feeling relieved to be no longer carrying such a large sum in cash in a strange city. He knew that he had deposited more cash than George wanted, but Peter felt that it was the right amount as he could never spend the remaining two thousand pounds shopping. While in the bank, Peter opened his own bank account with one thousand pounds and collected a cheque book. This was a longer procedure whereby they checked his passport and required an address to send all statements. He gave his parent's address in England as he did not want the Burmese to know he had a bank account in Hong Kong.

Peter then walked to the green painted Star Ferry to join the crowds sailing across the harbour to Kowloon. On the short journey, he sat in the front of the boat to appreciate the sea breeze on his face and enjoy the serene panorama of boats of all sizes crossing the harbour. He was particularly intrigued by the women in black trouser suits with babies strapped to their backs, paddling their small sampans rapidly across the bay. It required skill to make such a journey while avoiding the ships that criss-crossed their path. Then there were the huge junks with two or more sails and equipped with powerful engines that crossed the busy waterway. Many were flying different flags, including those of two sworn enemies, notably Nationalist China and the People's Republic of China. Watching over them were three Royal Navy motor gun boats and a frigate. The harbour contained cargo ships from around the world, including an American aircraft carrier, the USS Essex. These waters catered for all people the same way that the small colony thrived, by trading with all nations.

Once the Star Ferry docked, Peter joined the crowds rushing across the gangplank to Kowloon. Amid the hustle and bustle, Peter was afraid of being robbed, but he was not. So he returned to the Penninsular hotel and deposited five hundred pounds in their safe together with his air ticket and passport. At the same time, he converted two hundred pounds into Hong Kong dollars at the rate of sixteen dollars to the pound before going shopping. He asked at the reception desk where he could buy a good camera and was advised to go to the expensive shop known as Lane Crawford, but it only sold the best. There he purchased a Japanese Asahiflex 35-mm camera that gave excellent results, but was much cheaper than the German Leica. Now he could take photographs of everything he saw using Kodak Ektachrome slide film as it was the best or Kodak print film. So he purchased twenty rolls of each to meet his immediate needs. Next he purchased a Rolex watch for himself and a lady's version for Susie. They were expensive but were totally water proof and reliable.

He walked back to the hotel stopping to take photographs of the magic scenery and the people to be a record of his journey to show Susie. Then he phoned a contact at Kai Tak Airport to arrange to meet the Jardine Matheson manager of the small Hong Kong Airways, that was being reorganised as a feeder airline to take BOAC passengers to the Philippines and Taipei. That evening Mr. Barton, a senior manager of Jardine Matheson's air transport unit, visited Peter at the Penninsular Hotel. After a brief discussion about airlines, Hugh Barton and two of his colleagues took Peter out to the Floating Restaurant in Aberdeen harbour, for an exceptionally fine meal.

'We are always pleased to meet airline executives, especially those from neighbouring nations,' commented Hugh Barton. 'Though I do not understand what Burma Airways wants from us.'

'First let me thank you for such a superb meal,' replied Peter. 'I am here to check the overhaul facilities at Kai Tak run by HAECO and what your plans are now that you can no longer fly into China.'

'Luckily we have a very successful trade with China that benefits all sides. We market Chinese produce such as silk and furniture, while China buys western radios and electronic goods.'

'I am glad that your company flourishes under such difficult conditions.'

'Thank you. I can tell you that HAECO carries out the required overhaul of aircraft and their engines to meet international standards. At present, it is reconditioning some US F 51 fighter aircraft being sold to South Korea. I am proud to say their work is well respected even by the BOAC engineers. If you want I can arrange for you to be shown around their facilities.'

'I would like that very much, as UBA wants to buy bigger aircraft, that will need to be regularly overhauled.'

'Then I will send a car tomorrow morning at 10 to take you there as I too wish to see how they are getting on. As you have heard we are in discussions with BOAC to expand Hong Kong Airways in a joint venture using the latest medium range British aircraft.'

'Have you decided on which type you will buy?'

'We are considering buying an airliner which is well respected for reliability. So we think the choice is between the Vickers Viscount and the Handley Page Herald.'

'I do not think UBA will ever buy another Handley Page aircraft after the problems we had with their Marathons.'

'We prefer the Viscount, especially the type 700 that will fly at 300 miles per hour with a range of twelve hundred miles, powered by four of the latest Rolls Royce Dart engines to carry sixty-five passengers. Such an aircraft would allow us to fly to Tokyo via Formosa and Okinawa as well as to the Philippines,' boasted Barton.

'I must admit it would improve our services to Bangkok and Calcutta,' added Peter.

For the next few days, Peter visited HAECO and the offices of Hong Kong Airways. Later, he was taken around Hong Kong aboard Jardine's company ketch, Jardalinka. In this immaculate yacht, they visited many of the bays such as Tolo Harbour in the New Territories to swim, take photographs and enjoy a luxurious picnic. On the southern side of the harbour, Peter saw the green trains of the Hong Kong Canton Railway passing from Hong Kong to China at regular intervals. It was obvious that this was a busy and profitable route. He was surprised that in such a small country, there were still remote undeveloped places like Tolo Harbour where the Chinese lived in traditional houses and sold their produce, including fish at Taipo Market. On the surrounding hills, they saw black-clad Hakka near old walled villages and the many ancient tombs on the hills. It was an idyllic place to swim, with warm blue seas full of colourful fish of all sizes. Suddenly, he was called back to the yacht while a crew member pointed a rifle at the sea. He wondered if he was going to be shot.

'Sorry to rush you, but we have seen sharks coming our way,' Barton informed Peter.

A few minutes later, Peter watched a pair of large hammerhead sharks swimming well below the surface near the yacht.

'I thought sharks always swam with their dorsal fins above the surface.'

'Peter, that is a common myth as often they swim deep, especially if fish are around.'

Then they sailed back to the Hong Kong Yacht Club. After thanking his hosts for a lovely day, Peter returned to his hotel.

The next morning Peter started shopping for the family. First, he collected his suit from James Li along with three fine cotton tailored shirts. Nearby Peter went into a small shop full of the latest electronic goods. Here he had to bargain hard with the shopkeeper before buying a powerful radio and an electric record player together with some records to keep the family entertained for hours. These included classical music records as well as the latest American rock and roll tunes. In another shop, he purchased a pair of binoculars as well as a teddy bear and a toy car for Paul.

Susie and her father met Peter at Mingaladon Airport to rush him through customs. Once home, Peter showed Susie his purchases and gave her father a receipt for the six thousand pounds he deposited in George's HSBC account. Everyone was happy. Susie liked the record player and radio that would fill their home with music. After showing Susie the photographs of Hong Kong, she made him promise that one day he would take her there. However, first they had to prepare for his parents' visit and the birth of their new child.

# 44
## Lynette Returns to Burma

A BOAC Super Constellation at Mingaladon Airport.

It was dusk when the BOAC Super Constellation arrived at Mingaladon bringing Lynette and Paul Anderson to Burma. They were the first of the ten passengers to disembark and ushered to the Immigration desk where the officious passport officer checked and double checked their entry visas. The officer had rarely seen a visitor's visa as few foreigners were allowed to enter the country without work permits. Just when things started to get difficult, Peter arrived with George Tauk to verify that they were honoured guests. Then George guided them and their luggage through Customs where the awkward officers wanted to open every bag and confiscate whatever they wanted. It helped that George understood their greed by paying two hundred Kyat to an officer, who without changing his stern expression put the cash in his pocket, before releasing the luggage without examination. Then they were free to leave the airport.

'We were so glad to see you at the Immigration desk as it looked like we were about to be deported or arrested. They really do not like visitors,' commented Paul Anderson holding his wife's hand.

'Please remember that their behaviour is not personal, they are only obeying orders. Sadly, the government is scared of all foreigners, so they make it hard for them to visit. It is probably because they face too many insurgents,' George Tauk stated.

'I never thought my country would become a police state,' a sad Lynette said tearfully.

'Do not worry Daw Lynette, now you are in Rangoon no one will question your presence, and most people will welcome both of you. We Burmese have not changed, though nowadays we must be careful not to offend Prime Minister U Nu and his people. Luckily, the Buddhist values of charity and caring prevail to make Burma a friendly and beautiful country,' a smiling George added.

'I hope so as I want to see my sister and her family who are Karen and live near Lashio,' Lynette replied.

'I can try to contact them through my friends and family. However, I must warn you that the region contains Shan insurgents fighting the government. It may be safer for them to meet you in Rangoon or in a government-held city,' commented George.

'My sister is Daw Maung Win Mai and her husband Win Ba Tin, they disowned their son Ba Tin after he joined the Japanese.'

'Do they ever visit Rangoon?'

'Why should they?'

'Because Lashio is threatened by the Koumintang making it a dangerous place to visit.'

'That is bad news as I wanted to see my sister again after being apart for forty years,' Lynette replied sobbing.

'Then somehow I will make sure you meet her,' George replied reassuringly.

As they drove into Rangoon, Lynette's face beamed with excitement.

'The last time I was here was forty years ago with five other girls going to sail to England to become nurses. The wide streets have not changed much and still are lined with beautiful trees,' Lynette commented.

'I am sure the only difference is that the roads have more holes in them.'

'George, if I remember correctly, the roads were never as good as they are in England.'

They all laughed at how small things remind one of their homes.

Peter was upset at being reminded that the Devil's Helper was his cousin, but smiled to please his mum.

'Peter, I hope that you are not avoiding work just to help us,' Lynette required.

'Mother I have a month's leave to help you and be around when my son is born. My boss, Maung Maung Myint is a decent chap even though he belongs to a powerful family.'

'That's splendid news,' intervened Paul.

When they arrived in Golden Valley, they found Susie waiting in their house with her son Paul to greet them. Lynette felt relaxed when inside the house with her son and his family. The two women held each other close to feel each other's love. Then Lynette and her husband Paul went to bed to recover from the two day journey.

After breakfast, Susie went to Dr Lusk's clinic as she felt her baby was coming. After being reassured that the baby would not arrive for the next few days, Dr Lusk sent Peter away and kept Susie in his clinic for observation. Then

Peter guided his parents around Rangoon and took along his Asahiflex 35-mm camera to record everything.

The first stop was at the Shwe Dagon for Lynette to pray. Though she had often told Peter that it was one of the wonders of the world, she had never visited it. The long climb up the hundreds of stairs was problematic causing the older folk to have to stop to catch their breath. Eventually, tired but excited Lynette stood before the stupa holding tightly to Paul's hand. Then she proudly led her husband inside to kneel before the statue of Lord Buddha to present him as her husband and ask for his blessing. As she knelt with her head on the ground, Peter noticed a bright light shining around both his father and mother uniting them as one beautiful creation. He felt the goodness of his surroundings enter his body as he was lifted spiritually out of his body. Then he looked down from above on his parents who were kneeling surrounded by a bright light and the sounds of chanting accompanying the gentle sounds of the temple bells in the breeze. When Lynette stood up, Peter found himself kneeling, bewildered and yet exhilarated. Had he really been floating above everyone on a spiritual ether or was his mind playing tricks on him? Whatever it was he felt wonderful and full of love towards everyone.

When Lynette saw Peter coming out of a trance, she helped him to his feet and smiled knowing her son had inherited her spirituality. Peter looked into his mother's eyes as he tried to understand what he had just experienced.

'Mum, have you ever felt like you are looking down on everyone from above like a bird? I think that I have, to see things like never before,' asked Peter.

'Yes I have my dearest son. I think that you have become like Susie and me to learn how to let your spirit reach the world of your ancestors. I expect that you now feel a mixture of emotions that include contentment and surprise. I know that I always do. If you really concentrate on the goodness of God when you meditate, you will learn to see your loved ones wherever they are.'

'It is such a wonderful gift that you have given me.'

'One cannot teach someone to meditate and use their third eye until they understand the spiritual world and are ready to believe what they see. Sometimes you will see things that you do not like, but that is because our ancestors are warning us of what may, or may not happen.'

After leaving the Shwe Dagon, they drove to Tauk's shop on Sule Pagoda road. Once inside they were greeted by Ba Saw who took them into his garden where they drank tea and ate freshly baked cake. Paul Anderson was enthralled by the multitude of flowers and birds in the garden. There were the tame mynah birds living side by side with wild sapphire flycatchers, red whiskered bulbuls and blue-tailed bee-eaters along with large butterflies. Among all this beauty was a small golden statue of Lord Buddha surrounded by a pond with flowering water lilies. It looked like the Garden of Eden.

Then Ba Saw showed his guests around his shop. Lynette spent hours looking at the impressive array of precious stones, large black natural pearls and intricate silver work. She examined some excellent jade carvings before looking at the small fragile emeralds and the cheaper star sapphires. In the end, she decided that she wanted to own a ruby necklace as it was uniquely Burmese. No other rubies were so deeply red and brilliant when seen in the sunlight. Their colour brought warmth and happiness to the wearer, as though they were messengers of the gods.

'U Ba Saw, your beautiful gems must meet everyone's wishes,' remarked Lynette.

'Thank you, sadly we do not have any diamonds as they are not found in Burma.'

'Do you still sell many star sapphires?'

'Yes we do though mostly to young people who believe the star shape you see in them in the sunlight is a sign of a divine blessing.'

'I think they are lovely, but not as fabulous as blood-red rubies.'

'I must admit our blood-red rubies are our best seller, especially when purchased by the rich as a way of taking their money out of the country.'

'Just out of interest, how much is this ruby necklace?' Lynette enquired.

'Sorry Daw Lynette, but I cannot sell it to you,' a perplexed Ba Saw politely replied.

'Why cannot my wife buy the necklace. I probably have enough money to purchase it,' intervened Paul.

'I am certain Tauk would not like me taking money from his family. So if you want it, then it is yours with our love.'

'I cannot accept such a gift,' Lynette replied.

'Daw Lynette you of all people must know that inside our family no one pays for anything. It is our tradition that you must not ask me to break.'

Later, a very embarrassed Lynette left the shop holding a small parcel containing the necklace. Then she followed Peter into the Strand Hotel where they enjoyed a mild curry for their lunch. The meal was interrupted by the arrival of an excited George Tauk, who told them that Dr Lusk had phoned to say that Susie was going into labour. The doctor said that there was no need to rush as the baby was not expected for the next few hours. However, everyone decided to visit the clinic to be with Susie.

When they arrived in the clinic, they were met by an embarrassed Dr Lusk. He informed them that only twenty minutes earlier Susie gave birth to a daughter, and they were both very well.

'May we see Susie?' anxiously asked Peter.

'Of course you may, but only for a few minutes as she is very tired,' Dr Lusk answered.

'When can we take her home?' asked the ever practical Lynette.

'In three days time after I am certain that both mother and child are progressing well.'

Peter and his mother then visited Susie, who was nursing her baby at her swollen breasts. Susie smiled at them and handed her daughter for Peter to hold. It was a brief moment of joy that soon ended when they were told to leave Susie to rest.

That night Peter placed another jade leaf on the jade tree for the ancestors to know that his family had a new member for them to protect. Then he lit a joss stick while praying next to his mother for the health of his family.

# 45

# A Journey to Lashio

After weeks of waiting, George Tauk arranged for Paul and Lynette to fly to Lashio to meet her sister Daw Maung Win Mai and her husband Win Ba Tin. It took so long because George had to obtain special passes to allow the foreigners to visit a troubled area. After paying a few bribes and spending hours negotiating, he obtained the permits for the dangerous journey. George did not realise that everything was recorded by a few interested parties, including the state security police and informers of the Shan Army and their Koumintang (KMT) allies. George had unintentionally initiated a chain of violence that nobody could have imagined. Working for the Koumintang was Ba Tin, the Devil's Helper, who interrogated captured government soldiers. Though he was badly injured and close to madness, Ba Tin still enjoyed extracting information from his unfortunate victims, often leaving them dead or crippled. The Koumintang did not worry about Ba Tin as they knew he was wanted for war crimes and needed their protection even more than they needed him.

By the time Peter purchased the air tickets for his parents and himself to Lashio, Ba Tin had already put into operation his plans to destroy all his family. He had convinced the military head of the Koumintang that the capture of British people associated with the Burmese government would get them both information and ransom. So the KMT started to move their troops into safe areas near Lashio and ordered their informers to report the arrival of all foreigners at the airport and the Rest House.

When Peter's boss Maung Maung Myint heard that he was taking his family to Lashio, he was extremely concerned. So he informed his cousin, General Ne Win and asked him to increase the number of Burmese soldiers in Lashio and around the Rest House. Ne Win sent fifty of his best commandos to Lashio under Captain Tun Tin to establish concealed positions near the government Rest House. The general considered that if the insurgents were going to attack the British visitors, it would be a good opportunity to destroy some of them. At the same time, Brigadier Tommy Clift dispatched six Seafire fighter aircraft to reinforce the UBAF based at Lashio airport. Then the scene was set for a very violent confrontation in a large and mostly peaceful city. During the day, the city was quiet as the Burmese military was in control, but after sunset, everything changed. After the soldiers retired to the safety of their strongholds, the insurgents infiltrated into the city to buy essential goods from their fellow Shan tribesmen. Only occasionally did the two opposing sides meet, but when they did, it always left too many casualties.

A week before Peter was to travel to Lashio; George received an unexpected visitor. It was after dark when an old Jeep drove up to his house bringing an anxious Pip Palmarino.

'George, I apologise for visiting you so late in the day, but I have something very important to tell you,' stated a breathless Pip.

'Sit down my friend and have a whisky. Nothing is so important that it can't wait for a few moments while you relax and enjoy my fine mature genuine Scots whisky.'

'Thank you George, I could do with a stiff drink,' Pip replied taking a cut-glass goblet full of whisky.

'Well what is it that you want to tell me?'

'I want you to warn Peter that he may get a dangerous reception when he reaches Lashio.'

'What makes you come to that conclusion?'

'One of my friends tells me that living at the Koumintang base near Lashio is Peter's nemesis, Ba Tin also known as the Devil's Helper. Ba Tin is very dangerous and quite mad.'

'I thought Bo Ba Tin died during the war.'

'Sadly he survived, and some say is worse than ever before.'

'That is terrible news, but there is little I can do to stop Peter going there.'

'Maybe you could send one of your bodyguards to protect them,' suggested Pip.

'Of course, I could send Ye-Hut, who has family nearby.'

So two days later George sent Ye-Hut to Lashio to arrange the security for Peter and his family. George also warned Peter that Lashio was a violent city but did not tell him about Ba Tin being alive. So Peter took his Walther automatic pistol, in case he needed it during his visit knowing that no one would search him. However, he was surprised to find that half the fellow passengers onboard the UBA aircraft were Burmese soldiers travelling with all their kit. The stewardess said that recently they had carried at least twenty soldiers on each trip to Lashio because the government was reinforcing the garrison following recent attacks against the town by the Koumintang. Peter remembered that during the war, Lashio was controlled by General Stilwell and his Chinese Koumintang (KMT) army, and so they knew the area. It was believed that the Koumintang ran the opium trade with the Shan resistance assisted by the American CIA who refined the raw opium in factories inside Thailand. This was why all flights in, and out of Lashio were made around noon after the army had cleared the area of insurgents.

When Peter saw the green hills around Lashio, he suddenly experienced a strange feeling of impending doom. He started to sweat profusely as he tried to calm himself not realising that his ancestors were warning him of a nearby enemy. During the flight, Peter was invited into the cockpit by the captain who was his friend Aung Gyi. While there they saw an unmarked aircraft flying a mile away on their starboard side.

'Peter, do you see the ghost aircraft. It is one of the American Fairchild Providers often seen in this region. We call them ghost aircraft as they have no markings, not even a registration to show where they come from,' Aung Gyi commented as though such aircraft were normal.

'Do you report the ghost aircraft?' asked a concerned Peter.

'Yes we do, but they avoid our fighters and never respond to radio calls.'

'Who do you think the aircraft belongs to?'

'I am reliably informed that they operate out of Laos taking weapons to the Koumintang and return full of opium.'

'That must be a costly enterprise.'

'I am told it is run by the American CIA agents based in Bangkok. That is where the opium is processed into heroin and exported on government aircraft to the USA to avoid their cargo being examined by US customs. We pilots call them Air America, because only such a country could run a drug cartel that exploits their own people.'

'So that is why the Koumintang is so powerful and remains in Burma?'

'I think so and occupy the same bases they built during the war that are difficult to destroy.'

'Do you expect any difficulties during this flight?'

'It is just a routine flight with the weather ahead, and the situation in Lashio is reported as peaceful. So I expect to arrive on time. So enjoy the flight and your stay in the most Chinese of all Burmese towns.'

So Peter returned to his seat and noted that his parents were engrossed in looking down at the green lands of the southern Shan province. Lynette was busy pointing out the rivers and hill top temples as well as the winding roads to Paul. The sight of familiar scenery brought back a flood of childhood memories that filled her with hope and love towards everyone. She was going to see her family knowing just how much she missed them as they were very important to her.

On landing at Lashio airport, they were met by Ye-Hut with a large Humber car and drove them to the government Rest House. They drove past many shops and only a few people in the market before reaching the official guest house. To enter this old colonial building, they had to cross a check point where armed soldiers searched everything before allowing them inside. Peter was surprised to see so many soldiers. Ye-Hut explained that Lashio was a town in the middle of a war zone where the army maintained a fragile peace. However, once inside the compound's high-wire fences, they found themselves in a haven of peace. Around the building was a large garden full of mature trees, and flowering bushes behind which the soldiers were concealed inside well-placed bunkers. It was not as secure as it looked because the dense foliage provided cover in which any attacker could hide. Inside the Rest House, the accommodation was excellent with all the rooms having a balcony, and a private bathroom complete with a shower with hot and cold water. Downstairs, there were all the facilities one could expect in a good hotel, including a restaurant, comfortable lounge and a bar that sold nearly every drink. This was unusual considering the government had banned the sale of alcohol, but it showed that here, the army ran everything. Some of the very expensive bottles of whisky and brandy were purchased long before any restrictions came into force. So Paul Anderson was delighted to find a twenty-year old Napoleon brandy next to a mature single malt Laphroaig whisky from the island of Islay in the southern Hebrides. For the first time since arriving in Burma, Paul enjoyed a glass of Laphroaig single malt whisky without water or ice, for such a great drink must never be adulterated with even one piece of ice.

# 46
## The Reunion

Next morning, Lynette came down to breakfast wearing a blue silk *longyi* and a beautiful red *aingyi* with her hair tied back and a white orchid in her hair. She was dressed as a high-class Karen lady right down to her leather sandals and single gold bangle on her wrist ready to greet her sister and her husband when they arrived for lunch. She was no longer Lynette Anderson but Daw Maung Win Lin. It was a lovely day with clear blue skies, and the air was filled with the fragrances of hundreds of flowers. The cool breeze rang the temple bells hanging from the hotel porch that asked for Lord Buddha's blessing. So Peter took photographs of the magnificent building and the multitude of flowering plants. Only when it started to get warm did he return indoors to get a cool drink and prepare to meet his aunt.

It was noon when Daw Maung Win Mai, and her husband Win Ba Tin arrived wearing their best clothes. The two sisters cried as they hugged each other not wanting to let each other go, while the men watched quietly. Peter was surprised to hear his aunt call his mother Daw Lin, as he never knew that was her Burmese name. Later, he was amazed to hear about their childhood stories, how they were educated by the Catholic priests. At fourteen, Lin went to work at the mission hospital while her elder sister started to study at the teacher's college. At fifteen, Lin was awarded a scholarship with six other Karen girls and a nun to travel to England to be student nurses. So Lin said goodbye to her family and friends and started her journey. First, they went by train sleeping for many days sleeping on the wooden seats before they reached Rangoon. There they stayed at a convent, were given European clothes and put aboard a ship sailing to London where they lived in two small cabins with bunk beds for the next three months. Every day started with a boiled egg and sweet tea for breakfast, some bread and soup for lunch and a dinner of stewed beef complete with vegetables and dumplings. It was not what they were used to, but they ate it as they understood that they must adapt to their new life. Some days they were allowed on deck to feel the sea breeze on their faces and watch the flying fish, and dolphins swim around the ship. Now Peter understood how his mother's beliefs helped her thrive under such difficult conditions. In England, three Karen trainees studied at The Florence Nightingdale School of Nursing at St Thomas's Hospital, London and became good friends and helped each other settle down to life in a strange land.

Later, the two sisters talked about meeting their husbands and setting up home. At no time did they discuss the war as it was too bitter a memory to talk about. All Daw Mai said was that life was never the same after the Japanese came and the British betrayed the Karen people by leaving them to be ruled by their pro-Japanese enemies such as Aung San and U Nu. However hard she tried she could not understand why this happened when the Karen had fought so fiercely against the Japanese and their allies. Daw Mai added that they felt safer among the Shan because no one cared that they were Karen, leaving them free to run their business selling clothes and building materials. She added that the problem of living in Lashio was that occasionally the town was attacked by the Chinese Koumintang. Luckily, the Koumintang was only interested in obtaining medical supplies and electronic goods that they did not stock.

After a while, they all went into the dining room where a banquet was waiting for them. The speciality menu was the best the Rest House cook could prepare, and it was delicious. The menu consisted of:

**First Course**

| | |
|---|---|
| *Chinyay hin.* | A thin soup. |
| *Mohinga.* | (A traditional Burmese dish of rice vermicelli in a fish broth and boiled eggs seasoned with garlic, ginger and lemon grass. |

**Main Course**

| | |
|---|---|
| *Seejet Khao swè.* | A popular Chinese dish of noodles with duck fried in garlic oil, soy sauce and chopped spring onions. |
| *Lahpet thohk.* | A Shan salad of pickled tea leaves, peanuts and garlic, toasted sesame, tomato, green chilli, dried shrimps and ginger dressed with peanut oil, fish sauce and lime. |
| *Wet tha hymit chin.* | A popular Shan recipe of pork with sour bamboo shoots. |
| *Nga Baung Doke.* | Fish cooked in Banana leaves served with bamboo shoots. |
| *Htamin.* | Boiled white rice. |

**Dessert**

| | |
|---|---|
| *Hpaluda.* | A popular Burmese dish of rose water, milk, jelly and grated coconut served with ice cream. |
| *Shan yin aye.* | Agar jelly, tapioca and sago in coconut milk. |
| Fresh fruit. | A bowl of fresh mangoes, lychee, bananas, pomela and papaya. |

Custom demanded that everyone wait for Paul Anderson to start eating as he was the eldest present. As soon as he started to taste the light soup the others followed. For the next hour, little was said as they all were too busy eating the excellent food placed in front of them. Occasionally, they stopped to drink fresh mango juice or iced-tea before continuing to savour their banquet. When everyone was finished eating, the waiter arrived with finger bowls of warm water and a towel to dry their washed fingers. Then he served fresh green tea with a piece of lime with a jug of condensed milk and a bowl of sugar.

Afterwards, they sat down in the lounge happily chatting until the noise of a passing parade interrupted their thoughts. So they moved to watch the three colourful dragons and two lions dance joyfully down the street. It looked so beautiful that even Peter was not worried.

However, Ye Hut asked them to move inside where it was safer.

'I do not know why, but I feel that something is wrong,' said Ye-Hut holding his automatic pistol in one hand.

'Don't worry Ye-Hut, it is only a Chinese festival,' added Peter.

'Maybe, but it is unusual for any celebration to occur during the afternoon.'

Then Peter noticed two Burmese soldiers enter the House to set up a Bren gun to cover the front door. Minutes later, two more soldiers arrived to defend the rear. It was obvious that they expected trouble.

# 47
## Bo Ba Tin Seeks Revenge

Only having one arm and one eye did not deter Ba Bo Tin from leading thirty Koumintang fighters into Lashio. Though his body ached, he was determined to destroy all of his relatives in one great assault upon the government Rest House. He was invigorated by chewing raw opium that took away the pain and made him feel invincible. Only when all his family were dead would he feel revenged on those who defied him. He planned the attack with great skill by creating a distraction in the form of a colourful and noisy parade. For this occasion, he recruited traditional Chinese dragon dancers as well as two smaller lion dancers to parade close to the Rest House, accompanied by the gongs and many firecrackers. The parade had official permission to take place as part of the celebrations marking the opening of the nearby Chinese Guanyin temple. Hidden inside the hollow bodies of the three eighty-feet long dancing dragons were Ba Tin and ten KMT soldiers, waiting until the dragons stopped in front of the Rest House. Amid the noise of the gongs and the explosion of hundreds of fire crackers, they slipped from under the dragon to hide in the deep drainage ditch running alongside the security fence. Afterwards, the dancers rapidly contracted the dragon to be fifty feet long while continuing down the street. However, Captain Tun Tin was suspicious, especially when he learnt the procession would go by the Rest House and take place in the afternoon heat. He allowed it to occur while alerting his Burmese commandos of the risks involved. Then he placed more men inside the Rest House and positioned forty men in two nearby houses ready to react when required. The intelligent and experienced colonel felt that if this was part of a Koumintang attack, it was better to know when and where it could occur.

In a nearby house, ten KMT soldiers set up three small mortars aimed at the Rest House. One mortar was to blow up the guards on the gate, another to explode near the building and a third to send smoke into the building. They all waited patiently for Ba Tin's signal to attack. At the sound of the firecrackers exploding in the street, Ba Tin signalled with a tin whistle for the attack to begin. While the mortars fired at the gate, the KMT soldiers rapidly cut through the security fence to climb into the Rest House grounds and hide in the thick vegetation. Then Ba Tin led his men slowly through the trees and high shrubs to the rear of the Rest House. They only came across two soldiers on guard in the back garden who were quietly eliminated. One was garrotted, while the other was shot at close range with a poisoned arrow from a small crossbow. After hiding the bodies in the undergrowth, the KMT waited until two cooks came out of the kitchen door to place the leftover food into the bins used for pig food. They were killed with a Garrot before the KMT soldiers stealthily entered the kitchen from the garden. Inside the kitchen, they silently killed the workers, one at a time, until an alert cook saw them and threw a knife into the neck of one of the attackers killing him instantly. This angered the attackers so they raked the area with bullets alerting everyone in the Rest House of their presence. The attackers killed everything that moved including a cat, but failed to see a young cook who dived behind some bags of rice to hide and remain silent, though terrified. Then the Burmese soldiers reacted by forming a protective circle around the guests and issuing them with gas masks while pointing their guns at the kitchen doors.

Peter instinctively touched his jade leaf for reassurance only to feel the presence of a deadly enemy. So he held his automatic pistol while kneeling near his parents who lay cuddled together on the floor. When a smoke canister came in through the window, Paul picked it up and threw it out through the front door. In doing so he gave them a few more minutes of breathing clean air, but succeeded in burning his hands.

There was a pause as Ba Tin waited for the mortars to open fire with rounds of mustard gas, and for his men to wear their gas masks. It never happened because Captain Tun Tin's commandos had captured the mortars and eliminated the KMT in the house. The Captain radioed to his men inside the Rest House to say that he was coming in through the front door with twenty men. By then all the Burmese soldiers wore white patches on their arms and helmets to be recognised as friends. When they arrived inside the building, they took up concealed positions to fire on anyone entering from the kitchen, while others went behind the Rest House to catch any of the attackers who might try to escape. The Captain told his men that he believed the insurgents were led by the war criminal Bo Ba Tin who must be killed whatever the cost.

Having lost the element of surprise, Ba Tin led his men firing blindly through the wide kitchen doors. They reached the empty dining room having only lost two men before meeting any serious resistance. The main force of KMT attackers moved on towards the lounge full of Burmese commandos, while Ba Tin went to the far end of the lounge to part the wooden screen separating the lounge from the dining room. While the fierce battle raged, Ba Tin slipped into the lounge unnoticed. After seeing Peter facing away from him, Ba Tin ran towards his target with such hatred that he failed to see the soldiers surrounding him.

'Hi Chichi, I have come to send you to hell,' yelled Ba Tin in a high-pitched scream. Peter was so shocked when he saw the ghastly form of Ba Tin with one eye and one arm coming towards him that he hesitated and froze. The deformed face of Ba Tin and his staring eyes was a picture of evil that reminded Peter of being tortured. The sudden appearance of this monster surprised the commandos long enough for Ba Tin to come within ten feet of Peter.

'Peter, the Devil's Helper is coming to kill you,' yelled Ye-Hut remembering what Bo Ba Tin had done to his friend Ba Saw.

Then Peter fired several bullets at his enemy who was close and raising his Sten gun to shoot, it took three bullets to stop and kill the powerful Ba Tin. His mother lay and cried out with horror on seeing what her once handsome son had become, but was relieved that he could no longer hurt anybody. Her body shook at what she witnessed as her husband held her close. Daw Mai knew her son was evil but had never imagined how terrible he looked with a badly scarred face and one eye. He was not the son she once loved and who she regretted spoiling.

'Daw Mai be strong and remember that this monster is not the son you remember. The son you loved died long ago when he joined the Japanese. Be grateful that at last your family honour has been restored, and you can again be proud of your family,' stated Captain Tun Tin with a reassuring smile.

Daw Mai did not reply but simply nodded her thanks for what the good captain, and his men had done for them.

Then a soldier appeared carrying a tray with glasses of the finest brandy that he handed out to each of the civilians present. 'My captain says that you must drink this brandy as it is the best cure for brave people after experiencing the horrors of war. Everyone needs help to return to normality after being so close to death,' commented the young soldier. While they sipped their brandy, people removed the bodies and swept away the debris. Within thirty minutes, everything inside the Rest House looked normal, except, there was no longer a front door. The young cook was discovered alive behind the bags of rice and helped to recover by some of his friends. Though still in shock, he insisted on preparing food for the guests as if nothing had happened. The body of Ba Tin was removed to the Police station to be photographed before being secretly buried in a grave full of lime to destroy his human remains. At the same time, the wounded were admitted to the town hospital before they removed the dead for burial.

I have ordered my car to take Daw Maung Win Mai and Win Ba Tin back to their home where two of my men will protect them for the next few days. I will remain here with some of my men until you depart tomorrow for the safety of Rangoon. Peter, I am sure Maung Maung Myint will be delighted to hear of your safe return,' stated Captain Tun Tin.

Then the Rest House manager told them that the evening meal would be delayed as they had to bring in more cooks. However, in the meantime they would be served a pot of tea and fresh jam sandwiches. It reminded Peter, how resolute and adaptable the Burmese people had become.

Back in Rangoon Susie woke up with a start having dreamt of the fighting in the Rest House. When awake, she spent the night praying in front of her jade tree and did not stop until she felt her family was safe, then she managed to snatch a few hours sleep before feeding her baby. She sometimes wondered whether having the power to see things occurring many miles away were a good or a bad thing. This was especially true as she was too far away to send help or change the situation. Maybe it prepared her to face Peter and his parents when they returned. Then in need of guidance she opened her bible to read the Songs of Solomon. This reminded her that a godly wife was at all times to be a comfort for her man when she read. 'My beloved is mine, and I am his: he feedeth among the lilies. Until the day break, and the shadows flee away, turn, my beloved, and be thou like a roe or a young hart upon the mountains of Be-ther.' Then she went on to read 'Set me as a seal upon thine heart, as a seal upon thine arm: for love is strong as death; jealousy is cruel as the grave: the coals there of are coals of fire, which hath a most vehement flame. Many waters cannot quench love, neither can the floods drown it. It would be utterly condemned.'

Suddenly she knew that nothing could destroy her love for Peter and vowed to show him how much she missed him on his return. Her body was his, and their lives joined by their eternal love.

That night the Burmese troops attacked the Koumintang forces gathered by the river to advance towards Lashio. The UBAF Seafires flew low over the town to strafe and bomb the enemy before the Burmese army drove them back to the hills. Afterwards, the Burmese collected all the KMT weapons that were a mixture of brand new American MI-5 machine guns and AR-16 armalite rifles together with boxes of ammunition. This was a valuable addition to the Burmese arsenal in a long-running and bloody campaign. Soon the local Burmese commandos carried the captured AR-16 rifles on long range missions as they were lighter and had more fire power than their old Lee-Enfield rifles.

By the morning Captain Tun Tin was delighted to hear that the Koumintang was driven out of Lashio to the distant hills. It was as much as he could have hoped for especially considering that the visitors were safe and his casualties light. So he escorted Peter Anderson, and his parents back to Lashio Airport and onto the UBA flight to Mingaladon. He would not return to Rangoon until he had improved the defences around Lashio, especially from the Salween River.

Peter and his parents were glad to be back in Golden Valley where Susie waited for them with a fine dinner. Lynette was happy to have seen her sister but wished the circumstances were different. While Paul ate carefully as the blisters on his hands still hurt from throwing the hot smoke canister. Susie did not ask about the fighting. As she felt that Lynette understood she had seen what had happened in her dreams, or were they nightmares!

Susie went upstairs to bed first and fed her daughter from her full breasts. Afterwards, she was so aroused that she had a shower and put on her most sensual perfume to lay naked on the bed to wait for Peter. When Peter arrived, he found Susie smiling at him and squeezing her nipple to express some milk.

'Darling you must come here and kiss me. I need a lot of comforting as I know how close I came to lose you.'

'Dearest, you can never lose me until I die of old age,' he replied.

'Well I hope you are right, but knowing that you take too many risks, you must give me another baby.'

'Isn't it too soon after the birth of our daughter?'

'Maybe, but at least you could try until you succeed. I need to know that you still love me as a woman and not just as a wife.'

He slipped into bed next to his wife and kissed her hard. She opened her mouth to show him how much she loved him while her hand stroked his manhood until it was big. Then she put his mouth on her nipple to suck the milk from her full breasts and shuddered with delight at how he made her feel. The taste of her warm milk aroused Peter so much that he started to touch her between her legs until she shook and purred like a grateful cat. He looked at her lovely face to note her flushed cheeks and soft large lips. Her eyes were wide-open staring at him as if pleading to be loved. When he made love to her, she responded by moving her body with his. She started to cry out so loud that Peter had to put his hand over her mouth to keep her quiet as he did not want to waken their baby or his parents. Too soon the excitement was over as an exhausted but satisfied Peter lay by her side as she held him in her arms and gently kissed his forehead. In many ways, they were the perfect couple united in both body and mind by love and a real understanding of each other's needs. When Susie got up to feed her daughter, she discovered how sensitive and swollen her nipples were. It made breast-feeding her daughter a sensuous delight that was so intense it made her proud to be the mother of Peter's children. Whatever happened, she knew that she would gladly die to keep her loved ones safe. However, she prayed that she never would have to do so.

A week later, Lynette and Paul returned to England taking two small packages of rubies to sell in London for George Tauk, who had told them to keep half of the proceeds for themselves. The balance was to be deposited in George's account in the City of London branch of the Hong Kong and Shanghai Banking Corporation. George gave them the address of Eli Shaw Jewellers of Hatton Gardens who always paid the best price in cash for George's Burmese rubies without asking any questions about details such as export permits or import duty. In this way, George Tauk built up his 'retirement' fund that would support him when he could no longer happily live in Burma. Lynette often wore the ruby necklace that George gave her as a reminder of her family in Burma, especially her grandchildren.

# 48
# A New Beginning

By 1958, Peter and Susie found life extremely difficult because nothing in Rangoon worked properly. The electricity often failed during the night to engulf everyone in darkness, unless they had a lantern ready to light. To make matters worse even the water stopped running through the taps, but this did not affect Peter as his house had large water tanks that stored the monsoon rain collected from the roof. Now Peter was forced to obtain the petrol for his cars from the military at Mingaladon as the supplies of fuel in Rangoon were unreliable. When fuel was available, it was very expensive and involved waiting for hours in long queues.

George Tauk explained to Peter that Burma was bankrupt, and everything was falling apart. He was told that Prime Minister U Nu had lost all control over the nation's finances so that many officials went unpaid, so most public services stopped working. The ruling AFPFL party had divided into two factions that refused to cooperate with each other so that effectively no one ruled the nation.

'Peter you must be careful as Rangoon is now a dangerous place where gangs of desperate vagrants have come from the countryside to take what they can. You can see how nearly overnight the wide streets have become lined with squatter's huts and the police no longer patrol the streets. Whatever you do, do not allow Susie to go shopping,' Pleaded a worried George.

'Thanks for the warning. However, I must get to work,' Peter stubbornly replied.

'Then you must be careful and not stop for anyone or anything. I am told the mobs attack cars and there are over twenty murders reported every night.'

'I knew things were bad but did not think the city was in such chaos.'

'Surely you see the piles of rotting garbage at the sides of the roads that fill the drains and the packs of rats and rabid wild dogs roaming the streets.'

'Yes I have seen them, but I thought it was just a temporary happening because the workers had not been paid.'

'Peter, you are correct. However, it is much more serious because diseases are spreading like wildfire throughout the city killing hundreds.'

'Why is it all happening?'

'Burma has no money to pay for even the basic facilities having spent too much on hosting the Buddhist Conference and on the Prime Minister's overseas trips. So no one sprays the ponds and stagnant water with insecticide, so they become breeding grounds for millions of mosquitoes. On top of this, sickness is prevalent as epidemics of cholera, dysentery, malaria and typhoid rampage through the population. Even the incidents of leprosy and filariasis (elephantiasis) have rapidly increased. Sadly, the under-financed hospitals do not have enough medicine or beds to treat everyone so that many die without any medical assistance. Life is now worse than it was during those dark days after the Japanese left.'

'Do you think it will get better?' asked Peter.

'I believe the President will be forced to act to stop Prime Minister U Nu destroying what is left of our Burma.'

That night Peter was very careful when he drove home from the airport. He now noticed the mobs on every street corner. He slowed down to drive cautiously past the packs of wild dogs and people walking in the middle of the poorly lit roads, while avoiding the many deep pot holes. It was a mistake because as the car slowed a mob surrounded it trying to overturn it. In an attempt to escape, Peter blew his horn and noisily drove forward as fast as he could through the crowd. When the crowd saw the military number plate on Peter's car, they became afraid and parted to let him drive through, though he still knocked down two of the more aggressive people. In his rear mirror, Peter noticed that other cars were attacked and some set on fire; however, the mob allowed their occupants to escape. Clearly, the mob was angry at how the rich were treating them, but did not want to murder anyone, as their Buddhist beliefs forbade killing of any kind.

Peter was very angry that there were no policemen or soldiers on the streets to maintain law and order so that at night anarchy ruled the city. He decided that at the first signs of trouble, the poorly paid police vanished only to re-emerge when quietness returned. As he drove into Golden Valley, he was delighted to find the armed guards at the main gate had kept the mobs away, and it was peaceful. At least, his family was safe during these troubled times.

Luckily, the troubles were limited to the inner city where the number of squatter huts on the sides of the roads rapidly increased, and the temples were forced to close their gates at night. Even shopping for food was dangerous. No longer could Susie safely leave Golden Valley to go for a swim. Therefore, every Saturday morning Peter and his friends took their wives shopping for the essential food, when even rice proved hard to find and then very expensive. Peter always took his Naga watchman with them for protection, as most Burmese feared the 'wild' Naga with their tattooed bodies and fierce reputation as mighty warriors. This proved to be wise as everywhere they went, they were closely followed by beggars and vagrants looking for any opportunity to steal their purchases. So Peter purchased two-weeks supplies at one visit to meet the needs of his family and the household staff. Now he was appreciative of the hard work of his Naga gardener who produced enough vegetables and fruits together with chickens and eggs to feed the whole household.

The situation was totally out of control, in desperation President Win Maung asked Prime Minister U Nu to resign so that an interim government could run the nation. On 24th September 1958, Susie heard over the radio Prime Minister U Nu announce that he was resigning for General Ne Win could take over. He added that when life in Burma had improved there would be national elections to form another democratic government. Until then, he asked all of Burma to support the caretaker government. Susie and Peter felt that this was good news as Ne Win was related to the president by birth, being born Shu Maung. Suddenly, there was hope for a beleaguered nation where before there was only despair. It was as if the rains had come after a long drought to usher in life into the dried and barren land. Hope grew like fresh flowers to welcome a new dawn where things worked for the benefit of all.

Immediately, the efficient, though some said ruthless, Ne Win acted. He first appointed Colonel Tun Sein as Commissioner of the Rangoon Municipality to restore Rangoon to its former glory. Tun Sein used the army to remove nearly one hundred and seventy thousand squatters and vagrants out of the city to be housed in three rapidly built satellite towns near Rangoon. Then he initiated Operation Clean-up whereby the streets were cleared of garbage and poison bait placed to kill the packs of rabid wild dogs. Insecticide was sprayed on stagnant water and in drainage ditches to kill the mosquito larvae, and the swarms of dysentery carrying flies. The result was the death rate in Rangoon was dramatically reduced, and the drainage system worked during the monsoon to remove the surface waters and prevent flooding. With the return of police on the streets, supported by the army, people started to open their shops and business returned to normal, and the murder rate dropped. However, Colonel Tun Sein's greatest achievement was to obtain American assistance to supply equipment to improve Rangoon's water supply and sewage systems.

Life in Rangoon drastically improved when the army sold cheap meat and vegetables to the people to avert fears of starvation. Gradually, as petrol became available, the buses and lorries started to operate. They were supplemented by the arrival of Japanese two seater three-wheel motorised taxis, known as tuk tuks or trishaws, as a part of Japanese reparations. At the docks, ships arrived daily bringing new buses, cars and even trains that would improve communications. The government permitted UBA to take delivery of the four Vickers Viscount 760D aircraft from England. Suddenly, it looked as though Burma was being reborn under the leadership of Ne Win. To accelerate this modernisation, Ne Win asked all embassies to assist in recruiting skilled foreigners to help run his organisations and give scholarships for Burmese to study abroad to learn modern methods. Within six months many of them arrived and started to improve the efficiency of most concerns. Burma Oil Company increased its production to meet the nation's fuel requirements, and the tobacco industry started to export both tobacco and high-quality Burmese cheroots. Experts from the Colombo Plan supervised the operations of hydro-electric dams and together with WHO medics they modernised the hospitals.

Within months, Peter was flying the new Vickers Viscount aircraft to take forty-eight passengers at 350 mph to more destinations. He found the aircraft a joy to fly and highly reliable. One problem was that the Viscount's Rolls Royce Dart turbo-prop engines had to be regularly serviced in Hong Kong. However, there was no shortage of pilots wanting to fly the aircraft to Hong Kong to be serviced as it gave them a week to shop. The Viscounts flew to Calcutta, Bangkok, Hong Kong, Singapore and Dhaka. These flights proved very popular earning much needed foreign exchange.

By 1959, the expatriate population of Burma increased to around three hundred excluding diplomats. They came from all around the world making Rangoon society more cosmopolitan and less formal. Now the Kokine Swimming Club, the Rangoon Sailing Club and the newly reformed Pegu Club had more members, including Burmese to become profitable and important meeting places. Throughout Rangoon, people celebrated the new Burma at garden parties, dances and other social gatherings. However, the diplomats still behaved like greedy kings to demand whatever they wanted. Some were surprised to find that many locals and expatriates refused to be coerced or become their unpaid playthings. Their behaviour was to have long-term effects because many of the women they seduced later turned against them. Now the Burmese were exposed to having their children of both sexes raped by foreigners in the same way that the Japanese had done. It brought back floods of bitter memories and undermined the good deeds of the majority. The very tolerant Burmese kept silent as mistrust of all foreigners grew throughout the nation. Somehow the diplomats became arrogant and evil just like the old colonial administrators. They seriously misjudged the intelligence of the average Burmese mistaking gentleness and good manners for acceptance of their hideous behaviour.

# 19
# An English Engineer Arrives at UBA

In 1959, Peter met the aeronautical engineer Herbert (Bert) Meakins and his wife Peggy off the plane from Hong Kong. Bert was the new an advisor to the Union of Burma Airboard whose main function was to improve UBA. However, he initially reorganised the engineers working on the Viscounts and the stores before purchasing the necessary supplies. Both men got on well as they understood aircraft, Bert worked with Mitchell on the original Spitfires that Peter flew during the war and understood aircraft maintenance from working in BOAC and Hong Kong Airways. Inevitably, Bert helped the UBAF commander Brigadier Tommy Clift maintain their Spitfires and Seafires fighter aircraft. Though Bert was seconded from BOAC and recruited by the British Embassy with diplomatic privileges, the embassy staff unexpectedly refused to help him. So Peter arranged for Bert to rent a house in Golden Valley from George and helped purchase a Humber Hawk car.

The Meakins home in Golden Valley with the Humber Hawk complete with red headlights.

When Peter introduced Bert to Pip Palmarino, they discovered that Bert's father fought with Pip in the Great War. The two men became good friends making Peter realise how small the world was and how old friendships benefited all concerned. It was not long before Bert was a member of the prestigious Pegu Club where he relaxed with ambassadors and government officials. His straightforwardness and honesty helped him make friends as many knew of him as the man who built the Schneider Trophy winning Supermarine aircraft while working under Mitchell of Spitfire fame.

Peggy and Bert Meakins on the left next to Pip Palmarino and Margot Blanche standing outside the new Pegu Club in 1959.

At the Rangoon Sailing Club, Bert proved to be an experienced sailor and taught Peter how to sail. Here they brushed shoulders with diplomats, government officials and many of the better paid expatriates. One sailor was the reclusive General Ne Win, who always wore a plain white shirt and shorts with dark glasses when sailing and lived nearby in a large lakeside house. The General never entered competitions probably because he did not want to be beaten by a foreigner but sailed with Bert and Bert's teenage son, Robin. Strangely, Ne Win and Bert became friends, though they were never very close. It was probably because whenever Ne Win asked Bert a question, he always received an honest reply. The General found such honesty refreshing compared to the diplomats who constantly misled him.

While people sailed, their families relaxed on deck chairs by the water's edge drinking cool iced-tea and playing with their children. It was an idyllic way to relax on a Sunday afternoon and a different world from what they had survived only months before. Ne Win was sometimes accompanied by Brigadier Douglas Blake, but never by his family. His third wife Khin May Than (Katie

Ba Than) and family remained at home being too precious to be exposed to foreign influence. Many later said that while Katie lived, Ne Win was a nicer person as she kept him sane. Sadly, she died in 1972 leaving him alone to face his many enemies.

One day in April Bert and Peter were told not to travel to the airport as it was closed due to ice. That day hundreds of army lorries raced down the Prome Road to twenty miles north of Mingaladon to fight the advancing Karen Army. The fierce fighting lasted three days during which the Burmese Army, equipped with two Sherman tanks and artillery, forced the lightly-armed Karen Army back from the town of Insein. The casualties were so great that by the third night, a mutual cease-fire was declared so they could negotiate a settlement. Neither side trusted the other, and so they met in a tent in Insein, with the British Ambassador and Pip Palmarino acting as intermediaries. After two days, the Karen Army withdrew on the understanding that Ne Win's government gave the Karen people more autonomy and their wounded would receive medical treatment. The agreement worked, and the Karen wounded treated before being helped to return home. This fragile peace lasted until Prime Minister U Nu returned to power in 1960.

Meanwhile, this major event went unnoticed by most nations; it enhanced the reputations of General Ne Win and Brigadier Douglas Blake as able soldiers and negotiators. However, Ne Win still maintained military road blocks in Rangoon around all strategic buildings and on the main roads. All vehicles were forced to have the top half of their headlamps painted red to reduce their visibility. The government troops now regained control of over eighty per cent of the nation with the only exception being the Shan states where the Koumintang ruled. At last, the country was relatively peaceful, and communications improved as the railways were repaired to let the new Japanese trains operate. Improving the railways was difficult because many bridges needed rebuilding or reinforced to take the heavier Japanese locomotives. Slowly, the railways began to operate to most of the major towns over eighteen hundred miles of track, though during the monsoons and after attacks from insurgents, it often did not run regular services. People could now cheaply travel across the nation to sell their goods in the cities.

Peter found life under the Interim Government life was easier as the shops were well stocked, and the exclusive military commissary sold nearly everything. Therefore, the lucrative black market in alcohol and meat ceased to exist. The currency restrictions remained, as Burma struggled to obtain foreign currency as the Kyat was effectively worthless. On the black market, anyone with exchangeable currency could get a hundred times more Kyats than the rate offered through the banks. Sadly, few governments can control the excesses of their diplomats who purchased cheap Kyats on the black market to buy rubies they sold in Europe. These transactions were closely observed by the Burmese secret service that knew who was preparing to leave the country and who exported gems without a government permit. They soon discovered that the majority of the diplomats were involved in the illegal export of rubies and emeralds using the facilities provided for sending packages in the diplomatic bags. This loss of national resources infuriated General Ne Win, but he did nothing after being advised that opening diplomatic bags could have severe consequences. Anyway, it was difficult to find any embassy that was not involved. So he started a State Office to trade in gemstones where foreigners could buy the best stones and receive government export permits, though the purchaser had to pay for everything, including accommodation with dollar or pound notes. So Burma obtained more foreign exchange, but it was still not enough to buy what the nation needed. Ne Win assisted by James Barrington, the Head of his Foreign Office, initiated a diplomatic offensive to get international support. He received visits from the Duke of Edinburgh and his uncle Lord Mountbatten from Britain, with members of the Burma Star Association to visit the Imperial War Graves Cemetery near Rangoon. Then he received David Ben-Gurion from Israel and others from China and the USSR. However, the financial assistance did not materialise as the USA refused to admit supporting the Koumintang operations in Burma. So Ne Win ordered air attacks on the KMT bases at Mong Hsat, and along the upper reaches of the Salween River. This was in response to angry Chinese's complaints that the KMT in Burma was attacking border towns inside China.

Imperial War Graves Cemetery Rangoon 1959.

In December 1959, the Chinese decided to destroy the KMT by invading northern Burma. Within days, the Chinese People's Army had crossed the mountains to advance fifty miles into Burma before meeting any resistance. The well-armed Koumintang fled the region preferring to leave the Burmese to fight the invaders. When the news of the invasion reached Rangoon, Ne Win dispatched his fighter aircraft and more soldiers to repel the invaders with some degree of success. It was probably the first and last time the UBAF went into combat as it was rumoured that their Seafires fought Chinese Mig-15 aircraft. The Burmese strafed and bombed the invaders while their ground troops attacked them using every method possible.

Later, the Chinese complained that the Burmese snipers used crossbows with poisoned arrows to kill their men so silently that it worried even the hardest soldier. Such silent assassins were regarded as unacceptable as they could attack without revealing their position. The unexpected resistance caused the Chinese to halt their advance and propose a ceasefire. They sent their foreign minister, the impressive Chou En-Lai (Zhou En Lai) to Rangoon to negotiate with Ne Win. He was well received by Ne Win who was aware that USA and UK had not offered Burma any assistance when invaded. It had made him so angry that he wanted to expel all Americans from Burma, especially those who said the KMT were there to help defend Burma from any Chinese invasion.

Within two days, Chou En-Lai and Ne Win signed the Sino-Burmese Border Treaty that transferred four hundred square miles of Burma to China in exchange for much-needed aid. The Chinese agreed to build bridges, hotels and factories as well as supplying military assistance, in return for Burmese rice so that no foreign exchange was required. Furthermore, the Chinese agreed to train Burmese Army officers to fight insurgents, many of whom returned to become determined but ruthless leaders and undermined Ne Win. The long-term effect was that Burma and China became major trading partners, and Ne Win ignored America and treated UK with caution. Later, on October 20th 1962, the Chinese used the lessons learnt from invading Burma to enter northern India. After sending twenty thousand troops into India, the Chinese suddenly announced a ceasefire and withdrew their troops. They achieved their objective by warning India and other neighbours not to interfere with China and Tibet.

# 50
## The Rock and Roll Years

During the Interim Government, Burma was an exciting and pleasant land for foreigners to live in. The numerous embassies vied with each other to give the best garden party, where Russian and Chinese diplomats chatted to their American and British counterparts, while closely observed by the amused Burmese. Because the expatriate community was so small, most people were invited to the same occasions. The President Win Maung always attended the embassy parties dressed in national costume and proved popular with his cheerful nature. However, most of the Interim Government, including Ne Win stayed away except everyone attended the Independence Day garden party held by President Win Maung in the grounds of his official residence, Government House.

The once traditional western dances involving the waltz and fox trot suddenly were often replaced by the latest rock and roll music that had arrived from America. The energetic dances associated with the new tunes became popular among the younger expatriates at private parties and in the clubs. Soon the rock songs of Elvis Presley, Buddy Holly and the Crickets, Bill Haley and his Comets, Chuck Berry, and Peggy Lee resounded in once sedate houses, intermingled with a modernised version of the Tennessee Waltz, calypso music sung by Harry Belafonte and romantic songs of Pat Boone such as April Love. The most popular dance was Chubby Checker's The Twist that demanded everyone move up and down while swinging their hips to the tune. No longer did women wear long evening dresses as they were too restrictive, instead they preferred low cut short dresses with or without petticoats. The more provocative women loved to spin around to make their skirt rise so that everyone could see the tops of their stockings and panties, as they liked being admired. Some of them found the man of their dreams while others just made a lot of close friends. Importantly, everyone had fun while enjoying each other's company long enough to forget the dark clouds that were never too far away.

Every day there was a risk of being attacked or robbed, perhaps the biggest fear was that the communists would invade the city. Always, there were rumours of atrocities committed by the communists against foreigners, especially missionaries and priests. Therefore, most expatriates carried guns or other weapons on their person, in their cars or at home. Some kept Naga crossbows in the house as they were quiet, easy to buy and when used properly, deadly. The bamboo bolt from a crossbow could penetrate three inches of teak and kill any man or beast. The private clubs and cinemas showed films such as Brigette Bardot's provocative 'And God Created Woman' and the less shocking Glen Ford in 'Torpedo Run' along with Paul Newman in 'Rally around the Flag Boys.' There was no real censorship as the government only prohibited films that were considered to be political and against socialism. Brigette Bardot's sexual antics did not shock the Burmese as they were used to seeing European women in thin, nearly transparent dresses and considered nudity as natural. Anyway, some Burmese officials and many diplomats secretly had mistresses of all nationalities.

With the arrival of expatriate schoolchildren during the long summer holidays, the parents had to find things for them to do and places to see. They held parties for their children and friends who also helped to get the adults to know each other. So once a week someone held a party for their teenagers where they could make friends, dance and have fun. Often Robin Meakins went to the parties with Peter's son Paul, who was about the same age to become good friends and go on dates together to the cinema or swimming at the Kokine Swimming Club. Less regularly some children were taken on trips to places of interest. Luckily, UBA arranged flights and accommodation to safer parts of Burma, such as the white coral beaches along the Arakan coast or Mandalay. Once a week, UBA flew to Nagapoli airstrip on the edge of the Sandoway River where there were a few large bungalows for hire. They looked out over the Bay of Bengal to offer safe swimming, off white sands inside the coral reef. Here the fishermen sold fresh fish every morning, and the farmers sold an assortment of excellent fruit and vegetables. Others visited the ancient temples of Pagan and Mandalay. The development of a tourist industry brought much-needed money to remote and poor areas such as the Arakan coast.

In 1959, Bert Meakins took his family on a UBA Dakota for a two-week holiday to Nagapoli having hired a bungalow complete with servants near the beach. When they arrived at the airport, an ancient car drove them to the bungalow where everything was ready for them, including a fine dinner. Afterwards, they sat on the veranda to relax and look out over the beautifully serene blue seas of the Bay of Bengal. It was so peaceful that Bert started to relax now that he was away from the politics and intrigue of Rangoon. They all slept well under their mosquito nets as the rooms were remarkably cool.

Nagapoli Airport in 1959 with bus and passengers waiting for the plane.

Next morning Bert's two sons, David the eldest and Robin, were up at dawn to walk on the beach and explore the surrounding area. It was so peaceful that they could hear the noise of the waves lapping against the beach and the wind gently moving the palm trees to make a small whistling noise. Of course, there were the songs and colours of a dozen different birds welcoming in the new day. So they swam and were excited to see the sea was so clear they could see the shells and fish on the white sand under their feet. They knew to keep away from the spiney sea urchins, but no one warned them against the sharp coral that cut their feet. Afterwards, they returned to the bungalow to eat breakfast consisting of boiled eggs, freshly baked bread, papaya and mango juice.

The author's mother Peggy and his brother David in the bungalow at Nagapoli in 1959.

After breakfast, the boys walked down the beach to the nearby town. They saw no one until nearing the town, when they met the fishermen returning from a night's fishing carrying their catch. David was shocked to find two men carrying a three-foot shark caught inside the reef. Afterwards, David was not convinced that swimming was safe even after being told that only small, relatively harmless sharks could swim over the reef because all large dangerous sharks did not cross the barrier. On returning home the boys were offered the juice from a freshly cut coconut to drink that proved very refreshing.

The author drinking coconut milk with his family and the bungalow owner in Nagapoli.

During the next two weeks, they relaxed and explored the surrounding area on foot and in the local taxi. The taxi was an immaculately maintained black pre-war Austin ten with the glass missing from its windscreen. However, it worked when driven exactly as in the instruction booklet. On starting the car, driver opened the glassless windscreen before pulling out the choke to start the engine. With one loud cough and a cloud of smoke, its engine started to run smoothly like a well-oiled sewing machine. This much-loved vehicle carried the family up to the hills to look down over the Sandoway River, and visit the nearest temples and a nearby Baptist church. On the way, they passed a group of soldiers carrying rifles marching along the road. Afterwards, Bert said the soldiers were not wearing Burma Army uniform, and so were local militia or insurgents. Whatever was the case, they were lucky to escape unharmed. At the church, they met a young Canadian missionary priest who was cheerful but homesick and delighted to speak English. He warned Bert not to travel at night as rebel forces of the Arakan Liberation Party were active harassing the government soldiers. This confirmed Bert's suspicions about the militia they had seen and reminded him that even in this apparent paradise Burma was still a divided nation. They were surprised to learn that many of the people living on the Arakan peninsular were ethically Indian with many being Hindus or Moslem. The differences in religious beliefs and customs further divided them from the Buddhists, though somehow they lived together in an uneasy alliance. Too soon, the holiday was over, and they flew back to Rangoon refreshed and prepared for whatever awaited them.

# 51
## The Promised Elections

*When democratic processes fail because the people do not understand what they are voting for.*

Bert returned to find Rangoon was in turmoil as everywhere there were posters calling on the people to vote for a new government. The promised elections were taking place throughout the land even in places that the government did not control. It was an election campaign in which both sides sent lorries of supporters into the villages to gather their support making promises no one could keep. There was little discussion because few knew enough about what each side stood for. In the end, it was an election based on the personalities of the two leaders who both claimed to be the rightful heirs of the national hero Aung San. The people could only vote for either the Stable AFPFL represented by a grey flag and the Clean AFPFL whose sign was a white flag. The Stable AFPFL, President Ba Swe promised to send all army officers holding government positions back to their barracks and replace them with civilians. However, U Nu and his Clean AFPFL played to the mood of the majority by promising to re-instate Buddhism as the state religion and give autonomy to both the Arakanese and Mons peoples. It is important to note that he made no such promises to the larger Shan and Karen people, who he regarded as his enemies because they fought for the British against the Japanese.

On the posters supporting U Nu and the Clean AFPFL the predominant colour was saffron usually associated with the Buddhist monks and used in a successful attempt to get the support of the monasteries. Few people thought long enough to realise that U Nu would not continue the reforms Ne Win started as having already forgotten how bad things were before the Interim Government came to power. Meanwhile, the business community fearing their businesses and investments would suffer with a return to shortages, more export restrictions, and the banning of certain goods started to move their assets abroad. Other foreign companies stopped investing in Burma as they knew U Nu could nationalise their assets without proper compensation and deport all of their expatriate employees. This meant that the economy started to slow down as businesses rapidly trained up Burmese to fill the jobs that would be made vacant by the departing foreigners. However, many expatriates stayed in their posts hoping that U Nu had learnt from his previous mistakes and would build on the many successes of the Interim Government.

Most of the election campaigning was carried out by word of mouth combined with a massive poster campaign as many villagers could not read. The local canvassers made wild promises of peace and prosperity that only the ignorant believed. There was little discussion about the party's policies for governing the nation even in the newspapers or at meetings. In fact, no one knew what each group really believed in other than their wish to gain power and with it, wealth. The difference between the two parties was so small that no one party was expected to win an overall majority. The party that everyone expected to win the coming election was the Stable AFPFL who fought an honest contest, and before the election in February 1959 held the majority of the seats in parliament. The results from the election were unexpectedly decisive so that when declared in February 1960 U Nu's Clean AFPFL was victorious while the leaders of the Stable AFPFL lost their parliamentary seats. No honest observers believed the results thinking they were falsified, but there was nobody to complain to. It was an unprecedented landslide for the previously unpopular and pro-Japanese U Nu whose claims to have been a friend of the national hero Aung San was tenuous. Now the smiling, slippery U Nu would return as the next Prime Minister on the promise of a united Buddhist Burma run by Burmese. It was clear that he had learnt little during the past few years except to make rich friends and want to turn Burma into a closed society where all foreigners and other faiths were unwelcome.

Life in Rangoon continued as normal except that everybody started to store canned goods and alcohol, in case they were banned. Many packed up their valuables to ship back home or stored them in large cabin trunks. Then many people waited to see what happened before deciding to remain or leave Burma. It all depended on what the new government would do and who they would allow to work in the country.

Everything was peaceful even though the army was divided as to whether the nation was ready to return to civilian government. Most officers feared that the gains from the unification of the nation under Ne Win would be lost if U Nu started to sack foreigners, ethnic minorities and Anglo-Burmese from positions of authority. In many army bases, senior officers spent hours convincing their troops to give up power with the promise that if failed to rule the nation fairly, the army would return to power. This promise placated the disillusioned soldiers who felt that their three years working to rebuild Burma was being handed over to corrupt civilians. Similar feelings grew in the Karen states where they feared U Nu would renege on their treaty with Ne Win. So the Karen and other militant groups kept their weapons ready to use if the Burmese tried to take away their limited autonomy. Such a move would be resisted with all their military resources.

One of the final acts of the Interim Government was to stop military information reaching the insurgents. The Secret Service discovered that most troop movements were reported in the papers, especially in the Rangoon based Nation that was printed in both English and Burmese editions. So they warned the editor to refrain from publishing such detailed reports or risk having his paper closed and himself arrested. At the same time, they discovered that the CIA was receiving accurate information on troop deployments from American businessmen living in Rangoon that they relayed to the KMT. So the Secret Service monitored all phone calls from the homes and business premises of such people and recorded their movements. Then Ne Win re-enforced his bases near the borders in preparation for any military attacks when the new government took over. He feared that if U Nu won the election, he would rule all the states directly from Rangoon, especially those with limited autonomy such as the Shan and Karen States and by doing so break the fragile peace he negotiated. If this happened, the civil war would restart as both groups would receive arms from Thailand funded by the CIA and their highly profitable opium trade.

# 52

## The Teenager and the General

Every Sunday Bert Meakins took his family to the Rangoon Sailing Club on Victoria lake. They always arrived early so that Bert could obtain a good yacht to sail on his own or with his youngest son Robin. His wife and eldest son David would sit on the deck chairs near the bar to chat with their friends while being served drinks and snacks. It was a major meeting place and watering hole for most of the influential expatriates, especially the top businessmen and diplomats. Here they discussed business, including how successful the rebels were. Though they did not realise it, some of the waiters worked for the Burmese Secret Service and reported everything they heard while discretely saying nothing that would warn the visitors. After a few gin and tonics, many diplomats or their wives talked carelessly of secrets such as their country's attitude towards Burma not knowing that the information was within hours relayed to the government.

The Sailing Club owned twenty sailing boats moored by a small jetty next to the private ones belonging to the influential and rich. The Club was a convenient meeting place because it was close to the lakeside residencies of General Ne Win, Daw Khin Kyi the widow of Aung San, the American and British Ambassadors. So while sailing or just relaxing by the lake the diplomats could keep in contact while mixing with their people.

One morning General Ne Win greeted Bert as he was preparing to go sailing.

'Good morning Bert, it is a lovely morning for a sail,' remarked a smiling Ne Win.

'Good morning sir, are you going to sail?' a surprised Bert Meakins replied.

'I hope so. However, I need someone to be my crew. I wondered if you would let your son Robin sail with me and promise to return him to you safe and sound.'

'I am sure that he will be delighted to be your crew, please remember he is only a teenager, and sometimes he is not very tactful,' replied Bert.

'I am fed up of listening to diplomats and would like to know what people really think.'

So Robin boarded Ne Win's yacht to act as the crew. He sailed with his father, but never with someone else. Now he was excited about crewing for the general while apprehensive that he would make a mistake. The first thing they did was to practise going about to tack, or changing direction. Only after practising pulling the sail over to the other side when he heard the command 'Going about Lee-oh', did they sail out onto the still waters of the deep blue lake. For some time, they sailed in silence to listen to the wind in the sheets and the water lapping against the small yacht. They were both content to feel the cool breeze in their faces as the hot sun reflected on the water to form magical images. The General sailed the yacht across the lake to near his house that stood on the lakeshore before turning back while always keeping far away from any other craft as if they held danger, maybe they did.

'Well how old are you young man?' the General asked.

Sir, I was sixteen last week,' replied Robin.

'I remember when I was your age when I thought everything was simple. Don't grow up too quickly as being an adult can be very difficult.'

'I would like to be old enough to drive a car and do whatever I wanted.'

'Sadly few adults can do what they want as there are always friends and relations that need your help.'

'Oh, I never thought of that.'

'Few people at your age do. Just remember that your father's hard work and skills pay for your school fees as well as all your expenses. Do you like coming here on holiday?'

'Oh yes sir, Burma is the most beautiful place I have ever seen. Everywhere I go; there are fantastic colourful flowers, the golden temples and the bright clothing of her people. Everyone is very friendly so that I enjoy every minute.'

'I am glad you like being in my country. It proves that our providing first-class tickets for you and your brother to visit twice a year is a good investment. I like to think that flying for so long is difficult and the best seats make the journey more agreeable.'

'Thank you sir. The first-class service in BOAC is very comfortable and the food fantastic.'

'It is nice to know that some of the things I do are appreciated.'

'I am sure sir most people respect you and are pleased to see how well the country is developing under your administration.'

'Thank you. Tell me honestly from what you have seen, what do you really think needs improving?'

'I think most of the roads need repairing because they flood after the rains and have very deep pot holes, that is except for the Prome Road.'

'I agree, but such repairs are very expensive.'

'Surely sir the cost of not repairing them will be more expensive, if you include the damage to the vehicles using them.'

'That is a good point that I will discuss with my colleagues. I knew that by talking to you, I would learn things no adult would tell me. Thank you, young man. Are there any other things that I should change?'

'The customs and immigration officers at the airport are rude and frightening.'

'I did not realise they were so impolite, though you must realise they have a difficult job to do as smuggling has reached epidemic proportions.'

While sailing Ne Win pointed to the snake swimming on top of the water.

'See the snake swimming nearby. It is a water moccasin that is as deadly as it is beautiful. It is a reminder that even in lovely places, there are real dangers to be avoided.'

For a few moments, they both watched the snake rhythmically swim away into the distance before they continued sailing.

They continued to sail for the next hour before returning to the Club. Then Robin went to sit with his parents as the General left with an aide went home. However, before he left Ne Win asked Bert Meakins, 'I would like to take your son on an educational trip to visit the Imperial War Graves Memorial. Of course, you may come with us. Would Tuesday be convenient?'

'Of course, we will be delighted to come with you, sir,' a startled Bert Meakins replied.

'Then I will be at your home at 9 am before it gets too hot. You may be surprised to learn how much I respect your heroic soldiers.'

# 53
## A Stern Warning

At precisely 9 am on Tuesday morning, an army car arrived outside the Meakins house bringing General Ne Win and Brigadier Douglas Blake in full dress uniform. Within the hour, they were at the Imperial War Graves cemetery with Bert and Robin Meakins. It was situated near Mingaladon airport 21 miles north of Rangoon near the village of Taukkyan, so it is often referred to incorrectly as the Taukkyan War Cemetery.

Robin was overwhelmed by the size of the monument that consisted of beautifully maintained graves set out in rows with clean headstones surrounded by neatly trimmed bushes. Above this towered a series of pillars forming a rotunda on which were inscribed the names by regiment of all the Commonwealth soldiers who had died in Burma and had no grave. Ne Win led the group to the rotunda to stand next to an inscription that said in English 'They died for all free men.' Either side of this was the same message but in Burmese, Hindi, Urdu, and Gurmukhi.

'I find coming here a pilgrimage that reminds me of the twenty-seven thousand Allied dead that fought in Burma and Assam to defeat the Japanese. If you look carefully you will see they came from all over your Commonwealth to die in a foreign land,' stated the General solemnly.

'I did not realise that so many different nationalities fought here. According to this, they came from Britain, Burma, Canada, Australia, East, West, Central, and South Africa, with the majority coming from India,' replied Robin quietly.

'The numbers of your soldiers who died to free Burma is extraordinary high. It is a sacrifice that all of us must never forget,' commented Ne Win walking towards an individual gravestone.

At the gravestone Ne Win bowed his head before saying, 'Robin can you read the age of your fellow countryman?'

'It says he was seventeen, sir,' the startled Robin answered.

'It means he died when only a year older than you to liberate a foreign land. I hope he died quickly and has at last found peace,' commented Ne Win. 'Now you know how privileged you are to benefit from their sacrifices, and I hope that you never forget how they lost their youth, so we all could live without the fear of fascism.'

'I did not realise how many died until today,' commented a surprised Robin before asking. 'Are there more graves here?'

'There are six thousand graves with headstones and nearby a memorial for thousands more who were cremated as decreed by their religion. Every one of them died in a very cruel and bitter war that even today simmers on,' added Brigadier Blake.

'It is a sobering thought that they had so much to live for but were to die fighting miles from home to prevent the Japanese invasion of India. They started as an ill-disciplined rabble that was badly commanded and ended up as the best fighting forces the world has ever seen. I hope this memorial survives for a hundred years to remind everyone, especially the Burmese, of the sacrifices they made to drive the Japanese from our shores. Though I once fought for the Japanese before I learnt they were less trustworthy than even the worst British colonialists. It has affected me so much that every time I see their flag or meet their people I feel ashamed of the mistakes I made,' stated a serious Ne Win.

For the first time, Robin saw how complex and troubled the general was, but he said nothing as he dared not comment.

'Sir, I think that war changes everyone,' commented a serious Bert Meakins. 'I did not fight but organized the repair of RAF bombers and in doing so many regard me as part of the machinery that decimated German cities. While my own father, himself a soldier, never forgave me for not fighting. I hope and pray that there will not be another world war in which so many die.'

'Bert, I must agree that none of us want another world war, but we have no control over the weird behaviour of the USA and the USSR,' added Douglas Blake.

'Unfortunately the war in Burma did not end when the Japanese surrendered but continues as different ethnic groups fight the Burmese Army for independence and are often funded by western nations,' Ne Win added looking severe.

Robin took a series of photographs of the cemetery so that he would never forget all those who died to save the world from fascism.

Then they drove back to Rangoon to stop by a newly built pavilion inside a fenced area near the lake. The general led his party inside the fence so that they all could see the three elephants chained to the ground beneath a red wooden canopy near a group of pongyis that were praying. There were two large adults and a paler coloured baby elephant.

The baby white elephant with mother and another elephant in Rangoon, 1959.

'Friends what you can see in front of you is a rare and very sacred animal. It is a baby white elephant that in Buddhism signifies a gift from Lord Buddha to be cherished as a sign of peace and good luck. It is also a symbol of mental strength in Buddhism and in Hinduism represents the God Ganesh. The newly elected future Prime Minister U Nu says that it shows Buddha's approval of his victory and a sign of better days to come,' stated Ne Win.

'Some regard the birth of a white elephant as a mixed blessing. In the past, the kings of Siam used to present all such animals to people they did not like so that they had to spend a fortune looking after them without getting any reward. I think this is the origin of the British term white elephant to mean something of no value,' added Douglas Blake. Then he continued, 'They are very rare and when discovered must be kept for everyone to see and fed on special food. A white elephant brings good luck but also is very costly to keep. However, this one has been adopted by the pongyis of the Shwe Dagon who take care of all his needs.'

'May I photograph the sacred elephant?' Robin asked wanting a picture to prove that white elephants really existed.

'Of course you can but be quick before someone tries to stop you,' replied Ne Win.

After taking the pictures and making a donation in the offering bowl next to the pongyis, they drove to Golden Valley where the general left Bert and his son at their house before returning to the difficulties of running a divided nation.

A week later Ne Win accompanied by Peter Anderson visited Bert Meakins at his home. It was just after sunset when they arrived as Bert was relaxing after a very hot and tiring day at the airport. In minutes, the welcome guests were seated in the large sitting room drinking whisky with plenty of ice.

'Bert we have come here tonight to warn you that we believe the incoming government will expel all foreigners from Burma,' Ne Win stated. His face showed that he did not like what he was saying.

'Sir, I thank you for the warning but my work requires another year to complete,' replied a shocked Bert.

'I am afraid that is unlikely to happen as we believe U Nu intends to repatriate all foreigners from Burma, however, important they are,' continued the general.

'But why?'

'The reasons are not clear except that U Nu thinks he cannot unite the nation while there are so many expatriates and diplomats working throughout Burma. He believes that many support the insurgents and illegally send our wealth abroad as precious stones without paying tax.'

'There may be some truth to what U Nu thinks, but he should not blame all of us for the greed of the few,' a concerned Bert replied.

'Bert, I fully agree with you, and that is why I want you to resign and leave here in early September before U Nu is too powerful, and I can still arrange for your safe and easy departure,' insisted Ne Win.

'Surely my embassy will arrange everything,' added a worried Bert Meakins.

'I think your embassy will continue to ignore your requirements as they find your successes at UBA an embarrassment that upsets their plans to undermine Burma.'

'Sir, I fear that you may be correct as the First and Second Secretaries have recently been behaving more problematic and arrogant than before. Sometimes they make me feel as though I was their enemy and not to be trusted,' Bert added.

'I think they will try to destroy your reputation so that you will not be in a position to report their selling of visas, passports and smuggling of rubies to the Foreign Office in London.'

'I am afraid the general is right, and we all have much to fear from the two British Embassy men and their friends in the CIA. Both of us believe that the western powers support the new government but do not realize the depth of his hatred for all British and Americans who he has never forgiven for fighting the Japanese and supporting the insurgents operating in Burma. I too must consider my position but will not leave Burma until forced to,' intervened Peter Anderson.

'Surely Peter no one would want to deport pilots like you who are so vital to UBA,' stated a shocked Bert.

'I just don't know, but I am aware that many Burmese would like to replace me as the senior pilot.'

'This xenophobia will set the modernisation of Burma back many years.'

'I am afraid it is true,' intervened Ne Win. 'I believe such actions will isolate Burma further from the rest of the world while making it easier for the CIA to continue running the Opium trade both here and in Laos. Sadly, Prime Minister U Nu is too ignorant to see the cunning trap he is falling into.'

'How can the west be so vicious as to destroy this beautiful nation,' commented Bert.

'The answer is that it is simply a matter of divide and rule. Small nations must do what the west wants or it becomes subject to subversion, regime change or economic isolation. It is the worst sort of what some call neo-colonialism. Now that we have given you our sad news, I think that it is time we left. However, you must tell me when you are leaving so that I can see you safely off from Mingaladon and prevent any unpleasantness,' commented Ne Win walking towards the front door.

# 54
## The Departure of Friends and Family

In September 1960, Peter's life changed when many of his expatriate friends were expelled from Burma. Everyday more statements from the Prime Minister U Nu demanded that Burmese take over jobs held by expatriates under what he called a constructive programme of Burmanization. This he stated would return the wealth of Burma back to the people, though he did not add that the majority of new appointees would be both Buddhist and supporters of his road to socialism. In the end, it turned out to be another action that demolished many local industries and reduced Burmese exports.

Bert Meakins and family left Rangoon at the end of August aboard the BOAC flight to London. They were helped through emigration by Ne Win and Douglas Blake much to the annoyance of some customs officials who wanted to confiscate Mrs Meakins' pearl necklace and Bert's gold watch. As they were about to board the aircraft, Ne Win gave Peggy Meakins a small package.

'Please take this gift as a token of my thanks for all that Bert has done to help Burma. Do not open it until you are in the air as I do not want others to know what it contains. Remember that one day I will want you to return to continue building a successful Burma. Good luck and when you think of us always remember the good times.' Then the General watched the family board the aircraft and only left the runway after the aircraft door was closed, and the boarding steps removed.

Once the aircraft was in the air, Peggy opened the parcel to find seven pieces of fine jade mounted in a gold bracelet. It was a gift worthy of a lady, and she appreciated the gesture.

In the next months, many others left Burma; some willingly, others deported and a few escaped in desperation as the Secret police investigated their illegal activities. Gradually, Burma became a closed society with few foreigners and even fewer visitors.

One morning Peter discovered that his brother-in-law Tun Kyi and Maria with their children had fled to Thailand to continue working for the CIA in Bangkok to arm and assist the Karen resistance. He had been clandestinely helping the Karen Army for years by supplying information and medicines while officially travelling for George Tauk. George was shocked to learn of their departure that was made worse by a few visits from the Burmese counter insurgency agents who suggested he was also involved with the rebels. Luckily, they had no proof against George and after hours of interrogation decided to leave him alone. It was clear that George, and his friends were no longer safe in Burma, and so they made plans to leave.

George became aware his Burma was being destroyed by America for reasons he could not understand. He was shocked that the once brave Tun Kyi turned against his own people to become a paid employee of the CIA to live and work in Thailand. It was very likely that George would never see his youngest daughter and her children again. The thought of this separation brought tears to his eyes as his anger towards American grew. After praying for his family, George set out to reorganize his business empire removing all those with American contacts and starting to inform the security services of the names of all foreigners who purchased expensive gemstones from his shop. He hoped that with this information, the customs officers could stop them leaving the country, but he had forgotten about the sealed diplomatic pouches that transferred letters and packages from the Embassies back to their home nations. Sending gemstones in such pouches was against international law though quite common and difficult to stop without risking an international crisis.

Soon hundreds of frightened Burmese fled to Thailand by road, boat and even by air. Clearly, the CIA's large presence in Burma explained why the army had difficulty in locating and fighting the rebels. In fact, the rebels had better weapons than the army as well as more ammunition. At the same time, the Opium Trail through Northern Burma, Laos and Thailand proved highly successful. The raw opium from poppies in Burma and Laos was refined into heroin at secret factories around Bangkok before being exported to the USA. In America, it was used to supply the cravings of the poor, especially the black youth, in the ghettoes of Los Angeles, Chicago and Washington. It was an evil operation designed to destroy the minds and ambitions of a growing coloured and Hispanic youth. Some of the heroin was sold cheaply through trusted agents while the rest was sold to drug barons whose money funded the CIA activities in Indo China.

Within a year, Peter and his family returned to England where he worked as a pilot for a small charter airline taking holiday makers to Spain. They lived in a large house on the Sussex coast near his parents and London Gatwick airport. They never returned to Burma but did not forget the land or her people and kept in touch with their friends through letters and the magic of the jade tree.

# 55
## Military Rule and Isolation

Within six months of leaving Burma, Peter and Susie were joined in England by George Tauk. He had obtained his exit visa with the help of General Ne Win who was now president after leading a coup d'état in 1962 to remove his nemesis U Nu and initiate military rule. Within hours of taking power, Ne Win announced a Revolutionary Council to run Burma consisting of four brigadiers who replaced parliament and all state councils. He was determined to unite Burma even if it meant using military force. Next the Council stopped U Nu's prestigious projects and used the money to pay for agriculture to include irrigation and the building of a factory to produce insecticide. They followed this by declaring their belief in freedom of religion and a free press. These promises did not last long as by the end of 1966, all private newspapers were banned, and the presses nationalised. Ne Win also invited back some of the expatriates he trusted like Bert Meakins. However, very few accepted the offer after learning that many of the members of the military council were ruthless and having trained in China were anti-westerners.

The same year Burma signed an agreement with USAID for a loan of $3.4 million for land reclamation in the Irrawaddy and Pegu districts. This was followed by an agreement with the USSR for the construction of an irrigation dam and associated reservoir. In 1970, a former Prime Minister Bo Let Ya and the editor of the once prestigious newspaper 'The Nation' together with some ethnic liberation forces united to form the United National Liberation Front (UNFL) to attack Burma from bases in Thailand. Within months, they were killed or had fled back to Thailand. The UNFL was finally destroyed after Ne Win had an official visit to Thailand.

Soon Burma became an isolated nation ruled by an increasingly oppressive military regime that removed most traces of democracy and imprisoned or executed many opponents, especially those with western connections. At the United Nations Assembly in New York, they exposed the US involvement in running the Koumintang at the United Nations resulting in many of thousands of them being flown to Taiwan on US/Taiwanese aircraft. Though many remained in northern Burma to continue working with some Shan dissidents running the Opium Trail that still operates.

Ne Win purchased aircraft to modernise his Air Force and the state airline UBA with seven Fokker F-27, eight Fokker F-28 and in 1969, a Boeing 727 to replace the aging Dakotas. The Air Force was slowly supplied with jet aircraft such as the Lockheed Shooting Star trainers, and by the 1990s, they added Chinese built fighter aircraft. Soon Ne Win found himself with few friends and surrounded by over ambitious Chinese trained officers making him increasingly xenophobic and reliant on astrologers for advice. This became worse after the death of the wife who had guided him when he first ran the interim government. In an uncharacteristic gesture, Ne Win donated some of the surviving Burmese Air Force Spitfires and Seafires to the RAF with the help of the British Consul Henry Booth. The author knows they arrived in England because he saw and examined the log book of one ex-Burmese Seafire on display at the RAF stand in the Royal Tournament in London.

However, the relationship between Burma and Britain deteriorated even though the general still unofficially visited London for medical treatment for filariasis. Gradually, Ne Win changed becoming very troubled with few friends he could trust. The extreme elements among the senior officers demanded that he remove many of his loyal Anglo-Burmese officers such as Brigadiers Douglas Blake and Tommy Clift and replace them with Chinese trained Burmese.

In 1988, Aung San Suu Kyi returned to Burma to be with her seriously ill mother to live at their house near the lake close to Ne Win's home. Burma was again in turmoil as some generals formed a junta to control the ailing Ne Win as they set out to turn Burma into a military state. Knowing that he was powerless, Ne Win resigned as President in July 1988 and remained quietly in his house in Rangoon. During a demonstration following the general's resignation Aung San Suu Kyi addressed thousands of people from the steps of the Shwe Dagon pagoda encouraging them to believe that they may soon live in a free and democratic country. Shortly later, in September 1988, the military led by General Saw Maung toppled the BSSP government to replace it with the State Law and Order Restoration Council (SLORC) and rule the land with brutal force while punishing all opposition. Many projects such as building roads and digging trenches were carried out using forced labour whereby villagers worked without pay, failure to obey any command was severely punished. SLORC in 1989 changed the name of Burma to Myanma Naingngan (State of Myanma). They expanded the armed forces with aircraft and weapons purchased from China as well as selling them natural gas and oil as well as obtaining their support in all international matters.

When confronted by the opposition led by Ne Win's friend General Aung San's daughter Aung San Suu Kyi, the SLORC government feared her western education and her wish to remove them from power. Ne Win could do little to protect his friend's daughter as the military wanted her removed but dare not let her die to be a martyr. So they placed Aung San Suu Kyi under house arrest after she became chairperson of the National League for Democracy (NLD). This lasted from 20th July 1989 until her release on 13th November 2010. While under house arrest, she received many international visitors and was in 1991 awarded the Nobel Peace Prize for her work for democracy in Burma. After years of isolation, she was allowed to participate in the by-elections where her party won 43 of the 45 seats that were contested in the 2012 by-election. She won the seat for Kawhmu in the lower house of Parliament, the *Pyithu Hutla* and mediates with the government about a return to democracy and the end to military rule.

The ruling generals on 4th March 2002, placed Ne Win and his daughter Sander Win under house arrest in his home by the lake without adequate medical attention after accusing him and his family of plotting a coup and died on the 5th December 2002. Even in death Ne Win was a force to be reckoned with and so feared by the younger generals that they refused him a proper burial. In fact, he was the only member of the original Burma Independence Army leaders not to be buried in the Martyr's memorial. Eventually, his remains were cremated and his ashes cast into the Hlang River by his daughter Sander Win.

When Susie, Peter and George heard of Ne Win's death, they were sad to have lost a friend though aware he had become ruthless. So they sat together in front of the jade tree to pray for his spirit to be at last free from all fears and be reincarnated as a young man who would help Burma gain the freedoms he once fought for. They knew many would judge him for his actions as a dictator and forget all the good he did. Afterwards, George commented,' As Shakespeare wrote of Julius Caesar; The evil men do lives after them, the good is oft interred with their bones.' Peter felt this was true for both Caesar and Ne Win as strong men with too many enemies.

# 56
# Historical Notes

The War in Burma remains a topic of discussion and one in which there is much disagreement. There was no Peter Anderson but there were many like him. The armies of the British Empire with those of China and America fought a war against overwhelming odds to hold back the tide of Japanese expansionism. During the fall of Rangoon, the allies had less than fifty planes against an enemy of five hundred fighters and bombers. The role of the RAF is well recorded in 'The Forgotten Air Force' by Air Commodore Henry Probert, published by Bassey's Press (1995). The dated but still classic military text by Field Marshall Slim, entitled 'Defeat into Victory' published by Cassell (1956) is well worth reading, the most detailed account of all is Louis Allen's Burma – 'The Longest War 1941-1945' published by Phoenix Press (1984), though many find it too tolerant of the Japanese excesses. More importantly it deals with sources from all sides having the best researched material available.

Details of the air battles in Burma are few. The exceptional flying of the RAF, Indian Air Force, Flying Tigers, and later the USAF saved the day. The numbers of enemy aircraft destroyed are unreliable as many pilots failed to report their kills or the records were lost during the retreat. The battles around Imphal and Kohima were some of the bloodiest of the Second World War. All who fought in these campaigns were heroes. The first battle of Kohima, also known as the siege of Kohima Ridge, was the bitterest and the most heroic action of the Burma War, and one that the generals tried to forget. The famous painting of 'The Battle of the Tennis Court' by Terrance Cuneo depicts the second battle of Kohima after the siege had been raised, and not the original one. It shows tanks, and defensive barbed wire where previously there were none. However, it illustrates the intensity and destruction involved in those endless skirmishes over a long-forgotten tennis court.

The war destroyed much of the wealth and infrastructure of Burma. The British authorities in their improper haste to leave Burma, handed it over to the former pro-Japanese Burmese led by Aung San and U Nu. So the Pro-British Karen, Kachin, Chin, Naga, and Shan were to be governed by their enemies as their reward for supporting Britain. In the chaos that followed independence, Aung San was assassinated and distrust ruled a nation. The war between the Karen and the Burmese continues up to the present day.

As a teenager, the author lived in Burma to know at first-hand the kindness of the Burmese people. His father worked as an advisor to Union of Burma Airboard to improve the operations of the Union of Burma Airways. He knew and worked with many senior Burmese, including the then-Prime Minister General Ne Win, Brigadier Douglas Blake, Brigadier Tommy Clift, James Barrington and many others. All of them were honourable men caught up in an

East-West battle not of their choosing and striving to keep Burma free. The USA supported the former Foreign Minister of the Japanese government in Burma, U Nu, against General Ne Win and his people. They wanted to exploit the opium triangle of Burma, Laos and Thailand to fund the CIA covert operations throughout the region, and armed both the Shan army and the Chinese Nationalist Koumintang (now written as Goumintang) forces operating in northern Burma. Then the United Nations under Secretary General U U Thant intervened, forcing the USA to remove most of the remnants of the Chinese wartime Koumintang soldiers to Taiwan Formosa. The struggle against outside interference continues and so does the suppression of the liberal elements of the democratic opposition.

The author hopes that he has done justice to the bravery of people like ex-British Sergeant Major and elephant hunter Pip Palmarino, who befriended his family. Pip had fought with the author's grandfather in the First World War and treated the author's family as trusted friends. His story is true and like many others, he kept it, mostly to himself. Pip along with the artist Margot Blanche, Dr Lusk and James Barrington did walk out of Burma with women and children from Rangoon to Assam. They remained close friends for many years; James Barrington became the Ambassador for Burma to the United Nations as well as to the USA and Canada. Afterwards, he retired to Canada where he died leaving behind a daughter and grandchildren. The former Air Force commander Tommy Clift left Burma to work in Bangkok as a taxi driver and supported anti-Burma government resistance while his daughter lives in Australia. Likewise, the author has endeavoured to explain the Buddhism practiced in Burma, along with the traditions of her people, and the mysticism of the banyan trees and the jungle lights. They exist, if only one has eyes to see.

The vicious rule of the generals undermined the nation as the leaders of the SLORC namely Saw Maung and later Than Shwe crushed all opposition. During an uprising against the military rule in August 1988, millions of Burmese took to the streets to be confronted by an army who killed some 3, 000 people and arrested many others. There followed an election whose results were rejected by the military. In 2007, another major demonstration was put down by force killing 184 people while others were arrested and tortured. Afterwards, Aung San Suu Kyi was placed under house arrest for her peaceful political activities until November 2010 and months later SLORC was dissolved to be replaced by a new parliament with ex-General Thein Shwe as Prime Minister and President. Many people hope that Thein Shwe working with Aung San Suu Kyi will make Burma an open and democratic nation after sending the military back to their barracks.

One day the West must meet the Burmese half way so all will live in peace under a democratic government. The West started the opium trade in the nineteenth century, and some say still runs it. So it is time that one of the world's most beautiful nations is helped to become a united land of peace and prosperity. Maybe the heroic struggles of the Nobel laureate Aung San Suu Kyi will unite all the peoples of Burma and make it a real democracy where false imprisonment and torture are no longer tolerated. Though, by helping her, the western nations must not threaten the military that regards themselves as the protectors of the nation from foreign interference. It is a genuine fear because the West has at times armed the anti-government forces and fermented a bitter civil war. Now is the time for such interference to stop. Then there can be forgiveness and the reforms necessary if Burma is to become a paradise for her people. By 2013, the President of Burma Thein Shwe declared that Burma was moving towards a democratic state after holding talks with Daw Suu Kyi now a member of the lower house of parliament. A well researched account of modern Burma is Michael Charney's 'A History of Modern Burma' published in 2008 by Cambridge University Press.

Only time will tell if Burma becomes a land where the people are free to enjoy one of the most beautiful countries in the world. However, for this to occur, the nation needs international support and supervision without an influx of exploiters that could again destroy the nation. With the help of the thousands of Buddhist monks, the *pongyi*, and a nation that abhors violence together with the spirits of their ancestors, Burma will become the magical land the author loved and remembers.